the
BEGOTTEN
and
BLESSED

BOOK ONE *of* REVIVAL OF THE FALL

STELLA HOPE

Copyright © 2024 by Stella Hope.

All rights reserved. No part of this publication may be reproduced, stored or transmitted in any form or by any means, electronic, mechanical, photocopying, recording, scanning, or otherwise without written permission from the publisher. It is illegal to copy this book, post it to a website, or distribute it by any other means without permission.

ISBN: 979-8-9918400-1-9

This novel is entirely a work of fiction. The names, characters, places, and incidents portrayed in it are the work of the author's imagination. Any resemblance to actual persons, living or dead, events or localities is entirely coincidental.

Stella Hope asserts the moral right to be identified as the author of this work.

Book Cover by MiblArt
Copy editing by Nicola Hodgson
Developmental editing by Eleanor Boyall

First edition.

For my husband,
much of this is inspired by our love story. I hope that comes across
in the spaces between the words.
You're my soulmate.

For my son,
there aren't ninjas in my books, but some of my characters are
pretty close. I added in Carloff for you.
Love you, kiddo.

Acknowledgements

Thank you, Matt, for supporting me in making my dreams come true. I am reminded daily of how lucky I am to have found you.

I am deeply grateful to Eleanor Boyall, whose developmental editing turned my tangled threads into a cohesive story. To Nicola Hodgson, your straightforward copyediting and no-nonsense feedback helped me tackle my writing crutches head-on.

Thank you, Mark, you're the best beta reader ever!

And to my friends, you were my go-to for every monster concept, questions about weapons, and where to hide the bodies. Thank you for your endless support and your enthusiasm for my harebrained ideas.

Pronunciation Guide

Characters
 Cerys: "Kehr-ihz"
 Creiddylad: "Cree-thil-ahd"
 Glais: "Glice"; rhymes with "slice"
 Guillermo: "Gee-yair-moh"; Will's full given name
 Gwyn: "Gwen"
 Gwythyr: "Gwenth-yere"
 Nudd Llaw Eraint: "Nee-th"; the "th" sound is soft in "Thau-Errent"

Creatures
 Afanc: "Avank"
 Dullahan: "Dule-a-han"
 Gwyllgi: "Gwith-gi"
 Leshy: "Lesh-ee"; rhymes with "slushy"
 Púca: "Poo-ka"
 Trenti: "Trent-ee"
 Yaoguai: "Yao-gwai"

Other

Craic: "Crack," Irish slang for a "good time."
Cwn Annwn: "Coon An-noon," the hounds of Annwn
Sláinte: "Slawn-che," Irish way of saying "Cheers!"
Tylwyth Teg: "Til-with Teg"; the fairy folk of Wales
Wean: "Wayne," Irish word for "child."

Contents

1. The Sanctuary of Spirits — 1
2. Two Icebreakers Fights and Gin — 14
3. Footfalls and Fireballs — 26
4. A Dapper Hostage — 35
5. A Domestic Conference — 46
6. Cheers! Or Something Like It — 56
7. Emergence — 71
8. Night Intrusions — 74
9. What the Sun Reveals — 81
10. A River of Stone — 90
11. An Accidental Party — 93
12. Finger Pointing — 106
13. The Way Forward — 117
14. The Bastion — 126

15.	Twisted History	138
16.	Meetings in Triplicate	147
17.	Training with the Leprechaun	159
18.	Fear is a Catalyst	166
19.	Divulsions	180
20.	A Watery Burial	187
21.	Friends Chatting	190
22.	A Picture is Worth a Thousand Years	197
23.	Negotiations with the Dead	205
24.	Discipline in Motion	210
25.	The Hunt	217
26.	Gathering Allies	227
27.	Revelations	232
28.	Alia Iacta Est	247
29.	Halo and Horns	252
30.	The Ambiguous Morning After	260
31.	She Reads	271
32.	Fear Itself	274
33.	Scouring for Clues	278
34.	Sylas	288
35.	No Fire, No Escape	299
36.	Blursed Discovery	303

37.	Living is a Lesson	316
38.	Coming Clean(er)	326
39.	Varied Desires	335
40.	Details, Details...	342
41.	Rectifying the Truth	354
42.	Conversational Cookies	363
43.	Reconnaissance	363
44.	Dullahan	363
45.	The Fallout	363
46.	An Epiphany	363

The Condemned and Crowned Sneak Preview — 363

About the author — 363

Chapter One

The Sanctuary of Spirits

Somewhere in the mountains, the creature, a monstrous amalgamation of scales and sinew, surged through the rushing current of the snowmelt river. With each beat of its reptilian tail, each stroke bolstered by malevolent magic, the creature advanced. Hunger drove it through all the hours of the night.

The afanc, dissatisfied with the meager offerings of the forested tributary it had found itself in since its re-emergence, sought richer prey closer to human settlements—its hunting grounds of choice.

Eventually, a hapless deer cautiously approached the water's edge to drink. With barely a splash, the monster burst from the water, sinking its teeth and claws through the hide. With a speed matching its attack, it vanished with the deer, still protesting pitifully, below the surface.

Beams of moonlight lit the gory scene and led the monster on its way downstream, away from the mountains, where it could see the promise of hundreds of flickering lights in the distance: the promise of a full belly.

**

Esme

The bartender's left arm tingled as the familiar buzz of magic being used nearby danced across her skin. Though it appeared to be an ordinary bar, the Sanctuary of Spirits was anything but. True to its name, the space hidden from mundane eyes in the heart of downtown Seattle had become a haven for mages and magical beings alike.

The modern world was a far cry from the days of old. Magic, once wielded by kings and emperors to enforce their rule, had become little more than a tool to solve minor inconveniences. Mages now lived a rather ordinary life and used limited magic. They had to work regular jobs to support themselves. For them, magic had become about making their lives easier, about parlor tricks, and not much else.

Non-humans had it worse, scraping by in a world where their very existence was denied as a matter of fact. But Esme knew better. She knew how most of them, despite their ancient roots, had long since resigned themselves to being labeled myths. They saved their real frustration for the small indignities—like having to glamor up just to buy the latest smartphone.

One truth, however, remained constant across the centuries: regardless of species or magical prowess, everyone needed a place to unwind. They came to the Sanctuary to relax, to chat, and, more often than not, to drink.

Esmeralda Turner, ever watchful behind the bar, scanned the room with an ease born of years in the business. She wiped down the counter as the door's magic hummed again, signaling the arrival of the night's second group of baby mages. They stumbled in, most barely over twenty-one, and already flushed from drinking in mundane bars. Their laughter rang out as they filled a table near the back, probably trying to outdo the boisterous cheers of the night's first group of baby mages in rival university colors.

Beatrice lounged at the end of the bar, her pearlescent blue skin glowing faintly in the low light. Typical of a water nymph, she was always on the lookout for a date or at least someone to flirt with. Her azure eyes flitted from group to group, sizing up potential candidates while idly stirring her cocktail with a finger. The drink lazily twirled, forming an intricate mandala pattern in the glass—a small act of magic she unconsciously executed.

"Same crowd as always," Beatrice grumbled, not bothering to look up from her glass.

"Looks like it," Esme replied, glancing again at the table of baby mages who were now trying to impress each other with cheap cantrips. "No trouble tonight, at least."

"Amateurs," Beatrice muttered, glancing at the display with mild disdain. She sighed. "And too young for my tastes lately. Energetic but ultimately disappointing…"

Esme shook her head with a faint smile. "At least they're not setting the place on fire." She turned back to pour another drink, using just the faintest bit of magic to chill the glass as she filled it with a whiskey sour. No one expected flashy magic these days—just enough to keep things running smoothly, to earn a living like everyone else.

As Beatrice sipped her cocktail, Esme caught snatches of the usual argument from the chess table. Ivar the svartálfar and Carloff the gnome were arguing passionately, as always. Carloff's stubby fingers drummed on the table, his bushy eyebrows furrowed in thought. Ivar leaned back, arms crossed, with a smug grin on his craggy face.

"See? I told you, moving the knight to E5 was a terrible choice," Carloff complained, nudging the piece back into place with a wave of his hand.

Ivar rolled his eyes. "Oh, come on. You know my tactics are just a bit... unconventional. Keeps the game interesting." The two were perpetually at odds with one another. At this stage, Esme was certain it was the love language of those friends.

A mundane person couldn't stumble into the bar by chance. That was lucky too because Esme was about to serve a leshy—a deadly powerful one at that. Decades ago, a group of mages had collaborated to conceal the entrance to the meeting space, which had slowly transformed into their hidden bar. All outsiders would perceive was a twenty-four-hour, slightly run-down convenience store. If you possessed magical abilities and turned left by the donut display, you would walk straight into the bar. Without magic, you would be met with a wall of coffee and slushy machines, completely unaware of the magical space concealed beyond.

Drinks in hand, Esme offered them to the leshy, "Birch liqueur on the rocks for you and a Walnut Manhattan for the lovely lady. Nice to see you two still dating, Sylas."

Large gray hands reached out for her proffered drinks. "Thank you, Esmeralda." He was one of only a handful of people she allowed to call her by her full name, but he was like family to her. She winked at her customer and watched him return to the booth where his date, a tree spirit with wild green hair, sat expectantly. While the number of human mages far outnumbered the non-humans in the community, the Sanctuary of Spirits was the only place the non-humans could visit as their true selves. This resulted in an almost equal split of the clientele between both populations on most nights.

To Esme's left behind the bar, Will, her barback, balanced precariously on a ladder while attempting to restock the top-shelf liquors. His muscular tattoo-covered form contrasted sharply with the elegant, dimly lit, vintage interior of the bar. She sighed in frustration. Just because he was in a bar full of magic users didn't mean that he was invulnerable.

"Will! Am I going to have to bring Bert out to keep you from falling off that damn ladder?"

Bert was the most prominent troll in Esme's favorite conjured trio. Unlike most conjuration mages, she had a fondness for naming her summoned companions. It was an open secret that she was one of only a handful of mages on the entire continent that could sustain multiple conjurations at once.

It was simple for her to summon a trio of trolls, but she usually only needed one. Their abilities were simple. Their best work was holding things in place, which was convenient when a rowdy customer was problematic or when she had some handiwork to complete around the house. Secondarily, and only occasionally, they excelled at hitting things that needed hitting.

Rolling his eyes at Esme's jest, Will turned to place his now empty box off to the side of the bar. Esme could tell that he was suppressing a small smile when he said, "You never quit, do you?"

Nope. But it reminded her of something she needed to confront him about.

"Speaking of never quitting, can we take a break from you constantly setting me up on blind dates? I am not a dried up crone who cries herself to sleep every night—yet."

Will raised his index finger, wagging the point from left to right in a sassy show of defiance. "I'll quit when that harpy gives up on trying to outdo me in getting you on a second date. Money is on the line." The harpy he affectionately referred to was Abby, Esme's best friend, and powerful enchanting mage.

Esme admitted defeat, throwing her hands up in frustration, realizing she couldn't win with either of her friends. "The next one had better be smokin' hot, then."

Will grinned in a way that made her nervous. She pressed, "Gods below, what did you *do*?"

But just as soon as the last syllable left her mouth, a voice broke through the bar's noise, interrupting the grilling Will was set to receive. "Hey, charity case! Another round if you think you can manage to make it properly."

The dark cloud that was Maureen Mitchell had made her illustrious voice heard, and she expected it to be obeyed. It was a mystery to Esme why the woman spat venom at her specifically. Sure, Maureen was gruff and direct to the point of cutting. But she was rarely uncivil with other people; only Esme.

Esme muttered under her breath to Will. "I'll get this round. Since she loves you so much, you can make her happy at the end by taking care of the check."

Looking a bit too pleased that he'd escaped telling her exactly what he'd done to set her up while also evading serving Maureen, Will sauntered off to help other customers.

Hardly anyone called the shrew out on her verbal abuse of the bartender. Maureen's position as a seated member of the Northwestern Assembly of Mages, the group that held sway over the actions of all people possessing magic within their region, protected her from most rebukes. Each seated member of the Assembly was granted their position based upon the immense power that they held, magical or mundane, but usually a combination of the two. The Assembly's arbitration was fair, but their justice was swift and unforgiving, so it was no wonder most people were terrified of her.

The vitriol Maureen perpetually spewed conveyed her profound disapproval of Esme. Mostly her insults were personal, but Esme suspected that her condemnation was because Esme was mentored by two seated Assembly members who weren't overly fond of Maureen—Sylas, the leshy she'd served moments before, and Jacob, the bar's owner. She sensed there was some politicking going on between her mentors and Maureen, but she ignored it. Esme's life was complicated enough.

Concealing her anger, Esme smirked at Maureen. "Another round? You know, doctors say laughter is the best medicine, but I disagree. I think a good drink might do wonders for your disposition, too."

Maureen was a middle-aged woman with plain brown hair, recently turning gray. She sat primly at a table with her silent, almost mousy, husband. Beneath the softness of her face and femininely tailored cream-colored suit, a wicked witch with enough evocation magic to freeze a room solid lurked.

With a practiced hand, Esme measured and poured the cocktail into the chilled martini glass. She sauntered over to Maureen, holding the drink before her with a flourish. "One extra dry martini with no vermouth. Shaken." Embellished words to elevate what amounted to a glass of pure vodka. The drink fit the woman: A veneer of class on top of what was essentially pure poison.

Maureen stopped just short of snorting, unimpressed with Esme's comeback. "Save your wisdom for someone who cares, child. I'm not here for your thrilling conversation. I'm here for a decent drink. And that," she pointed disdainfully at the glass, "better be decent."

Esme quipped, "I'm here to serve. Don't worry, I won't burden you with my eloquence," while chilling the glass further with her hands.

Maureen took a cautious sip, leaving behind a ring of toxic yellow-red-hued lipstick on the rim. "Not bad, for a hanger-on."

Esme smiled prettily as she replied, "Next time you insult me, try to make it more creative." Then she whispered, "I thrive on challenges, you know."

Maureen spoke just loud enough that only Esme and her diffident husband could hear, "Creative insults? I don't waste my talents on charity cases. I suppose, in your world, serving drinks is a grand accomplishment."

Losing some composure, Esme almost hissed, but still quietly so that no one else could hear, "I should have let the rats eat through your walls."

Maureen's husband didn't react, other than to take another sip of his beer. He'd become accustomed to their dynamic.

Earlier that spring, the Mitchells had developed an enchanted rat problem. For obvious magical reasons, a pest control company could not be called. The Assembly tasked Esme with using one of her smaller conjurations to pull the rats out of the walls one by one. At least the tedious task gave Esme ammunition to bother Maureen with until another opportunity presented itself.

Maureen pouted. "But, darling, your services were so cheap."

Free. She meant free. The woman saw Esme as a tool to be used and nothing more.

Before Esme could reply, rapid movement caught her eye. Sylas frantically gestured to her with the universal come-here-quickly wave. Concerned, Esme gave Maureen a falsely apologetic smile and said, "Yes, well, I won't taint your presence any further. I'll ask Will to settle the bill."

On too many occasions to count, Maureen had derisively deemed Esme "tainted" within earshot. Sylas had given Esme the excuse she needed to remove herself before she said anything else—before she crossed a line.

When she reached their table, it was the immediate change in the leshy's smell that struck her first. Sylas usually had a pleasant pine resin scent that she loved. The fragrance transported her to hiking through a fresh forest, her favorite exercise. But now a strong odor of ozone and decaying plant matter filled the air. She hadn't known that the leshy's smell could change. Unease grew within her, pushing aside the defiant rage she felt just moments before.

Sylas protectively clutched his date's hands on the table between them, his metaphorical hackles raised. Juniper, a dryad who he'd been dating for a while, frowned but seemed to seek comfort from him. This was clearly not a lover's quarrel; something else was amiss. Esme had only seen Sylas upset once before, but never this angry.

The lines of decorum were slightly confusing for her with her mentor. He'd been a close friend to her family, especially her father, so she had known him since she was a teenager. Luckily, Esme understood rule number one of leshies, which applied even to usually friendly examples of their race. An angry or otherwise emotionally charged leshy was not to be trifled with—especially one powerful enough to be a seated member of the Assembly.

The tension spilling off Sylas was making her nervous. So she forced a fake smile and asked, almost begging, "What can I do?"

Immediately, a ward of silence surrounded the table. Esme hadn't even seen Sylas move, he was so fast to cast it. Still, she guessed that having lived for hundreds of years would provide enough time to practice. Taking a sip from his drink to cover his words from observers, his serious tone matched the gravity of his words: "Juniper has informed me of a heinous intruder stalking the Cascades."

Esme remained quiet, her silence urging Sylas to continue speaking.

His emotions were running so high that he struggled to keep his thoughts hidden. He chose his words carefully, speaking with a slow precision to ensure her understanding. "The intruder isn't my primary concern, but their presence nearby suggests a possible link to what I am truly worried about. Uncovering any connection is what I need from you, Esmeralda."

A grimace of pain streaked across his gray face. "We are about to ask much of you, but the situation is most pressing. A young child has perished in Juniper's forest. His parents reported to human authorities that everything was fine until he disappeared without a sound into the river's gushing torrent. I will not go into further detail because it is most distressing, but we fear that magic was involved."

Using magic to kill a child? Esme was horrified. She now understood why he'd looked so distressed; leshies cherished children of all varieties. The inviting smile she normally contrived to conceal the real reason she became a bartender in the first place, spying for the Assembly, dropped immediately.

"A similar incident occurred within our jurisdiction in eastern Oregon last week. While in Montana, a child and her mother were ravaged in what the human authorities considered a bear attack. We sent representatives to the locations of the deaths. Each found evidence of magic lingering in the area."

He looked at her squarely then. "I know exactly what is going through your mind, dearest. 'Why am I being told this?'"

He was right. Why her? She didn't usually do this type of job for them. Sure, she was technically an enforcer, but that didn't mean that she investigated murder cases. She didn't know who handled those, but she wasn't at that level—yet. Most of her work was in acting a bit like a thug, delivering reprimands from the seated members of the Assembly to badly behaved mages. Her conjurations gave her the muscle power and intimidation they wanted to get the point across.

"I am speaking to you because we would like a second set of eyes on the area. You are known to be an avid hiker, who just so happens to be in our employ. No one would tie your presence in the area to Assembly activity."

This was sounding distinctly close to political strife in the mage world. Despite her efforts to avoid mage politics, she couldn't escape the sinking feeling that this job would inevitably entangle her in them—if not immediately, eventually.

Sylas continued. "Similar stories have reached us from the East Coast. In the beginning, the victims were primarily located in rural areas; however, they have now been identified in suburban and urban settings. Esmeralda, the problem is getting worse and we do not know the cause. I currently have my attention focused on monitoring my forest. Tonight's foul weather has granted me this break."

She fought against the urge to raise one eyebrow at his assurances. The way he was describing it sounded like they had a mage serial killer on the loose. Which was way, way above her pay grade.

"Secondarily is the problem of this intruder. My Juniper has feared for her life. A devious Fae has threatened her safety. With fire! He said he'd burn her from the roots up if she didn't stay out of his business when all she did was go to greet her new neighbor!"

Esme probably should have been paying more attention to the word "fire," but she was mentally stuck on the Fae part of this problem. Everyone knew the dangerous varieties of Fae had vanished a thousand years ago. What kind of devious creature could make a gentle tree spirit fear for her life?

Before she could ask, Sylas, stormy-faced and completely serious, declared, "An insidious, heinous, detestable leprechaun! He may know something about the child's death."

Esme blinked. *Do not laugh, Esme. Do NOT LAUGH. Straight face, keep a straight face.* But, a silly little leprechaun, seriously? She bit the inside of her cheek to hold it all back.

Trying to compose herself, Esme turned to Sylas' date and said, "Juniper, hello! Happy to see you again. I am sorry to hear about your troubles." Then, facing them both, Esme asked, "So where did this leprechaun bother you?"

Still agitated, Sylas spoke up quickly, overriding what Juniper was about to say, "Near the hiking trail that has three waterfalls, even though humans refuse to number the falls properly."

Esme thought about the puzzle, then asked, "Are you referring to Twin Falls?"

He gruffly confirmed, "Yes, that's it."

Then, with a regretful face, Sylas apologized to Juniper. "Please accept my apologies, lady, for speaking in your stead." Grasping her hands more tightly, he continued, "I was too hasty with my words because I am protective of you."

Turning back to Esme, he whispered, "Esmeralda, I ask you to deal with this matter by tomorrow evening, as I do not trust myself to deal fairly with this fool."

Nodding in agreement to Sylas' demand, Esme said, "I will."

And that was that. When the Assembly ordered, she obeyed without hesitation or question.

Dealing with a troublesome magic user was right up her professional alley. She'd done similar work for the Assembly many times. Surveying a murder scene, not so much. She wasn't thrilled about the darker direction that the investigation might take her career in, but Sylas had been there for her when she needed it. She'd return the favor. If she looked on the bright side, giving a satisfyingly intimidating scolding to a pint-sized bully might be fun.

Sylas thanked Esme for the drinks and for being of aid, as usual. The couple gathered their things and left the bar just as the typical raucous din of laughter and glasses clinking was abruptly replaced by the sound of breaking glass.

Esme had been far too hasty earlier in announcing the night trouble free.

Chapter Two

Two Icebreakers

Fights and Gin

Esme

The bar's policy on fighting was crystal clear. It was even written on tasteful placards on nearly every wall in the Sanctuary of Spirits:

Rhetoric, Not Magic. Offensive Magic Prohibited.

One simply did not run into a mage fight, fists raised. A more thoughtful approach was called for. It didn't take the skill of a seasoned bartender to know that there was potential trouble when the voice of one combatant, a human—it was always a young human male—come out too slurred to be understood. *Damn baby mages and their university rivalries.*

At first, it seemed that the two hotheaded young men would keep the scuffle mundane, wrestling each other to the floor, the only real victim being the glass they'd smashed to pieces. If this was the case, Esme could conjure a few of her trolls to hold both offending parties in place until they calmed down. If that didn't work, the stench that she enchanted the trolls to emit usually did the job. Though she didn't like the extra work this method caused, she preferred mopping up vomit to hospitalizing someone.

But as Esme watched shards of glass rise from the floor in preparation for a telekinetic attack, she knew that a simple solution wouldn't cut it. It wasn't something she bandied about but, deep down, she relished a good bar fight. She was used to being underestimated, which added something special to the taste of victory after kicking a few asses.

With the situation now magically escalated, immediate action was necessary. Her trolls would have to wait for their chance to join the party because she needed something to cool tempers and absorb flying shards of glass first thing. December was months away, but Snowbert the ice elemental would make an early appearance that year.

Her conjured elemental's frigid form appeared in the center of the levitating shards of glass. He—because she thought of the elemental as a "he"—was roughly humanoid but lacked a head and stood at just over six feet tall. Snowbert resembled a thin, headless snowman that had sprouted legs. A solid ice structure formed the framework of his skeleton. On top of this was a thick layer of hardpacked snow.

With one swipe of his arms, Snowbert absorbed every shard of glass into his snowy outer layer. With that problem solved, Esme ordered him to cool off the fighters. He took a step closer to the pair, still struggling in a heap on the floor, and laid directly on top of them. As soon as she heard two yelps of pained surprise, she ordered the two trolls she'd conjured in the interim, Tom and George, to detain the two combatants.

Each troll stood over nine feet tall and was exceedingly hideous. She'd modeled them in the classic style of legendary trolls with thick armored skin, jutting lower tusks, and meaty extremities. Each picked up one of the two now half-frozen hotheads. Her two helpers approached the bar, easily carrying their charges as if they were small children. She only knew one combatant in passing, but neither would soon forget Esme.

Struggling vigorously, the smaller, more unfamiliar one, screeched at her, "Let me go, b—"

In a flash, a small purple pixie, whom Esme had named Irritella because she looked perpetually pissed off, appeared directly before his face, her wings flapping wildly. Irritella grabbed the offender's top and bottom lips and pulled each in opposite directions. With his arms still bound by the troll and his legs dangling in the air, he wouldn't be able to complete the insult.

"You," Esme commanded, holding up one finger as an angry mother might to a rebellious child, "can speak when you are civil." Esme's conjured pixie continued to pull the man's lips painfully apart. She turned to the regular, the larger of the two fighters, and much larger than her, and questioned, "Agreed?"

This one was calmer or smarter. He said nothing in response, but nodded in affirmation.

The bar was quiet as patrons eagerly watched the evening's entertainment, so Esme's voice easily carried to the backroom when she yelled, "Will!"

Strutting into the main room, he took in the scene before him and rubbed his hands together in unabashed glee. Reaching them, he asked, "Whatcha got for me tonight, E?"

She asked, "Which of these chuckleheads used magic in the fight?"

The exuberant expression on Will's face cleared as he concentrated. All mages could feel magic. They could feel it on their skin as it was being cast and the traces that it left behind. But Will was different. He wasn't the type of mage who could summon a cutting gust of wind or conjure a raging elemental. In those things, he was weak. But he was unique in the way he could experience magic. He could see it.

He described his sense of it as being much like how a bird can see into the ultraviolet spectrum, making the world more vibrant and colorful than a human could ever imagine experiencing. He could tell what type of magic had been used from the differing colors of the traces it left behind. With sight alone, he could track a spell's course back to its caster.

Will answered, "The smaller chucklehead."

Grumbling, she said, "That's what I thought."

At her order, Tom dropped the larger of the two men to the ground, the regular.

Evaluating him, she said, "Don't get pulled into a fight here again. Your cap is now two drinks per day. Still, thank you for keeping it clean. You're free to enjoy the rest of your evening." In The Sanctuary, "clean" meant using only fists and words.

"You," she snarled at the smaller offender, who George was still holding tightly in his bulky arms, "are banned for six months."

She heard some cheers and whistles from the onlookers. George carried the young man to the door and forcefully launched him out.

He would emerge back in the convenience store where the bar's entrance, battered, wet from Snowbert's icy embrace, and slightly stinky from the troll's odor. Esme had marked him with what she liked to call a "Badge of Dishonor." If he tried to reenter the bar, this magic would set off the barrier to repulse him with an exquisitely painful electric shock. She'd have to report this minor incident up the chain. It was funny how completing one task often created even more work.

Esme addressed the gawking crowd, "All right, show's over." Then she said more quietly to Will, "Why is everyone staring at me like I just sprouted horns or something?"

Will rolled his eyes dramatically and scoffed, "Chica, you're out here acting like it's no big deal that you have four conjurations just chilling, awaiting orders. Two of which stink, by the way. And you're not even sweating."

She silently mouthed an elongated, "Oh," and dismissed Tom and George, Snowbert, who was steaming in the warm interior air, and the angry-looking Irritella from service.

Glass shards clinked as they hit the floor where Snowbert had been standing. Esme had sort of forgotten that they'd been embedded in her ice elemental. She announced, "All right, the show is actually over now. The first person who cleans that up with magic gets a beer or a glass of wine for free!"

Three humans and a tiny bannik, covered in wrinkles, scrambled to be the first to do her bidding. The helpful Fae creature won, flashing her bright green teeth in a wide smile at her competitors. The bannik contented herself with a special mead that Esme had stashed away for favored guests.

Slinging drinks was a far cry from the mundane corporate path Esme's degree had charted for her. Most days, like this one, leaving behind that framed piece of paper seemed like a small price to pay for the excitement of working in a place where magic was common and people could be themselves, even if they had feathers covering parts of their bodies.

Without warning, Will snuck up on her and shrilled, "Esme! Sloe Gin is back again!" She almost dropped the Old Fashioned she'd been preparing.

His words caused an odd mixture of excitement and dread to bubble up inside of her. Staving off the unaccustomed feelings, she replied with marked dryness, "Great, a simple order that you can pour for me. He likes it neat."

Will replied with a grin that would appear menacing to anyone who didn't know him. "Neat? Maybe you should ask him if he likes it dirty instead," he swiveled his hips suggestively, "And see where that gets you."

Having been through this discussion with him a few times before, Esme exhaled, lowering her head and shoulders together in time with her breath. She took this moment to remind herself that she could not strangle her friend, her coworker, in public.

Making sure to sound long-suffering, Esme replied, "Gods and goddesses, grant me the endurance to slog through this man's bullshit with a customer-wallet-opening smile on my face."

Will smirked, flipped his bar towel over his shoulder, and performed his best strut to the storage room without pouring the requested drink for his bartender.

Typical.

Amid the tumult of the busy bar, Esme realized the only free seat for Sloe Gin was with her up at the bar. As he moved through the room, his presence silenced conversations, lowering the room's volume. This was nothing new. Regulars had always been suspicious of newcomers. Still, something about him demanded her attention as well, so she couldn't blame them for their reactions.

It was his third or fourth visit to The Sanctuary. Neither Esme nor Will had yet learned his name, hence the moniker of his preferred drink. On each prior visit, he sat by himself, sipping his gin, alternately observing the room and flipping through his phone, saying no more than necessary to order. He didn't seem unwelcoming. Rather, he looked like the confident type who was content with his own company.

That evening, Sloe Gin was dressed in a fitted gray raglan sweatshirt with blue jeans tucked into brown leather boots. Approaching the unoccupied bar stool, he untucked his hands from his jeans pockets to take a seat. Esme realized how tensely he had been walking through the crowd, with his broad shoulders held high and tight. It made her wonder if this was evidence of nerves or simply a dislike for the attention that came with being the new guy. Either way, she'd do her job and try to help him feel comfortable.

Perfunctorily drying her hands, she started with her usual opening line. "Hey there! What can I get for you?"

Esme couldn't help admiring how attractive he was as he raised his face to meet hers. She didn't try very hard to conceal her study of him. She figured a good bartender should read a customer's body language to gauge their mood before striking up a conversation anyway.

Untrained chestnut brown hair and a trimmed beard of the same color, with a few grays sprinkled in, framed his masculine face. His nose was slightly widened at the middle bridge, indicating at least one breakage in his past. His frame was solid, exhibiting equal parts strength and agility.

Gentle green eyes met hers as he settled into his seat and leaned his elbows on the bartop with tented hands. She mentally chastised herself for the sudden flutter in her chest. He's a customer, she reminded herself. But her smile widened anyway, despite her better judgment.

Her mind momentarily stumbled as she realized something she had previously overlooked. Gods above and below, his right hand was a prosthetic. It wasn't the type meant to mimic the look of a human hand, either. It looked like a piece of advanced technology.

The man noticed her glance at his hand, and a smile tugged at a faint scar on his cheek. Wiggling the fingers of the prosthesis, he said, "It's pretty neat, huh? Prosthetics are way better than they used to be. What you did back there was impressive. Four conjurations at once."

She hadn't noticed him in the crowd during her conjuration sideshow. Her cheeks warmed at having been caught gawking, but the laughter in his eyes freed her to smile again. That was one point she liked about him already: He didn't take himself too seriously and could share a laugh with a stranger, even if it was at her expense. Plus, he had complimented her, and that deepened the blush on her cheeks.

Meanwhile, Will swaggered back from the storage room with a fresh bottle of sloe gin. Exaggerating his actions like a mime on the Las Vegas strip, he opened it and poured two fingers into a glass. That clown was lucky that Esme loved him enough to put up with his constant buffoonery.

Returning her full attention to the man she hoped wouldn't be a stranger for much longer, she reached out her hand and said, "Hi, I'm Esme. Nice to meet you..." lengthening the last word to elicit a response. She restrained her excitement, making a conscious effort not to bounce even a millimeter on the balls of her feet. Some people found her "joie de vivre" to be a bit much. It was pointless to scare him away before knowing his name.

"Miles," he replied and gripped her hand in his bigger one.

As the pair shook hands, Will slipped behind Esme and plopped the drink down squarely in the space between them. Peeking over Esme's right shoulder, Will whispered just loud enough that Miles would most likely overhear, "Dirty. Get it? Dir-ty."

Groaning internally, Esme briefly considered conjuring Bert to harass her barback until the end of his shift. Then it hit her: this was the set-up Will had been alluding to earlier.

Esme rolled her eyes at Will's antics as he walked away to handle some request, but when she glanced back at Miles, she found him grinning. "Your friend's subtle, isn't he?" Miles chuckled softly, and the warmth in his voice put her at ease.

"You have no idea," Esme replied, matching his grin. It was a small moment, but it felt like they were sharing an inside joke already.

"Thank you for the drink. This is perfect. Either you are very good at your job or I am a creature of habit."

She answered, "Why not both?" His change of subject offered them a welcome diversion from the uncomfortable position Will had put them in, and she was grateful for it.

Esme wanted to know more about Mystery Miles. She reasoned that her curiosity was purely innocent; it wasn't a common occurrence to have new faces in the bar, after all. Besides, the Assembly might show an interest in knowing more about a mage new to the area before he formally introduced himself at the next meeting.

"So, Miles, you're pretty new here. Are you traveling or are you a recent transplant?"

"Did the accent give me away? I moved here a few weeks ago for work."

Esme had noticed his slight accent. Seattle's population had mostly moved there within the past few decades, resulting in a subtle Pacific Northwest accent that differed from the stronger accents found in Texas or northern Minnesota. Once she gave it some thought, she recognized he was different in some way. Perhaps his suggestion was correct; perhaps what she had noticed was as simple as the accent. Perhaps. Or perhaps it was how incredibly hot he was. Gods and goddesses, she needed to get a hold of herself.

The few words he had spoken exhibited an interesting mixture of cosmopolitan and rustic sounds to her untrained ears. With increased interest and one eyebrow raised, she asked, "Accent?"

"I feared that something I said gave me away. Every once in a while, my singsong Welsh joins in the conversation, uninvited." He sighed. "It's been years since I lived there, but it refuses to leave me completely." Waving the topic away, he said, "Ancient history now."

Hoping to give him a chance to try his drink, but also not ready to end the conversation already, Esme cheekily asked, "So, Miles, what day job moved you out to Seattle?"

He laughed a little, confused at her choice of words. "Day job?"

She swirled her finger around in the air, gesturing at the magic-filled surroundings.

"Ah, yes, that. It's easy to forget that this—" he said, mirroring her gestures, "—Isn't exactly normal. I'm at the hospital on Madison Street."

Before Esme could respond, she was distracted by a beckoning wave and a request for a refill. She gave Miles an apologetic smile and said, "Let me check on a few things real quick."

Miles had noticed the calls for her attention too, turning around halfway in his bar stool to see what the commotion was. Plopping down more cash than the drink was worth, he stood up, preparing to leave. She was glad to see him looking more relaxed, his shoulders no longer as tense as when he arrived at the bar. Maybe a bit of her bartending magic had worked that evening.

"No problem. I see you are a wanted woman. See you soon, Esme," Miles said softly, his gaze lingering on her for a heartbeat longer than necessary. He winked, turned, and left.

She watched him leave, and though she knew she had customers waiting, she couldn't help but hope that 'soon' would come sooner than later. Deep down, she hoped the wink meant that this was the start of something promising.

She'd been so engrossed in the conversation with Miles that she'd forgotten that Will was standing only a few feet away during this exchange. Will surprised her by saying, "I'll take care of the refill if you want to handle the waver, boss." Then, mimicking Miles in tone, he said, "I'll see you soon, Esme," and winked for effect.

She made a strangling gesture in her coworker's direction.

Esme allowed the rest of the night's whirlwind of tasks and engagements to serve as a distraction from thinking any more about the handsome mage with gentle green eyes. It was also too easy to get bogged down in worrying about the assignment Sylas had given her. As long as she wasn't attacked by this serial killer he talked about, scouting the area for more evidence would be straightforward. But she needed information on how to deal with a pesky leprechaun before engaging him.

Normally, she went to Jacob for advice, but he was in California visiting with the leaders of the Southwestern branch of the Assembly and wouldn't return to Seattle until tomorrow evening. Jacob was a man with many roles. He was not only the elderly owner of the bar, but also the de facto leader of the Northwestern Assembly, and her mentor in all things mage.

Sylas was another person she also frequently turned to, but he seemed more in the mood to suggest murder than to offer advice.

She had few direct contacts for jobs within the Assembly. This was necessary to maintain confidentiality about her clandestine work for them. With limited time, she would have to handle this task alone.

Weren't leprechauns supposed to be difficult to catch? None of them lived in the area, so she'd never bothered learning much about them. Instead of tucking into bed with a new book as she'd planned that night, she'd be reading up on trickster Fae.

Chasing a leprechaun through a forest seemed like a losing strategy. She'd have to gain his attention through her own trickery first. A plan was already coalescing in her mind. Once she got him talking, she could see if this annoying but mostly harmless Fae knew anything about the child's death. She'd top off the day by issuing a stern warning against any additional bad behavior.

She had too much to do and too little time to do it. On top of the reading, she also had to pack for a hike because the area where Sylas said the child disappeared and the leprechaun lived was only reachable by foot.

The morning would arrive too soon. Still, she was confident.

Checking out the area where the boy died would only be a problem if she slipped on a rock and fell into the river. And surely she could handle a silly, errant leprechaun alone?

Right?

Chapter Three

Footfalls and Fireballs

Esme

Esme was a late bloomer. Not physically. Unfortunately, she'd had to wear a bra by her first year of middle school. Magically.

Her parents waited until they couldn't deny it any longer to reveal her magical birthright. By that point, she was already well into high school. Most mages grew up knowing exactly what they were. They even threw quasi coming of age parties with their mage friends to celebrate their magic manifesting.

She probably would have figured it out sooner if her parents hadn't chosen to live on the periphery of the mage world. She would never know the reason since her parents passed away unexpectedly while she was in her second year of college. The contagious enthusiasm for life that defined her personality up to that point vanished in her mourning. Grief painted her world gray at most times and red with anger at others. In the process, she angered friends and gained a few enemies.

When Esme's world fell apart, the Assembly stepped in, guiding her through legal proceedings and offering her a place in their community. But that was just the beginning. Jacob had taken her under his wing and taught her most of the magic that she knew. Without his mentorship, her magical abilities would still be infantile and potentially dangerously unpredictable.

Similarly, Sylas, disguised using his very average-looking human glamour, had left his precious forest for weeks to sleep in her living room because she couldn't bear the thought of being alone. He'd become something like an uncle to her over the years. Without the warmth of Sylas' presence during the hardest time of her life, there was a genuine threat that she might have given in to the grief to become a dark shell of a human being. Because underneath her outgoing, friendly exterior, something darker had always lurked, waiting for its turn.

Eventually, Jacob offered her a position at the bar. The bar had transformed into more than just a job for her. It was a sanctuary where she found belonging, a second home. It's people, her people. Without the Assembly, she would probably be the worst thing imaginable - alone.

In retrospect, it was evident when the Assembly sought a return on their investment in her. At first, the requests were mostly innocent. "Esme, darling, we're very worried about Gerald. Could you discreetly inquire about his health the next time he comes in and let us know how he is doing?"

After a year of this, they began asking her to make further "inquiries" outside of the bar and started paying her "for her time." It helped that the stipend made living in a city as expensive as Seattle, on a bartender's wages, doable.

Bit by bit the requests escalated, so slowly that she barely noticed the change. A decade had gone by, and the responsibilities she carried out for the Assembly had gnawed at her moral foundation. Because she had lines she refused to cross, even with the Assembly's cajoling for more, always more, she could still look at her reflection in the mirror the morning after. She would be lost if she couldn't do that.

Something told Esme that if she were to budge even an inch in her convictions, she could lose a part of herself that would be nearly impossible to get back.

To put it simply, the Assembly had been there for her when she needed it most. All of that, starting with her parents' death followed by the Assembly swooping in to save the day, was how Esme found herself groggily hiking up a steep mountain the morning after a very busy night of both bartending and researching - hoping to find clues and a troublesome leprechaun. The problem was that working for them felt like she was part of a family that was held together by silence and a niggling sense of distrust. Lately, she's noticed that they provided her with sufficient details for the task, but not enough to understand the situation.

The spring melting had begun, swelling the Snoqualmie River to its banks. Even the most able swimmer would lose their fight against the rushing rapids. But a child? There was no chance. The wheel marks from off-road vehicles nearby and a line of spray paint on the rocks proved that police or search workers had been in the area recently.

While exploring, she searched for typical signs of foul play, such as a discarded backpack, tools, or even blood trails from the water. Professionals had already searched the area, but she still felt the need to try. All she found while looking for mundane clues was a few energy bar wrappers she picked up to trash later, and a prevailing feeling of defeat.

Sylas knew that sensing magic wasn't her greatest strength, but she did her best to feel around the area. She discovered weak magic traces near the shoreline, as he had suggested. However, the magic was so faint that she couldn't discern any details about its use.

To ensure she missed nothing, she walked about half a mile along the riverbank. She nearly twisted an ankle twice while trying to right herself after the unstable rocks and eroding edges of the river shifted underfoot. The third time this happened, she fell, shifting her feet and catching herself with her hands just in time to prevent a bloody nose. Her face landed near something resembling dark green plastic debris.

Instinctively, she reached out to pick it up so that she could pack it out to a proper wastebin. But instead of the smooth plastic that her fingers expected to feel, she realized she was holding something that felt and looked a lot like a piece of a fancy leather purse.

She wracked her brain for the term she learned in biology class years ago because it wasn't a scale exactly. It looked almost exactly like a scute from an alligator but it was impossible for one to survive this far north. And it definitely wasn't processed leather either. Opening herself up to the magic, she was taken aback by the powerful sensation radiating from it.

Realizing she wouldn't return empty-handed, she experienced a strange mixture of satisfaction and fear. Whatever left the scute behind was practically soaked in magic and was apparently connected to a killer. Instead of answers, she would be returning with another mystery. Still, the day wasn't done. She still had to track down the pesky leprechaun who might know something about the kid's death.

Esme easily found the leprechaun's stomping grounds thanks to the familiar magical sensation tingling on her skin. Allowing the sensation to lead her, she ventured off the main hiking trail and bushwhacked through the forest. The sounds of birds chirping filled the air as the world around her stirred awake for spring. The scattered deciduous trees were showing signs of new life with their sprouting leaves, and she noticed a few trilliums budding.

She'd read that Fae dwellings were notoriously difficult to find because of the spells that they used to disguise their homes from human sight. At first, the straightforward discovery of the leprechaun's front door felt too easy to her. But once she got close enough, she realized the door was disguised using magic strikingly similar to the spell that concealed the entrance to the Sanctuary of Spirits.

Esme would have to press Jacob for more information on this connection later. Especially since he seemed so loath to depart with its magical process. Unfortunately, the circumspect way Jacob said, "We'll work on it later," in his posh accent made her think she needed to pass some sort of test first. Despite being 31 years old and having worked for the Assembly for years, she still hadn't passed his test, assuming there even was one. The realization reignited years of pent-up frustration she'd held towards the Assembly.

Pushing the annoyance aside, she approached the door. Everything she'd read about leprechauns said that they were nearly impossible to catch. Given their specie's reputation for hoarding, she bet he had countless alert wards on his house. What easier way to get his attention than try to break in?

It worked a bit too well.

She'd grown up like any other American child, hearing tales of jaunty green-suited leprechauns. The stories had described leprechauns as diminutive man-like Fae hailing from the Emerald Isle. They were known as treasure hoarders, mischievous shoemakers, or purveyors of children's breakfast cereal.

However, her research had left her unprepared for the reality of the leprechaun she faced. He was close enough that Esme could tell that the physical description from her research was mostly correct. With his blond hair and slightly pointed ears, he appeared nearly human. He was taller than expected, closer to four and a half feet tall than the two that books described.

It was what Esme didn't know about this leprechaun, or rather, what information she had dismissed as unimportant from Sylas' demand for action, that nearly filled in the cause section on her death certificate. The leprechaun paused, seeming to ponder whether the human mage was stupid enough to break into his home. Then, no longer in doubt, his hands sprouted flames.

Her eyes widened, taking in the flames and recalling Sylas' words. It came streaming back to her then. "Her safety has been threatened by a devious Fae. With fire!"

What the actual fuck?

Fight or flight kicked in. Without hesitation, Esme immediately bolted. If discretion was the better part of valor, she was happy to look like a coward if it meant that she wasn't going to die in a blaze of disgrace. Without speaking a word, the leprechaun zealously unloaded fireballs in her direction.

She weaved through the trees, hoping they could provide cover from the rain of fire. Esme was flabbergasted. How could a leprechaun have such a talent for fire magic? She mentally kicked herself for dismissing Sylas' mention of it.

Esme had experienced her fair share of bizarre occurrences in her work for the Assembly, but this event stood out as being outrageous. She knew that a great deal of information about magic had been lost to time, war, and human folly since the Extinction. But a leprechaun with fire magic?

If she had seen the situation from a calmer perspective, she would question why such immediate violent hostility was coming from him. Leprechauns were known for being mischievous tricksters, not outright gangsters. It wasn't until later that she realized his aggression meant something more.

Feet pounding and lungs heaving with the effort from the intense sprint, she tried to disguise her fleeing form with an illusion spell. The problem with running away was that her ass might still get burned.

Esme's illusory effort did nothing other than change the color of her hiking jacket to a shade of military green. Noticing her failure, she berated herself for botching the spell, with aplomb no less, as fireballs were flung her way. She should have relied on her strength in conjuration, but her father's teachings in illusory magic surfaced in her mind during her mad dash.

Hoping for a moment of concealment, she paused behind a nearby tree trunk to catch her breath. Fireballs whizzed past as she gulped air into her lungs like a dying fish. Was this guy ever going to succumb to magic sickness? Esme wryly pondered the cascade of failures that resulted from her supposedly exceptional tactical planning.

All she needed to do was keep it together. Despite recently reaching the age where endless energy was no longer a given, she refused to let being sleepy from an all-nighter make her sloppy.

She could feel the impact of the magic and smell the smoke coming from the burning bark as a fireball hit the other side of her hiding spot. Nearby wet leaf litter steamed anemically in the misty drizzle. This was not how she had envisioned the morning going.

Concealed behind the tree, she was suddenly struck by a realization. Despite a few fireballs coming somewhat close to her, none had come close enough to singe a single hair on her body. Either the leprechaun's marksmanship was severely lacking or he shot to scare, not kill. Regardless, the potential danger meant that she could not afford to gamble her skin on that thought.

As her breathing slowed, she considered her options. Charging the leprechaun, Joan-of-Arc style, was indisputably out of the question for her, as death by third-degree burns was likely and therefore not appealing. The best approach was to keep distance and strike him with something or someone.

Esme cautiously glanced out from behind the tree, not wanting to push her luck. Sure, she wanted a second glance at her foe, but she also needed to see the area that she was working with around him. Time to play smarter, not harder.

Ensuring that all of her precious body parts were tucked safely behind the tree once more, Esme visualized the leprechaun and soundlessly moved her lips in the call for Bert. Another quick peek from the refuge of the tree proved to her that the conjuration had worked as intended.

Just as quickly as she poked her head out, she swiftly yanked it backward as a fireball whistled past where her face had just been. The last missile was dangerously close. It was time to make a move. She dashed to the closest large tree, giving the mental command, "Knock him out, Bert!"

All of her plans hung in the balance. This attempt had to succeed. Following this command without hesitation, Bert lifted his meaty, wrinkled club of a fist and jabbed at the leprechaun from behind, smacking him face-first into an adjacent tree trunk with a resounding thud.

Proceeding with all the caution that walking onto a battlefield engenders, Esme sidled up to the leprechaun to check him over. She was relieved to find him alive. If she could avoid it, she would never cross that line. He was unconscious and certain to have a nasty bruise when he woke up.

Relief and the remaining adrenaline surged through her. She hadn't come here to fight, yet here she was, standing horrified over the body of an unconscious leprechaun. What had she gotten herself into?

Shock and self-doubt hastily filled the hole where the adrenaline waned. Esme did not have years of crisis response training like the human military or mundane police. She was a conjuration mage who felt obligated to assist the Assembly in return for everything that they had done for her over the years. Everything that she knew she had learned on the job. It was a complicated situation that had gotten out of control. Indecision gripped her as she mulled over her options.

Despite her frustration with the Assembly and her uncertainty about what to do next, Esme would be damned if she didn't do something. She'd be doubly damned if she didn't do the right thing.

Chapter Four

A Dapper Hostage

Esme

Esme had to protect herself first. She rummaged through her day pack and found a rope. She tied the leprechaun's hands and feet and instructed Bert to carry him. Back at the leprechaun's home, she finished the cantrip to unlock the door.

With the door ajar, Esme could see that Fae magic expanded the interior of the home well past the volume that the laws of physics would allow the tree to contain.

His house perfectly fit the stereotype of a leprechaun's home. The arched-top rustic door opened into an interior that blended homespun comforts with pops of gaudy glitz. Rustic, hand-hewn support and ceiling beams bracketed the whitewashed cob interior. Heavy wooden furniture supported gaudy golden tableware, candle stands, and knickknacks. Every inch of the interior was lit by enchanted candles and a fireplace that never needed to be fed, as it had no apparent fuel. It was a subtle yet powerful display of the Fae's magical mastery.

She instructed Bert to gently lay the leprechaun on what looked like his bed. Determined not to make a completely preventable mistake that day, she left the leprechaun tied up as he dozed. If he tried to sling fire, he'd have to set himself ablaze first.

The leprechaun wore sturdy brown woolen trousers, a brown leather belt with a golden buckle, and a crisp white shirt sporting golden buttons. Appraising her charge, Esme stopped just shy of laughing aloud, thinking that he looked far too dapper to be so murderous at that hour of the morning.

She sat down on an undersized chair placed at an ornately carved desk nearby and waited for the leprechaun to wake. She left Bert standing like a hideous statue nearby.

During the wait, she had little to do other than glance about the room, and she started pondering the series of blunders that led to her having fireballs flung her way. At the forefront of her mind was the realization of how precarious her current situation could be. She had been lucky when Bert's offensive move worked and knocked her opponent out. What else could this leprechaun be capable of? He had already shown mastery over fire magic—something wholly unexpected for a leprechaun who should have used tricks or misdirection instead.

She thought through the situation and filtered all her issues down to the most basic problem. She—and really all mages—was out of practice when it came to dealing with aggressive magical types. This leprechaun was certainly acting like a malevolent, which was confusing in itself. She still wasn't certain if he had missed her on purpose during their altercation.

Sitting down to wait was fine for the first few minutes, but after that it became tiresome, so Esme cautiously explored the leprechaun's home. She didn't know what she expected to find, other than the obvious gaudy decorations. But she expected something with a personal touch. No friends or family photos or paintings adorned the walls. The fireplace mantel wasn't adorned with a family crest or heirloom. There was nothing of note whatsoever.

Her walls overflowed with family photos and mementos. After her parents died, she couldn't bring herself to take them down. They were a celebration of their life together. But this leprechaun had none of the same. From what she knew, their culture wasn't significantly different from human culture. They had nuclear family units and extended families that kept in close contact. The undecorated walls and pictureless furniture surfaces left her feeling rather morose about the leprechaun currently tied up, unconscious.

The home appeared to have only one room, but then she noticed a door at the back. She glanced at the leprechaun before carefully opening the back door. As she did, the smell of diatomaceous earth mixed with woodsy and floral notes struck her nostrils. Her sense of smell alerted her to what was beyond the door before her sight could give her any hints.

She opened the door all the way to see a conservatory of such magnificence that it could stand as a proud addition to the glass houses at Kew Gardens. Magic maintained the different biomes in each corner of the large room. On the left was a display of tropical splendor featuring dwarf banana plants and sandalwood. Next to that was a graduation of subtropical zoned plants, spanning from birds of paradise and palms. Then came the temperate area, featuring dwarf apple trees and roses in full bloom. Finally, the smallest area was what she assumed was tundra or arctic. Here, small shrubby plants that she couldn't identify sat under clouds of frigid air and low light.

The conservatory was a marvel of magic and maintenance. How was it possible to create a space of that size with magical lighting within the confines of a tree? The magical prowess needed to fabricate it was mindboggling. It had to be at least a thousand square feet of just gardens, plus another four hundred for the interior of the house crammed into less than five square feet on the outside?

Gardening on this scale and with such precision took genuine passion and delicate care. The evidence she saw made her reconsider the leprechaun's character. Someone who was truly evil, like a malevolent, wouldn't care so much about so many needy plants.

As far as she knew, all the seriously dangerous, malevolent magical beings had disappeared sometime following Arthur's death and Merlin's departure from Camelot and its subsequent fall. The reason for the malevolents' disappearance was a matter of lively debate among mages. They called it the Extinction.

The history of human literature provided clear evidence of the Extinction. Following the medieval period, there was a sharp drop in stories of fantastical magic and otherworldly creatures. Perhaps this decline in "fairy tales" was because of human civilization entering the Renaissance, followed by the age of enlightenment, industry, and technology. Or, from the perspective of those in the magical world, few fresh stories were being written because the terrible monsters lurking in the watery depths had vanished alongside those that swooped down from the skies to rend flesh.

Since no one needed to worry about being a wyvern's next meal, mages could once again live as ordinary individuals instead of society's protectors. Later, the Inquisition and witch hunts around the globe instilled discretion into the daily lives of all mages. No one wanted to be hunted for the power that they inherited when they had the choice to live, mostly, like mundanes. Now magic was something only seen in movies and read about in books unless you were within the community.

Given the thousand years of peace since the disappearance of malevolents, magekind had become relatively soft. The art of fighting with magic had all but been forgotten. Few mages regularly used offensive spells. She knew of a few adrenaline junkies who had joined the Navy Seals or Marine Recon teams, but they couldn't do anything too flashy without risking revealing their powers. Fire magic was mostly useless, aside from lighting candles and campfires, so no one trained to become a highly skilled pyromancer.

Esme left the conservatory, as it had no doors other than the one she came in through, and re-entered the main room of the leprechaun's home. She made one more circuit around the room looking for evidence of his character, then retook her seat. Other than the flamboyant decorations and impressive magical feats of engineering, she had found nothing of note. It left her feeling a miserable mix of melancholy and angry. Why did he have to attack? Why could they have not talked it out peacefully?

Peace was the key...

Only nonviolent creatures, like leprechauns and sasquatches, had survived the Extinction. Humans no longer needed to fear marauding ogres, the fairy queen, or the Wild Hunt. A person could walk down the street to grab a cup of coffee without worrying about being attacked by a griffin. She knew one thing: the world would be very different, and not in a good way, if the Extinction had never happened.

Eyeing the still form of her captive, Esme wondered somewhat hysterically whether the Extinction had accidentally skipped one jauntily dressed, petite savage.

She was woefully out of her depth in knowledge and training against this Fae. As if his fire magic wasn't enough to convince her of this, his enchanted house that defied physics certainly made that clear.

Still, she had started the fight, and now she had a job to do. She couldn't leave just because she was starting to have regrets about her actions. The best she could hope for was a truce, allowing her to leave his house unharmed. The worst...Esme would not be deterred by the worst-case scenario.

Sure, she was ill-equipped to handle a dangerous Fae, but she had made her friend Sylas, and by extension of his position, the Assembly, a promise. While she didn't always agree with them, they had earned her loyalty.

At long last, the leprechaun woke, breaking Esme out of her reverie. Sighting the human mage sitting nearby, the leprechaun vigorously tested his bonds. Afraid of what he might try, she spoke up, "Trying more fire would burn you before it could reach me. Calm yourself. I'm not here to hurt you."

There, she thought, chuckling internally at her folly and the ridiculous situation that she found herself in: Maybe if she didn't mess this up any further, she could redeem her self-esteem.

Despite his vulnerable state, the leprechaun still glared at Esme. He finally spoke in a lilting Irish accent, saying, "You're out of luck, lassie. I don't have my gold here."

Esme couldn't help herself. She barked out a laugh, putting on a display of looking around at the gaudy golden accouterments gracing most surfaces. Returning her focus to him, she set her face in her best impression of a bad bitch, honed over the years while cutting off other magic users at the bar.

A bit snottily, she said, "Well, that would certainly make my life easier. I'm not here for that either."

As if taken aback, the leprechaun's sneer dropped and a mask of icy reserve took over his face. Only in hindsight would Esme recognize that this shift in attitude hinted at something deeper happening with the leprechaun. Unfortunately, she was too preoccupied with thinking of her next words to analyze why his expression changed.

Lacking any better ideas, she took the direct route. "Let's get to it then. I'm going to ask some questions. You will give me answers. Then we'll part ways, safe. Got it?"

The leprechaun rolled his eyes, then nodded unenthusiastically.

She pressed on, "Why are you here? I know that your kinfolk rarely leave the isles and when they do, they are seldom seen far from the east coast of the US."

In her opinion, things were going well. He hadn't tried to attack her yet, and the house wasn't on fire. Her standards and expectations for this encounter had become quite low.

He replied in a rather haughty voice for a person tied up, "You, acting the maggot, asking me questions! Sneaking around in my domicile, up to no good. Why should I talk to you, mage?"

Tales of leprechauns were consistent in one thing: They could be caught and held. None of her research mentioned that leprechauns could fling fireballs. Proceeding blindly had yielded poor results for her so far. She needed to find out more while giving away as little information as possible.

Humans weren't the only ones who felt the need to fill a weighted silence with chatter. So, she sat quietly and eventually gestured at his bonds. She shrugged and kept her silence.

Puffing out his breath, the leprechaun eventually said, "'Twas time for me to move on. Nothing more to it."

Hoping to maintain the little momentum that the conversation had gained, Esme said, "Fine. Then tell me, why would you threaten a tree spirit with your fire? They are the picture of kindness if you leave them be. That seems like being a puppy kicker to me. Are you a dirty puppy kicker, leprechaun?"

"Puppy...what? Tree spirit?" Then, after a second of thought, he raised one eyebrow and asked, "You some sort of mage police?" For a fleeting moment, there and gone again, the leprechaun's expression changed from stink-eyed effrontery to cautiously eager.

Esme did not move. She sat still and stared at him, keeping her expression schooled to blankness, which was not an effortless task for her.

"I did nothin' to that tree spirit. She just saw my flames and got frightened."

It seemed like he thought that he'd said enough and feigned interest in studying the ceiling. His lack of eye contact convinced her he was hiding something.

Esme credited the leprechaun with a bit of truth. Sylas had said that Juniper was merely afraid, not harmed by him. But why would he use such a display to keep a harmless tree spirit away? That made no sense.

"You travel thousands of miles, leaving home and family behind, because it was 'time to move on'? No, I don't think so. You also threaten an innocent with fire. What are you hiding, leprechaun? Were you involved with the child's death in the river? We found magic where he entered the water."

At first, the leprechaun's eyes grew wide at the mention of the child who had died. Then he eyed the troll looming in the background, motionless, expressionless, but still vigilant, awaiting further orders.

Noticing his glance at the troll, Esme added, "I don't want three wishes either and I know enough to keep my eyes on you until you are no longer of use. I have a travel mug of coffee and a gigantic bag of trail mix to keep me content. I'm willing to wait a long time. My troll—yeah, the one who knocked you out earlier—can keep watch while I rest. So, what do you know about the child's death?"

"Giving me no choice, then. And no offer of your name," he prompted, once again gazing at the ceiling.

Modern mages might lack in magical education compared to the greats of the past, but one fact was handed down through the ages: Names have power.

Using silence as a weapon again, Esme knowingly lifted one eyebrow and stared at the Fae.

Finally, turning his gaze to meet hers, he asked, "Do you give your binding word of promise that all you seek from me is this information?"

Seeing a chance to get out of the leprechaun's home unscathed, Esme nodded sagely in acceptance. "You have my binding promise. You did not harm the tree spirit, so I will accept your word that you were simply trying to scare her."

A mage's bound word was nothing to take lightly. That was another piece of knowledge passed down through the years from one mage to another since Camelot's fall. The consequence of breaking a binding promise would be a complete and utter loss of magic. Once a promise was broken, the breaker's magic would join itself to the other bound person—like a cosmic rebalancing of the scales. Most mages would rather lose a limb—and some, undoubtedly, their life—rather than live without magic.

With the formalities aside, Esme exclaimed, "Now, spill it!"

"I'm wise enough to see that ya have me at a disadvantage for the moment. But mind you, I'm not without other tricks. Free me and I guarantee your safety until sundown, unless ya start somethin' first."

Well, well. She didn't expect a leprechaun to play the verbal games that were the sport of the defunct Fae courts. Wary of the leprechaun's wily nature, Esme needed more from him before she could accept this pact.

So, Esme asked, "Let's be clear here, Mr. Pot-O-Gold. Do I have your binding word to speak completely to the limit of your knowledge? I freely give you my promise that I came here with no desire to fight, steal from, or harm you. I just wanted to have a chat about your unacceptable behavior toward the tree spirit and to get some information that could help save innocents."

With a nod, the leprechaun gave Esme his promise. He wouldn't lie to her. He couldn't—all Fae were bound to speak only the truth. The promise was the cherry on top of their deal.

Weariness was settling into Esme's bones. This situation had gone so far beyond her expectations that her natural sarcasm took over.

"Well, I'm looking forward to wrapping up this conversation. So, why are you here?"

He let out a deep breath, his face growing deadly serious. "They're being drawn back somehow."

Impatiently, Esme rose and stepped closer to him. "Who?"

"Those who are supposed to be banished! Not three moons ago, I saw a banshee with my own eyes, lassie. And I suspect that somethin' similar is afoot in the river below."

Intellectually at least, Esme knew Fae could not lie but her brain would not—could not—accept the words.

"Okay, where do you keep the whiskey, Leprechaun? It must be good stuff, because you're talking nonsense."

The leprechaun replied, "I heard tales 'bout sirens and boggarts on the continent. Truth be told, I had doubts, thinking like you. That maybe the tale spinners might've been indulgin' too much in the whiskey. All I know is what I've seen. The 'how' and the 'why' and the measure of it all? That's a mystery to me."

The tone of his voice changed from unabashed effrontery to a softer, more haunted sound as he kept talking.

"In Wicklow, there she was, just gliding like a patch of darkness over the bog in the moonlight. Her wailing would put any hungry tot to shame. It cut through the night air and seemed to freeze the blood in my veins. It was like she wore a cloak of darkness. I could feel the grief pouring off 'er. I decided then and there that I wouldn't be taking part in that grief."

Eyes closed, face averted, he whispered, "I came here to hide, to get away, as far and long as possible. Now I may need to pull up stakes again because I felt the darkness again not two nights ago. Something wrong. Something nasty. Something lookin' for meat."

It hit her then. Before he looked away, his face and the uncharacteristic seriousness of his tone revealed the truth. She believed him. She had to. Fae could not lie.

There'd been a banshee in Ireland and something looking for blood not a mile away. His words hinted rather strongly at the return of malevolents. She felt uneasy about the idea of providing Sylas with nothing more than a magical scute as flimsy proof of what might be happening. She could already imagine the dismayed look on his face when he realized they were no closer to the truth of the child's death.

Just as Esme was mentally teetering on the abyss, waiting for the floor of her world to crumble at the news of returning malevolents, the leprechaun dispelled the seriousness of the moment.

Openly leering at her chest, his face brightened. "Now, lassie, I could really use a hug after reliving that. But you'll have to untie me first."

"You've got to be kidding me!"

Chapter Five

A Domestic Conference

Esme

Frantic anxiety buzzed through Esme's mind at the thought of what she'd just learned. But fretting after a long hike and a firefight wouldn't get her anywhere. It was time to untie the little creep and get home.

The fighting spirit she'd previously seen in her captive was gone. Esme was pretty sure that his creepy request for a hug was just his way of messing with her head before she left. That behavior fit everything that she had read about his species.

Their binding promise assured her there would be no more fighting, but the relief allowed guilt to trickle in. Despite the fact that he'd tried to burn her alive, a sliver of compassion crept in.

She couldn't place all the guilt for her actions on the shoulders of those who ordered it. Ultimately, she chose her actions, not the Assembly. She had to live with what she had done, even if how she had handled the leprechaun wasn't the worst of her sins.

The list of sins she had accumulated that day wasn't long, but each one felt like a burden she didn't want to carry. Instead of waiting to speak with him first, she had impulsively tried to break into his house, unnecessarily escalating the situation. Winning the fight had left her with a strange feeling of guilt. She regretted pressuring him to confess his shame. She recalled the leprechaun blushing before his confession. Was he ashamed of fleeing his home? Or was he ashamed of being caught?

Empathy and guilt dragged at her; inconvenient emotions for an enforcer. She brushed off the creepy hug comment because that was just a leprechaun being a leprechaun. First, she untied his feet, then his hands. Standing from her crouch, Esme said gently, "There. That's done. Unfortunately, this is all I can do for those rope burns." She dug in her pack and pulled out her hiking first aid kit to hand him some ointment.

Their eyes met. She looked intently, but detected no cowardice behind his eyes. She concluded that his embarrassment was because of getting caught.

Unbound, he nodded slightly, pursing his lips. He sat up quickly, gripping the mattress edge with both hands as though it were the only thing keeping him upright. Maybe it was.

Esme grabbed her pack, walked to the door, and without turning around said, "For what it's worth, I'm sorry," then left.

The hike back to her car was uneventful, aside from the internal torture caused by her overactive brain. Scenes of goblins tearing people apart and boggarts abducting children while they played haunted Esme's every step. Thoughts of drowned dead rising from Lake Washington colored her commute home as she drove into Seattle over the floating bridge.

Back in the city, the mental assault of her overactive imagination didn't cease. Later that afternoon, walking up the front steps into the small bungalow she'd inherited from her parents, mental images of harpies snacking on her neighbor's sweet tabby cat assaulted her.

She'd had enough of the mental torment. Further thinking would only do more harm than good. She dragged herself through the post-hike routine—shower, dinner, pajamas—and collapsed into bed.

The last thought she had before falling asleep was the realization that she'd forgotten to ask the leprechaun about the scute she'd found. Maybe that was for the best, though. She hadn't completely trusted him, even if she had felt guilty for all that she'd done.

The sun wasn't yet up when Esme finally awoke. From the slight stiffness in her muscles, she figured she must have slept eleven or twelve hours straight. Taking off her sleeping mask, she turned to grab her phone to check the time. Only then did she realize she wasn't alone.

She scrambled upright, limbs tangled in the duvet, screeching, "What the fuck!"

The same fireball-happy leprechaun from yesterday was perched nearby on top of her dresser.

The lack of wards on her house would have to be fixed as soon as humanly possible.

His expression radiated smug satisfaction, which, once she thought about it, was infinitely better than an expression of murderous glee. For an indeterminate amount of time, the two sat there, facing off, neither moving. Had Esme been more awake, she might have used magic to knock him out again, but she didn't consider it in her confusion.

"Alright, I'll speak first, Esmeralda," he said, acting as if his every word was magnanimous. Seeing her response to his use of her name, he added, "Yes, I know yer name. Humans have it written everywhere in their homes. Easy." He snapped his fingers for effect. "You get it for free for nothin' but a glance."

The logical part of her brain had just begun to wake up because the admission of his activities while she slept made Esme reevaluate their current standoff. Sure, the leprechaun that she had tied up the day before had been in her house, watching her sleep. That definitely tipped the scales into creepy territory. However, he'd been there long enough to find her name written somewhere and had done nothing to harm her. Nor, after a glance around herself, had any of her stuff been tampered with.

The moment that the sun dipped below the horizon, they'd fulfilled their binding promise. The leprechaun had free rein to harm her at any moment if he wished to. But he hadn't.

"My name's Fionn. Finnegan or Finn, for you Americans."

She raised an eyebrow at that. He had specifically said "my name". A true name freely given by a Fae was not something to take lightly. It was the magical equivalent of handing your foe a weapon during hand-to-hand combat.

Clearing her throat of sleep, Esme pulled the duvet close to her chest and asked, "So, umm, Finn…what brings you to my house?" Glancing down at her bedding she said, "As you can tell, I was not exactly expecting company."

The hellion's response was to laugh uncomfortably long and loud. He fell sideways off the dresser in his mirth, appearing not to be affected by his fall as his giggle fit continued. She watched on, amused.

He recovered slowly from his convulsions of hilarity. Once he did, he sat up from his spot on the floor and said, "I had to get you back, lassie. The look on yer face!" Then he fell back into another round of hysterics.

Esme realized then that she had unwittingly started a game of a leprechaun's favorite sport: tricks and mischief.

"I'm so glad to make your day, Finn. Watching a woman sleep is super creepy, by the way."

He shrugged, continuing to smile, with laughter glimmering in his eyes.

Still clutching her duvet, Esme said, "Fine, this round to you, Finnegan! So, did you come here just to get that prank out of your system or is there something I can help you with?"

His face lit up dreamily as he exclaimed, "That was the most fun I've had in ages."

After a long moment of reverie, he proceeded in a conversational tone, "I've seen enough and done enough over the years to own up that ya got the best of me yesterday. The way you did it showed me you aren't the wicked sort of human. I also came to apologize for my...over-the-top response to yer presence at my home." Carrying himself with a self-assured air, he climbed to his feet and stuck out his right hand. "Truce."

Was it wise to trust a creature who had slung fire at her less than twenty-four hours ago? He could have hurt her already if he'd wanted to. What was he after now?

Then she remembered something her mother had said when Esme asked her for advice. "Sometimes the only way out is through." With that thought, she decided that the best way to determine what he was after was to accept. A bonus to this would be an end to her cringe-worthy predicament of hiding clumsily behind her bedding.

Esme awkwardly released the grip that she held on the duvet with her right hand and offered it out to Finn. Finally, the pair shook hands.

Emphasizing the 'out' in her request, Esme said, "Great, now that that formality is finished, do you mind getting out of my room so that I can freshen up? Since I suddenly have a guest to entertain and all. I'll meet you in the kitchen in ten minutes." Under her breath she added a mumbled, "creeper leprechaun" at the end for good measure.

She was fairly certain that he heard the last bit because he smiled mischievously before leaving the room. Waking up to a leprechaun gleefully swinging his legs while sitting atop your dresser was more than enough bullshit for any person to deal with before their first sip of coffee.

While she went through her morning ablutions, she heard pots and pans rattling in the kitchen. She wondered what additional chaos he could be up to.

Prepared for the worst, Esme stepped into the kitchen—and immediately questioned her sanity. He was cooking breakfast in her kitchen. She intentionally paused her entry to stem off an overblown reaction to his shenanigans. The pause gave her just enough time to recognize that she could either treat this as a problem or as an opportunity.

"Finn, my new buddy, being in your presence makes me wonder how many times I can unironically say 'What the fuck' in one day. However, I will forgive your use of my stuff without asking," she pointed at the scrambled eggs and pancakes cooking on the stove top and continued, "if you plan on sharing that with me."

He responded promptly from his position in front of the stove, "A bargain accepted!"

This was not the subdued leprechaun that Esme had met yesterday. Finn was full of energy; Esme felt her spirits lift in response. That might also be because of the unexpected meal she didn't have to cook for herself after a long night's rest.

She said, "Great, I'll make us some coffee and set the table. If you drink coffee."

"Aye, I'll admit to enjoying a proper Irish coffee occasionally." He waggled his eyebrows.

"Well, you're in luck, because I'm a bartender." Decision made to see this truce through and simultaneously find out all that she could from him, she got to work whipping the cream for their coffee.

"A bartender? Lassie, I do believe we'll get on splendidly."

Pouring the lightly whipped cream over her plain coffee and his spiked, Esme commented, "I didn't even know I had eggs. Pretty sure I put them on my shopping list."

That now familiar mischievous glint appeared in his eyes again when he said, "Ya didn't."

That's when Esme noticed the orange fur decorating his slacks. Putting two and two together, she accused, "Did you steal these eggs from my neighbors?!"

Laying his accent on thick, Finn replied, "I'll have you know I was ever-so-kindly invited into the house by a 'Mr. Snuffles'. We became fast friends. I simply popped over to grab a few eggs and popped back. Nothing else. No harm done."

Esme had to remind herself that she was dealing with a leprechaun. Petty acts of misplacing things and playing pranks were fundamental aspects of their identity, even if it was annoying. She accused, "I can see that your idea of harm done is ambiguous. You stole!"

"Nay, lassie, I *traded*. I left Mr. Snuffles a marvelous piece of fish that I found in your icebox. The humans won't notice a few missing eggs."

Fish? Then she realized what he was referring to. "That was a very expensive piece of halibut that I was saving for dinner with my friend tonight!"

That same satisfied look from earlier came over his face again. "Well then, Mr. Snuffles got quite a good deal for his trade of eggs."

Placing the coffee, plates, forks, and maple syrup down a bit too forcefully, Esme sat down at the small dining table in her kitchen. Then she considered and stood to grab a bottle of whiskey to correct her own coffee. She would roll with the punches.

Finn served out the food and joined Esme at the table. History repeated itself as the pair stared at each other, at the plates, everywhere, not moving for a few moments. Just in case, Esme grabbed his plate and switched hers with his. He grinned and said, "Smart, but not necessary." He reached over and grabbed some egg from the plate that she had stolen and shoved the bite into his mouth. Then he did the same with the plate in front of him.

Stranger things had happened. Her gut told her that this was the right way to build a bridge toward peace. Sometimes the only way out was through.

So she picked up her mug for a toast and said, "To the truce and whatever comes after."

Finn lifted his glass and replied, "Cheers to that!"

To her surprise and delight, the food was excellent—better than most restaurants, in fact. Finn equally enjoyed his coffee. The pair said little beyond "Can you please pass the—" and other simple pleasantries about the meal and the weather. Despite his mischievous behavior, she found it amusing how normal their meal together was.

Moments after she finished eating, Esme received an unexpected phone call. She read the name on the screen and immediately knew that it would be a quick, but necessary, conversation.

She apologized to Finn and stepped out of the kitchen and into the living room. Happy for the momentary diversion from the still slightly awkward situation, she answered brightly, "Hey, Abby! What's up!"

Abby, Esme's best friend and fellow mage, replied, "Hey, lady! I know it's early, but just wanted to double-check if we're still on for tonight while I have a quick break to call you. This shift sucks."

There was one easy way that she could think of to get the leprechaun talking more about his run-in with a malevolent. She purposefully pitched her voice louder, hoping that Finn could overhear this part of the conversation. "Anyway, about tonight, would you be up for meeting me at the bar instead of our dinner date at home? The fish I planned to cook won't work. Plus, I have a new friend who enjoys tasty beverages that I would like for you to meet."

Abby instantly replied, "You had me at tasty beverages! See you at eight?"

Pleased with her hasty planning, Esme bid Abby goodbye.

Abby's family had stronger ties to the mage world than Esme's. Perhaps Abby would know something that would rationalize Finn's story once she got him talking.

Esme returned to the kitchen to see that Finn was at the sink cleaning the dishes from their breakfast. Maybe it was the whirlwind of the past twenty-four hours or possibly the spiked coffee, but Finn was starting to grow on her. Sure, he was consistently mischievous. Yet, he had also offered his name and a truce to her freely. Those were not minor acts to mages. Next, he cooked breakfast and cleaned the dishes. Sadly, the leprechaun had already done far more than most past boyfriends had done the morning after.

"Finnegan, would you like to share a few drinks with me and a friend tonight? Don't worry, it's a mages' bar, so no glamor is needed."

He puffed himself up, still at the sink, and replied, "I'll have you know I am a giant of a leprechaun. I can pass as a little person if I wear a cap to hide my ears."

"Oh, is your favorite cap red?" She couldn't resist a little gallows humor in referring to the once-murderous dwarves called Redcaps who wore hats soaked in their victims' blood. Although, on second thought, after his declaration yesterday that the malevolents of legend were coming back, perhaps she should amend the "once" part.

Finn slapped his knee and said, "Haha, I knew I'd like ya. I do enjoy a tipple. See you tonight."

Then he disappeared. Like, *poof*, actually disappeared from Esme's sight and senses, both magical and mundane.

It suddenly hit that her she hadn't told him where the bar was.

Chapter Six

Cheers! Or Something Like It

Esme

Esme checked herself in the mirror one last time before leaving her house that evening. She liked to dress up a bit and do her hair if she ever visited the bar while not working. That night, she opted for a sleek black dress with a belted waist and heeled boots. It was refreshing to be viewed as a woman, not solely a bartender.

As she stepped outside to leave, she noticed the interior light was on in her hatchback. Hoping that her car battery wasn't low, she walked to the vehicle. She opened the driver's side door and squawked like a dying bird from surprise. Finn sat in the passenger's seat, laughing at her. Again.

Rejoining the game of tricks and mischief, she said, "Shouldn't you be sitting in a booster seat? Or at least in the backseat?"

Grinning, he replied, "I suppose I deserved that for surprising you. Point to you. I can't say that I didn't enjoy your squawkin', though."

She recovered from her surprise, sat down, and pulled on her seat belt. "Look at you, absolutely rakish, Mr. Finnegan."

He wore a midnight blue fedora, slung low over his ear tips, with matching trousers, a white shirt open at the collar, and suspenders.

His cheeks turned pink. "Thank ya. I considered complimenting yourself but thought twice before opening my gabber. I can occasionally make wise decisions."

Shooting him an impish side-eyed glare, she replied, "Smart move after the whole leering hug comment yesterday."

His tone made it clear that he was offering an unspoken apology. "I didn't mean a thing by it. I was just tryin' to ruffle yer feathers."

She replied truthfully, "I know."

For the first few minutes of the drive, they were quiet. Once they turned onto the highway, Finn broke the silence. "I could stand to meet my new neighbors if I'll be here for a while. So, thank you for the warm welcome."

She replied, "You know that we'll have to tell the story of our meeting. So, be prepared for that and play along. Maybe you'll also get a chance to apologize to Juniper."

"Juniper?" he asked.

"The tree spirit you terrified."

"Ah, yes, that. That I'll do."

He seemed sincere, so she figured she could be honest. "I'll try to keep her leshy boyfriend from gutting you."

"Leshy?" His skin paled. So he was familiar with leshies. Good; it was only fair that he marinate on the possible repercussions of his bad behavior on the drive.

When the pair arrived at the convenience store, Finn had no problem finding his way through the secret entrance to the bar. He received only a perfunctory second glance from another customer as he made his way through the store, glamorless.

As they crossed the magical threshold, they were surprised to find almost everyone they wanted to speak with that evening—plus one unexpected addition. Abby and Miles were sitting together next to Sylas and Juniper.

On the table in front of them, a tiny man crafted from a folded napkin danced a waltz with a napkin woman. It was exquisite, intricate magic—Abby's work. The demonstration of such precise control was awe-inspiring. Juniper must have used her magic to create a giant tropical leaf, which served as the podium for the enchanted dancing couple.

Miles appeared relaxed, sitting with his shoulders slouched, watching the display of magic. He must have come to the bar straight from work, judging from the steel gray button-up shirt with black trousers and polished black leather shoes. He looked ready to walk into any business and start ordering people around.

Abby stood up to embrace Esme while Sylas sat at the table, seething.

"Miles," Esme said, breaking the embrace, "what a surprise. I didn't know that you and Abby knew each other."

Abby interjected, "So you two have met! I thought I told you about the doctor that I met at the hospital a month back. We talked a bit, and I knew that he'd love it at the bar."

Abby forgetting to tell Esme something was not an unknown occurrence. She worked as a nurse in the ER, so her waking hours and Esme's waking hours as a bartender did not always align. Lifting an eyebrow at Miles, Esme poked, "Oh, Doctor Goodwin, is it?"

Miles smirked. "Unfortunately, we didn't get that far last time."

His smile made Esme mentally kick herself for checking him out again. His unexpected presence made it hard for her to focus. She couldn't help stealing glances at him when she should focus on why she was there.

"Everyone, this is..." Esme turned around to introduce Finn to them, but came up short. Finn had disappeared.

Instead, she saw Will carrying a drinks-laden tray toward their table with Finn at his side. As Will set the drinks down on the table, Finn said, "Worry not. The first two rounds have arrived. I got the proper black stuff, the beer for you Americans, and a peaty whiskey."

Will stood with his now empty tray grasped by one hip, his face questioning what in the hell was going on. Esme introduced Finn to everyone. He avoided more than a split second of eye contact with Sylas, who wore an expression of undisguised malice.

Will glanced around at the awkward social dynamics and gave Esme another questioning look. He shook his head in reluctant resignation when she shrugged and returned to the bar. She understood all too well how he felt after his first run-in with Finn; she'd fill Will in on everything later.

As they took their seats, Finn's gaze lingered on Abby, smitten. Esme didn't think the leprechaun even noticed his ridiculous beer foam mustache until Miles broke the silence, saying,

"Mate, you've got something..." motioning to his upper lip. Startled, Finn abruptly shifted his attention and acknowledged the other mage's presence.

Finn froze like a stunned deer upon setting eyes on him, really looking at him for the first time since sitting down. Miles slouched back in his chair and gave a small, nervous chuckle.

Finn took a moment to collect himself before resuming his friendly and generous demeanor, making sure to offer drinks to everyone. To Esme, his behavior confirmed his sincerity in integrating into the magical community. After serving out everything, he cleared his throat and bowed decorously in Juniper's direction.

Esme learned years ago that when you make non-human friends, especially long-lived ones, you had to expect some antiquated social behavior and flowery language. The bow suggested they were about to hear a speech. Esme was uncertain whether she wanted to cheer him on or groan for what could be long-winded.

Not raising his head from its lowered position, Finn said, "My dear lady, I must humbly beg yer pardon for the ill-bred actions I made in your presence. My ungentlemanly behavior toward a gentle spirit as yourself was inexcusable. I deeply regret any offense that I have given you. I am ashamed that I acted out in fear, and I hope you can find it in your heart to forgive my foolish behavior. Please accept my sincerest apologies. I will do my utmost to ensure that such a breach of decorum does not occur again."

His apology was more formal than his usual mischievous demeanor. Esme pulled her jaw off the floor as Finn straightened and handed Juniper a small potted sapling. Had he somehow transported the pot all the way from his conservatory to the bar, with no one noticing? If so, it was more evidence that this leprechaun had serious magical chops.

His apology worked. Juniper accepted the sapling, immediately handed it to Sylas, and dove straight for a hug with the leprechaun. Their height difference meant that she had to crouch awkwardly to succeed, but she went about it enthusiastically. Finn, seeming surprised, accepted the embrace from the dryad but still eyed the leshy from over her shoulder.

Sylas' face remained clouded, but the faint ozone smell was fading. Esme was relieved not to see any signs of immediate homicide in his eyes. Leprechaunicide? She realized she had been holding her breath and finally released it.

Settling in again, Esme faced the challenge of juggling her obligation to report accurately to Sylas while keeping her covert assignment hidden from Abby, Miles, and Finn. She hadn't told Abby about her work for the Assembly because she was unsure if she could handle her judgment once she discovered the truth of everything she had done for the Assembly. The recent broken collarbone and dislocated shoulder were just one example of many missteps she would rather forget.

She explained away their meeting by saying that she "stumbled upon the front door of that leprechaun" while hiking who "Sylas mentioned was being a brat." Sure, it sounded kinda lame, but Abby knew she hiked for exercise frequently, so it was plausible. Esme squeezed every drop of humor out of the story and skipped the firefight part.

She intentionally left out having Bert knock Finn out and then subsequently tying him up so that she could question him. Instead, she explained he thought that she was trying to break into his house. Naturally, he took it personally because that was something that happened to leprechauns. To get her to stop, he had threatened her with fire. She did her best to downplay the danger and his aggression. By saying the right things, she persuaded him to stop the fireballs and talk. She smiled through the awkwardness, hoping the hogwash she was selling would seem like a good deal. Occasionally it worked.

At the end, Esme eyed Finn, hoping that he wouldn't reject her alterations to the story. Esme knew what was going through Abby's head—dismay at how stupid Esme had been to make it seem like she was getting anywhere near a leprechaun's gold, and surprise at Finn's reaction to it.

Abby sat upright from her hunched over position and shrugged dramatically, remarking, "Esme, you've always been the kind of person who collects friends like it's an addiction. So far, you haven't been wrong about any of them. Even our own púca."

Miles nearly spat out his beer. "Púca?"

It was said that the only reason that púcas had survived the Extinction was that they never killed their victims, only terrified them to a state of blubbering confusion.

Esme groaned, hiding her face in her hands. Abby ignored it and kept going. "Wexley had been coming into the bar for weeks disguised as different people each time, running up their bar tabs. Esme noticed that each time one of these 'people' came in, they always avoided ordering from her."

Abby laughed and continued. "So Esme spiked his drink with an anti-glamor potion. Then she talked him off the metaphorical cliff when he realized that he'd been discovered. It turned out that he'd fallen into using old Fae tricks because he was struggling with food and housing. Now he's the chef here a few days a week. And thank goodness for that, because we love his cooking!"

Then, probably to appease the embarrassment she knew Esme felt, Abby added, "I trust your gut. I trust you. That was a long way of saying 'welcome,' Finn." Somehow, she conveyed both resignation and hope simultaneously in her closing words.

Finn raised his glass in salute to her welcome. "Sláinte! To new friends!"

Esme gave Abby a grateful smile. She was the considerate friend that everyone needed in their lives. Her acceptance of Finn changed the energy of the conversation back to a more convivial one.

The initial phase of Esme's plan had been a success—making Finn feel at ease. Admittedly, her role was mostly limited to making introductions and a few verbal missteps. Now she faced the second stage of her plan with a mix of anticipation and dread. Now she needed to get Finn to open up.

The unexpectedly large audience was intimidating, but it also offered a unique opportunity to clear her tormented mind of doubts. She had a few-hundred-year-old leshy, a dryad, and a leprechaun of indecipherable ages, an enchantress with a deep magical family history, and a doctor sitting at the table with her. Would she ever have access to such an experienced group again?

Waiting for a natural lull in the conversation, Esme forced herself to sound less tentative than she felt. "You know how I said that I didn't blame Finn for his reaction? There's more to it."

She addressed him, "Finn, because we all know that Fae cannot lie, could you share the story behind your move here?"

Finn sat up straighter, appearing to be none the worse for wear after several drinks, which was impressive considering his limited stature. He gave her the assessing look that she was just starting to associate with his shenanigans. It made her wonder how he would get her back for putting him on the spot.

He cleared his throat and affirmed, with a here-and-gone-again smirk, "Aye, I suppose I can. I packed up and moved from old Wicklow because of the pesky new neighbor. Ya see, it just didn't sit right with me to have a banshee walking across the bog like she owned the place. I'm not the first, nor will I be the last, to move because of problematic goings-on in the neighborhood. My own eyes convinced me that a certain subset of the malevolent variety was poppin' back into their old haunts. I was havin' none of that."

Eyeing Abby, he finished, "I can't say that I am unhappy with my decision. Had I known that this area hosted such lovely landscapes and creatures," he drank a long, thoughtful swallow of his beer and smiled mischievously while staring at Abby, "undoubtedly rife with secrets to discover, I would have come years earlier."

Esme rolled her eyes. How did Finn not see Abby was with Miles? She wondered how long this little crush of Finn's would last. Abby shifted forward in her chair, maintaining eye contact with the leprechaun for an awkward moment. Esme cheered Abby on for her tacit rebuke of Finn's rakish side getting the best of him.

The tone of Finn's story differed slightly from his original telling of it, but all the important parts were there. He placed his hand over his heart and said, "I swear on my mam's heart that I was not off my head with drink. Nor," he rolled his r's dramatically, "am I taking the piss with you."

Esme studied those around her. Abby looked confused. Juniper tilted her head to the side, pondering. Sylas maintained a grumpy grandpa's expression.

Miles surprised everyone by speaking after his prolonged silence. He asked, "Your magic isn't fully Fae, is it?"

She hadn't watched him while Finn spoke, but he sounded more interested in the leprechaun than the shocking news of a banshee, something that should be extinct. Maybe an academic interest in magic was something he and Abby had in common.

Thrown off balance, Finn answered simply, "No, sir, it is not."

Sir? Wait, what? Esme was confused. What did he mean by "not Fae magic"?

Initially, she couldn't figure out why Miles would ask a question so far off-topic. The implication was that if Finn's magic was not fully Fae, he could be exempt from the "no lying" rule.

Finn went on, "Well, as you know, magic is part of a leprechaun's very bein'. We can't escape that fact like you humans. Was it my devilish good looks or my respectable stature that gave me away, sir?"

Miles replied succinctly and without emotion, "Neither."

Esme couldn't help herself so she asked, slightly indignant, "The fire? Finn, have you been taking the piss with me this whole time? I really hope that you haven't been lying about everything because you're not bound to Fae laws."

Juniper's equanimous voice, like the rustling of leaves in the wind, interjected while Esme stared Finn down. Its effect was akin to throwing a bucket of sand on a fire. "Regardless of what he is or what magic he has other than Fae, the laws still apply to him. So, no, dear Esmeralda, Finnegan has not been lying to you."

Finn scooted his chair back and stood, again bowing at the waist in Juniper's direction. "The lady is correct." Sitting back down, he continued, "Since it is a hot topic, pun intended," he chuckled at his joke, then nodded at Miles, "Ask any of the little folk and they'll tell it true. We're all bards at heart with varying degrees of talent. Meself, well, it's a habit that I won't be breaking now. An ifrit, in all her fiery glory, made a promise that she couldn't keep to a leprechaun she'd crossed paths with."

Esme's breath caught in her throat. The implications of that single sentence were staggering.

Unaware of her struggles, Finn pressed on, speaking dramatically. "Magic is a merciless mistress. We all know the fee that her justice takes upon those who break such a binding. Yours truly became the vessel for what was once his. Yes, I can summon fire."

He showed a small flame sprouting from his upturned palm, which he immediately doused.

"But magic's justice is also blind. The fire demon's magic didn't stop there. I suppose it needed a larger container," he slapped his leg and laughed, "because it made me grow to double the man that I once was."

Countless thoughts ran through Esme's head; it was hard to keep them all straight. If he had truly made a deal with an ifrit, Finn could be over twelve hundred years old. The math was simple because all the ifrits disappeared during the Extinction. Or could he have encountered yet another of the returning malevolents? It was just as rude to ask non-humans their age as it was humans, so she'd have to reserve that question for when she knew him better.

How could a tiny leprechaun survive any sort of encounter with an ifrit? Esme felt seriously out of her depth and exceedingly grateful that they had declared a truce.

It took some effort, but she eventually extricated herself from her spiraling thoughts and stepped back into the present. "Finn,

I apologize. I should not have been so hasty in accusing you of lying. I was rash and reacted emotionally before thinking. Also, thank you, Juniper, for your clarification."

Unconsciously, Esme glanced at Miles after she finished. She couldn't deny that she cared what he thought of her, but she could delude herself into thinking that it was because he didn't know her yet and not because she was wildly attracted to him.

Finn, showing his less formal side with Esme as compared to Juniper, waved his hand in a wiping away motion. Then he said, "I can't say that I blame you for it. Being able to admit your mistakes in judgment reveals much about your quality. I thank you for the apology, Esmeralda."

He continued. "Speaking of my magic, I've no wish to dance 'round words. Rest assured, I harbor no ill intentions toward any of you. So," a flash of light emitted from his palm as he slapped it lightly on the table, "take that as you will. I'm here for the craic and the company."

Looking thoughtful, Abby said, "Esme, you wouldn't have asked me to meet you two here if you didn't at least believe his story somewhat."

Esme agreed, "Right, but I also know that if Finn believes he saw it, even if he actually saw something else, he is not technically lying. No offense, Finn."

After a moment of thought, Abby stated, "As far as I know, having an actual banshee in your backyard should be impossible. Could it have been a conjuration like Esme's beloved trolls?"

Esme wasn't certain if Abby was playing devil's advocate or if she was trying very hard to be unconvinced.

Finn shook his head. "Nay, it didn't feel the same, not by a long shot. I know what the general sort of magic feels like. I know what Fae magic feels like. But the banshee was different. In the way like recognizes like, she felt like my fire."

Finn looked at his half-empty beer glass and said, "I know that sounds crazier than a parcel of rabbits hiding up a tree." Then he sank back in his seat, looking more guarded than before.

Esme suggested, "Maybe we should see if his tale could be substantiated."

Sylas nodded.

An errant curl drifted into the space between Abby's eyes as she shifted restlessly in her seat. "No," she said. "I mean, yes! It seems fairly obvious to me that this should be brought to the Assembly's attention. Officially, that is." She finished with a glance at Sylas.

"Yes," Sylas confirmed, "we'll convey this to the Irish Assembly and discuss it internally."

It was a clear indication that the matter was closed as far as he was concerned.

Finn stood formally again with one arm braced at his waist in the front and one braced at the back, and said, "I'd be more than happy to lend a hand with anythin' if my presence would prove beneficial. Also," his tone and expression changed almost imperceptibly but Esme recognized it from him during his bound confession, "I would be delighted to find out that what happened was not exactly as it seemed."

Finn quickly regained his poise and added, "Though I'll confess a touch of hesitation in meetin' your Assembly. How would they take the likes of me? My magic's got a twist to it, so factor that in before you respond. But then again, I suppose I'm a bit late on officially announcin' my move."

Sylas' face contorted with disdain as he struggled to hide his dislike of the leprechaun, but he managed to rasp out, "You are late to follow the custom. We have noted your presence even if you haven't announced it." Warming to his topic, he continued, "The Assembly will not be calling a special meeting to address the mad ravings of this creature. A regular meeting will occur in nearly a month's time. We shall see you again, then."

It made Esme wonder if Sylas' response was because of his continued dislike of Finn or, more troublingly, if the Assembly was actively trying to stifle the news of returning malevolents.

Juniper, looking noticeably more at ease than her date, stood up and joined him. Sylas added in a deeper, threatening voice, "Kin of the ifrit, of you I will remain wary. There are many things that are precious to me…"

Esme stood, both to bid the couple farewell and to hasten their exit. She could see that it was necessary to halt the mounting anger within the leshy. "May we speak briefly before you go?"

Sylas and Juniper donned their glamors. Sylas' elongated gray body and antlered head changed to look like a tall, slender, white male wearing nondescript jeans and plaid flannel. Juniper's luminous bark-brown skin softened and her bouncy green locks morphed into intricate black braids. She wore a pink flower-patterned smock dress that made Esme wonder if someone needed to remind her that humans still needed coats this time of year.

Once they were away from the table Esme said, "I scoured the riverbanks and hiking trails and found lingering traces of magic."

Sylas seemed almost hopeful, albeit briefly. She pulled the shed reptilian scute out of her dress pocket. "Plus, I found this."

She placed the evidence in his human hands. As expected, the news did nothing to soften Sylas' demeanor. Without hesitation, he returned the piece to her, suggesting she discuss it with Jacob instead. She bid them farewell.

Once Esme returned to the table, Finn handed a red rose to Abby, and a yellow rose to Esme. She smiled with her secret knowledge of their source. Finn had chosen two beautiful roses from his secret conservatory to share with them. The only thing that kept the affected expression from her face was her confusion about where he'd been hiding them for the past few hours.

"Um, thank you?" Abby turned the statement into a question. Esme schooled her face and gave Finn a flat look to disguise her appreciation of his hobby.

"The small card attached has my mobile number, so you can reach out to me whenever the need arises. I know Esme pledged to see me to the Assembly. I'll be around to help her keep to, uh, her obligations," replied Finn. "Now, I must go. Toodles," he said, and disappeared.

Used to this disappearing act by now, Esme didn't react. Abby's mouth hung open at the casual display of power. Her expression quickly changed from stunned amazement to disbelief. "He has a cell phone?!"

Shaking her head, Esme replied, "Absolutely nothing surprises me about him at this point."

Miles added, "I like him."

Smiling, Esme replied, "Me too."

Chapter Seven

Emergence

Gwyn

At first, time had passed slowly for him. Days turned to weeks, weeks to months, months to years, and years to centuries. Eventually, time became meaningless.

His state of mind progressed in much the same fashion as time. His thoughts of plotting revenge turned into planning escape. The escape strategies he had devised became despair, and ultimately, nothing at all. He stopped thinking and merely existed.

A crack had slowly snaked its way through the magic binding him in the void. Its progress had been ongoing for centuries, but he hadn't noticed. He had started the crack a long, long time ago, but then he had forgotten about it, and everything, completely until the day his prison shattered.

It had been so long since he considered freedom a possibility that once it happened, he simply continued to exist as he had for so long, as if nothing had changed.

An unpleasant sensation, a cyclic here and gone again feeling of discomfort, steadily roused him to consciousness.

His eyes rejoined his mind in wakefulness. He looked for the source of the discomfort.

A barberry bush. The long spikes on the stem of one branch had moved with the wind to scratch at his arm. For how long? Long enough for his skin to bleed, to scab over, again and again, many times over. His arm was streaked with scratches and some dried blood.

He looked up from where he sat cross-legged on the ground to see the sky. Slivers of brilliant blue peeked out between the edges of the blanketing clouds overhead.

He remembered pieces then.

He remembered his name and why he had disappeared from himself. But not why he had disappeared from the world. He remembered why his skin should not have shown a scratch and why he should not have bled. But bled he had. Who, what, was he now?

Gwyn ap Nudd stood and started walking. The sound of water was a siren song that he could not deny. Behind him, a small patch of frost covering the new spring grass where he had been sitting slowly melted.

The Dullahan

Half a world away, a headless horseman stumbled to his knees, his head dropping to roll on the lifeless ground. His stallion faltered, first falling onto its hocks and then fully onto its side. The debilitation of the vertigo and disorientation was overwhelming.

The Dullahan crawled on hands and knees, toppling forward and sideways in its quest to retrieve its head. The magic holding its body together called out for its eyes and mouth, rotten as it was.

Regaining its other half, the creature, once a man but cursed to live a second undead life as something else entirely, dragged its body across the arid pasture it found itself in to lean against the billowing ribs of its horse, still lying on the ground.

The scraping of rocks on his armor sent harsh sensations throughout his body. The weakness, the enfeeblement of his limbs, was a foreign thing. Giving a name to the feeling was, in itself, a struggle. The simple act of feeling was foreign to the Dullahan.

The undead knight felt utterly empty. His thoughts, once exclusive to his duty, undivided and all-encompassing, now drifted. Where, who, was he?

He remembered snatches of his past. Once he was a man, a powerful mage, who slew scores of his foes on the battlefield. Until he didn't. How had he, a conqueror, suffer such a complete defeat that he was beheaded?

His recollection shifted to the desperate and relentless search for his missing head. And anger, so much anger. He remembered that emotion. That anger had transformed him into a creature beyond recognition. It had given him a purpose, his duty, his brethren.

Glimpses of riding through verdant countryside for hours on end, his stallion exhaling puffs of smoke from its labors, flitted in and out of his mind. All this to speak a single name and send that soul to the place beyond life.

Now, his whole being felt as devoid as the landscape he found himself in. The connection to his brethren, the connection he once felt to the place beyond all life, was gone.

All that he understood was lost. He was lost.

The Dullahan lay there for hours, confused, trying everything it could to reestablish the link it once had to the other servants of death, but failing each time. So he did the only thing that he could do. He regained his seat upon his stallion, pointed the beast toward the setting sun, and started searching.

Chapter Eight

Night Intrusions

Miles

Pained wailing pierced the darkness that flickered with torchlight.

A banshee?

No, the cries of a young child.

No soothing, motherly sounds cut through the anguished sobs.

Miles, no. Not Miles, someone else, yet still him, was awoken by the piercing cries.

The wool-topped rush mattress gave way to his shifting weight as he sat up in bed. The air was cool but not frigid as a fire smoldered in the hearth.

His movement roused the wolfhound that had been dozing on the woven rug to the left of his bed. Always by his side, the king's loyal companion rose to join him.

Donning his nightcoat, Miles, still an unwilling guest in the king's body, left the king's rooms with his hound matching his stride in search of the source of the cries. Within a few paces, he encountered his first guard.

"What is it?" he demanded.

"Sire, they are in the great hall."

Departing with his thanks, he made his way through the stone halls of his keep, following the increasing sounds of pain to reach the great room.

Male figures standing in the shadows of the firelight stood over the source of the cries. One turned at the sound of his slippers on the wooden floor. "Sire! The child, we thought she was too far gone to disturb you," the guard pleaded.

"The strength of her lungs would say otherwise, Glais." The king pushed his irritation aside and strode forward.

Miles could only watch, trepidation gnawing at him. He wished he could help, but as always, he was nothing more than a witness. As the king and loyal hound reached the trundle that contained his patient, the guards parted for him.

The air was tinged with the unmistakable tang of iron and salt. Blood. He could smell it before he could see it.

A small girl, maybe eighteen months old, with flaxen hair and the lungs of a court singer, lay before him, covered in blood. Pain contorted her angelic face. But she was a fighter. Her left leg was mangled, torn open, with deep wounds running along both sides.

"Sire, her mother tried..." Glais started, but stopped.

Not-Miles replied, "Her mother, Glais, speak plainly! Is her mother in a similar state? Where is she?"

"Forgive me. An afanc, the reptilian demon....her mother fought desperately to save the girl, but she succumbed to the beast."

That explained the twisted bones and gashes on both sides of the child's leg. The afanc's gruesome fangs had ripped through the girl's flesh as the mother twisted and wrenched her free from the monster's jaws.

The king spoke then, in his typical prosaic fashion, "When we are done, I must know the name of the mother with a warrior's heart. For now, hold the girl still."

The king reached down toward the child with hands, one perfect and the other silver, emitting a soft glow...

Miles startled up, his alarm blaring its call to rise. It took a moment for him to shake off the disorientation and snap back to the present. He'd been stuck in a dream. Again.

While he was in it, his thoughts intermingled with the thoughts of his host, an unknown king. The king was distinct from himself and yet indistinguishable. Mind still torn between the world of the waking and the world of dreams, Miles wondered if the little girl had survived. It was cruel that the vision had not revealed her fate.

Fighting the dream was impossible. Usually, the same number of dreams and nightmares would cycle through his mind while he slept. After experiencing countless nights like this, Miles had learned that the only way to escape the dream was to allow it to run its course. On rare occasions, like the one that he had just entered, the dream would be completely new. He'd had another new one the first night he'd talked to Esme at the bar. Was it becoming a trend?

Only once before had Miles been able to pinpoint exactly which event during his waking hours was the trigger of his nocturnal visions. It was the day he lost his hand. As if the trauma of having his hand blasted off while on a tour of duty during his stint in the military was not enough, he had relived his dream king's brutal amputation the night after waking from his surgery.

The wail of the child in the dream had reminded him of a banshee. The retelling of Finn's encounter from the night before had prompted this new vision.

So, what did losing his hand and hearing the story of a malevolent encounter have in common? His sleep-addled brain could not form any connections between the two waking events or between the two dreams. Perhaps it was simply a coincidence...

The name! The realization snapped Miles fully awake as surely as a bucket of ice water thrown upon his head would.

The dreams had haunted Miles' nights and shaped his days since the moment that his magic awakened as a young teen. Yet, this was the first time that a name had featured in one. Glais, the guardsman, he thought. Who was he? Could the name of a single guard, if that is who he was, help Miles identify his dream king?

As if the king were real.

Miles doubted it. Logic suggested that his brain used the dreams to deal with situations that came up in his waking life. What little science existed on the topic suggested the same. He and the king had far too much in common for it to not be a fabrication of his own subconsciousness. They'd both lost a hand, they both had a wolfhound, and from the clues he'd picked up on over time, they were both Welsh.

Still, what could account for his brain's fixation on a single set of characters for over twenty years? He knew it wasn't normal to dream like he did.

But neither is your healing magic, came the unbidden reflection. But that was a secret, known only by a few.

Miles did not linger in his bed, allowing the thoughts stemming from his dreams to occupy his attention no longer. His time in the military had eradicated such "self-indulgent" behaviors from him—their term, not his.

Plus, Lily was staring at him with her big, solemn eyes. The houseboat was small for such a large dog, but man and hound made it work for them both.

He swung his legs over the side of his bed, gave Lily scritches, then donned his coat and boots. Miles left his hand charging on the nightstand nearby; he didn't need it yet. He clipped the dog's leash onto her collar and the pair left the dock, headed for the nearby grassy area to allow her to do her business. Lily's leash was mainly for show; she was the most placid dog that he had ever known and would stay by his side without instruction.

That morning's fog was heavy, even for Seattle. The mist laid upon the lake before them like a heavy shroud, smothering the nearby buildings and hills from sight. Even the seagulls were subdued. Typically, he would wake to their incessant calls to one another. The mornings were slowly getting warmer by degrees with the increased sunlight. Soon he wouldn't have to bother with a glove and hat.

"Lil," he mumbled as they walked lazily along the lakeside pedestrian trail.

Yes, Miles talked to his dog like she was a person. No, he didn't care who heard him do it.

"It's going to be a long day. I have a short morning of work and then I have work. Will you come with me to do some work this afternoon?"

Lily huffed out her cheeks and yipped, almost daintily, for such a large dog.

Man and hound walked back to the houseboat together so that he could finish his preparations. The lingering mist remained undisturbed except for their movement. Stepping back onto the deck, Miles was greeted by the gentle sway of the water beneath his feet.

As he began his preparations, he mused on his good luck. Last night's chance meeting at the bar had been an unexpected gift. When he received the text from Abby asking him to meet her for a drink, he figured it would be a pleasant night of friendly conversation at a place he already frequented. Plus, there was always a chance that he'd gain relevant information on a night out surrounded by mages.

But then Esme had walked in with the leprechaun. It was as if the stars and planets had aligned to make his work for the Corded Brotherhood that much easier.

He wasn't certain if his cell phone would work where he was headed that afternoon, so he double checked his GPS unit to ensure that it was fully charged and loaded with the data of his target's location. Esme had also inadvertently supplied that information to the Brotherhood. She was proving to be...useful.

She was beautiful. There was no doubting that. He stole secret glances of her each time he'd been there. Her radiant personality drew others in, her warmth a magnet for attention. For him, a man too used to living alone in the shadows, it was impossible not to be drawn to her.

His mind and senses battled each other in their opinion of her. To his magical senses, Esme felt ever so slightly odd. There was a subtle offness to her magic. The strangest thing of all was that meeting her tugged at the edges of his memory, like he should be able to place her face to a name from his distant past. Perhaps it was the peculiar nature of her magic that caused his déjà vu. In any case, she was something to study. Any magical irregularity was worth investigating to the Corded Brotherhood.

He packed away his sealed kit of butterfly syringes, skin tape, and packets of local disinfectant. The fact that she, a person of interest, had brought his original quarry, the leprechaun, within his reach, without him having to lift a finger, made him beyond pleased. Their impromptu get-together had provided him with an opening that could fill two needs with one deed.

He went to his small kitchen and grabbed an empty plastic bag and put some ice in a second one. These he tucked into a tiny insulated container next to the field IV kit and saline bag he stored in the smaller section of his hiking pack. Everything was ready for later that afternoon.

Being on the water always soothed him. As he sipped his mug of coffee on the porch, Miles reflected on how important it was to have some time for relaxation the morning before you confronted another killer.

Chapter Nine

WHAT THE SUN REVEALS

Esme

"Jacob...Jaaaacob! Wake up!" Esme waved her hands and snapped her fingers in front of the old man's face, hoping to rouse him from slumber. Despite her efforts, Jacob remained slouched in his favorite recliner, mouth slightly agape, his chest rising and falling in the rhythm of deep sleep. He looked peaceful, the imposing aura that often filled the room when he was awake turned down significantly. His wiry hair stuck out in wild tufts, contrasting with the neatly arranged books lining the walls of his otherwise impeccable library.

This wasn't the first time she had found him there, sleeping. Given the hour of the morning, this was not a napping spot—he'd been there all night. It was a mystery to Esme why the old man chose to sleep in the ratty recliner in his library, which stood out incongruously given its comfortable surroundings. Especially when she knew he had several comfortable bedrooms to choose from.

To enter, Esme first used the mundane key Jacob had given her. She had purposefully announced her presence several times upon entering the house, but Jacob was slightly hard of hearing. Which, she realized belatedly, was probably why he hadn't yet roused.

Then she used the mage's hidden entrance to his library to ultimately reach his "bedside." This reminded her that Finn had used magic nearly identical to the bar's concealment spell. She bit her lip to stop herself from cursing aloud. For years, Jacob had guarded secrets as closely as his precious tomes, but now... now was her chance to pry one loose. She took a page from Finn's book and impishly hatched a plan.

Conjuring a feather and sending it to wiggle ever so slightly under his nose felt like a tiny slice of justice for her. The feather worked where her words had not. First, Jacob tried twitching his nose to dislodge the bothersome sensation. When that didn't work, he raised his hand to swat at it.

Esme was ready for this.

Mid-movement, she hastily conjured another feather that appeared upright in his raised hand. Feather number two succeeded with aplomb. He snorted half of it into his nose and finally roused, sputtering, with pieces of the downy barbs lodged in his facial scruff.

Beaming with her triumph, Esme said, "Good morning, Jacob." The feather's barbs stuck to his face slowly disappeared into the ether. Pursed lips and the beginning of an assessing gaze appeared on his grizzled face.

But then, just as quickly as the look appeared, it disappeared. It was replaced by the happy grandpa expression of his that Esme had grown so fond of over the years. Their relationship was more familial than professional, and she had grown comfortable with it. Hence, she knew before she even started the magic that he would dismiss the childish prank with a smile.

Still, deep down, Esme knew Jacob had a hard side. Albeit frail of body at his advanced age, Jacob was indisputably a presence in any room. There was something hidden in his eyes that made others wary. An impenetrable shield obscured whatever it was, but she knew she only caught rare glimpses of its edges. She had seen his domineering side come out occasionally during Assembly proceedings, but with her, he had always been more like family. The way others treated him with deference, even if they knew nothing about him, was further evidence that something about Jacob set off people's instincts.

He'd been her employer at the bar and for the Assembly, as well as her mentor in magic and in life. Jacob had become so important to her she couldn't help but feel betrayed. Sure, it was a small thing, hiding a magical secret from her, but it mattered because of the nearly unbearable reasons that might be motivating his silence.

Jacob replied to her greeting, his voice filled with mock affront, "Esmeralda! You devilish girl. I see that you've let yourself in and acted as my alarm clock."

He gestured at the wooden stool at the study desk nearby. "Oh, do sit! Don't stand there with a sour expression. If you are going to take part in hijinks at your age, commit to them fully."

Esme relished how indignant his posh upper-crust English accent sounded when he was surprised. She couldn't help but feel a surge of warmth in her chest at his endearment, "devilish girl." Still, the familiarity between them couldn't erase the nagging thought from her mind.

Esme couldn't help herself. She felt like a child confronting her parent during an argument as she blurted out, "Oh, at my age, huh? That's funny. You've been pushing off teaching the bar's concealment spell to me for years. Why?" She crossed her arms and sat down, annoyance clear in her body language. The time to have a frank, direct discussion was past due.

However, as soon as she sat down, Esme regretted her outburst. There was a fine line between candor and rudeness, and Jacob didn't deserve the latter. "I'm sorry. That was a lot to spring on you with no context. I came to speak with you, not berate you. How are you, Jacob?"

"Awake, apparently." The sparkle in his eyes hadn't disappeared. He was always quick to forgive her for any missteps.

She pressed on, "I'm here on Assembly and on personal business. Do you know what Sylas requested of me?"

Jacob's reply was dismissive, "That whole business with the leprechaun that he was raving about? Yes, I know of it. I assume the situation is well in hand, since you sit before me unscathed."

"But Sylas also asked me to check out the riverbank where the boy disappeared. That's where I found this. It's buzzing with magic." She pulled out the scute, holding it out as if offering evidence at trial.

He grabbed some glasses from the table nearby and peered at it. "So it is, my dear, so it is. I'm uncertain what this is from. I'll have someone look at it. This could be helpful, so thank you." He slipped the scute into the drawer of the desk.

It was annoying her that she couldn't tell if Sylas or Jacob were giving her the brushoff, so a bit of chaotic humor colored her tone when she said, "Unscathed?" She chuckled and went on, "Just barely. I nearly died from third-degree burns and I hog-tied an unconscious leprechaun to interrogate him." Sarcasm leaked into her tone. "But I made a new friend! So, you know, it was a big win for me."

One bushy eyebrow lifted as Jacob asked, "Oh, that's all?"

She snapped back, "No. Why didn't you tell me that the bar's concealment spell is Fae?" It was too much for her to contain any longer. The only explanation she could come up with for his long silence was that *she* was the problem.

Jacob's dismissive attitude disappeared. She could tell that he wasn't upset by the question, just surprised. "Well then," he said, standing slowly, resigned to the impending conversation, "might I at least have a morning beverage before we get into it?"

They traveled to the kitchen, where they sat down in a comfortable breakfast nook with mugs in hand. The trip took just enough time for her anger to dissipate. Knowing Jacob, he'd planned the move the second she opened her mouth to complain. He was always two steps ahead.

She didn't realize the level of frustration she had reached until she unintentionally brought up the concealment spell. Her exasperation at the Assembly's persistent demands to "Jump!" while keeping her in the dark had finally reached a boiling point.

Her palms were a little clammy and her heart was beating too quickly for only having had one cup of coffee so far that morning. Anxiety over what he had to say had replaced her anger. She shouldn't be nervous to be the one asking questions of him for once, but she was. Her nervousness stemmed from a simple fear: She didn't want to jeopardize their relationship.

She had nearly rallied her courage to be the first to speak when Jacob placed his mug on the table and asked, "So, you made a friend? Good, good. The leprechaun you brought to the bar last night?"

How could he already know? Esme wondered. The answer was as plain as her reflection in the mirror. She was not the only set of eyes and ears that spent time at The Sanctuary. But who could it be?

Jacob didn't wait for a reply, since he seemed to know the answer, anyway. "That reminds me. Have I told you about my mate from university? The pech fellow? Surely you remember the rock-skinned, cavern-dwelling gnomes of Scotland? No? Well, he was as ugly as a waterlogged boot, but the glamor he used made him into a brightly shining Adonis. He was irresistible to the ladies. That is, until he inevitably started blathering on about rocks and bored them to death. Some excuses that the ladies came up with to leave the conversation had me in stitches. Once a woman pulled a crumpled-up piece of paper from her purse and practically shouted, 'paper beats rock!' as she slapped it on the table, and fled the scene. So. What has this leprechaun been blathering on about that made you bring out the feathers like the girl with the paper in my story?"

Esme had a feeling the story was fabricated to calm her anxiety, but she could never be sure with Jacob. He was always full of surprises, so it was equally likely that the story was true. She didn't relish the idea of telling the whole narrative, especially since she knew it would make its way back to him from Sylas at some point. She jumped straight into was bothering her instead.

"I feel you've been dangling this carrot in front of my face for a decade now. You know I've always been curious about the concealment magic. So when I find the leprechaun's home and see that he used what is essentially the same spellwork to hide it, I'm puzzled. Why? Why hide it from me for this long?"

To her immense surprise, his answer was immediate and without disassembling. "The damn Californians!"

Of all the things that Esme expected Jacob to say—that he didn't think that she was ready, that she wasn't strong enough to pull off the magic, or, deep in her heart of hearts, she feared he didn't trust her—she expected this answer the least.

She allowed a small laugh to escape from her, releasing some of the tension that had built up from her earlier nervousness, as she asked, deadpan, "The Californians. What?"

"Yes, the Californians! Esme, it's all politics!" he said, swiping his hand in the air. "If the Assembly in California knew that our secret, superior concealment magic was from the Fae, they'd have a field day! I've had just about enough of their uppity behavior for one lifetime!"

Esme buried her head in her hands and silently groaned. Politics. It was ridiculous the lengths to which the Assembly would go for politics.

He studied her momentarily, and then unexpectedly apologized. "Esmeralda, I'm sorry. I should have explained sooner. I wish I had understood that my secrecy troubled you as much as it seems to. It will be rectified today. I promise you."

On the upside, this was a far less hurtful answer than she had emotionally armored herself against. Knowing that her loyalty hadn't been misplaced was a comforting relief. She felt relieved as a hidden burden was lifted.

Face still buried in her hands, she heard him ask, sounding almost impressed with his belated realization of what she'd casually mentioned before. "Wait, hogtied. What is this about hogtying the leprechaun? What on earth did you do?"

This time, the groan coming from her was louder. She succinctly retold the story of finding Finn's home, the confrontation with fire and trolls, and finally, her questioning him while he was tied to his bed.

After she finished, Jacob commented, "And then the next evening you met with Christi's daughter and the new mage, Miles, at the bar."

Christi was Abby's mother. She sat in the Assembly with Jacob.

So Jacob was on a first-name basis with Miles. Interesting. Esme asked, "Have you already spoken with Sylas about this?" She wanted to know if there was another Assembly spy at the bar or if Jacob's communication with Sylas was simply that frequent.

Jacob didn't answer. Instead, he asked another question, "This banshee, the leprechaun didn't mention interacting with it at all?"

"He claimed to have fled from it all the way here, only to feel another evil presence near the river."

"Well, that's neither here nor there. Esmeralda, this story is so bizarre that I feel as though I am still catching up. You mentioned fireballs. But how could the scoundrel wield the power of fire magic?"

"Scoundrel?" Esme questioned with a lift of one brow, prodding him.

Knowing what she was getting at, he replied, "Very well then, I formally withdraw the description of your 'friend' as a scoundrel. Although you must admit that leprechauns have the most mischievous nature. But this fire. Do you know its source?"

Esme wasn't certain if it was better to tread lightly around the topic or risk sending the elderly man into heart palpitations with the truth. After all, the whole reason that she was disgruntled right now was the Assembly's tacit dishonesty with her.

"A broken binding promise granted him the powers of an ifrit," she said, mind made up.

With a surprising nonchalance, he uttered the words, "Well, that's an unexpected twist," as if it were just another everyday occurrence. He continued, "It explains the fire. We all have our unique heritage."

Something about how he said the last part left her with a tingling unease. She pondered why his seemingly innocent statement had evoked such a response in her.

Jacob broke into her reverie, asking, "Do you think he is dangerous?"

"Unprovoked? No. I think he just wants to have a bit of fun."

He looked thoughtful, then replied, "Perhaps, just in case, spend some more time with your new friend. I appreciate your certainty of his harmless nature, but the Assembly will require zero doubts. We'll make sure any time off you need from the bar will be taken care of."

Mulling it over, Esme could see the logic behind their request. Having her keep an eye on Finn made perfect sense, and spending time with a new friend was no trouble at all.

"Done. Any suggestions?" she asked.

He replied, eyes sparkling, "Under no circumstances should you feed him after midnight."

Esme rolled her eyes and stood to hug Jacob goodbye.

Had Esme's focus not been split by her own troubles, the whispers of malevolent resurgence would have surfaced in her mind. By the time she realized the price of that distraction, it would already be too late.

Chapter Ten

A River of Stone

Gwyn

Night had fallen in the time since his reawakening.

The descent from Dinas Emrys was nearly the same as it ever was. Trees and bracken still grew on the rocky slopes, and Gwyn could hear the familiar bleating of grazing sheep in the distance.

But much had changed during the years of his imprisonment. The Glaslyn River beckoned to him with its thirst-quenching waters. Beside it, a dark river of stone stretched as far as the eye could see. He could make out perfectly straight white lines demarcating the outer edges and the middle of the stone river.

Surely these were the work of a great mage demarcating the boundary of their holdings? If he stepped foot on the border, would an alarm be raised and knights be called up to meet the intruder? Could it be a warded boundary, designed to defend against any outsider with a swift and deadly attack?

As he neared the boundary, the absence of any magical energy became more noticeable. There was no prickling sensation on his skin and his stomach did not tie itself into knots on approaching it.

His body's need for sustenance was evident from his hunger and thirst. Despite his lingering weakness, he would have to take the chance. If it came to death, he would happily oblige his attacker with a fight.

Memories of his wrongful imprisonment and the time before were still trickling back. Yet, the small flickers of his slowly returning memory paled in comparison to the immense scale of the loss. In his current state, he had no hope of reaching the heights of his former life. He was greatly diminished.

One step, followed by the next, took him across the river of stone. No alarms were raised, and he met no resistance.

The first drink from the river was better than any wine served at one of a hundred kings' tables. He splashed his face and looked for sticks to make a fire. He still possessed a sword, so he made use of it.

His heart grew bitter and cold, sensing deep down that the betrayal that brought him to this place came from within his own family.

A curious lamb, fluffy with its coat of fresh wool, wandered over. Gwyn imagined his father's face in place of the young animal's as he snapped its neck.

With his thirst and hunger sated, he fell asleep.

Gwyn saw his first automobile the morning after he awoke in the field. His startled amazement at the creation was quickly overcome by fear, real and visceral, of the unknown, as dozens barreled by him at speeds no horse could manage. A person piloted each and each wholly lacked the telltale feeling of magic. Nothing in his mind could explain what he was seeing.

And so he hid in the fields. He survived for two days by slaughtering lambs, foraging for greens, and sleeping under bushes. Already a faint reflection of the person he once was, he became a shadow of his former self. He felt like a draugr wandering in the sunlight, if not in body, then in mind. The weariness besetting his soul consumed him completely.

He roamed as far as his legs could carry him. But the spaces that he once knew as wild were tame. The hills, the stream, the animals, and the sky were much the same as they were before his imprisonment. Everything else, however, was changed to a state of unrecognizable obscurity. He didn't know this world any longer.

The only thing that could have changed his world so much in so many ways was time—a great deal of it.

Unsure of what lay ahead and with no clear destination in mind, he pressed on. Spurred by his confusion and restlessness, he walked along the edges of the river of stone. The air was filled with a monstrous roar as a metal carriage sped by, blaring a sound that overwhelmed his senses and made him stumble backward. The anger that shot through him at the indignity snapped him out of his walking slumber. His hand wrapped around the hilt of his sword, ready to meet the insult. Just who were these humans to do such a thing to him?

As the offensive car sped away, the reality of his newfound situation brought him low once more. Humans.... He could curse them for their low behavior, but he...he was human again.

He was left with nothing, as everything and everyone he had known was gone. Overwhelmed by sorrow, Gwyn felt his legs buckle as he realized the magnitude of what he had lost. With a broken sob, he collapsed to his knees, tears mingling with the dirt beneath him as despair threatened to take over his soul.

Chapter Eleven

An Accidental Party

Miles

"Really, you think that putting me through this twice in one week is gonna get me in the right mood for talkin' with you?"

Magic allowed Miles to control his bionic hand with a precision equal to that of his flesh. He tightened the ropes holding Finn in place with practiced ease. His intention was not to create an adversary or a corpse out of the leprechaun, so he worked in silence. Lily lay half awake but watchful on the floor of Finn's house, facing the door.

Finn carried on talking while Miles checked his bindings. "I can't say I'm thrilled, but it worked for Esme, didn't it? I'll be honest, she may be young, but I would have preferred being conscious while she tied me up instead of you, beggin' your pardon." The leprechaun suggestively waggled his eyebrows.

The Fae's words caused him to pause in surprise. Esme had tied him up? But Finn continued speaking, cutting off any further exploration of that question.

"Bejasus, I surely didn't expect the likes of you, bein' yourself and all, to attack me outside my own home. But lo and behold, here we are. I suppose I ought to consider myself fortunate to still be drawin' breath."

To gain clarification on whether "being yourself and all" pertained to his role as a Brother or something unrelated, Miles inquired, "You know about the Brotherhood?"

"Of course I do. Yeah, let's just both keep pretendin' that's what I'm talking about."

Miles waited patiently, fixing his eyes on the leprechaun who sat before him, tied to the chair.

Finn saw right through the ploy because he smirked and remarked, "I suppose that being upright while tied up this time is a welcome change."

It wasn't worth the effort needed to get the trickster to open up, so Miles stuck to business instead. "I say it a third time to bind: I have no harmful intentions toward you. I represent the Corded Brotherhood. If you know of the Brotherhood, you know that I have a job to do, no matter what."

At this, Finn burst into peals of chaotic laughter. Miles failed to see the humor in the situation.

So he shut out the sound of the rain outside, straightened his back, and prepared the sodium thiopental.

Esme

Esme hesitated before starting her car, quickly typing out a text message to the number Finn had given her on the rose. She explained she would drop off a package at his house and asked if he would be home. Cheekily, she added a promise not to break into it this time.

The weather that greeted Esme on the trail was not ideal for hiking. The fog that laid over Seattle in the morning turned into rain mixed with a few late-season snowflakes in the mountains. She checked her pack—waterproof, thankfully—every mile or so to ensure that the homemade cookies and a bottle of whiskey were still intact.

Even days later, she couldn't shake off the mixed emotions from her first encounter with Finn. Her actions were morally gray—a place she was becoming rather accustomed to as of late.

Esme eventually reached Finn's house, excited to see him. Right away, she could see that Finn's front door had changed since the last time that she had been there. The color was the same, but what was once a solid rustic door now had a halfmoon-shaped pane of glass at the top. It wasn't surprising to her that he could make such a change after witnessing the awe-inspiring magic inside his home.

But what she heard in the last few feet to the entrance made her steps slow in interest. She heard two voices. Finn was not alone. Unable to deny her curiosity, she listened more intently. Both were male. Both voices were calm—no shouting or commotion.

Still, a sinking sensation settled into her chest as she stepped closer to the door. Finn's voice didn't sound right to her ears. He'd replied to her message earlier, saying that she was welcome to come over, but he hadn't mentioned a visitor.

Her mind turned over the facts. Finn said he didn't know anyone in the local magical community at all. So who would visit a leprechaun who professed to be in hiding?

A quick peek revealed an unfamiliar large gray dog, sprawled out asleep near the doorway. Nothing alarming about that. But then her eyes landed on Finn. He was bound to the chair where she had previously questioned him. His head was loose on his shoulders, as if holding it upright took too much effort. That probably meant this wasn't some freaky leprechaun BDSM thing, right? From where she was, she couldn't determine if he was injured.

The other unidentified man was hidden from her view by the door's angle. Were leprechaun treasure hunters really a thing? It was surreal that she had to worry about this in real life, but nothing about the situation made sense.

The urge to rush in, to confront whoever might hold her friend captive, swelled within her, but logic and anxiety restrained her from acting. Logic urged her to wait, to listen and try to steal another peek, to gather more information before acting. Her anxiety whispered of the potential loss of face with Jacob and the rebuke of the Assembly for acting rashly if she did more harm than good by failing a new member of the community. Plus, there was a legitimate risk to her safety if she got involved with the person holding Finn captive.

She couldn't quite make out the words of the conversation; she could only take clues from the tone and cadence of the speech. But her instincts nagged. They screamed at her, above the din of logic and anxiety, to act now. It was this that finally pushed her over the edge.

This wasn't a situation where she could hike back to a place with a phone signal and beg for orders: there was a real possibility that Finn was in danger. She needed a plan, and quickly. As a conjuration mage, she could make her own backup. She summoned her trolls. Her favorite trio was as stupid as they were ugly, so she needed to strategize carefully because she would have to navigate their actions without knowing her opponent's intentions or capabilities.

Tactically, she needed the conjurations to distract and, optimistically, detain the unknown male speaker while she helped Finn. The entryway was narrow, so she'd have to stagger them in, one by one. They weren't immune to magic or physical attacks. If hit hard enough, they would eventually lose corporeal stability, and her shield spell wasn't strong enough to be of much use. Unfortunately, there were no available improvised weapons at hand, as the nearby fallen branches and sticks were too small to do much good.

A dangerous smile broke over her face when she realized that this impromptu home invasion wouldn't be all that different from handling a pub brawl. She appeared to have developed a liking for the chemical rush caused by the thrill of a fight; by the risk and the excitement of danger.

She chanted the call for her minions. They appeared with no sound, having no breath of life in their bodies. Bert was the tallest and appeared the oldest, covered in fat folds and wrinkles. Tom scratched at his beard, awaiting orders, while George, the dirtiest of the trio, idly watched a slug slink across the forest floor. Usually, each of her conjurations stood still, exactly where they were conjured, arms limp at their sides and mouths hanging open, eyes vacant. Were they changing or had she altered the spell without noticing? Regardless, it wasn't the time to be having an academic debate on spellcasting with herself.

She ordered her minions, then hid behind a tree in view of the door. Time was indeed cyclic because here she was, again, hiding behind a tree outside of a leprechaun's house, awaiting action. Following instructions, Bert was the first to turn and approach the door. The sound of splintering wood echoed as Bert's fist crashed through the door, shards flying. It broke into three large pieces, only partially still hanging from the frame. She cringed as she realized the door would be unsalvageable. Unfortunately, she didn't think that she could buy a door for a magical Fae house from a hardware store.

So much for her promise not to break into Finn's house this time...

Following the crash of the broken door, a single bark rang out. She reassured herself that the dog would be fine. Her trolls lacked the autonomy to defend themselves aggressively or take independent action. Their instructions were to guard Finn and handle the dog with care. She was being purposefully less specific about the handling of the other unknown male. As far as she was concerned, he deserved a bit of rough treatment.

She heard a sharp command for the dog to sit from the unknown voice. Only a few movements' sounds reached her ears before she spotted George emerging from the entryway holding the shaggy gray dog. Seeing that it was unharmed and appeared to be enjoying the troll cuddles, she set aside her worries for the poor creature. She could sense that her conjured helpers had captured the male, but his appearance remained unclear due to the interference of the Fae magic in Finn's house.

Walking over scattered door pieces, Esme's eyes adjusted to the candlelit interior. Her breath caught in her throat as her eyes locked on Finn cradled in Tom's arms, still tied to the chair, half-conscious and smiling like a fool. He twitched his fingers up from their spot on the chair's arm to her in greeting.

Between one heartbeat and the next, she realized her mistake. She was so fixated on checking on Finn, the primary object of her concern, that she dropped her guard. What she saw next ensured that she would not be making that mistake again.

Miles.

There he was, dangling aloft in Bert's arms, his expression inhospitable. His eyes weren't the gentle green that she had seen before. Instead, they were the green of frozen evergreens in winter. The eyes belonged to someone she barely recognized: indifferent, calculating.

The inexorable circle of time spun again as she said, this time rather sadly, "You've got to be kidding me."

It would have been logical for a member of the Assembly to show up at Finn's house, uninvited. She knew they rotated through a few of their heavier hitters to "greet" new magic users to the area. It was a method that left no doubt as to who had the power and who had to ask permission, but one of these visits would not have rendered Finn in such a state. After all, a person must be lucid to be properly intimidated by a guest.

Her gut had told her all of this as she debated whether to break through the front door. Now her stomach was churning and, somehow, that made her impossibly more angry than she already was. She was utterly pissed off. But really, what had she expected when she saw Finn bound to a chair through the window?

Not Miles. That was certain.

Her anger only got worse. Why should she be uncomfortable when she had done nothing? She hadn't drugged the leprechaun with whom they had spent a convivial evening not so long ago. Miles had.

She wanted to punch him in his indifferent face.

Snarling, she let out the first thing that came to her mind. "What the flying fuck, Miles?" Her voice was sharp, but inside she felt a mounting panic mixing with her outrage.

To his credit, he didn't flinch from his position within Bert's clammy embrace. His already indifferent expression tightened and his jaw clenched.

He replied, "You still have the option of turning around and forgetting this unfortunate…party."

Esme crossed her arms over her chest. "Oh, I'm sorry, was that a threat coming from the guy who seems to be dangling in the air right now?"

Despite his tight expression, he spoke in a calm tone: "It's not meant to be a threat, just a recommendation."

Her patience snapped. Vision narrowing, she barked back, "What exactly is wrong with Finn? What did you give him?" She was walking in circles between the triangle of trolls and talking with her hands. Perhaps she appeared slightly insane, but moving was her only way to refrain from punching him.

Silence. Miles said nothing and didn't shift his expression. That was it. She was going to pop a blood vessel in her forehead. A small growl escaped her lips.

The growl unlocked something within her; it unleashed a wave of anesthesia. It dulled the connection she felt with her body and obliterated her emotions.

Her entire focus sharpened to one thing. Her goal was absolute. Nothing else mattered.

A whisper of alarm skated across the surface of her thoughts, barely breaking through her deadened state. The piercing sound of the alarm vanished, floating away like dandelion fluff on the wind.

The unnatural, cold, relentless numbness had won control over her.

From this place of detachment, she said, "I swear on my parents' graves that if you don't tell me how to help Finn, I will give the order to have your ribcage crushed until your insides are indistinguishable from the outside."

A small part of her brain did a double take in shock at what she'd just said.

Miles looked at her then—really looked at her, studying her face, studying her eyes. To his credit, he didn't try to deny his actions. "I administered a very small dose of sodium thiopental. He may experience some somnolence and retrograde amnesia, but no other ill effects. Yet, with him not being human, I can only extrapolate."

There was a threat in her words when she asked, "You can only extrapolate?"

"It was a very small dose. His liver will process the drug. I noted no signs of overdose and monitored his heart rate." Miles lifted his chin slightly and said, "He appears to be sleeping it off now."

Esme turned and noted that Finn's head was lolling to the side. A puddle of drool was working its way down the front of his shirt. His chest rose and fell with each slow breath.

Observation made, she snarled, "Why?"

This time the response was quick and served flippantly. "Constraints seemed to work for you, so I gave it a go."

How did he know?

Esme ordered her minion aloud, even though the verbal commands were not required. Sometimes, all it took was the threat itself to get her mark talking. "Bert, slow and steady squeeze, please. Reverse at my signal."

Her detachment had rendered the difference between right and wrong meaningless to her. She watched, emotionless, as Bert began on his work.

"I'm willing to watch your eyes pop."

Miles struggled to breathe. Nevertheless, he held her gaze, but remained silent.

Then, from her left, she heard a quiet, anguished howl. The dog's wail jolted her back to reality. It was a dose of sobering clarity, provided by the mournful cry of a dog for its master.

The person she had been a few seconds ago, the person who suggested that they'd watch a man's slow death by their order, wasn't who she was. She snapped out of the state that had overcome her. Was the thrill of conflict really so irresistible to her that she was willing to cross a line she had made for herself?

Esme immediately signaled Bert, and Miles inhaled a full breath. She covertly studied his breathing to assure herself that her order hadn't done any serious damage.

"Well done, Miles. Your deflection of throwing my own sins back in my face was a direct hit." It was the truth, but she still needed more answers. Once Finn and she were safe, she could deal with the numb state that had taken over her.

Regrouping, coming back to herself more as each moment passed, she realized something. Her voice softened, but a tinge of anger lingered in her tone as she asked, "Why didn't you put up a fight?"

Feeling more herself, she waited patiently for his response. From the subtle emotions flickering across Miles' face, he appeared to be struggling with how to reply.

Finally, with something close to the truth in his expression, he answered, still slightly out of breath, "Combat with three conjurations would be too risky."

"Fine. Why drug Finn? What does this sodium thio-whatever do?"

To her surprise, he answered quickly this time, "I needed the truth, not the Fae 'close enough' version of the truth, and the drug could ensure that. It used to be used for general anesthesia for surgery but has the useful side effect of decreasing higher cortical brain function while reducing inhibitions—a truth serum, basically."

She used her voice like a knife. "What truth? Why do you need it?"

The space between them was charged with tension, and she tried to piece together the scattered information in her mind. It didn't help that Miles had remained inscrutable, inching her closer to the certainty that something more clandestine was at play.

Half accusatory, half regretting his answer before it was even given, she asked, "Did the Assembly send you?"

Insecurity was a liability that she should extinguish at every opportunity, but it kept popping up. She had to remind herself that Jacob had, only just that morning, offered a long-held secret to her. Her mentor would not have sent Miles to double-end her work. If there was division brewing at the top, a political play against Jacob could explain Miles' presence.

Miles answered her question with one of his own. "Did the Assembly send you?"

Finn giggled in his sleep from his bindings on the chair, still held aloft by George.

Inspired by the Fae trickster, she tried for reluctant cooperation. "Tom, set the chair down gently." Then, to Miles, "You could say that or, equally, you could not."

Succinctly he replied, "Same."

So, he was keeping secrets. That much wasn't a surprise. Unfortunately, his response to her question gave her nothing to work with.

He hung his head for a moment and clarified. "Look, we both know that the Assembly has a strong influence on your actions. I can't ignore that fact when talking to you."

So he knew. Was this another deflection or, more troublingly, was this a sign that he was an agent of some competing faction? She needed to be two steps ahead instead of behind in the future. It was becoming clear to her she'd have to be proactive to make that happen.

"And I can't ignore the fact that you drugged Finn to extract information," she retorted. "That doesn't scream 'do no harm' to me, *Doctor*."

Guilt flickering on his face, he nodded once, acknowledging the truth.

It had been much easier to stare daggers at him when he wasn't being so forthright.

Miles sighed, which seemed like a rather easygoing response for a man dangling helplessly in the air. "I won't pretend that my actions were completely justified. But I had reason to do what I did." A degree of warmth returned to his glacial gaze. "I think that we both know that there is something bigger at play here."

She smirked, skeptical. "So, because there might be some big bad things out there, I'm just supposed to trust you and forget about all this?"

"No."

She threw her hands in the air. "Finally, something we can agree on! Do you have anywhere that you need to be in the next few hours?" She thought twice, then said, "Scratch that. I actually don't care. We," gesturing between them, "are going to hang out until Finn can fill me in on a few things. Especially on how things went before your 'retrograde amnesia' drug kicked in."

She'd been overly confident because, without warning, a shield spell materialized around Miles. She hadn't even heard or seen him cast the spell. Bert's arms widened to accommodate holding the shield in place of a man; he was holding the shield up as if it had actual mass, not just magical properties.

Normally when she tried to touch a defensive shield with her hands, it was like an invisible force field existed outside of the visible part of the shield, stopping her hand before it made contact. During practice sessions with Jacob, her conjurations' blows would simply bounce off. She hadn't considered that her conjurations could interact with solid magic in a way that living flesh could not. She'd have to think of applications for that little nugget of information when her prisoner wasn't escaping.

The shield appeared and vanished in a flash, almost as if it had never been there. Miles fell to the floor while Bert's arms moved in again to detain him unsuccessfully. No wonder Miles had seemed so easygoing just a moment before.

Sedately, he walked to the nearby bed and sat down.

Bert hadn't been ordered to recapture the man, so he stood there dumbly. Esme couldn't help but do the same.

Lacking any hint of a threat in his voice, Miles straightened his jacket and said, "Then let's talk while we wait."

Chapter Twelve

Finger Pointing

Esme

Esme gaped. "Great. So you could have broken out of that the whole time."

Miles replied—rather confidently, she thought wryly, for a large man sitting on a child-sized bed—"I wasn't certain, but I had to take a chance. Can we agree to a temporary armistice?"

His calm invitation to chat, with no hint of threat, fractionally lessened her nerves. Esme's troll trio, with Bert at the forefront, remained in place, awaiting orders. Miles had surprised her too many times for her to be comfortable without protection.

Esme pulled a chair over, crossing her arms as she sat down. "Alright, Miles, let's entertain a conversation. But first, how about one of my friends unties Finn so that he can wake up in his own bed?"

She took it as another good sign that Miles readily agreed. After completing the task, he repositioned himself to sit across from her, taking the place of Finn in the chair. Within moments, the leprechaun was fast asleep, lying on his side.

Esme spoke first. "Does Abby know? I get that the relationship is still pretty new, but this—" she pointed at the broken restraints lying in a heap on the floor, "—is a whole hell of a lot to be concealing from a girlfriend."

He asked as if he already knew the answer, "How did your last boyfriend take it when you told him what you're up to in your spare time?"

Well, she had walked into that response by asking such a personal question first thing during a tense conversation.

She relented. "Fine. Sorry. It's just that Abby is my best friend and I genuinely don't want to see her hurt." She'd done enough lying to Abby for two lifetimes. But acknowledging that aloud would be all but confessing her role with the Assembly to him. She wasn't prepared to do that yet, even though he seemed to have already deduced it.

A rogue smile played at the corners of his lips. "I assure you that Abby is safe from me."

She pinned him with her eyes, disbelief plain on her face.

Hands in the air, he said, "We're not together like that."

"Good." The number of times that Esme had turned Abby down for a hangout or lied to her about where she'd gotten a new bruise was astronomical. On top of all that, Esme was relieved to not have to lie about her boyfriend.

Esme's relief had layers. On the surface, she was glad to avoid a messy situation that involved either more lying to Abby or breaking her heart. Below that was relief that she didn't need to get any more involved with this dangerous man. Even deeper still, she couldn't suppress the glimmer of hope that she would be further entangled with him.

Miles massaged his beard thoughtfully. Esme watched as the muscles in his forearms flexed and relaxed with each motion. He broke the nervous movement, saying, "My turn. First, can your conjuration put my dog down? Lily will not attack you or the trolls."

Gods below, she had forgotten about the dog! But, looking over, she realized that her concern was in vain. The dog—Lily, he'd called her—lay half asleep in George's arms. Her eyes barely cracked open when she heard Miles say her name, quickly shutting again when she realized that nothing exciting was happening. Seeing the hound acting so normally, as if nothing was amiss while it lay in the hideous troll's arms, unraveled a knot of tension on Esme's spine. If Lily could relax that much, Esme could try mellowing out too.

A bit of her normal good humor returned. Allowing the smile she felt when looking at the dog to show on her face, she said, "I dunno. She seems fairly content to me."

George bent down and placed the gigantic dog on the ground. At Miles' order to lie down, Lily circled three times in the same spot where she had been dropped by the troll and fell back asleep.

Dialing back to Esme with his characteristic focus, Miles asked, "Why did you come here?"

"To answer that, I need to grab something from my bag. I'll send George. Yes?"

He held her gaze and tipped his head up slightly. He was extending a lot of trust to her after she'd just threatened his life. The troll dutifully walked outside and headed to where she had left her bag behind the tree.

In the meantime, Miles wondered aloud, "Keeping three conjurations sustained for this long must be quite taxing for you."

Was it supposed to be draining? Jacob hadn't mentioned in their training sessions that she'd need to ration the time for which her conjurations were active. She barely felt any strain from maintaining the magic. She'd thought it was that way for most people when they used their magical specialty. Not wanting to reveal her inexperience or ignorance, she simply said, "Nope."

A small "huh" escaped with Mile's next breath.

Before there was time for a follow-up question, George re-entered through the shattered door. He handed the pack to Esme, who looked to Miles for assurance that her opening it wouldn't restart hostilities between them. It felt a bit like waiting for the cop's permission to retrieve registration papers from a dark glovebox. First, she pulled out a plastic takeout container; next, she pulled out a familiar bottle. "Cookies and whiskey."

A quiet voice rose from the small bed. "Wha-wha-whiskey?"

"Finn!" Esme exclaimed.

The leprechaun gradually reached a sitting position, taking breaks between each movement of his body.

She nudged Finn good-naturedly. "Apparently 'whiskey' was the magic word with you, eh?"

Miles interjected, "A depressant would not be a healthy idea right now, but the cookies might be good for blood sugar stabilization."

Finn looked over at Miles, the drug belatedly causing him to register his presence with disdain. Voice still weak, he accused, "Ya maggot. Comin' in here!"

"Whoa, Finn," Esme soothed, "You're safe. We're going to talk this through."

She could hear Finn grumbling, "So, I've got not just one noooo, but two of ya after me. Just my luck." He spoke up, asking, "Pass the cookies if you can't trust a grown man with a tipple or two."

Miles frowned slightly, reluctantly admitting, "You recovered from that faster than expected."

"Yeah, no thanks to the likes of you. I burned your drug away." Finn lit his palms on fire as a demonstration. Esme suspected that it was also a thinly veiled threat because the leprechaun was glaring.

Finn picked up one of the oversized chocolate chip cookies and started stuffing it into his mouth like it was the only thing standing between life and death for him. "These are delicious," he muttered. "I suspect that I have the lady to thank for them."

Esme nodded and leaned over to grab a cookie for herself. "Got any milk?"

Without saying a word, he jumped up and hurried to a wooden cupboard. A cool mist escaped as he opened it. How did he have electricity in a tree trunk? He returned to the table with two glasses full to the brim.

The leprechaun ate the cookies like a ravenous bear. After his third, he spoke again. "Esme, tell me I haven't erred here and that you're not a Brother like this one?" He pointed at Miles, who had remained seated with one ankle perched atop the opposite knee, the picture of relaxation.

Her head tilted to the side, puzzled. "I'm an only child. Miles, is he still high?"

Miles looked skyward beseechingly and sighed. "She is not a Brother."

As he mumbled through a mouthful of cookie, Finn said, "If I'm high on anything, it's these delicious cookies. Thanks for coming, lassie."

Esme furrowed her brow and shifted her gaze between Finn and Miles. Finn's mouth briefly devoid of food, he gestured to his arm, outlining a line along his upper bicep. He said, "A chara, my friend. You know, the Corded Brotherhood?"

Esme did not know. She was in yet another situation where she lacked the necessary knowledge, and the frustration she thought had been quashed when Jacob told her the truth of the bar's concealment spell returned. It was easy, and usually right, to blame the Assembly for being tight-lipped on important matters. But, as much as it pained her, she couldn't deny that her parents bore some responsibility for her ignorance.

If they hadn't secluded themselves from the mage world, how much more confident might she be when questions like this arose? At the very least, her foundational knowledge would've been sturdier if they'd taught her more.

Esme watched as Miles shifted, uncrossed his legs, then crossed his arms. It was clear that whatever the Corded Brotherhood was, talking about it made him uncomfortable. Which provided the perfect exposed nerve to prod. "Finn, I know nothing about this Brotherhood. Since you were able to burn off the drug, maybe we should open that bottle of whiskey after all and you can tell me all about it."

Finn's reply was immediate and wordless. He popped up from his spot on the bed for a second time to open the bottle. Seeing him as spry as ever was reassuring.

Miles uncrossed his arms as Finn poured out glasses for him and Esme. With the confidence of a decision made in his voice, Miles said, "I came here for the Corded Brotherhood." Almost instantly, a third glass appeared before Finn and he filled it, too. Honesty had earned Miles a share.

The leprechaun grinned and handed over the drinks. "Ah, the truth, a grand and beautiful thing. Sláinte!"

Each slowly sipped their beverages. It reminded Esme of another time when they had all sat together sharing drinks—an easier time.

Perhaps remembering that pleasant evening was why Esme's voice had less of an edge when she spoke next. Or, perhaps it was her guilt over her similar actions toward Finn that eased her anger. "So, this Corded Brotherhood ordered you to come here and drug Finn?"

"Not precisely. I was given no orders."

His ambiguous answer at least clarified that Miles was higher in the pecking order of this Brotherhood than Esme was in the Assembly. She hoped that meant he had the authority to answer her next questions.

"What kind of organization is this Brotherhood? What do they do?"

Miles was clearly reluctant to tell her why he had come after Finn, but if she knew more about his organization, then maybe this situation would start to make sense.

He said, "You'd be able to ask your Assembly contacts once you leave here anyway. I suppose it would be better for a member to set the record straight rather than hear it from someone else."

So he'd already decided that she'd be leaving here after their truce was over. Fantastic news.

Miles looked at Finn as he spoke. "The Corded Brotherhood was established some time before the fall of Camelot. The trials of Sir Gawain inform the moral code, but the—let's call them escapees—of the Extinction provide our mission. I came here to recruit Finn."

Finn spluttered, spraying a small amount of whiskey out in his exasperation. "Ya what?"

With a self-assured smirk, Miles replied, "You're a good fit."

Finn turned a new shade of red. "Ah, now, tyin' a man up and druggin' him was a grandly unconventional way of extending an invitation, I must say. But sure, go on about the lady's question, won't ya?"

Looking not the least bit contrite, Miles continued. "In the story, King Arthur is challenged by the Green Knight to strike him once, setting in motion a year-long pact for a retaliatory blow. Gawain, one of Arthur's knights, fears risking his king to the challenge. So he volunteers and chops off the Green Knight's head, thinking that will end the whole situation.

"But instead of dying, the Green Knight puts his head back on and promises to wait to return Gawain's blow in kind. Gawain, a man of honor, rides to fulfill his agreement even though it means his death. On his journey, he is attacked by beasts, suffers from starvation, and nearly freezes to death. Those are his tests of physical fortitude.

"Eventually, Gawain finds refuge at a lord's house, where he is then tested in spirit. The castle's Lady tries multiple times to seduce him. He refuses her each time. Yet, he agrees when she offers him the green girdle, claiming it will shield him from a fatal blow. This is his one moment of weakness.

"Gawain leaves the lord's house to meet with the Green Knight at the agreed upon chapel. He presents his neck to receive the prearranged fatal strike. But the Knight only draws a bit of blood with his blow.

"The Green Knight reveals he was the castle's lord. Knowing that Gawain hid his acceptance of the girdle, he made the cut.

Gawain humbly acknowledged his lack of bravery in accepting the girdle.

"Nevertheless, the Green Knight regards Gawain as noble due to his endurance in trials, his commitment to doing what is right, and his honest admission of his flaws. Ashamed, Gawain begins to wear the green girdle on his upper arm as a mark of his dishonor. When he returns to Arthur's court, he tells the story of his journey, his successes, and his failures. From that day forward, the knights of the court wore a green cord as a reminder of the personal weaknesses that they must overcome and a reminder of the importance of humility."

Miles rolled up his left sleeve, revealing a tattoo of a green cord encircling his muscular bicep. It was half an inch wide and very well drawn. The location of the tattoo was exactly the same as Abby's singular tattoo. Hers was of a delicate green vine, which she said was a mistake from her misguided attempt to rush for a sorority before she met Esme. The unkind part of Esme's mind suggested that maybe their similarity wasn't a coincidence, but she pushed the stray thought away forcefully. She would not start projecting the guilt that she felt over keeping secrets on her best friend like that.

Rolling his sleeve back down, Miles spoke again. "Of course, the Brotherhood has changed over time. We're less concerned with temptation and old-fashioned 'virtue' than we used to be. But we still value compassion, resilience, and integrity. At the center of all of this is an acceptance of the complexities of morality and everyone's imperfections."

When it was clear that he was finished, Esme commented, "Damn, you really have that speech down, don't you?"

Miles replied wryly, "I may have explained it a few times."

Adjusting her position in the too small seat, she asked, "And you wanted Finn to join? Explain that."

"Initially, we heard of a leprechaun who had eliminated the threat of a roving banshee. That piqued our interest."

That piqued Esme's interest too. Finn told her he simply ran away from it. "Eliminated" did not sound like running away to her.

Miles continued. "The Round Table is gone, but our mission has remained largely the same. When it comes to causing trouble, it's usually humans who are the culprits. The Assembly typically deals with those bad eggs." He paused and sent Esme a knowing glance. She tried not to squirm in her seat.

"You could say that the Brotherhood is something like the special forces of the Assembly. Separate, but still connected in secrecy. What we do shouldn't see the light of day. Every once in a while, a malevolent will pop back into the world. That's where we come in. And that's where I was hoping Finn could help the Brotherhood out. As things stand today, the malevolent problem is growing increasingly difficult to contain."

Esme felt overwhelmed absorbing all of this information at once. First, there was a clandestine magical group. Second, surprisingly, their ideals resonated with her. Third, it seemed a considerable number of people knew malevolents hadn't been entirely eradicated—possibly even the entire upper ranks of the Assembly.

Was she going to find out that Santa Claus was real next?

Unable to completely let go of her grievance with Miles, even after all that he'd divulged, Esme said, "I have to agree with Finn. Drugging him wasn't exactly the most effective way to invite someone to join a club."

Miles replied coolly, "As I said, I needed to be certain that Finn wouldn't circumvent the truth. You seemed on good terms with him following a confrontation and he honestly offered his help to you. That spoke in his favor. But," he looked directly at Finn as he continued, "then he divulged his possession of malevolent magic from the ifrit. I don't take chances when I don't need to."

That was...fair and logical. Damn.

She would keep asking questions as long as the information kept flowing. "Finn, I'm assuming that you can remember what happened before he drugged you. Can you verify his motivations in any way?"

Polishing off a fifth cookie, crumbs falling all over his bed where he still sat, Finn answered. "Aye, I must admit that he gave me a promise of three that he would not harm me. To the Fae, a promise made thrice is near to a binding one." He offered one of the oversized cookies to Miles, something that neither he nor Esme had done up to that point.

He continued. "Aye, I can remember it all. He asked if I had killed the banshee. I beg your pardon for keepin' that part to myself, Esme. He also asked what I reckoned about the Brotherhood's mission. Then you showed up, bursting through the door with yer trolls."

With eyes sparkling and laughter breaking through his words, he added to Miles, "Since we're all bein' so honest, I'll admit that I set ya up, Brother mine. I knew Esme was comin' from a text she sent me." The snickering that escaped his lips, just short of a genuine laugh, sent cookie crumbs flying through the air, despite the leprechaun being likely drained from the interrogation.

Esme studied him, but Miles didn't seem perturbed by Finn's admission. His only reaction was to swiftly cover his glass and the cookie box, guarding against any leprechaun-spit-contaminated flying crumbs.

As far as she could tell, Miles had laid his cards out on the table. Finn had revealed the truth of his actions before coming to Seattle. And Esme's role with the Assembly was all but admitted aloud between the three.

She did the only thing that she could do.

"How do we move on from here?" she asked.

Chapter Thirteen

The Way Forward

Miles

Miles fought to keep his guard up, but he was losing the battle. Esme's sudden acceptance of the truce without further threats made it difficult to reconcile the friendly woman before him with the one who had just threatened his life. He needed to stay focused, despite the conflicting emotions she stirred.

But he was realizing that nothing was simple for him when it came to Esme.

The night he spoke with her for the first time at the bar, he'd experienced a new dream. He dismissed its significance at the time, unable to link it to any event in his day. But the question she had just asked revealed a connection that made him wonder if his dreams were becoming prophetic. Which he dismissed as a ridiculous thought, but still...

As he pondered her words, the memory of the dream rushed back with startling clarity.

Between the snow-laden boughs of the forest, a dozen sets of glowing eyes pierced the darkness of the night. A bone-chilling sweat broke out on the king's skin as the anticipation of battle gripped him—Miles felt it too. Surrounded by his guards, the king stood alert, awaiting the demonic howl that would signal the assault of teeth and claws.

Miles' gaze shifted to the guard on his left, who, out of instinctual fear of appearing weak, attempted to disguise the rattle that invaded his every breath. Here, a sword bobbed while its wielder attempted to keep it at the ready, the steadiness of the soldier's arm sapped of its strength. There, a carelessly placed boot slipped as the snow compressed into a sheen of ice underfoot. Every man was emptied down to the last dregs of their energy.

Within the dream, the king's memories invaded his own. The night before, a runner, covered in deep cuts on his shoulders and back, had arrived, bringing news from a hamlet down the coast. Describing a scene of outsized hounds with glowing eyes, the battered young man recounted the harrying of the local people. The king drew his sword upon hearing how parents sacrificed their livestock, and with them their food for the entire winter, to protect their children from abduction. However, what made the already troubling news more disturbing was the runner's frantic account of being pursued by a group of them as he raced to the fortress.

Not one to shirk his duty to protect his people, the king roused a group of his men from their beds to join him in pursuing the monsters. They arrived shortly after dawn on foot, having left the horses tied out of harm's way in the nearby forest, to a scene of destruction usually only seen during times of war. The few men left standing in the hamlet cheered the king's banner as it entered the gathering of buildings.

The king's men fought the monsters for half of the day. The dogs the runner described turned out to be gwyllgi, the massive black mastiffs of the Wild Hunt, whose flaming red eyes burned brightly with malevolent magic. Lack of organization was evident in the monsters' erratic behavior. The feral group of gwyllgi had left a trail of destruction, attacking anything and everything in their path.

Miles felt a surge of fear from the king through their connection as he remembered the unsettling rumors about the Wild Hunt's lack of a leader. This attack was proof that the Hunt was unchained once more. The king's fear abated as he reassured himself that fate would soon bring forth a new leader for the Hunt.

The men devoured their rations and retrieved the offerings of grain from the townspeople for their horses. In order to avoid burdening the hamlet's residents any further, the king decided the soldiers should leave for the fortress immediately, leaving them with only two hours of daylight for their journey.

They expected a dark ride home for the last leg of their journey. However, in their fatigue and haste, Miles realized they had forgotten the runner's warning of the stalking score of hounds. Once again, they were prepared to fight for their lives, so soon after the battle in the village.

Breaking the tense silence of the forest, the chilling resonance of a gwyllgi's howl ripped through the unmoving cold air of the woods. Hellish growls and grunts echoed in response from the rest of the pack.

The men's unsteady arms raised to form a shield wall as the shaggy black forms of the mastiffs thundered toward them. Each man braced for the leaden weight of the beasts as flesh hit metal. A sword met the feral hounds' muscle and bone when an opening appeared. But the men were breaking. Already two men had to rotate to the interior of the shield wall so their weakness would not prove to be the death of all.

Feelings of certainty came from the king—it was time. His breath billowed out before him like misty clouds as he readied the last effort to save his men. The shield would prove effective at guarding the group until dawn, but after maintaining it for that long, he would be comatose for a full day and night. His vulnerability would become his men's vulnerability. His mere presence had already endangered all of his men. Malevolent creatures were drawn to his power. The less intelligent beasts sought his flesh while the intelligent ones sought his unwilling slavery.

Standing at the center of his men, the king prepared the magic that was their last hope. He prayed that the time until dawn would be enough for the beasts to lose interest. Peering between the gathered shields, he saw the mangled bodies of two of his men on the ground, already surrounded by several broken gwyllgi corpses. Casting powerful spells required time, and those men had already paid the cost.

He watched on in dread as a beast wrenched a young guard forward from the front line, his feet swept out from beneath him. A sickening popping, squelching sound came from the place where the gwyllgi's fangs dug into his flesh at the ankle, dragging him from the circle of men. Trained to react, the men filled the gap left by the fallen soldier.

Still, the king's attention lingered on the fallen knight as the man's weakening fist rose to smash at the attacking hound's face. If he broke off his concentration for even the smallest moment to save one man, he'd damn them all. So the king continued his preparations, holding his gaze on the knight's eyes that eventually met with his. He gave the man, who he knew was a new father, a small nod of respect for his sacrifice as he lost in his struggles, his lifeblood spurting to coat his attacker's muzzle.

A string of strangled yips cut through the noise of the battle. The pained sound coming from his foes made his heart fill with hope that the tide of the battle was turning in their favor. He had his own son, now a strapping youth who any father would be proud to return home to.

Without warning, one unbound beast broke through a gap in the line created by a faltering knight. The unchecked predatory instinct drove the hound toward its prey, the king. A guttural snarl ripped through the air as the impact of the hound's body knocked the guard closest to the king off balance.

Before the guard could find his feet, the hound lunged into the space behind the shield wall, pinning the king to the ground with the full force of its massive body. As the king's spine met the frost-hardened ground, the air whooshed out of his lungs, leaving him nearly stunned. The hope that had built up within him for their survival fled his body, along with his breath. All of his efforts to prepare for the aegis were destroyed. The certainty that he would join his men in the afterlife filled the space that hope had abandoned.

Miles, watching it happen through the eyes of the king, exerted his full strength against the beast, but it was futile. His lungs, arms, and legs scrambled to keep the hound from ripping out his throat. The monster was unnaturally strong this close to the solstice. Confusion rattled him as a hot flash of something wet hit his chest. Suddenly, the massive weight of the gwyllgi heaved to the side as a blade pierced all the way through the beast's chest. The king disregarded any questioning thoughts and took in a deep breath of cold air.

There, standing above him, was the smirking countenance of his unexpected savior. The king recognized her. He had denied this same hero a position in his service just days before. Then, he had justified his denial, claiming that her gender and parentage presented insurmountable obstacles. Was a lack of noble birth truly a barrier to military service for this king? It seemed preposterous to Miles, but he supposed he was a man from a different time.

The woman, clothed in hardened leather, with hair the color of winter honey, held his gaze through the king's eyes challengingly for another moment, then left to continue her bloody work. Her eyes were the striking amethyst of Esme's. Her broadsword cut through the remaining mass of gwyllgi one by one. Witnessing her sword cut through the flesh, the king reconsidered his choices and came to one conclusion. He would not deny this woman again.

As the last of the demonic hounds fell before her, the woman wiped her blade clean on the fur of one body. The snowy ground of the forest was decorated with garish red stripes. Sword as clean as it could be, she stood to her full height and addressed the king, bowing slightly, "Your majesty."

The king motioned for his men to part so he could speak to her directly. "I see that the weight of my misjudgment has been thoroughly demonstrated today."

With another smirk, she wiped the sweat from her eyes and said, "Yes, this was not a bad showing for one as unworthy as myself." Her tone was laced with indignity, but the smallest quaver in it hinted at her feelings of vulnerability.

A guard took issue with her disrespectful tone toward his king, but was dismissed by him. The king cut through the growing tension, saying, "We are grateful for your intervention, my lady. I have wrongfully dismissed you based on your blood. I hope you can understand that it is a difficult thing to ignore completely."

She swallowed and nodded. "The stain that no one can overlook. My blood may be tainted to your kind, but battle knows no pedigree."

Her unusual choice of words, referring to the nobility versus peasants as "your kind," struck Miles as peculiar, but he was just an observer.

The king replied, "Yes. Death does not discriminate. Without you, we would have met that fate today. I apologize for my errors and thank you for coming to our aid, lady. We are in your debt."

The king bowed deeply. After a puzzled moment, his guards followed suit. The action seemed to have struck the woman like an arrow to the chest.

Regathering her wits, the warrior looked around her as if expecting another attack. "Your majesty, this place is not safe. I can feel evil about us. What is the path forward?" she asked, her tone slightly less acerbic.

The king replied, "I hope your sword will remain as sharp as your tongue. If you will stand with us, the way forward is together. We shall face whatever awaits us."

The timing of the dream might be a coincidence, or it might not. Something urged Miles toward the latter. This world had magic, so why not? But his rational side grappled with the foolishness of such a thought.

In the endless cycle of his repeated dreams, both times he'd experienced a new vision recently, she'd been there. Esme was the key, the catalyst. Also his lucky charm. He felt himself walking dangerously close to the line separating rationality from superstition.

The logical conclusion for his new dream was that she was just one part of the enormous change that he'd made in his life by moving to Seattle. But he couldn't shake the feeling that he'd known her, or someone just like her, long before their paths crossed.

It was odd. In the dream, he sensed the king had the same feeling of something slightly off about the warrior woman, just like Miles did when he was near Esme. If she stayed close, perhaps he could determine why. Besides, he had already planned on bringing Finn into the Brotherhood.

She'd asked how they could move forward.

So far, the king of his dreams hadn't guided him toward disaster. So, inspired, he answered her question that felt like it had been asked an eternity ago, "Together."

Warming to the idea, he spoke more quickly. "The situation has become more challenging of late. The Brotherhood is struggling to keep up with the increasing frequency of malevolent emergence. We can't recruit or train members fast enough to deal with the threat ourselves. In the past month, three members of various Mage Assemblies had to manage the threat entirely without our aid. The problem is growing. Eventually, keeping it a secret will become unmanageable. You've read the stories. You know who the favorite victims of most malevolents are."

He let the answer simmer in their minds before finally saying, "Children. And if that's not enough to convince you, anyone could be their victim. Even the strongest mage."

He consciously stopped himself from nervously crossing and uncrossing his legs. "I'm operating alone here. I don't know the town or the surrounding areas and I'm not enough. That's why I came here to enlist Finn. Even if I mucked it up. I need help."

Esme raised her hand and asked, deadpan, "If I want to help, I don't need to get the tattoo, right? I honestly don't have the guns to pull off the look." She raised one arm to flex her bicep.

He chuckled despite himself. The tension from her earlier threat lingered, but her unexpected humor made it hard to hold on to his worries. Was she trying to disarm him with charm?

Finn joined in the banter, saying, "Aye, I think my tattoo artist would have to use a magnifying glass to get the detail in. But, lassie, I think yer trolls could sport the look well, no?"

Esme raised her right hand in the air, slanted toward him, ready to receive a high five from the leprechaun.

Finn eyed her raised hand and asked, "Ya got a question, dove?"

Deflated, she sat back and crossed her arms in defeat. "Well, that failed spectacularly. No, no question."

Miles felt a twinge of guilt for misinterpreting her earlier. This wasn't manipulation; it was just two friends being themselves. With a small smile, he decided to bridge the gap and lift her spirits. Miles tentatively raised his hand to give Esme the failed high five.

She perked up, grinning. "Oh hell yeah!" and completed the celebratory gesture. "You see that, Finn? That's a high five."

It seemed like the leprechaun was trying to piece together what he had missed out on, his brow furrowed in confusion.

Finally, Esme answered his question. "Miles, we both mucked this up in different ways. I, cautiously," she emphasized the last word, "think we can work something out."

"Aye," Finn agreed. "Wouldn't do for me to get too bored 'round here, anyway."

"How do you feel about following me in your car to meet the Bastion of the Corded Brotherhood?" Miles suggested.

"The...what?" Esme asked.

"The other option is that you follow me to the cars, I inject myself with a low dose of the leftover sodium thiopental, and you drive us all there. If you're not comfortable with it, you can push me out of the car into the driveway and speed off." He knew it was radical, but he wanted her to trust him.

She stared at him as though he had suddenly developed a second head. Then her look became more contemplative. He found he appreciated her attention on him. Evidently, his attraction to her ran so deep that not even a death threat could shake it. He was already halfway gone for her and he barely knew a thing about her. He was like a teen boy struck with, possibly ill-advised, puppy love.

Finn nearly squealed with excitement as he said, "Oh, please tell me I'm invited to meet the Bastion, Esme!"

Chapter Fourteen

The Bastion

Esme

Esme and Finn followed Miles on the hike back to the parking lot, staying ten paces behind. She wanted to keep him in sight, but she also didn't feel comfortable having a drugged-up man in her passenger seat—as much as he would deserve it for drugging Finn. Even though he had shared far more information with her than she could have expected, she still couldn't bring herself to trust him.

He pulled out of the parking lot and she followed with Finn along for the ride. After driving down too many familiar roads in Seattle, she had a sinking feeling she knew where they were headed. But she denied it until she watched as Miles reached out of his car window to type in a gate key code she had used herself many times before. Everything she'd known about her world was unraveling, and now, for the second time, its foundation crumbled as she drove into her usual parking spot.

Esme paced between the lined-up chairs in the Bastion's library. When she spoke, she sounded a bit hysterical, even to her own ears. "Jacob, you know me. Right now, I want to be mad."

Lily was curled up next to Finn on the chaise lounge while Jacob sat comfortably in his favorite chair. Miles perched on an uncomfortable but beautifully carved wooden chair that he had pulled over from a nearby desk. Jacob's presence made her feel like she could let her guard down around Miles, as she trusted her mentor implicitly.

Flinging her arms in the air, defeated, she continued speaking. "But I can't. I want to be mad, but I get it. I understand why you didn't tell me. It sucks being out of the loop, but I get it."

She felt halfway to delirium from the day's revelations. "My back and my feet ache when I wake up in the morning. I recently had to switch my makeup to accommodate dry skin. And now I'm suddenly used to accepting half-truths. Am I...am I getting old?"

A low, resonant sound punctuated by small intakes of breath cut through Esme's musings. Miles was laughing at her! Of course, the first time she heard him laugh, it was at her expense, but she couldn't blame him. She knew she was being ridiculous.

Jacob tried to reassure her. "Darling, you are a stunning specimen of womanhood. If you're old, then we should have ordered my urn many years ago. Esmeralda," he huffed out an undignified breath, "You are making the end of my life very interesting."

Still pacing, she shot a look of disapproval his way. "That's not funny at all. Finn is the joker here."

Finn stayed unusually quiet, clearly trying to disappear into the background. He most likely did it to fully enjoy the unfolding drama without any hindrance.

Jacob responded, "I am one hundred and six years old. I think I've earned the right to make light of my own mortality."

She looked at his patchy white hair and wrinkled face, but her mind snagged on the power she felt from him. There was no way a one-hundred-and-six-year-old body could burn with magical energy like he did.

"You're eighty-five, tops," she suggested skeptically.

"Esmeralda," he said with long suffering evident in his voice, "you know that we tend to live longer than humans without magic. What year did the Second World War end?"

"1945?" she answered, hoping she was correct. She glanced hesitantly at Miles, who she suspected was suppressing a grin.

"Glorious. Now do the maths given the current year." He pointed at his military awards hanging on the wall near his Oxford banner of arms. "Was I in a nappy when I earned those?"

Although it made complete sense, it was emotionally challenging to come to terms with his advanced age.

The leader of the Northwestern Assembly of Mages and apparently secret Bastion of the Corded Brotherhood was too vivacious to settle in her mind as a centenarian. The sentimental part of her wanted to reject the information as false—losing Jacob would be a blow equivalent to her parents' deaths. Over time, he'd become like a grandfather to her. She eventually relented and admitted to herself that she was being stubbornly, willfully ignorant of his age.

"Well," Jacob said, slapping his knees and rising, "I'm going to make us all some tea so you can tell me exactly what happened. I know you don't like caffeine in the evenings, my dear. Peppermint for you? Miles, if I recall, you're a traditionalist like myself."

With their agreement, Jacob left the room.

Esme turned to face Miles squarely and spoke quickly, her voice slightly lowered. "Bastion? What the hell is that? I know Jacob and I have since I was quite young, but what the hell do you know that I don't?"

Miles shrugged. "He is exactly who you think he is and maybe more too."

That was a strangely comforting, if incomplete, answer.

"Go on," she urged, raising her eyebrows and tracing a gentle circle in the air between them with both hands. "Right now I need the Miles who opened up out of nowhere and told me all about the Corded Brotherhood while sitting in a leprechaun's house. I need the Miles who was completely transparent with me earlier."

He smirked at her. It made her irrationally mad. But he spoke again before she could. "By this point, you know that the Brotherhood is all about symbolism. The Bastion is the person who embodies the principles of the Brotherhood and who can stand alone as its last defense if need be. From the stories I've heard, Jacob is an institution in his own right."

"So he's like an officer or something?" Esme asked.

"More like the guy yelling orders at the front of the battalion while he mows down the enemy line with a machine gun."

"Oh," was all she could say as Jacob walked back into the room carrying a tea tray laden with mugs and cookies.

Jacob served the beverages, as genteel as always, and made himself comfortable. Esme, mentally fatiguing from the stress pacing, pulled up a chair and sat down with her mug in hand.

Smacking his knees again with both hands, Jacob interrupted the brief peaceful moment, saying, "So, you're here together. There are only three scenarios I can think of in which that would be the case." He held up one finger. "I'm in trouble." He added another finger. "You're in trouble."

"And the third?" Esme prodded.

His eyes twinkled in response. He shook his head, dismissing her question, and asked his own. "So, which is it? Do I need to prepare for my verbal lashing, or do I need to grab my shovel, tarp, and some rope?"

"Jacob!" she mockingly reprimanded him. "Wait, on second thought, depending on the person, the shovel might be the preferable end of this evening. Also, it's wonderful to know that you'd be willing to help me cover up a murder." She jumped up and gave him a hurried hug. He returned it with alacrity.

"Miles," she said, raising her mug smugly in his direction, "this is your show. I didn't know that we'd be speaking with the illustrious Bastion of the Corded Brotherhood tonight. I'll be happy to fill in any sodium-related details you leave out."

Miles was direct and to the point in his reporting of the day's events. Jacob didn't bat an eye at Miles' interrogation methods and he didn't seem surprised that Esme had intervened. The surreal conversation had almost taken on a commonplace, everyday feeling.

At last, Jacob asked, "Esmeralda, would you like to continue working for the Assembly?"

"Yes!" she answered, too quickly to really think about her answer.

He nodded. "Good. So Sylas has unwittingly brought you in on what is going on. I highly doubt that he expected it to proceed to this degree, but here we are. I don't know what urged that leshy to...well, that's neither here nor there now. Yes, we know about the phenomenon of malevolents returning to the world. We've been able to stay on top of the problem so far. We must continue that work."

Changing topics, he said sharply, "Leprechaun, don't think that I've forgotten about your presence. I know that you're trying to pull a Fae charm on me to make me overlook you."

Finn became much more noticeable to Esme as he said, "Oh, alright, can't blame me for tryin'."

Jacob's response was haughty. "I can. Pull that again in my household without permission and you won't like what happens."

Then he rummaged around in the desk drawer muttering something about his "glasses" and pulled out the piece of shed reptile skin she'd found while searching for clues. He held it up in the air and said, "This was your find, Esmeralda. Miles could use the backup. Well, now that the afanc, or bunyip, I suppose, is out of the bag, let's have you all handle this."

Esme asked, for the second time that day, "The...what?"

"And the leprechaun can be bait."

Finn's accent was thick as he nearly shouted, "Just what now?"

***

The next evening

Esme couldn't believe what was about to come out of her mouth, but, damn it, it felt necessary to say. "I swear by all the gods and goddesses, if you come out of those bushes looking like Abby, I'm going to explode."

"Jus' hold on to yer bonnet, lassie."

She huffed out a breath and whisper-yelled back, "Ugh, update your comebacks to the twenty-first century, please."

Esme felt stuck somewhere halfway between elated and panicky at being included in a monster hunt. Jacob wasn't certain what type of creature the scute was from, but he'd narrowed the options down to a Welsh afanc, an Australian bunyip, a Himalayan buru, or an Egyptian sobek. From the little reading that she'd done on the way out to the river, she hoped it was a sobek, because those seemed to be the most neutral of the four options. They mostly left you alone if you left them alone. But given what had already happened, she guessed that it was one of the other more aggressive creatures.

Esme suggested that if the malevolent creature resembled a crocodile as they suspected, it would face difficulties getting past the hydroelectric dam, whether in water or on land. To her amazement, everyone had agreed. So she, Finn, and Miles traveled downstream from the place where she'd found the scute.

They discovered a path leading down to a sizable rocky sand bar along the riverbank, on the outskirts of Snoqualmie. The city was situated at the point where the Cascade mountains first began to rise noticeably. Because the area was somewhere in the middle of suburban and rural, they had to work to keep a low profile while they were out in the open. It was also why they'd gone out well after dark.

Miles hid fifty feet away near the river's waterline, downwind, ready to give orders with a walkie-talkie to Esme at any time. So, he couldn't see Esme's mouth hanging open as she stared at the gorgeous, compact woman who walked out of the bushes where Finn had hidden.

"Hoh, mama. Who are you supposed to be?" she asked. Finn was glamored to look like a tan beauty with silky black hair and expressive eyes. She was wearing a bikini top and a sarong slung low over one hip.

The disparity of his natural voice coming out of a beautiful woman's mouth rattled Esme's brain. "I just looked on my phone for hot eighteen..."

"Oh my gods, do not finish that thought or mention this ever again!" she commanded.

He tittered like a schoolboy. He'd been hoping for that reaction from her. "Do ya think Miles will like it?" He swiveled his hips suggestively.

She scoffed. "Probably. Anyway, weirdo, you're supposed to be nubile bait if this is an afanc. Go sit by the water and look like a helpless, delicious meal."

It was near midnight. The air was chilly, and the sky was cloudy with early spring rain. The gorgeous woman that Finn had become walked primly down the rocky shore to dip her feet in the water. Finn found a patch of moonlight and began humming a song that Esme didn't recognize. She knew he wasn't wearing a coat under his glamor. Maybe his ifrit magic kept him warm.

Esme's role in this scheme was to create a few small conjurations that could "play" in the water near Finn to act as further magical bait. Jacob had explained that malevolents seemed to be attracted to the use of magic. So, the more she used near Finn while he had a glamor on, the better chance they'd attract it between them. If the creature got too close, Finn could quickly pull his disappearing act or, conversely, put a fireball in its face.

Miles' role was to put the creature down. She hadn't asked how. She'd been too nervous about what she was about to do on the drive over to think to ask. Plus, she still felt uneasy around him. Not too long ago, she'd threatened to kill him, and now

Jacob had thrust them together as if they were a team. Esme found it difficult to trust Miles due to his actions, and she suspected he felt the same way about her. There was going to be an adjustment period—if they made it through the night alive, that was.

Esme conjured three copies of the elves she used to liven up the bar at Christmastime. The magic was the important part, not what they looked like, so she didn't bother to change them out of the festive attire they usually wore for entertaining guests. She ordered them to skip around in the shallows like children on a summer day.

The scene before her was beyond belief. A buxom, scantily clad beauty lounged in the moonlight, singing with an Irishman's voice, while three of Santa's elves played in the gushing Snoqualmie River at midnight.

She discovered a neat hiding spot among the trees on the riverbank, giving her a clear view of Finn and her magical creations. She left them working on a loop, so they'd require less mental power, while she grabbed the thermos of hot tea she'd brought along for the wait.

Her mind strayed back to her new "partner." She wondered what Miles was doing over there in the shadows. She wondered how he would end the child-killing malevolent. He seemed so confident, yet all she knew about him was that he could cast a powerful shield. What else was he good at?

It took her about an hour to realize why detectives on cop shows always complained about stakeouts. It was mind-numbingly boring. Finn had swapped to an improvised song that switched between, "Tis' borin', it's almost mornin'," followed by something longer in Irish that she couldn't understand, but she deduced it was bawdy.

She had just picked up the lyrics that Finn was singing when she felt the water shift unnaturally through her elves. She clicked the talk button on her walkie-talkie three times in quick succession to alert Miles. Nervous, she stood and unconsciously took a step forward, nearly stepping out of her hiding spot. Her pulse thundered in her ears, drowning out the river's rush. Miles sent two quick clicks back in receipt.

Then absolutely nothing happened for the next fifteen minutes. Esme felt no change in the water current around her elves, didn't hear or see anything out of the ordinary. Her heart rate reduced to its normal cadence and, eventually, she sat back down. It was a false alarm. She thought she was making the right call, but now she just felt silly.

But there it was again, that same unnatural change in the way the water moved around her conjurations. She almost clicked the walkie-talkie three times again, but hesitated. She didn't want to be the silly newbie alarmist. It would be too embarrassing.

A splash of water preceded the monstrous amalgamation of scales, fur, deadly teeth, and claws as the bulk of hundreds of pounds of afanc crashed through the water, trying to take Finn unawares. Esme's legs started running while her mind dismissed the frivolous elves. She had to warn Finn.

His name ripped out of her mouth as she tripped over a large rock in the darkness. As she fell, she didn't see Finn vanish just in time before the afanc crashed down.

A hissing sound came out of the creature's throat, like the noise she associated with dinosaurs in movies. She scrambled to her feet and watched in horror as its form barreled toward her on four crocodilian legs. Like the sound it made, its fangs belonged in the Jurassic period, not in a living, breathing creature.

Its beaver-like head, filled with monstrous teeth, snapped toward her. The creature had reptile-like armor on its spine, but its torso and legs were covered in coarse mammalian fur.

Instinctual fear made her turn and run. She could hear it behind her, gaining ground over the loose rocks with far more efficient strides on land than something of that size and shape should be capable of. It used its paddle-shaped tail like a fifth leg, propelling itself with blinding speed toward her. There was no way she could outrun it.

She heard a pop of air around her ears as she tripped, yet again, plummeting to the ground near the treeline. Her face bounced off a rock, hitting it like a butcher tenderizing meat.

The pain started unexpectedly with stinging, melting heat near her feet. She squirmed to get away from it, but she was stuck under the bulk of the creature. Freaking out would just make it worse, but she couldn't stop her limbs from scrabbling for freedom.

She quickly realized that there was a small pocket of air around her holding the weight off of her body. A wave of relief and gratitude washed over her. Miles had shielded her.

She began to cry hysterically, but squashed it down with the realization that she had to get out from under the afanc before Miles' aegis failed. While she was no expert, she knew the shield was taxing to maintain and far from impervious.

The burgeoning claustrophobia from the body pressing above her was almost too much to take. She needed to move. As soon as the panic built inside her, the creature whipped forward in a blaze of motion, relieving the pressure off her and the aegis at once.

She took in a big gulp of air and clambered upward. The afanc was slowed, dragging its heavy body across the rocks.

Miles was standing still on top of a large boulder in front of it, concentrating on something.

Move, she thought.

But then she saw it. He was preparing to launch three floating knives and was holding two more in his hands while still maintaining her personal shield. He loosed the knives in a flurry of flying blades. They rocketed across the rocks and gravel. One dagger hit home on the afanc's furry shoulder; one bounced off the scutes along its spiny back, and the third barely sliced a glancing blow along its flank.

This seemed to have confused the creature just long enough for Finn, back in his natural form, to return, each hand spraying enough heat at the creature for two bonfires. It must have been his magic that she had felt while under the creature, using it to bait it off her.

The leprechaun's face, lit by the fire streaming out of him, was a mask of intense focus. She gawked, awestruck by the power pouring out of his hands. He burned and burned, and didn't cease until it slowed nearly to a stop in front of Miles' boulder. All of this took less than thirty seconds.

Miles sprang off the boulder and landed, thrusting the two larger knives that he was holding downward on top of the afanc's back, presumably where its heart lay. He rolled off and jumped up into a ready crouch, leaving the knives behind. Twin handles heaved upward a few times as the afanc made its last struggles before death overcame it. Then the charred carcass lay there, unmoving.

As Esme touched her jaw, the bruise swelling from her fall, she realized she had the answer to her musings about what skills Miles possessed. He could maintain the strongest personal aegis that she'd ever experienced, even stronger than Jacob's, while performing telekinetic magic, and then do a blockbuster-worthy flying leap to kill a monster with a dagger in each hand.

Gods above and below.

Her respect for Finn had skyrocketed as well. Not only had he disappeared in the blink of an eye to avoid the afanc's attack, but he'd thrown more fire at the creature than she knew one person could be capable of without passing out or dying first.

She owed them both, big time.

And what had she done? Played with elves in the water. Ran out of her hiding place, yelling, nearly getting Finn killed. Then she'd run from their quarry and tripped, awaiting death.

Failure stacked on top of failure. This was not a good first showing for Esmeralda Morgana Turner.

Her face throbbed in time with her heartbeat, but the embarrassment? It was fading, being replaced by something colder, harder—resolve. She wasn't going to let this defeat her. She didn't have to be perfect, just better.

Chapter Fifteen
Twisted History

Gwyn

Gwyn had no choice but to rejoin civilization. There were no more wilds of Wales for him to hide within. The entire landscape looked completely occupied by human activity. The world, his place within it, and even he were all changed beyond recognition.

At first, his anger was indiscriminate. Without exchanging a word with anyone in those early days, his hand twitched toward the pommel of his sword more often than not. At every turn, he foisted the loathing he felt for himself, for his lowered circumstances, unjustly onto strangers.

Once he left the fields, he found ruins to sleep in at night and studied the people who came to gawk at them during the day. His magic, the only shred of hope for his survival, allowed him to apply a simple glamor to disguise his dirty leathers and hide his weapon. It felt anathema to him that no one in this age armed themselves.

The need for food and shelter urged him to resume his roaming. Early on the second day of walking through the day and night, a vehicle slowed, keeping pace with him. Stopping would only make him an easier target. Gwyn kept walking, his hand steady on his concealed sword.

The glass separating the driver from Gwyn lowered to reveal the merry face of an older gentleman. Wearing a mask of disinterest, Gwyn faced him. The man spoke unintelligibly at him, smiling all the while. The discrepancy between Gwyn's aloofness and the man's open, congenial attitude was jarring for a man brought up in a royal court. His arm itched to strike out at the man, but that was his misery trying to rule him.

If he were to kill this man just for talking to him, he would deserve the imprisonment he'd endured. So, grudgingly, he tried to communicate in his native language first. When that didn't work, he tried the tongues of the Britons and the Picts, but each time his words were met with confusion.

Eventually, the man gestured that he was going to pull over to the side of the road. When he exited his car, Gwyn detected no magic from him and concluded that he was likely a scholar or priest based on his build. So he tried a greeting him in Latin. Success! The man's face brightened at hearing a familiar language.

Gwyn's first conversation in eons was mediated by a talking box.

The older man pulled an object from his pocket that glowed with the light of a candle and spoke with the voice of a woman. Its pronunciation was odd, but it spoke perfect Latin. He felt no magic coming from the translation object, yet he couldn't imagine what else could create such a wonder.

The man, who called himself Edgar, admitted that he'd seen Gwyn walking the past two days and wanted to know if he needed a meal and a place to sleep for the night. Gwynn's fingers slowly loosened on the hilt, stunned by the stranger's unexpected generosity.

Following some back and forth with the translator, Gwyn took a chance to get into the car with the man. The experience in the vehicle was surreal to the point of nausea. The man stopped the car in front of a series of stone cottages and showed Gwyn to a room.

Before Edgar left to allow him to get settled in, he turned on the overhead light, making Gwyn jump in surprise. The man must have taken his shock at the use of electricity as a sign of fear because he used his translator to assure Gwyn that he was safe at his inn for the night and that a meal would come soon.

Gwyn explored the room. He flicked the lights off and on for a period far longer than he would admit to any living person. An hour later, Edgar returned to his room with a tray of food and an armful of towels. He deposited the tray on the desk and left the towels hanging over the bathtub. Once the man left again, Gwyn ate the food like a ravenous dog. It was a mutton stew with the finest bread that he had ever tasted and a glass of very strong ale.

Curiosity brought him to the room where Edgar left the towels. It didn't take long for Gwyn to discover the glory of a hot bath. He remained in the water until his skin was as wrinkly as a banshee's and the water was cold. He washed his repulsive leathers in the water and hung them up to dry near the small fireplace in the room. That night, he slept like the dead.

The next morning, the innkeeper brought him a set of clothes that were stuffed into a backpack with some food and an aged book, saying, "*Tū accipe librum.*"

It was a Latin–English dictionary, probably a relic of the man's youth. Gwyn's desperation won out over his pride, permitting him to stay at the inn for one additional day and night.

He remained in the room while his leathers dried and spoke with Edgar only when he popped in to deliver food. The innkeeper offered another night's stay, but his pride refused. Instead, Gwyn accepted a ride into Liverpool.

He'd already benefited from Edgar's kindness in far more ways than the man could ever understand. This simple, mundane, human kindness was how Gwyn was able to launch himself into the new world.

Once again, he faced challenges after beginning anew in Liverpool. His lack of language skills and utter ignorance about how this new world worked led him to rely on magic to steal food. Eventually, he found a shelter for unhoused men to sleep in, but it came with its own set of problems. During the weeks that he spent like this, he felt the cold, now rancid, loathing for everyone and everything return.

The only bright spot of this time was that his long periods of inactivity granted him the time to study the language and observe human interactions. He pored over the dictionary until he could say two-word and eventually three-word phrases in English. In the middle of the day, he studied the people as he walked down the streets. From the subtle gestures of greeting to the unspoken rules of etiquette, he absorbed every detail with keen interest.

Matching the cycle of day and night, his mind oscillated between the light and the dark. In the morning, he woke up vowing to pay back Edgar at his first opportunity. In the evening, he cursed his father's name for condemning him to such a life. The question kept repeating in his thoughts: How could it be that a stranger could extend a hand of compassion, while his own father, an ascended man of great power and supposed wisdom no less, had either locked him away for no crime or turned a blind eye to it?

Regardless of his inner turmoil, if Gwyn was anything, he was adaptable. He quickly found a source of income that had spanned the ages: gambling. He discovered that fooling the people of this era was much simpler than it had been before, because no one looked for magic. Gone were the days when people viewed him with suspicion or admiration upon recognizing his noble lineage. Appearing like any other man, he could quietly and discreetly walk away from the gambling table with all the night's winnings, leaving no one the wiser.

He found much to appreciate in the current era. The people were fat with prosperity and leisure. Engineering and technology had built marvels and made the lives of all easier. The world had become, in a word, luxurious. But he was shocked to learn that the common man did not even believe in the power of magic. In this time, it was almost as if magic was dead. He feared he was the last magic user left in the world because he hadn't encountered any mages.

By early summer, he was truly finding his footing in the modern world. He split his time between cities in the north and the midlands of England. Given the questionable legality of his money-making methods, he reasoned that a transient lifestyle afforded him the best chance of evading too much scrutiny.

Manchester shattered his fragile new world for the second time later that summer. In every city he visited, Gwyn spent a great deal of time in libraries. At first, it was because it was a free space to spend time in while learning the language. But then his curiosity got the best of him and Gwyn did as any curious man would do: he looked himself up. He had hoped that delving into the histories would jog his still empty memory, but what he read had sickened him.

By then his reading was skilled enough that he could understand most of the histories with his dog-eared dictionary in hand. Some stories described him as a divine warrior and a hunter, as a bull of battle, protecting all and dispersing armies single-handedly. These were easily his favorite. Others painted him as the king of the Tylwyth Teg. They were the group of human children brought to the land of the Fae in exchange for changelings in their cradles who could bless you or curse you in equal measure.

But he nearly wept while reading the stories of the brave soldiers who fell in battle whose souls he was said to have escorted from this world. This he could remember as the truth. The hows and wheres of it were a mystery, but even through his transformation back to human, that much of his ascended life had remained stitched upon his heart.

He took great pride in the fearsome reputation he had earned among the Celts. To them, he was the huntsman who rode a demon horse at the front of the Wild Hunt, leading a pack of dogs from hell. Gwyn had fragments of memories of the gwyllgi. From hell, they were not, but neither were they domesticated. He knew they would act as malevolents without a leader of the hunt guiding them.

Of what he could remember, some pieces of these stories were true, some false, and still others embellished beyond recognition. History had equally praised him and condemned him as a villain. The stories of his triumphs and prowess were a painful reminder of how far he had fallen. The unsettling gaps in his mind left him searching for missing pieces, trying to complete the picture of how everything had truly unfolded. He needed to remember more.

However, his stomach churned as he delved further into the lore. Book after book after book all said the same thing. They claimed he was obsessed with his sister and stole her from her betrothed so that he could have her for himself.

It was untrue, disgusting, and shameful.

The memories from his human years were far better preserved compared to the jumbled flash of images that made up his ascended years. Creiddylad was not his sister. She was Nudd's ward, fostered by her family there to ensure peace between her father's kingdom and his. She had no blood relation to him whatsoever. The idea that generations believed the lie curdled in his stomach, turning his shame into something toxic.

Being of the same age, they had shared tutors for their lessons and slowly their hearts became entangled with each other's. Nudd had never approved of his relationship with her. In the end, happiness together was not to be. Marriages were made for political alliance, not love. So, she was married off to one of Arthur's knights.

Gwythyr, her new husband, repeatedly raised his hand to harm her. In desperation, she reached out to Gwyn, using her handmaiden as a messenger. That part of the story was true. He had rescued Creiddylad from her abusive new husband.

But then things became complicated for Gwyn and Creiddylad. Not long after he removed her from Gwythyr's household, Gwyn had followed in his father's footsteps to ascend. He became something more than a man, more than a mage, but not quite a true god. The bards sang of it as a touch of divinity, and maybe that was true. He couldn't remember the truth of it. Only the barest fragments were left to him of his ascended life.

But one thing about his history rang true in his thoughts. His father often disapproved of his actions. He knew saving Creiddylad was never a choice: It had been his duty.

When he first emerged from his magical prison, he remembered the unsolicited feeling of certainty that betrayal came from within his own family. Had he held onto that feeling throughout all the years of his isolated agony for a reason? Anger at his wrongful imprisonment was quick to burn and slow to cool.

Surely he was missing something, some piece of information that would tell him why he'd been imprisoned. He couldn't shake the feeling that Nudd had something to do with it. It had been one of his first thoughts after his emergence into the modern world. Had Gwyn done something terrible that led Nudd to lock him away?

He stared into the grimy mirror of his temporary accommodations, wiping vomit from his chin before flushing away the evidence. In his anger, he inadvertently used magic to strengthen his hands. The porcelain sink cracked under the pressure of his grip tightening on its edges. If not Nudd, then who? If he could regain even a fraction of his memories from his ascended life, maybe he could make a better guess.

Still, that self-righteous fool was surely to blame for the lies about him. History was written by the victor, after all. Now the world saw Gwyn mainly as a monster, as a creature of darkness with twisted incestuous intentions and ties to hell. The rage within him simmered. Looking back at the mirror over the cracked sink, he vowed he would reclaim his name, even if just for himself, even if he could never regain all of his memories.

Gwyn had to do something about it. He'd already spent far too much time poring over books, pining over the past that was now lost to him. If Nudd was unaltered by whatever magic he used to condemn Gwyn, the king could still be alive. With his mind more than half gone, Gwyn needed to find Nudd and ask the most important question of all: Why?

Even if no one else who knew him as Gwyn ap Nudd still existed, the value of his name mattered to him. Forever a warrior; a hunter at heart. He wouldn't stop until he found his quarry. Perhaps Nudd's answer would be satisfactory. Perhaps it had been an accident. But if so, why hadn't he done anything to save his own son?

He wasn't naïve enough to relinquish all thoughts of revenge. His lifetime in a royal court had taught him to be cautious; suspicious.

If his own father had done this to him without a single conversation, then Nudd had become corrupted in some way. One didn't throw out the entire fruit because it showed a single blemish. They used a sharp blade to slice away the rot, leaving the rest to be enjoyed. If Nudd was the rot, then Gwyn would be the knife. It would be called justice for more than a thousand years of wrongful imprisonment.

If anyone possessed knowledge of Nudd's whereabouts, it would likely be a mage. Gwyn was willing to bet that if there were any constants throughout history concerning mages, it would be their tendency to organize themselves based on rank. People at the top got noticed. Nudd would be hard to overlook.

The problem was that he needed to find one to ask first. Either modern mages were exceedingly rare, extremely good at covering their use of magic, or they rarely used it.

It was time for a hunt.

Chapter Sixteen

Meetings in Triplicate

Esme

Over the next few weeks, Finn became a regular fixture during Esme's shifts, his easy charm turning the bar into his personal stage. She watched him thrive, amused by his antics as he flitted from group to group, the perfect social butterfly. Always settling his tab with cash, Finn never hesitated to buy rounds for those he mingled with, solidifying his role as the life of the party. Every time Esme saw him he was chatting up a new person, alternating between animatedly telling stories to rapt audiences at tables, laughing uproariously, and once even leading the late-night crowd in an a cappella rendition of "Molly Malone."

Finn always checked in with her to see how she was doing. He dropped by to say hello a few days before the next Assembly meeting, just as she expected. She'd promised Sylas the night she'd brought Finn into The Sanctuary of Spirits for the first time that she'd accompany Finn to the meeting.

Finn said, "I came to talk to ya 'bout the old geezer, Sir Jacob, or whatever you lot call him."

"Sir Jacob," she tittered. "I can't wait to see how he'll respond when I try that one on him. Alright. So?"

"We chatted a bit. Now, there's no need to worry your pretty little head about it, but I thought ya should know."

That was cryptic. It was either an unspoken warning of something she needed to worry about or, more likely, bait for a trick. The safest route for dealing with him was through humor. She replied in a pouting voice, "Aww, thank you. You're right, my pretty little head is best kept empty."

"Dove, we both know that's a load of bullocks," he said with a grin. "Anyway, would ya like to meet for coffee before the meetin'? Yer friend Abby would be most welcome."

"Abby might sit in on the meeting, so I'll ask." She thought it would be best to warn him. "You're barking up a tall tree with her, my friend."

His challenging grin devoured her warning. It made her wonder if he was trying to cause mischief between her and Abby. She just hoped she figured it out before it was too late.

Warning given, she answered his question. "My answer is yes to coffee, if you can answer one thing for me."

"Aye," he replied, a little too trustingly given their history of shenanigans.

She had many non-human customers who didn't maintain a human alter ego, so she'd wondered, "You always pay in cash. How?"

He quipped, "Maybe you were right 'bout needing to keep yer head empty." Then he looked at her, exasperated, "Lassie, I'm a friggin' leprechaun. I've got gold and Seattle has pawn shops."

As she peeked through her fingers, palm covering her face to hide her rising blush, she saw his grin had expanded to maximum capacity. He'd won yet another round.

Modern money wasn't made magically. Everyone had a "day job," as the magical community liked to call it, so Assembly meetings were held on weekend mornings.

Esme and Finn probably looked like quite the pair to anyone looking at them when they walked into the sleepy coffee shop. Finn strutted in, the rhythmic tap of his ebony walking stick echoing off the cafe's tiled floor, its golden lion-head topper gleaming under the warm lighting. His navy blue pinstripe suit was perfectly tailored, the matching fedora tilted at just the right angle to obscure his pointed ears.

Next to his flamboyant display, Esme felt frumpy in her white silk blouse, pencil skirt, and heels. At least she had put some effort into her hair and accessories. She'd tamed the waves in it with a curling iron to give it a nice bounce and she'd put on a few pieces of her mother's jewelry since she'd be on stage briefly.

"It's not that formal of an event, you know," she said, a hint of amusement coloring her voice.

He shrugged. "Well, I wasn't sure. It's better to be over-prepared than under."

"Lose the walking stick," she suggested.

"But it complements the cufflinks!" He showed her the tiny lion heads adorning his cuffs.

She chuckled at his affronted reaction. "I love how into fashion you are. I thought you were supposed to be obsessed with shoes, not fine fabrics. Anyway, the walking stick is kind of Jacob's thing. You'll see."

The leprechaun put on a show of looking around for someone else.

"Oh, Abby's not coming, but she'll be at the meeting. She's helping her mom through a rough patch right now."

His face fell, and Esme, hating to see his usual good cheer falter, quickly added, "We should drag her out for a drink sometime. She could use a break."

This improved his mood.

Regular hotel meeting rooms worked perfectly for the Assembly, with wards of silence placed upon the doors, windows, and walls. Entry into the area was restricted to magic users, enforced by the presence of protective barrier wards. These wards were more repulsive than illusory. She observed a few mundane hotel workers cautiously approaching the room, ready to offer assistance. But once they reached for the door handle, they would suddenly snap their fingers in recollection of something overlooked and swiftly change direction.

Inside the meeting room, Esme scanned the crowd, looking for familiar faces. She spotted Christi sitting at the head of the room with some of the other seated members. She was looking thinner than she had even just a few weeks ago. Abby, looking glum, caught her eyes a few rows ahead. Esme extended her forefingers and thumbs, joining them together to create a heart shape in the air, a silent reminder to her friend that she would always be there for support.

When she sat back down, she saw Sylas and Jacob, but not Juniper. She was probably at home in her forest, since she had no obligation to show up to these meetings. Esme herself only came when Jacob bugged her about it enough. She looked around for Miles, thinking that he should be in the line-up to formally introduce himself to the community as well. In all honesty, she'd been avoiding him since the fight with the afanc. Her embarrassment over her showing during the fight hadn't yet abated over the last few days.

Finn muttered beside her, "Uff, of course we're both wearin' navy blue. I shoulda gone with the dark gray suit, I knew it!" He slapped his knees in frustration.

She started to say, "What are you on about?" But then she saw him. Miles was also dressed in a navy blue suit, although its effect on her was quite different than Finn's impressive fashion statement. Gods and goddesses, a work of art had been hiding under his casual clothes the whole time.

Jacob called the meeting to order and Esme was thankful for the timely distraction from her ogling of Miles.

The first half hour nearly put her to sleep. Christi slogged through a count to ensure that a quorum of attendance was met. Next they went through the motions to deny a reading of the last meeting's minutes, thank goodness. They breezed through reports on the budget and projects. All very businessy and all very boring.

Introductions followed, breaking the monotony of business as the new arrivals took the stage. During the quarterly meetings that took place in the summer and fall, this part could last over an hour, as multiple families always moved to the area while their kids were on summer break. Luckily, this was the spring quarterly event, so the number of newcomers was usually quite small.

Some single guy who worked in the city's technology scene was first. He seemed to be a few years younger than Esme, and was cute in a "I'll build a robot for you if you need help around the house, honey" kind of way. She wondered if they'd meet personally at the bar soon.

Next up was Miles, poised to deliver his prepared speech just like everyone else. Esme settled comfortably into her seat, eager to hear what Doctor Goodwin would share from the stage. Unlike many others, Esme had been spared the awkward tradition of self-introductions at this Assembly. As a teenager, her parents had handled the introduction on her behalf.

Miles began, "Respected colleagues, I am deeply honored and humbled to address this esteemed gathering of individuals who have devoted their lives to the pursuit of knowledge and the progress of our craft. As both a doctor and a proud veteran of the coalition of troops allied with this great nation, I am honored to address you."

She hadn't known he was in the military. Maybe that explained his hand.

Miles continued, "As I stand before you, I am reminded of the boundless potential that lies within each of us. Let us embrace the challenges that lie ahead with courage and conviction, knowing that our collective efforts have the power to change the world for the better."

He ended the speech with a flowery pledge to work with the mages of the area and offered his expertise to any who sought it. The crowd clapped when his speech ended—that never usually happened.

During the applause, Finn pulled a face and whispered, "Uff, the golden boy has spoken."

Esme snickered. Miles was a golden boy, wasn't he? She should just start calling him that and get on with it.

Last came Finn. Esme's position at the bar made her a highly visible member of the mage community. Despite having detractors like Maureen, she was generally well-liked. Empowered by the confidence her reputation gave her and how amazing her butt looked in this skirt, she escorted Finn to the stage. Her role wasn't to speak, so she gave him a big hug and walked offstage.

She understood that non-human introductions had slightly different rules. Not being the dominant species on the planet, they had to disclose different information about themselves. Because he was Fae, Finn only had to give his commonly used name. Similarly, he had to explain why he'd moved to the area, along with his plans to occupy his time. The last was to reassure the community that the Fae would be too preoccupied to stir up trouble. It was a discriminatory act but unfortunately necessary, as history had shown repeatedly.

Esme had forgotten all about the explanation part of his introduction. So few Fae lived in the area that it had barely come up in the past decade. She started sweating through her antiperspirant; the silk blouse would be ruined. He was in the spotlight and unable to lie. How would he spin the banshee story?

He smoothed out his accent to suit the audience and said, "I come from Wicklow County in Ireland. I left Ireland due to troublesome neighbors. I decided to settle here after seein' pictures of the wondrous landscape. My garden and my friends will be my diversions." He'd played it right by keeping it simple—or so she thought. Esme's relief was short-lived.

An all-too-familiar voice shouted, hissing venom, "Your leaving has nothing to do with your tainted magic?" Maureen had a habit of using that word for anything she disliked, including Esme. How had the woman known?

Esme shot to her feet, anger flaring at Maureen's audacity, the heat of it burning away any trace of nerves. The meeting room full of powerful mages erupted into discussions, both whispered and shouted. What she could make out through the racket boiled down to a few simple lines:

"Tainted magic?"

"She means malevolent!"

"What?!"

Esme stared each detractor in the eyes and didn't sit back down. Some stared back with barely veiled hatred. She wished she could shout in their faces. The way they treated her friend made her furious. She felt Miles' eyes on her, but she didn't look away from the hateful mages.

Finally, her voice shaking slightly from the adrenaline of her mixed anger and nervousness, she said, "He's shared laughter and swapped stories with dozens of us over the past month. He was acceptable then, but now he's not? What is this really about?"

No one answered her.

The noise subsided as each person noticed the hunched old man come to a stand in his black robes of the office at the center of the room. The hush became absolute as he struck the base of his gnarled wooden walking stick on the floor. Despite her efforts to calm herself through measured breathing, Esme still shook with fury.

Jacob's cultured voice, barely diminished by age, lifted across the audience. "Let it be known that I vouch for this man, this leprechaun. Your concerns are valid, but he has been tested. Multiple times, in fact. He stands before you today because he has passed each one. The source of his magic is old—a broken promise.

"Finnegan of the Irish Isle, I welcome you to the Northwest Assembly. Keep the peace and be received as one of our own."

Jacob slammed the butt of his short staff on the floor again, signaling the end of his speech.

And that was that. Maureen sat there, tight with tension and disapproval, but blissfully silent. It was impossible for Esme not to feel some smug satisfaction at that.

Retaking his seat in the audience, Finn whispered, "To be sittin' so close to a bona fide gorgon in the flesh—well, I feel like that was a resounding success."

Esme couldn't agree more about the monster in the room. The success part...they'd see about that.

Sometime later, as Jacob took the stage again, Finn whispered, "I see what you mean about the stick, though. That codger's puts mine to shame."

She whispered back, "Yours is so fancy though!"

Jacob's was gnarled, pale, and plain.

Finn made a dismissive sound, then said, "Aye, but his...his most certainly has a story."

Whispering, Esme remarked, "Well, that's exceedingly cryptic."

Scratching his beard in confusion, the leprechaun asked, "Ya can't feel how special it is?"

"No?" she hissed. "I mean, I can feel magic like anyone else, okay, but apparently not like that."

He lowered his face and shook his head slightly. "What are they trainin' ya, lassie? How can ya not sense it?"

That was a good question. Even in a whisper, his tone suggested she was woefully lacking in a basic skill. Ever since he had walked into her life, there were more questions than answers for Esmeralda Turner.

***

Barely forty-eight hours had passed since the Assembly meeting when Esme received a text message from Jacob "summoning" her to a meeting at his home. He emphasized how he'd "condescended himself" with great reluctance to send her a text message. She vaguely remembered him calling it something like a newfangled, low-brow method of communication. After scooping her jaw off the floor, she realized that such a momentous act for him must have something substantial behind it.

When she arrived, a bedraggled Jacob greeted her at the door. Instead of being led to the library or to the comfortable breakfast nook that she shared with him so often, they went to Jacob's office. There she saw what, or rather who, had sapped Jacob's energy and was the likely instigator of the text message.

In one of the conference seats across from Jacob's desk sat the irrepressible ball of energy that was Finn.

The leprechaun had evidently been there a while because a plate covered in muffin crumbs and an empty tea mug sat before him. Jacob took his place at the desk and motioned for Esme to sit next to Finn, who greeted her with a small standing bow. He rarely used such formal manners with Esme, so she knew that something was up.

"I know an ambush when I've walked into one. Jacob, what is this? Last time I checked, I don't need an intervention." She said this last with a touch of humor in her voice, relieved that she didn't have that familiar sinking feeling in her stomach that often heralded bad news.

Jacob motioned for them both to sit. "Well, actually, in some ways you do. Finn and I have been chatting."

Was this about the afanc? The pit in her stomach opened up. Her performance and, frankly, that mission itself still kept her up at night. She'd had to face the undeniable fact, squarely in its monstrous face, that malevolents were actually back in the world. Not only that, but she was still grappling with how close she'd felt to death under one of their claws. But what was worse was that she'd also put Finn and Miles at risk with her poorly thought out choices.

Having had sufficient time to reflect, she realized that their teamwork should have been better. Miles had been too tight-lipped about his role in the scenario for her to have reacted appropriately. Plus, she hadn't known that Finn could disappear as quickly as he'd proven. But she'd bring that up once she knew what Jacob wanted to say. They'd have to improve if they worked together again.

Tapping a pen on the desktop, Jacob subtly revealed his agitation. She was most likely not the whole reason why Jacob's hair was sticking out in all directions, as if he had run his hands through it in frustration. He enjoyed his thoughtfully structured life, free of unchosen complicating factors. Finn was the exact opposite of the order that Jacob treasured.

The elder mage gazed at his apprentice and coughed, a hint of his familiar steadfast energy coming back. "Esme, darling, I am getting old and tired, and my duties have multiplied. Your potential is deserving of more attention than I can grant. No," he said, waving away her rising objection. "I've barely taught you a thing in years. I've done you a great disservice and I apologize for that, truly. It's past time for a change."

Taken aback by his surprising words, she responded, "Jacob, a disservice? Truly, no one has helped me as much as you. Not even my parents." It hurt to say, but it was the truth. Maybe part of moving past the pain was accepting that.

"And I know they did the best they could have given the circumstances. Esmeralda, you are far too promising to languish from my negligence. If you accept, Finnegan will be able to give you the attention and guidance required to fully develop your talents. If you agree, I'd like for you to focus on your growth, not what you can do for the Assembly, for a while."

She could not fathom what had occurred between the leprechaun and the Bastion that convinced her mentor to give up his teaching duties, but she had a feeling it concerned her lackluster magical performances. Perhaps Finn had impressed Jacob with his magical prowess, or perhaps it was his ability, and willingness, to kill malevolents that proved invaluable to him.

Jacob had a strong mind and even stronger magic. But he was one hundred and six years old. Maybe he needed a break. She noticed how paper-thin the age-mottled skin on Jacob's hands was. It was Esme's turn to try to pay him back for everything and make his life easier. She said, "A leprechaun mentor is rather unconventional. But if you think it's a good idea, I'll try it."

Chapter Seventeen

Training with the Leprechaun

Esme

Esme quite enjoyed her training with Finn. His methods were sometimes bizarre, but they had shown results.

One of the first things that he went about "rectifying," as he called it, was her weakness in sensing the differences in magic. Like any other mage, she could sense magic, but she discovered she had been blind to its subtle nuances all her life.

Proffering a black scrap of fabric, Finn announced, "Alright, lassie, time for the blindfold."

She groaned as he placed the blindfold back over her eyes. It was the fifteenth, if not the sixteenth, time she'd repeated the exercise in the past two weeks.

Each time Finn had explained the differences in magic like this: General magic was the type of magic that anyone could use. It was the magic of all things, in all things. Fae and malevolent magics were variations, both twisted in their unique way by millennia of alterations and "taint," as some would call it. That Finn could use all three varieties made him the ideal teacher.

The Fae probably predated humans, and that had left its mark on the magic that was uniquely theirs. Their natures varied, and not all of them were malicious; most had survived the Extinction. Over eons of malicious intent influencing it, malevolent magic had transformed into a distinctive strain from the rest.

Hearing her groan, he replied, "Well, it wasn't working the clean way, so we're doin' it the messy way."

At first, he tried infusing bowls of sand with the magic of each variety. She dipped her hands in each and attempted to feel the subtle differences. But that didn't work. She failed every time.

Then he got the bright idea to infuse something "with a memory of the magic of life in it." So he presented three bowls of oatmeal, or porridge, as he called it, that had been cooked with milk. She had to dip her hands into each gloopy bowl until she could announce the type correctly.

"Ugh, this is so gross. You don't plan on eating this afterward, right?"

"Uff, no."

She rolled her eyes under the blindfold and said, "Knowing you, I thought it was necessary to ask."

"Enough stallin', lassie. Get to dippin'. Here's the first two."

As her fingers squelched into the bowls of anonymous lukewarm mess for the second time that day, she had a breakthrough. She wiggled her hands in the goo one more time for reassurance and triumphantly announced, "The left one is Fae!"

Finn sounded proud as he said, "Aye, spot on! Any idea what the other one is?"

Reluctantly, she admitted, "Not yet." But she had correctly identified one. She could do it again.

"Alrighty, let's compare the other two." He grabbed the hand that had been in the Fae bowl of oatmeal and wiped it clean with a towel. The once warm and smooth glop had now turned cold and slightly hardened as he dipped her cleaned hand into the second bowl.

She squelched the goopy slurry in each of her hands, trying to feel a difference on her skin or with any of her other senses. After holding her hands in the bowls for nearly ten minutes she finally admitted, eyes still blindfolded, "I noticed the Fae bowl felt foreign, sort of like how putting on gloves for the first time each winter feels—kind of weird and tingly."

She scavenged her mind, trying to think of a similar analogy. Unthinking, she barely stopped herself from grabbing the blindfold with her sodden hands when she said, "I'm going to use another clothing metaphor, so stay with me. But these two feel like putting on another pair of comfortable cotton socks. They feel like nothing new. I suck at this."

Finn had been quiet for a long moment. Esme started pulling her hands out of the bowls so that she could clean them and end this farce. How could she not feel the difference between general and malevolent magic? It should have been easier than identifying the Fae.

In a tone that she'd not heard from Finn before, he said softly, "Wait now."

She paused in removing her hands.

Slowly, he said, "I can see where it might be confusin' for ya. Let's think of it another way. Think of the porridge as your emotions. Which porridge wants to slap that puffed-up gorgon we met at the Assembly meetin'?"

It was such a ridiculous question that she should, by all rights, be laughing at his joke, but his somber tone was undeniable. She couldn't read his face, but she suspected that his expression matched the tone.

"Okay." She considered the gloopy oatmeal, "I guess the bowl on the left might want to spill itself all over her fancy pantsuit."

He clapped his hands once and shouted, "Bingo! So now ya know what to look for. You did it!"

She smiled and felt around for the towel to wipe her hands. Finally, a minor victory was in the books for Esme.

With his help, she had also recently learned to stop "gabbing her plans for all the world to hear," as he called it, while she cast. She could now cast silently, reliably, without moving her lips. She was starting to feel like she had finally graduated from mage primary school.

During another one of their training sessions, she pointed out to Finn that she felt like her conjurations were changing, noting their fidgeting and how the humanoid ones occasionally wore readable facial expressions.

After conjuring her troll trio to demonstrate, he asked, "Aye, so what were they like before?"

She explained that they used to stand there dumbly, without expression, and with arms hanging limply at their sides. "Now they feel...more alive?" she stated questioningly.

"It's simpler than ya might think. Yer improvin'. You've put a wee bit of you into them. They are more alive."

He warmed to his topic. "They come from somewhere else—where, I dunno. But, here," he pointed stiffly at the ground, "they need a connection to you to exist and to think. Yer connected to them like a puppet with strings. Ya just can't see it."

He clapped his hands excitedly and continued, "And ya fed them a bit o' consciousness without even knowin' it. Yer a natural! I'm not skilled in conjurations like you, but I'd wager that if you can remember the string that binds them to ya, those dimwits will be sharper than ever."

His advice had shown its worth. The next time that she conjured her troll trio for practice, two of them had moved defensively without orders to dodge an unexpected fireball that Finn had flung their way.

For the first time in years, she couldn't stop smiling as she practiced. Magic felt alive in her hands again. The possibilities that smarter conjurations offered for combat or more menial work were endless. It could be the edge that she needed to stay ahead of the malevolent threat.

He'd specifically requested that they meet at his house instead of hers for their next series of lessons. She found that to be odd, but Finn was a bit odd in any case, and his hair-brained training ideas were working well, after all.

Their newest project together was diversifying her conjurations. He'd remarked that she was too predictable in her choice of summoned minions.

"Why limit yourself? Why not try somethin' new?" His expression changed to one of mischief then, puzzling her at the implications. "Do ya remember how we talked about your emotions with the porridge?"

How could she not? Her memory of it had been amplified by the unpleasant sensation of her hands sitting in clumpy goop for hours. It had been a moment of great triumph for her. She was all for pushing her boundaries, so she'd try anything.

He suggested, "Take some of the emotion that ya felt in the malevolent porridge and use it to create somethin' new." He thought for a moment, then offered, "You're a cat lover, so why not that? Let's start small though, alright. No bigger than yer neighbor."

Esme peered at him dubiously while standing in a clearing some distance away from the hiking trails. Skeptically, she clarified, because it sounded absurd, "You want me to conjure a cat from my angry porridge emotions? Mr. Snuffles?"

He nodded, smiling reassuringly.

It sounded crazy, but his bizarre methods had worked many times before, so she readied herself anyway. "Alright, one angry oatmeal cat, coming up!"

It became clear why he'd opted to teach at his house, in an isolated location, when she saw and smelled her latest creation.

The conjuration she summoned broke ruthlessly through the unseen barriers between reality and unreality. Its shadowy essence mingled with the stench of rotten eggs in the air. Before them stood a creature of blackest black, standing arrogantly on four tiny paws. Its eyes were swirling silver, lacking the familiar definition of feline-slitted pupils. But it somehow still held the imperious gaze that only one familiar, pint-sized, self-conceited creature could muster: the common house cat.

Esme stared at Oatmeal, as she had already named "her" at the onset of her conjuration, with a mixture of pleasure and dismay. On one hand, she had created something entirely new. Oatmeal looked impressive, albeit small. The swirling smoky shadows that made up her body billowed softly in the breeze, but she remained whole. Her eyes looked menacing, and giving the mental order, Esme inspected Oatmeal's teeth. Poking one with her fingertip, she found that they were, in fact, sharp.

On the other hand, Oatmeal smelled absolutely horrible. It wasn't even something that she added to her conjuration like she did with the trolls. The smell was part of the cat's essence. No matter how hard she concentrated, the stench wouldn't go away.

Giving up on clearing the smell, she said to Finn, "Ta-da! Meet Oatmeal."

In a manner most unbecoming of him, the leprechaun rubbed the stubble on his chin, worriedly, with both hands and said nothing.

Was he disappointed in her for doing exactly as he asked? She felt the need to defend herself. "I did what you asked, and I produced something workable." She mentally ordered the cat to run in a circle and jump up in the air, as she'd seen Mr. Snuffles do when he tried to capture a flying insect.

Finn nodded slowly. "Aye, so ya did." It seemed as if something rare, something usually eclipsed by his good humor, flickered behind his eyes as he studied the cat and then Esme for just a moment longer. Yet, that feeling dissipated once he reverted back to his pedagogical, albeit slightly mischievous, self.

He said, "But I think we can make 'Oatmeal' here a wee bit more impressive, don't you?"

Esme was all in. "One big, honkin' scary shadowcat comin' up!"

Chapter Eighteen

Fear is a Catalyst

Esme

Anyone sitting in The Sanctuary of Spirits would think that Esme was simply chatting up a customer, if rather closely. The man taking up all of her attention was maybe ten years her senior, impeccably dressed, and graying at the edges in an attractive, silver fox kind of way.

Even though Jacob had practically ordered her to work less so she could focus on her magical training, she still covered shifts for friends and worked at the bar when she was able. So her presence there that night wasn't particularly noteworthy. Propping her chin on one hand, Esme leaned over the bartop, feigning interest in the man's tale just as Miles walked through the door.

Their target was currently eating out of her hands—and looking down the front of her blouse. Her prior experience with this sort of assignment left her more at ease than she had been when facing off against a real-life monster.

She sent Miles a fleeting sideways glance as he made his way to his typical table. In that brief moment, she noticed his unease, a stark contrast to the confidence he typically displayed. She could understand the sentiment. Their last mission together fighting the afanc had been a tidy moral black and white. This one was an indeterminate shade of gray; dealing with humans always was.

A day before, Esme had witnessed the uncommon sight of Jacob losing his temper as he explained the details of this particular case. She'd gone to visit him for breakfast and, as a courtesy, she'd brought his newspaper indoors with her. But Miles was there, sitting at their breakfast nook. Esme was mature enough to acknowledge the pang of jealousy she felt seeing that. When she set the paper down on the table, she noticed a familiar face from the bar staring up at her from the front page and pointed it out.

Jacob said, "Yes, darling, that's precisely why you're both here."

With those words, butterflies with poison stingers took flight within her belly. It had only been two weeks since their last disastrous, for Esme at least, assignment together and Jacob was already pushing her to do another one. She'd considered gracefully backing out of it until she bore witness to the extraordinary sight of what came next.

"The blaggard has started cutting corners, and it nearly got someone killed! He's always been a bastard, but this is inexcusable!"

Esme nearly jumped as Jacob slammed his walking stick on the floor in anger, his face flushed and hair in disarray.

The person in question was Philip Luis, a real estate developer with a city contract to construct affordable housing. The problem was that he'd started using illusions to conceal the shortcuts he'd been taking to save money during inspections. A section of one building had collapsed during construction, leading to one man having a leg amputated. Using magic to circumvent mundane laws was a serious violation of Assembly edicts.

It left her speechless. Nothing ruffled Jacob. He had to visibly gather himself to explain.

"This only came to our attention because Philip has spent outrageous sums recklessly over the past month. His odd behavior, plus the illegal use of magic at the construction site, caused us to dig deeper. The reason both of you are here is that one of our operatives found evidence of malevolent magic at Philip's house."

Miles shifted uncomfortably in his seat. She thought he was the only Brother in the area. Was he the operative who had done the digging?

Jacob had continued. "We cannot allow anyone not in the know to look into this. Something smells bad about this situation, so I want you," he looked directly at Esme as he said this, singling her out, "to perform a little test so we can see what happens afterward. Miles will be there as backup."

Instead of asking, "Didn't I screw up the whole malevolent thing well enough last time," like she really wanted to, Esme quipped, "Just how many times have you ordered some goon to go through my stuff, Jacob?"

Maybe he was coming off of being angry, but he surprised her by answering her sincerely: "We've never felt the need. Your parents, however..." never finishing the thought.

Esme desperately wanted to grill him on what he'd meant about her parents, but not with Miles in the room.

Esme knew her customers. Philip always came into the bar on Wednesdays following the weekly meeting he held with his building materials contacts in China. Her role in this scenario was to deliver a handwritten reprimand before he left the bar that evening. Then Miles would follow him home and do some hands-off surveillance of his activities that night. What Philip did and who he contacted might lead them to discover what exactly was "malevolent" about this peculiar situation.

Looking at Philip through her lashes, she couldn't see him as being capable of feeling guilt over his actions. He simply didn't have the self-reflection necessary for genuine change. The politics at play made Esme ill.

She'd learned that his standing in both the mundane and the mage world apparently excused him from public embarrassment. She wanted to stand up at the bar and welcome everyone to a special story time, where she told them all about the dirtbag who put profit above people's lives. It would give her a sick sort of satisfaction to ruin his day.

This was the kind of job that irked her. It almost made her feel dirty. Why should this creep get off without public shame when his greed had permanently maimed a man? It would take months, if not years, of recuperation for the injured man to get back to work.

Discreetly delivering the reprimand should be easy. Philip usually only drank one cocktail during his weekly visit, but she'd keep him there for two or three if possible. That way, he would need to use the restroom before leaving. While he was taking care of his business, her orc, Chuck, would block Philip's exit with his hideous face.

She only used Chuck for Assembly jobs, hoping it would allow her to maintain some anonymity. Her orc would offer the letter in a delightfully menacing way, and then her part would be done. The only problem was that the more she thought about it, the more she was curious about Miles' role and the more she wanted to join in on his surveillance.

Making the excuse that she needed to get help to serve other customers, Esme offered Mr. Luis a free mocktail to keep him well-hydrated. He seemed happy with the drink, so she confidently walked to the back room and summoned two helpers.

A wrinkled, bald elfin creature clad in a red tunic and trousers, walked out of the bar's kitchen. Sitting on its left shoulder was the same purple pixie, Irritella, that Esme had used to harass the college kid who got in a fight the night when Miles had first introduced himself to her. She then returned to her spot in front of the older gentleman, resuming her flirtatious stance.

The elfin creature carefully and slowly picked up the glass of sloe gin and placed it on Miles' table, just outside of his reach. The pixie flitted off the creature's shoulder and grabbed the napkin from the tray. It struggled to stay aloft, beating its wings wildly, as it held up the napkin for Miles to take.

He took it from the pixie and noticed the writing Esme had left there for him.

> *I'm coming with you tonight.*
> *Drink's on the house.*

As soon as he was finished reading it, the pixie disappeared. The elfin creature turned sedately around and returned the serving tray to the back room.

Miles took a sip and saluted her sideways glance with a nod of assent. He hadn't said no. She wanted to jump and clap in victory, but kept her cool. Miles cracked open his phone and tucked in to wait for her to be finished.

Later, when she noticed Miles covertly studying her performance, Philip excused himself to the restroom, walking cautiously to avoid seeming intoxicated. It was game time.

Once again, she excused herself to the backroom and summoned her orc to do the honors. She was free to conjure helpers in the main bar area, but this needed to be discreet. Before the bar opened for the day, she had hidden the letter of reprimand on top of the mirrors in the men's restroom, just out of sight for anyone but an eight-foot-tall orc. She'd placed a sticky note with the words "Read me and he'll disappear" on the outside.

Esme had already convinced another bartender to take over for the rest of the night so she could join Miles. She wiped down the bar preparation area while her conjuration did its work and walked over to Miles' table. While picking up his glass, she quietly asked, "Meet me outside the shop in ten-ish?"

He placed a twenty-dollar bill on the tray with the used glass and replied, "Yes, thank you."

She wanted to argue that the drink was free, but it was simpler to allow him this one small thing. It was a weeknight, so her coworker should be fine flying solo for the last few hours of the evening. She quickly cleaned up and did some prep for the next day to help out.

While she couldn't precisely see through her conjurations, she could sense what they were experiencing like an echo, a disconnected and subtle representation of their experiences. When she could sense that Mr. Luis had crumpled up the letter and thrown it into the trash bin, she dismissed her orc. It took about five minutes for the man, veins visibly pulsing in his forehead with fury, to burst through the restroom door. To her relief, he marched straight toward the exit doors and disappeared.

After delivering the reprimand, Esme quickly moved to prepare for the next phase of their mission. Motivated not to miss out on the surveillance work, she walked out of the bar in record time. Turning the corner outside the convenience store, she expected to see Miles leaning on the wall somewhere waiting, but he wasn't there. Maybe he was still in the bar?

Esme watched the crowds of people standing around the restaurants and mundane bars nearby. There must have been an early-season baseball game going on at the field a few blocks down. Holding her purse close, she walked around the corner of the building to see if Miles was waiting there.

The face that greeted her was not a friendly one. It was Philip Luis, and he was still furious.

His clenched fists and tight posture broadcast the anger burning through him. The air around him practically vibrated with barely confined magic. All she could hope for was his continued restraint. He knew just as well as she did that any use of magic with so many potential mundane witnesses would not end well for either of them.

"This was you, wasn't it?" he snarled. His face distorted briefly, as if broadcasting on an old-fashioned television that was losing its signal. Strange.

Crossing her arms defensively, she replied, "Maybe that last cocktail was one too many." It would be best if she could diffuse this moment hastily. She added in a dismissive tone. "Need me to call a rideshare to take you home to sleep it off?"

Faster than her mind could process, he pushed her to the shadowed wall just around the corner of the building. Her spine hit the bricks hard as his breath, reeking of alcohol, entered her nostrils.

He growled, "You think you can do that without consequences?"

Philip's hands pinned her arms below her shoulders against the wall and his torso was pressed into hers, leaving her unable to kick upward in defense. A torrent of fear coursed through her veins. Her heartbeat raced and her palms became clammy with anxious perspiration. She had never felt so vulnerable.

She watched in astonished relief as a clenched fist quickly dragged across the left side of the man's neck that was now a stark white—not a color her brain could associate with the man she'd chatted up in the bar. She saw a flash of chestnut brown hair as her attacker was dragged backward, choking off of her.

Miles slowly sank to one knee, holding the human-shaped thing up by its neck. Miles had his head tucked safely behind its shoulders, out of the range of any potential oncoming blows. The thing's face was broadly human, but the nose was not much more than a hole, the mouth lipless, and the eyes a solid black. Its face, which was once as white as snow, was now turning a pale gray color, likely due to blood flow slowing between its brain and its heart.

Horrified, she watched as the inebriated creature struggled feebly with its sinewy hands around Miles' compressing arm, attempting to harm him and free itself.

She glanced around and noticed that their scuffle had attracted no attention. The thing must have cast an illusion around them as it attacked her. The illusion was still active, so it must be maintaining it.

Miles quickly asked, "This guy is supposed to be human, right?"

Esme slowed her breathing, still standing next to the brick wall. "Yeah, yes. One hundred percent. And he—it—is casting an illusion around us."

Miles dragged the nearly limp body, still in a chokehold, behind one car parked in the small lot next to the convenience store. He made it just in time for the illusion the thing was casting to drop, allowing the world to see and hear everything near them once more.

Esme walked to the other side of the car to survey the scene of horror. Miles was crouched behind it, still holding the neck of the alien-looking creature.

Miles ordered, "Open the trunk."

She pointed at the car they were hiding behind. He nodded. She clicked the trunk release button. It popped open soundlessly.

From his place on the ground, Miles said quietly, "I know this is against the edict of not using magic in public. But," he breathed out as he clenched down harder on the thing's neck, "I promise that this won't blow back on you. Can you," he breathed out again and tightened yet again, "cast a small illusion around the car so I can get this into the trunk?"

She nodded dumbly. Her father had been an illusion specialist, so her early training with him was enough to get them through this.

"It's ready," she said, turning back to Miles. He slowly removed his arms from their locked position.

"Is it knocked out?" she asked.

Illusion in place, Miles heaved upward, using his legs to propel himself and the alien body off the ground. Holding the limp body like a bundle of firewood, he stuffed it unceremoniously into the trunk of the car and closed it.

Even though he'd reassured her, the potential repercussions of using magic in public made her immediately drop the surrounding illusion.

He finally replied to her earlier question. "Dead."

Gods and goddesses below, he'd killed it. Right there, in front of her. Well, technically, she was probably turned around when it died, but still.

Miles studied her as if checking her over for injury. She expected the first thing to come out of his mouth to be, "Are you okay?" But what he said instead blindsided her.

"Take a quick stroll with me?"

Surprised, she mumbled in reply, "Yeah," then more firmly, "Yes." Shifting her purse back onto her shoulder and straightening loose strands of hair, she started walking.

For a while they walked in silence, remaining a short distance apart. As they reached a tree-lined square a few blocks down, she finally opened up. "Thank you."

He said nothing, only nodding in acknowledgment.

Once they rounded the baseball stadium, they turned around, retracing their steps. She was itching for him to say something; anything.

"I hope that was your car. I wasn't paying attention back there," she remarked, finding a small glimmer of humor in the darkness. She asked, "That wasn't Philip Luis, was it?"

"No," he said in a low tone, "that was a doppelgänger. A malevolent. Philip Luis is probably long dead somewhere."

After a few more steps, he continued, "We're lucky it was drunk. Otherwise, things could have turned out very differently. I don't understand how it could mask its malevolent magic from an entire room of mages like that."

Esme considered this, then suggested, "Maybe it used Philip's magic instead of its own?"

He shot her a considering sideways look that made her feel like maybe she had a functional brain after all. "Huh. Maybe."

The implications of what had just happened were incredible. A malevolent was in the city, in the freaking Assembly, hiding in plain sight.

Suddenly, Miles stopped walking. It took Esme two steps to stop and turn to him. He asked, seeming frustrated, but with his voice still pitched for just the two of them, "So the Assembly never taught you physical self-defense?"

Well, that certainly got her hackles up. But damn it all, he was right. She couldn't be cross with her savior for asking a valid question.

"No," she answered, shaking her head in disgust at her inability to defend herself. As if being a woman didn't involve enough self-flagellation, this felt like yet another mark against her.

His gaze roved over her face, seeming to evaluate her state of mind. He said, "Let's do something about that." His tone wasn't reproachful or condescending. He was offering a solution to a problem, not poking at an open wound.

They resumed their stroll and eventually made it back to the parking lot. He held out his keys, showing them to her. "Need a ride?"

"I'll be honest," she whispered conspiratorially. "I kinda want to see what you're going to do with the body."

He snorted out a quick, throaty laugh, and the knot at the base of her spine unraveled. He said, "I know a guy."

She smiled softly, genuinely, for the first time that night. "But I totally would have had him, you know?"

"I have no doubts about that. I've seen what you're capable of," he said as he opened the passenger door for her.

Since the body in the trunk answered the question of how Philip Luis' odd behavior and the malevolent magic at his construction site were related, they didn't need to do any surveillance.

It turned out that Miles did know a man who ran a mortuary south of the city. He assured her that he would turn a blind eye to the activities of the Brotherhood if enough zeros were on the check afterward. Miles called ahead to alert him of their arrival.

Their talk about everything other than malevolents on the drive south calmed her nerves and brought her back to herself. It helped that it was easy to talk to him. He was easygoing and well-rounded enough that he could talk about any topic that came up.

Miles backed the car to the rear of the building. Esme practically jumped out to help. She grabbed the feet as Miles took the shoulders. Together, they carried the body through the open back door.

The beady-eyed, rather languid man who greeted them barely counted as a mage, but he liked their money well enough because that was the first thing he inquired about.

Miles replied cryptically, "Himself will take care of it by tomorrow, I'm sure." This made her wonder if Jacob was bankrolling this endeavor or if there was a line item in the Assembly's accounts for "Biological Disposal" or something equally sketchy sounding.

The beady-eyed mortician huffed, "He'd better," and waved Esme and Miles away briskly. He barked, "I've work to do. Be off!"

Miles stared the smaller man down for one moment, then turned to leave with an unusually silent Esme in tow.

Once back in the car, Esme remarked, "So, that's the whole morally gray part of being a Brother, isn't it?"

He pursed his lips as he drove out of the parking lot, saying simply, "We do what we have to."

As Esme ended her night, she reflected on the drive home with Miles. It seemed like such a small thing, but after experiencing true terror in the clutches of a malevolent for a second time, she appreciated his businesslike approach to careful driving.

When he parked in front of her house, he gave her the contact information for a self-defense instructor, stating that he trained at the gym when the time allowed.

Trying not to drop her phone on her face as she lay in bed, she combed the gym's website, learning everything she could about what they taught—subconsciously hoping to find some sense of safety in her planning. She'd already checked the wards on her doors and windows, but even then she couldn't escape the awful feeling that something, anything, could be out there just waiting to do one of the million things that she'd imagined had happened to Philip Luis.

Feeling defenseless had been utterly terrifying. A malevolent had overwhelmed her both times she'd encountered them. And the last one had worn a human face. If Miles hadn't been there…

Well, she'd just have to use that feeling as motivation to get to a point where she wouldn't ever feel that way again.

She realized that the lingering distrust she'd held for Miles had all but disappeared. He'd saved her from a thousand different horrible possibilities, not once but twice. He'd been open, honest, and unjudgmental during each of her failures. They'd even disposed of a body together. If that wasn't a sign of true friendship budding, she didn't know what was.

Another realization struck her, and she sat bolt upright in bed. *Damn*. She'd have to tell Jacob exactly what had happened that night.

Eventually, she put down the phone and set her alarm for her meeting with Jacob the next morning. It would not be fun telling him that a malevolent had assaulted her in the middle of downtown Seattle. Not only that, she'd have to inform him that a malevolent had taken the shape of a prominent mage and done who knows what while impersonating him. She would have to do it alone too, because Miles was busy. She let out a long breath, trying to center herself and calm down.

If all of that was already happening, she couldn't be completely unprepared for what else might be coming. The Assembly and the Brotherhood couldn't go on like this; as if nothing was happening. They needed to act proactively instead of simply reacting to sightings.

There was no doubt in her mind that malevolents were coming back in droves, and it was probably far worse than anyone had suspected.

With her mental list of things to talk about compiled, the last thought she had before falling asleep that night was a question. How much of Philip's behavior was because of the doppelgänger and how much was because of the evil part of human nature? Sometimes it was hard to tell the difference.

Chapter Nineteen

Divulsions

Esme

How did you go about telling your boss with a straight face that monsters were most likely hiding under a few Assembly beds? Esme was about to find out because she had zero plans on what she was going to say during this encounter. She took a deep breath, steeling herself for the conversation ahead. Miles had to work that morning, so she would be reporting alone. The hours he kept made her wonder if he ever slept.

After each mission, job, assignment, or whatever they called it that day, she always reported to Jacob at his home. Rather than a formal business-style report, they treated the meeting as a relaxed brunch. It made reporting to him more enjoyable, but she doubted others in her position were served breakfast sandwiches with coffee by Jacob's house staff the day after getting their butt kicked by a doppelgänger.

She sat across the table at the breakfast nook with Jacob. She'd probably been staring at him too long, considering what to say, because he asked, "Do I have something on my face?"

"What? No."

He frowned quizzically. "What is it then? What's keeping you from inundating me like usual?"

This was it. "I, uh, handled the Philip Luis job last night."

The smile that he gave her was innocent. "Well done. I'm sure you did a fine job."

"He's dead."

A furrowed brow and squinted eyes replaced his smile. "Come again? I think I might have to replace a hearing aid battery."

She repeated it louder, enunciating each word, "Philip Luis is dead."

Jacob replaced his coffee cup on the saucer. She felt a ward of silence envelop them. He'd been quicker and more subtle than Sylas in casting the complicated magic.

He placed his hands in his lap, face scrunched into a gut-wrenching expression of sadness, and asked, "You?" He didn't look reproachful, like she feared he would. No, this was Jacob awash in remorse that ran so deep that it seemed to touch his soul. He thought he'd sent her into a situation where she had no choice but to take a life.

Esme shook her head. "Not me: Miles. Well...it's...fu...shit! Ugh, again, damn it! Sorry for cussing, Jacob." Any eloquence she possessed had escaped her.

Determined to showcase her stability, she spoke with a steady voice and requested, "I'm not doing a great job of reporting this to you, so can I start at the beginning?"

He said, "Please do," with a sad tone that carried a heavy weight.

Her mind raced, weighing how much to say, but under Jacob's unwavering gaze, she knew she couldn't keep it all hidden. She expected a response from Jacob at this, but he didn't seem to disapprove of the idea. In fact, he made no reaction as she told the story until the point that "Philip" restrained her bodily. He pushed the table away, standing with alacrity, demanding, "What now?"

A small spark of warmth entered her heart at seeing his concern. "It's fine; I'm fine," she said, trying to calm him back to sitting. "Miles handled it."

He regained his seat stiffly, still incensed.

Then the rest of it came spilling out. About Miles strangling the doppelgänger, then shoving its body in the trunk and disposing of it. At the end she added, "Miles said that the real Philip Luis is probably dead somewhere."

Jacob's lips formed a thin, unyielding line. "Yes, Philip is most certainly no longer with us. That's how doppelgängers work. They kill and wholly replace the person they've chosen. I'm so sorry that you were a party to this."

Esme left his last statement unanswered because she wasn't sorry that she'd gotten involved. Her life had been going nowhere fast before Sylas dropped a problem involving a deceased child and a troublesome leprechaun in her lap. The feeling that she had something to work for, to improve herself for, was something she hadn't realized she'd been missing. This life, however brutal, had given her purpose.

Hands trembling, she flattened her hands on the table to spread out her napkin. "I need you to hear me, Jacob."

He wiped at his face with his. "You know I'm listening."

Taking a deep breath, she said, "I'm no expert, but I think it's clear that what the Brotherhood and the Assembly are doing isn't enough. Look at what happened with Philip. A malevolent murdered and replaced one of your own mages, a top dog, with no one noticing it. This should be a wake-up call for everyone in the know."

He sat back in his seat and breathed out heavily, but she continued. "It's time to be proactive instead of waiting for someone to be killed or a disaster to occur. At the very least, we need to find some way of detecting the malevolents when they first appear. Get them before they can get us. You say that we have to keep it a secret, but what good is that doing?"

He looked grim, like a demanding teacher attempting to impart a lifesaving lesson. He was metaphorically standing on his lectern as he spoke. "I agree. We need to do more. A proactive approach is precisely what we need. But first," he raised one warning finger in the air, "just think of the implications of this information getting out, Esmeralda. All it takes is one wrong person knowing about it to create panic. Think of the mundane doomsday preppers out there now! What is the mage's equivalent?"

He allowed her to ruminate on this for a moment, then asserted, "Horrors! They would create nightmares to protect themselves. There would be an arms race. We know from history that when mages feel the need to defend themselves with magic, the other, less desirable, traits of our kind follow. What traits, you might ask. Power has a way of making its holder desire ever more of it."

A shadow of something dark and painful moved across his face—memories. He turned somber and introspective as he explained. "We talked recently about my time in the last world war. I remember your reaction to learning my age. Anyway…at first, I deferred my conscription so that I could complete my studies at Oxford."

She knew he'd attended the university. It was impossible to miss the banner of arms sitting above the mantel in his library.

"But then my baby sister and mother were killed in the Blitz."

Gods. She had not known that. "I'm so sorry. I didn't know."

He sighed heavily and dropped his napkin back on the table with some force behind the movement. "Spurred by grief and anger in equal measures, I found my way onto the lines in Tunisia and Italy. Everyone has a few turning points in their lives. My mother and sister dying was one of mine. But what I did in Italy was another."

The look of shame she saw in his eyes made her unsure if she wanted to hear the rest.

He continued. "I am not proud of the story I am about to tell you. It may shock you. But I must get my point across."

All she could do was nod.

When he began, he avoided making eye contact with her. "Everyone was doing it. They were our enemy, so what was a bit of looting of what we considered 'ill-b—, ill-gotten gains' during war? Esmeralda, magic has a way of tempting the soul. It makes the exact same promise of safety that money and power offer."

A hint of regret, or maybe something else, something darker, clouded his distracted gaze for a second time. When he returned his consideration to her, she was gripping her coffee mug as if it were the only thing keeping her from running away.

He finally met her eyes. "I see that I have your attention. Yes, I have made my fair share of mistakes. As far as I know, I was the only mage in my regiment. I, like anyone, wanted nothing more than safety and, honestly, revenge. I desired freedom from my constant state of fear.

"Desperation can make any man dangerous—a mage, even more so. A good deal of my strength in magic has its roots in destruction; in death. It should come as no surprise to you that I used magic to save my life. I also used magic to take lives."

She listened intently, acknowledging the significance of what he was sharing with her. While it was logical that being in a war meant that someone might have to kill another person, hearing Jacob admit it outright was another thing altogether.

"While officers were cutting paintings from their frames, I sought something else. The magic practically called out to me from the stables behind the estate we were in. "

He took a deep breath, reliving the moment in his mind before continuing. "There, curled up in a corner, covered in hay, was a dying man. He clutched weakly at a gnarled wooden staff in one hand. The staff practically vibrated with magical energy. The man, probably a mage, looked as though he had part of his head smashed in by a horse's hoof or perhaps, more darkly, he had been turned on by his employer. Either was likely given the chaos of the invasion.

"To my mind then, he was an enemy, part of the reviled Axis forces. I reasoned that there was nothing I personally could do to help him. So, I did what I believed at the time was the next best thing. I killed him. Even though he might have survived, albeit with grave injuries, I killed him because he had something I wanted."

Esme tried, and mostly succeeded, at hushing the sharp intake of breath that came unbidden. She asked, "Your walking stick?"

He nodded slightly and spoke in a bleak, matter-of-fact tone. "The very same. After I had taken his life, I took the staff from his grip. Esmeralda, sometimes the pursuit of magic, like any power, can lead us down paths we never intended to tread. I removed a dead man's prize possession from his still-warm hands because inside I was still a frightened little boy. I was scared. I wanted the safety that its magic promised me.

"The staff," he motioned toward a wooden artifact leaning against the wall of the room and levitated it toward them to grab it from the air, "is a reminder of a choice made in the darkness of war; a choice that I must live with today.

"That man was not the first, nor was he the last, whose life I will have counted against mine in the afterlife. I have done far worse in my days; worse during the war. Fear, anxiety, and revenge—all things that come from knowing that the monsters are real—are mighty motivators. If we can help it, I'd prefer that we create fewer human monsters while in pursuit of the malevolent ones. The secret must be kept. Do you understand?"

Gods below. She did.

She thought that she also truly, finally, understood Jacob.

Chapter Twenty

A Watery Burial

Miles

The summer night was oppressively hot, the air heavy and stifling. The winds shifting from the sea to the land meant that the salty breeze from the nearby Sound no longer provided relief. With each breath, Miles' nostrils filled with the rich, earthy, nearly rotten, smell of the wetland's mud. It was impossible to mask the soft creak his steps elicited on the weathered wooden planks of the boardwalk.

During the day, this park was filled with strolling families making their way along the path to reach the driftwood-laden beach below. Parents, children, friends shared sandwiches and lemonade while they watched boats drift past. With the sun long past setting, Miles hunted a creature that would seek to rip away the chance at making those happy memories. Too many years of life granted the yaoguai sentience, and now it was free to inflict chaos and pain upon its victims once again.

It was tempting to rely upon the echoing symphony of frogs to drown out the sounds of his footsteps, but experience told Miles that it would not be enough for this quarry. Then he saw it—the movement of all-too-familiar gray fur at the edge of his vision. The creature had clawed over the surface of his mind to find a disguise. Aware of the power of confusion, it aimed to create an opportunity for escape. He'd been warned not to bring Lily or anyone else on this hunt, and that advice was now paying off.

As Miles approached the spot where it was last seen, he froze with his hands resting on his hips—not in shock, but in a moment of strained concentration. His other sense could reveal what he couldn't perceive with his eyes, ears, or nose. Some might refer to it as a sixth sense—the ability to perceive the intangible energies permeating the world. Others might label it intuition or mere instinct. For Miles, however, it was unmistakably the sense of magic.

This yaoguai excelled in concealment, remaining invisible to all his mundane senses. But there, with his sixth sense, he could feel that it was close enough that he should be able to feel it breathing. On one hand, it was fortunate that this yaoguai still had enough control not to attack him without reason. But on the other... Miles gripped the push dagger at his belt and punched downward, using his entire body to amplify the strength of his attack.

He glanced down at the creature still impaled on his blade. In its final, desperate moments, it transformed, adopting Esme's anguished visage. Her face twisted in unbearable pain. Her mouth bled cruelly as the creature opened it, as if she, it, hoped to speak to him. Its intelligent eyes locked onto his, searching through her violet eyes for his protection and healing.

Even though he knew it wasn't real and that what he did was right, he felt something within him break. For far too long, he held a dying Esme in his arms. His...his what? His friend? He'd been keeping her at arm's length, trying to remain professional; to not follow the path that his dreams had led him down when it came to her.

But the agony he felt as he watched the light slowly fade from her—no, from *its*—eyes, convinced Miles that his determination to maintain strict professionalism with her was doomed to failure.

Slowly, too slowly for his sanity, each of her features melted away. The face of a lion, misshapen and too small, stared back. His dagger protruded from the place where its mane met the scaled reptilian torso. Its serpentine tail remained still and lifeless. This monster wouldn't drain another human life; another child.

After severing the yaoguai's head, he tossed its lifeless body into the water below and swiftly made his way across the boardwalk to the shore. There he threw his grim trophy, the head, into the waves. If found, the separate halves of the monster would not seem to be connected in any way. With any luck, the tides and nature herself would dispose of the remnants before the beach filled up the next morning.

He walked back to his car feeling hollowed out, wishing that it was as easy to dispose of his psychological scars as it was corpses.

Chapter Twenty-One
Friends Chatting

Esme

Before she knew it, it was midsummer in Seattle. The days were long and the weather was glorious. Esme was enjoying only working a few shifts per week while she focused on her magical and physical training.

Jacob hadn't ordered her out on another mission in what felt like forever. Esme bartended and trained. Finn did whatever hijinks a leprechaun got up to on a normal day when they weren't training together. Miles doctored and probably did super-secret Corded Brotherhood stuff on the side.

Since the doppelgänger job, Esme and Miles had become something like acquaintances, maybe even some version of friends. He'd came into the bar once a week while she was working. He'd always order the same thing, chat with her for a few minutes about her training or whatever else was going on in the world that day, and then leave. If Finn was there, Miles would share a drink with him or they'd play a game of cards. Not once did he ever bring up the Corded Brotherhood, malevolents, or even Jacob while at the bar. He was very good at the whole covert thing.

Sometimes she got the feeling that he was purposefully keeping her at arm's length. Not that she could blame him. First, she'd threatened to kill him. Then, as a reward for his moderation, Jacob had burdened him with her as a newbie to malevolent hunting and investigations. She'd screwed up both jobs and had almost gotten killed or hurt in the process. In spite of that, Miles had become surprisingly friendly with her. Even if he was keeping her at a distance, she felt like he was a much better acquaintance to her than she deserved.

It was a weekend night when Esme, Abby, and Will sank into the overstuffed cushions in Esme's living room with a shared sense of relief. Abby and Will clinked glasses with her before sinking into the overstuffed cushions, propping their feet on the coffee table and springing the footrest in unison.

In one small way, Esme and Will were lucky. Last call at The Sanctuary of Spirits was midnight, not 2 a.m. like most places in Seattle. Still, bartenders at those establishments were not burdened with grumpy dwarves demanding "a wee taste" of the latest beer, refusing to accept each was the new one until they'd drunk an entire stein's worth without paying or leaving a tip. Did customers think they used magic to clean all those glasses?

Abby had joined them after work to adjust her sleep schedule in preparation for switching to night shifts for a few months. A coworker was about to go on maternity leave and Abby was the first to volunteer to help cover her absence. While she mainly did it to be kind, the bump in pay for the shift change didn't hurt either.

Will was his usual lively self. "Esme, this prosecco was exactly what the doctor ordered: crisp, clean, and refreshing. I spilled an amaretto sour on my apron earlier and I thought I was gonna gag from the smell of the egg white on it for about two hours during our rush. I had no time to change!"

Esme added, "If it helps, I didn't notice."

"Girl, it does not," he declared, miming a gag as he delicately held his glass. Immediately, knowing what was coming, he held up his index finger, holding Abby off. "Ms. Nurse, nuh-uh. Do not even come at me with some disgusting story of body fluids you had to clean up. I," he gestured at his muscled physique, "was not built to handle that nastiness."

Abby reddened slightly with guilt. Honestly, it wasn't much of a feat because almost any emotion would show brightly on her fair skin. "Fine, party pooper."

Will playfully groaned in disgust and covered his face with a nearby pillow. A sound of muffled dread came from behind the stuffed decoration and finally, "You still managed to use that word, you harpy!"

Abby brightened considerably, knowing that she had won their little verbal sparring contest in the end. Esme watched on, content, thinking how good life could be if you just gave it a chance.

"Speaking of your body," Esme winked at Will. "How was your date with that lawyer? He did not seem like your type."

Abby and Will traded knowing glances. It was Abby who spoke for the two of them. "No way; you are not deflecting right now."

Will added, "I will personally die if you do not tell us how this morning went."

Esme had been caught. She tried to stop it, but she could feel her face betraying the truth of her attempt at deflection for all to see, burning pink.

That morning, she had attended her first sparring session with Miles. Her instructor said that she had excelled in her training and that she was at a point where she could try casual sparring with a more skilled opponent. Miles had brought up the idea before, so she took him up on the offer of training together. She found she was—and this was putting it mildly—unprepared for his abilities.

A bit grumpily she said, "Well, first of all, no one told me he was in the freaking special forces while he was in the military. Obviously, I got my ass kicked."

Esme shot Will a warning glance, knowing that he would probably take that as an opportunity to mention her or Miles' derriere, or conversely, about his willingness to be involved in anything involving Miles' behind.

More seriously, Abby prodded, "Elaborate."

Esme thought for a moment then said, "Uh, how do I say this? He was hard on me with the training in a respectful way—if that makes sense."

Will leaned forward in interest. "Hard, you say?"

Her mood not dampened by this in the slightest, she shot back, "Are we certain that you're not a nymph in disguise or something? Because sex is on your mind twenty-four seven!"

In reply, she received only a handsome grin. Abby playfully smacked his knee and reprimanded him, "If you don't shush, we won't get the full story out of her!"

Esme clarified, "I say he was hard on me because if I messed a move up, he didn't ignore it. He showed me the correct way, and then we worked on it together. He never acted like something was beyond my capabilities." Unable to contain her excitement, she wiggled in her chair and finished by saying, "It was fun."

She had been nervous during the entire first half of their sparring session, constantly fearing that she might kick him in the face or do something equally regrettable. But something about him, something about the way he approached everything so methodically and yet so openly, overcame her nerves.

"Anyway," she tried to disguise her eagerness, "I think that we're going to make it a regular thing since we train at the same gym now."

Will asked primly, "So, when are you meeting the parents? Oh wait, you still don't have a passport." He frowned. "Remember, you need that so we can go to Cabo together."

"Ugh, I've said this a million times already. We. Are. Not. Dating." She threw a pillow at him. Abby plucked it from the air with magic before it hit his wine glass.

"My gods, you two, behave!" Abby then pushed Esme impatiently. "If you're not dating, what is this, then?"

"Just training! I swear! Am I not allowed to have a new hobby?" Esme asked with a bit too much pleading in her voice.

Will practically snorted. "Yeah, your new hobby just so happens to be one where you rub different parts of your body all over a sweaty, delicious man."

"Honestly, I thought Abby was dating him on the down low for a while!"

Abby gasped and didn't attempt to stifle her laugh, "Seriously? *Me*?"

"I know, I realize now that it was silly. He's not exactly your type—too straight laced."

Abby gave her a "duh, that goes without saying," face.

Neither of her friends knew of the eventful past between Esme and Miles. From their perspective, they saw two single adults spending time together outside of a professional setting. To them, the sparring session looked like a date, or at the very least, the precursor to one.

Esme felt a twinge of guilt at lying to her friends by omission, yet again. They didn't know that it was purely business for her and Miles. That they both led second, secret lives.

Abby looked at her in the way that Esme knew meant trouble. Her tone was persuasive when she asked, "Does it *have* to stay that way?"

Really, how could she respond to that? Her emotions were all over the place. Maintaining her current relationship with Miles was maintaining the status quo. That should be fairly easy unless something drastic happened. Only, she'd already taken steps away from the stagnant course her life had been on, doing the same jobs for the Assembly, working the same nights of the week at the bar. So making another change was tempting.

After taking a fortifying sip that bordered on a gulp from her drink, Esme finally admitted. "Well, I guess not. We'll see what happens." Whenever she could, she granted her friends the truth.

Abby pointed at her with her now empty wine glass. "Right answer. I am all for this pairing, and I don't mean the wine and snacks."

Miles had the looks, the job, the personality, and he possessed the sharpest mind of anyone she'd ever met besides Abby. It was nearly impossible to see herself as someone worthy of his interest. He was everything that a woman could want in a man. The only thing that gave her hope was the way she'd seen Miles looking at her when he didn't think she was watching. Whenever she noticed it, anticipatory butterflies took wing within her. It was a look that balanced something like hunger and tenderness so precisely that a new word would have to be made to describe it.

Esme couldn't know the truth behind his glances until she opened herself up to the real possibility that they meant something. She had a choice. She could stand in her own way like she had been for months, or she could allow events to unfold organically. Abby was right. Things between them didn't have to remain the way they were, as nothing more than casual friends. She just wondered what event would tip them over the edge into whatever came next.

A moment later, as planned, startled shrieks ripped out of both Abby and Will.

Bert had silently entered the living room carrying a bowl of popcorn in one hand and a tray of water glasses in the other. Neither noticed until a dark form blocked out the light from overhead. Hunched over behind the pair on the couch, his hideous face was just inches away from theirs as he waited to lower the tray and bowl to the coffee table in front of them.

Esme grinned in delight. The leprechaun was rubbing off on her.

Chapter Twenty-Two

A Picture is Worth a Thousand Years

Gwyn

"Trent! I've been looking everywhere for you." Gwyn rushed to push the child away from the woman whose skirts he was about to tug at. He feigned a genial smile for the show. "That's not your mother, dear."

He whispered as quietly as he could into the ear of the creature that only appeared to be a child, allowing the promise of his threat to seep into his tone. "I swear by the earth and sky, if you lift one dirty fingernail toward that woman again, I will burn it off."

The child didn't fight his interference. Instead, it allowed him to push it along down the platform. The awful creature probably thought that looking like a preschooler would allow it to get away with the act, but Gwyn sensed the magic and stepped in, pretending to be its father.

Needless to say, Gwyn wasn't lucky enough to find a tolerable human mage or other non-human as his first magic user.

Instead, he ran into a perverse Trenti while it was attempting to accost a woman in the Piccadilly Circus tube station. He mentally patted himself on the back for how far his skill in the language had come in the past six months. He'd made it through putting on a show and a full threat without a hitch.

The glamor the Fae from northern Spain was using was weak but effective. Without the glamor, the creature would be quite small, with elfin features in a dark wrinkly face and green eyes. Their kind had the bad habit of pinching women's legs or pulling on their skirts. Gwyn wasn't certain if it was a perverse inclination or an instinctual naughty behavior, but he wasn't keen to find out either way.

Gwyn guided it off the platform and up the escalator to the street above, where there was enough traffic on the walkway to muffle their conversation. It was just turning to autumn in London. The air was cool with a gentle breeze but thick with humidity from the recent rain.

"Trenti, I have no desire to put up with your half-truths, so tell me one thing, and we can forget about this loathsome episode." Although he would prefer to be indoors with a warm drink at a gaming table, he couldn't pass up this long-awaited opportunity to speak with another magic user.

The Trenti turned its glamored pug-nosed face upward to look at him squarely. Petulant, it replied in a whistly voice, "That depends. Your silence to the Assembly will buy my frank answer."

Assembly? He was dying to know what the Assembly was, but he'd made a deal with a Fae. He'd been foolish in his choice of words. Because he'd specifically said "one thing" he bound himself to one and only one answer for the exchange.

"I am a foreigner. Tell me exactly where I can meet a gathering of mages."

His hard work was finally paying off. Once he met a few mages, he'd be able to find out what this Assembly was without having to make another deal with an odious creature.

Through the glamor, the Trenti sent him the type of beatific smile that only children are capable of. It grabbed his hand as a child would hold their father's and started leading him through the streets. He sent the creature a malicious smile in return that was dressed up to look like a grin of acquiescence.

What the little Trenti didn't know was that Gwyn ap Nudd would kill it if he didn't approve of where they were headed.

Nearly a month had passed since the Trenti saved itself from a premature death by leading Gwyn to a pub reserved for those with magical abilities. Being in the company of so many magic users felt comfortably familiar to Gwyn. But he couldn't deny the striking disparities he noticed when looking back on his former life.

During his time, mages were venerated. Their power, actual and political, set them apart from the public. It supplied them with lives of relative luxury. But here, now, the average person enjoyed the luxuries afforded to them by technology. Yet, mages were not granted the respect that their power should confer to them. The mundane population didn't even know they existed. Mages lived equal to peasants.

There was nothing luxurious about this secretive public house in London. The floor was dirty, the chairs uncomfortable and aged, and the ale, though plentiful in varieties, lacked character. It was neither bready nor pleasantly smoky like he was used to.

He watched as mages streamed into the pub, the autumn rain dripping from their coats. Gwyn judged that the scattering of people he'd chatted with during his time at the pub were wholly unimpressive. Was it now common for the average mage to have skills equal to that of a mere child from his time?

Perhaps it was unfair to judge the soft, well-fed mages of peace that surrounded him against the hardened soldiers of magic from the past. It was a shock to his very core when he learned that when he had vanished, all the vicious magical creatures of the world had vanished with him. These modern mages called it "the Extinction." He could see the truth of it at the beginning of his own journey in the modern world. Not once during his time sleeping outdoors had he been pounced on or attacked by a predatory beast. So soon after his reemergence, he'd been too disoriented to notice their lack.

The timing of the extinction event made him wonder if he'd been mistakenly counted as one of the malevolent creatures. The accounts of those he had spoken to varied, but one thing was clear: All malevolents had mysteriously vanished, leaving behind no evidence of their existence.

While they shared a similar experience, the malevolents had not returned like he had. There was a time when he would thank the earth mother for his return, but now he realized that she had done nothing while he lingered between insanity and death for more than a thousand years. The goddess would hear no further words of gratitude from his lips.

While he felt like he was a man apart from these modern people, he found that being alone, being lonely, was too close to the madness of his imprisonment. To that end, he decided to order yet another drink. Perhaps he would also have the delightful fried root vegetables with a spicy sauce that he sampled during his last visit. But that would have to wait until he completed the very necessary step of relieving himself.

Gwyn had become an aimless man, reduced to seeking the comforts of his human body. The search for his father had turned up nothing. He pored through hundreds of texts on the time before his imprisonment, but none had a single word about the fate of Nudd. That he was far more famous than his father did brought a small smile to his face, but that was poor recompense for his lost memories, power, and life.

Lacking purpose and direction, Gwyn reached for another beer. It would either serve as a bitter reminder of his own failures and shortcomings or drown those thoughts out just a little more than the last one had—he hardly cared which.

His nights were still haunted by the grim, spiraling thoughts of his betrayal. He could tell that they had poisoned his spirit, but he felt helpless against their onslaught. Perhaps it was a side effect of the imprisonment magic. Perhaps he was far more vindictive than he'd believed himself to be. Or perhaps he was a lonely man with nothing else to occupy his time other than survival and dark thoughts.

Gwyn stared at the wall, teetering slightly to the right and then to the left as he scanned the photos. He hadn't noticed the panorama of pictures between the toilet rooms before. It was a collage of mages with accompanying accolades below their pictures. "Best in Show—Illusions—Creature Category" stuck out to him as being overly specific. Did these weak mages dole out commendations for every inane feat?

But his heart began to beat a battle song when his eyes settled on the image of a man near in age to himself. He bore an uncanny resemblance to the man who was Gwyn's namesake: his father.

"Miles Goodwin." The unfamiliar name tasted like bile in his mouth.

Sobriety washed over Gwyn as he made his way back to the bar on steadier footing. If his picture hung in this establishment, someone would know where to find Nudd. He forced himself to steady the battle song pounding in his chest. If he let his rage take hold now, it would burn through both his composure and the roof over his head—and ruin any chance of finding answers. Death had once been as familiar to him as life. But his death now, while he was reduced to a state of humanity, would be his last.

"Excuse me, sir," he said politely. "I have a question about the wall of pictures."

The bartender, a stout, balding man with a genial countenance, ambled over to Gwyn. "Aye, what'll it be then?"

The man's accent was subtly different from most of those Gwyn had encountered in the city. The bartender's amiability helped to cool some of the fire burning within him. He knew that harming this servant would not help in his quest to find the man responsible for all that had befallen him. Gwyn determined not to muddy his path to revenge or redemption, whichever fate had granted him, with petty acts of anger.

"I saw a picture of a man on the wall who I have not seen since my school days. A 'Miles Goodwin.' It would be a pleasure to...see him again. Where might I find him?"

"Ole Miles! That chap scooted off to America months ago. Hold on, let me check with Nigel in the back. I think he knows exactly where he might be now. Miles helped heal him up after he fell through the bloody floor! These old buildings.... Anyway, I think they still email back an' forth occasionally. Be back in a jiffy."

The bartender, whose name Gwyn never learned, shuffled through a door behind the bartop. He'd said that this Miles had healed his coworker. Was his healing mundane or magical? Was healing magic as rare in these times as it was in his? If so, this Miles might be the man he was looking for. There was much to consider, but he finally had a lead. He sipped on his refreshed ale as he waited for the bartender to return.

The beverage was half consumed when the bartender ambled back to Gwyn. "Sorry 'bout that. Nigel had to charge up his phone to open his email. But he's only got his old work email address, so we can't help ya with a new one. Seems Miles is in Seattle, of all places! You'd think he'd move somewhere sunny with his fancy doctorin' job, but no, he moved to another place with too much rain."

Gwyn had found more pieces of the cruel puzzle that his life had become. No longer aimless, the pieces clicked together in his mind.

The Dullahan

As the Dullahan ventured deeper into the rugged terrain, the landscape gradually shifted. Orchards gave way to rolling hills covered in timber stands, which gave way to towering trees and jagged rocks. The place was greener, more lush with life than where he had awoken.

The concentration of humans increased with the lushness of the land. He no longer felt the need to harvest—he required a leader for that. So he avoided their notice, slipping through the mists of magic when no other choice presented itself.

Compelled by his confusion and the overwhelming feeling of isolation, the Dullahan pressed forward following the setting sun. In times past, he disdained the mortals for their compulsion to maintain their pitiful existence through food and drink. Except he discovered that both he and his horse could now fatigue.

The traveling was difficult on their bodies. Nothing was as it had been. They now required sustenance and rest. They even breathed like men. While he rode or while he walked alongside his horse, each of these novel things became a battle to be won.

Cresting a blustery mountain pass, he sensed another—a brother, a fellow rider, in the distance. Did his brother also sense him? He spurred his steed onward, energy renewed. The clop of hoofbeats quickened in time with his lately beating heart.

Together with his brother, he had a chance to reclaim some of his old power. Together, they could resume their purpose: the harvest of life.

Chapter Twenty-Three

Negotiations with the Dead

Jacob

An outside observer would see an aging man reading a book, enjoying his retirement on a pleasant day. However, if your eyes could pierce the veil of magic, you'd see that the aging man was holding an ancient tome of spell fragments he hoped to work on restoring to something like their former glory, not the newest self-help bestseller.

Jacob sat bundled under an electric blanket in a comfortable Adirondack chair in his rear garden. Magic could solve many problems, but technology had done a splendid job of solving cold legs. It was a rare cloudless day in autumn, which meant that the temperature was far below normal. Not being one to pass up a day of pleasant weather, he resolved to endure the cold in exchange for some sunlight on his face.

Suddenly, and without warning, his pleasant day out of doors came to an abrupt end. A bone-chilling wind whipped the blanket nearly off his lap and flipped the pages of the decaying tome to a frenzy. It was an effort of body and spirit, but Jacob quickly came to standing. With a heavy sigh, he set the tome down on the nearby table and awaited the inevitable confrontation. He couldn't be certain what would appear, but he knew it would be unpleasant.

His power attracted them.

He winced as the chrysanthemums surrounding the porch, planted just last week by his gardener, froze solid. The temperature remained far colder than it had been, even after the frigid chill caused by the nether prison breaking abruptly ceased. With a subtle wave of his hand, the air surrounding him became charged with pure magic, forming a shield. It was no use preparing any offensive spells until he knew what he was dealing with.

In one blink of an eye, a Dullahan astride a black stallion with glowing eyes appeared before him. From shoulder to toe, the rider donned heavy armor in black and silver. With his head tucked under his left arm, the dead knight wielded a whip crafted from the spine of a fallen man in his right hand. For Jacob, the creature's arrival at midday was fortuitous.

"You chose an interesting time to visit," Jacob remarked, looking up at the sun overhead. The strong light of day weakened them. Its sudden arrival back into the world of the living should also confuse it. Or so he hoped.

Normally he'd have a "whopper" of a spell working, as Esme liked to call them but, the sunlight had lifted his spirits and inclined him to humor before getting down to business.

A rasping sound, like the scraping of a dull ax on a sharpening stone, came from the head that was still held under the Dullahan's left arm. "Elder one, I came...not seeking thou."

The Archmage in all but name, the powerhouse that was confined to the failing body of an old man, hesitated. The Dullahan had spoken to him. Legend universally held that their kind spoke nothing more than the name of their victim. As the foul smell of the head finally hit his nostrils, he nearly gagged.

The head opened its mouth again, moving the neck up and down grotesquely on the arm, saying, "Spared. If..." the head was struggling to continue speaking, "find my brothers." It paused, confused by its current situation.

Jacob patiently waited to see what would happen next. He'd already learned one thing from his forbearance; Dullahan rode together. The histories had always described a single rider.

After the extended pause, the creature seemed to conclude, "Or the leader of the Hunt... the attendant to the threshold."

Its broken way of speaking initially prevented him from connecting the offer of being spared to his ability to locate some supposed leader or attendant. The title the creature had given this attendant sounded eerily similar to descriptions of a psychopomp, whose role was to escort newly deceased souls from Earth to the afterlife, or to the leader of the Wild Hunt. Throughout legend, many names were attributed to the leadership position, so he couldn't be certain who the undead knight meant—if it was even sane. The very notion that this monster implied a mythological god might walk among ordinary people was too absurd to entertain.

Carrying on with the farce, Jacob said, "You'll find neither within a week's ride from this place." It would be most expeditious to end the discussion immediately with a violent application of magic, but the unique opportunity to glean insight from a confused malevolent stilled his hand once again.

He said, "Noble Dullahan, you seek leadership. Lacking a brother and with the whereabouts of the attendant unknown, who will you seek next? Perhaps I can guide you to another instead."

The body stowed the ghastly whip in the saddle and shifted the head between its hands. He took these as signs that it was becoming less vigilant with him.

It said, more lucidly this time, "One like myself, a brother to the infernal...or one of great power."

For a moment, the words forced Jacob's mind to wander to the image of a smiling young woman standing next to a young man blessed through some mystery of magic. While he still lived, he would not regret the small moves that he had made in nudging them toward each other. Each deserved a long story, even if it held the possibility of cutting his already long one shorter.

Jacob's hand rose again, waving a last farewell to the Dullahan as he burned it back out of existence. In its surprise, the undead knight had no chance of responding to his swift and decisive gesture.

As the magic faded, warmth slowly returned to the garden. As Jacob regained his seat, the tome returned to his hands, levitating through the air to spare his body the effort of moving. He resumed his work on restoring the spells as the magical energies dissipated into the once again tranquil air.

Still, he couldn't quite shake the lingering sense of foreboding the encounter had left him with. What it had said was something to consider for the future. Esmeralda and her beau would eventually have to be told of their vulnerability, but today was not that day. He had just ensured it.

The only tangible remnants of the encounter were frost-burned flowers, a bit of soot, and the mage's aggrieved sigh.

To be the first to see a Dullahan meant that your death was approaching. One didn't reach the ripe old age of one hundred and six without feeling its pull. Jacob sighed again. This time contentedly, back again under his heated blanket.

He was keenly aware that his end, his death, could be right around the corner. While it wouldn't be tomorrow or even next month if he could help it, he'd ensure that his days ahead would count, just as he did on this one.

Chapter Twenty-Four

Discipline in Motion

Esme
A few months later

Esme looked at her reflection in the mirrors lining the gym's walls. She gritted her teeth and flexed like a goofy bodybuilder on stage, just because she could, and no one was watching. Her eyes traced the new contours of her body, now surprisingly well-muscled. The progress that she had made in training was unexpected, considering that barely four months had passed since she had made it a focus.

She'd gone from struggling to lift forty pounds over her head to lifting a hundred, with only a bit of effort. Her mile time had dropped from twelve minutes down to only seven. Miles said he'd never seen anything like it, but she figured he was just trying to make her feel better.

At least her progress in the gym was something to celebrate. While her biceps were bulging, her bank account was dwindling. Her parents' life insurance policies had paid off the house, but she still had to pay property taxes, insurance, and the list went on. Her basic monthly stipend for being on the payroll from the Assembly wasn't quite cutting it either. If Jacob didn't start sending her out on jobs that came with bonus checks again soon, she was going to have to beg for shifts at the bar.

The weather had become chilly and gloomy again following the picture-perfect, albeit short, summer that Seattle typically enjoyed. Esme watched the rain lazily drip outside the gym's windows as she waited for Miles to arrive at their planned sparring session.

She had a hunch that he regularly paid the owner of the small mixed martial arts gym under the table so they could train there outside of normal hours. That or, equally possible, he charmed his way in for the two of them. Either way, she was grateful. Working with Miles had made all the difference in progressing her physical combat training.

The moment she made the decision to be open to deepening their relationship, she became acutely aware of the vulnerability she felt whenever she was around him. It was how he looked at her, like he could peer into the deepest depths of her being. That feeling had become progressively worse as time went on and they spent more time together training and chatting.

Having someone to be real with, who knew what she did for the Assembly, had felt like peeling away a mask that had become painfully fused to her face. She felt like a tightrope walker, teetering between the conflicting emotions of wanting to keep him at arm's distance, because anything more could be terrifying in its intensity, and wanting to pull him in to get to know him better.

As soon as she had the thought, he materialized before her through the gym's window, his hair concealed by a gray hoodie and a gym bag nonchalantly draped across his shoulder.

"Sorry we're late," he said, stepping inside and slipping off his shoes to avoid dirtying the mats.

Quick on his heels patted in Lily. She waited patiently while Miles cleaned off her paws. Knowing that the dog would promptly prepare herself for a nap in the entryway, Esme bounded over for some puppy kisses. The owner of the gym had a veritable zoo at home, so one dog visiting was of no concern to them.

Glancing up from where she was crouched with Lily, she saw Miles shove back his hood, revealing dark rings of fatigue around his eyes. She playfully scruffed the dog's fur around her ears, saying in a baby voice, "Daddy looks like he's ready to get his butt kicked today, doesn't he?"

Miles scoffed good-naturedly and replied, "That is becoming all too much of a possibility for my pride to handle some days. Today might be that day."

Standing, Esme said, "Doubtful. Also, you're always here before me, so I should thank you for making me look good for once."

She watched him wrap his hands to prepare for donning gloves, studying him to gauge where his mood and energy level were at. He was as methodical as always, and he seemed to have an air of determination about him. Maybe she was seeing things that didn't exist.

Esme practically bounced to the mat in her zeal, readying herself for the fight. They circled each other, starting with their usual warm-up of light sparring. Each movement was a carefully controlled exchange of blows. It was as much a mental game of predictions as it was a warm-up for their bodies.

She read in the subtle shifting of his muscles his intention to jab and he read her intention to rear hook. Back and forth, their movements intensified until, with a smirk in his voice, he laid his accent on thick and asked, "Feeling feisty today?"

She clapped her gloves together and, with a falsely calm voice, careful not to reveal her excitement, said, "Bring it."

She often wished that she'd started training years earlier. She wished she knew how fulfilling training her body could feel. Blocking his first blow, she felt herself inch backward from the impact, even though she'd been braced for it. His look of fatigue was deceiving, because that hit proved Miles was there to work.

So she matched him. Hard and fast, she surprised him with a roundhouse kick to the left side of his ribcage. But he was quick on his feet and took advantage of the opening that her raised leg afforded and struck her exposed inner calf with the hard bone of his shin. Miles attempted a cheeky cross while he was within striking distance, but was barred by Esme's left-handed block.

Rebuffed, he attempted to take advantage of her closeness by going in for the clinch. This was basically an aggressive hug. He used this grappling technique to limit her ability to throw another painful strike his way. His quasi-embrace allowed him to control her movements by trapping her in the circle of his arms. Holding her head and neck close, Miles tried for a classic knee strike against her.

That was a mistake.

As soon as his right leg lifted off the ground to strike her side, she hooked her right calf around his supporting leg and pulled. Destabilized, Esme dumped him onto the mat, back first. Not wasting a second, she passed his legs expertly, moving to pin his shoulder blades onto the mat with her weight and counterforce. Here she circled his upper body with one arm wrapped around his neck and the other grasping tightly over the opposite arm, pressing down to avoid getting mock-punched.

Despite his efforts, he found himself on his back with Esme now in a dominant position. Miles, never one to back down, pushed up with his hips, lifting her off the ground with him and simultaneously using his forearm to push her neck away. Esme resisted, leveraging her strength and technique, but it still wasn't quite enough. With a sudden burst of energy, Miles managed to shift their positions, transitioning smoothly into a grappling mount, him above with his legs straddling her hips and his feet hooked behind her raised calves.

She didn't know why she consistently felt surprised at just how strong he was. Uncertain if they were done, Miles remained with his chest down and head tucked into the space between her ear and her shoulder. It was the safest place for him to avoid any mock punches she might aim at his head. With him nestled so sweetly into her neck, she completely forgot to tap out of the fight.

Breaths coming heavily, they remained there, body to body, with no space between them, for ten more indulgent moments. Coming out of the daze, she murmured near his ear, "I guess today wasn't the day for hurt pride." She gave the universal double tap with her hand to end the match. Quickly—perhaps a bit too quickly—Miles practically jumped out of the mount and began to clean up their equipment.

For the next few minutes, all that could be heard was Lily's soft panting and the swishing sound of cloth on leather as they diligently cleaned their gear in preparation to leave. Esme felt as though they were in the awkward space between amicable silence and "Was that intense for you too" with neither being willing to ask aloud.

As they packed their bags, Miles said, "Last night, I received word about a 'red-eyed demon dog' in the mountains north of Skykomish. It might be nothing or it could be some sort of hellhound—there are multiple varieties. Since it's black, I'm guessing that it's a gwyllgi." He pronounced it like "Gwith-gi."

"A gwyllgi?" Esme's mouth failed to do the unfamiliar word justice. She was relieved to be talking about something tangible that she could put a name to, even if it was a monster. Because what she'd felt in those ten indulgent moments with him was as intangible as the space between them now.

He explained. "Your run-of-the-mill hellhound. Finn and I are planning on investigating tomorrow afternoon. Luckily, it is far enough away from human settlements that it shouldn't prove to be an issue yet."

Her mouth went dry, partially from the dehydration of heavy training but also from burgeoning unease. While she was quite new to the club of people who knew about the malevolent problem, it seemed like there was a lot of them popping up in the area in such a short time. They had to figure out some way of tracking them or predicting where they'd emerge soon.

She asked, "Another malevolent. Already?"

He replied, "I hope not, but either way, we could use your help."

"My help?" She wasn't certain if she should be ecstatic or terrified. She hadn't been a whole lot of help the last time they'd dealt with a malevolent. A suspicion wiggled its way into her thoughts. "Did Jacob put you up to this?"

"Jacob? No, I doubt he even got word of this. We don't know a lot about most varieties of hellhounds because there are so many of them. This one might be immune to fire and, well, you know that's our best weapon with Finn around. You could be the key to our success," he looked chagrined as he continued, "or our survival. You've lived here the longest, and having a local's help that far away from civilization could be useful."

He straightened to his full height and gave her the look that made her feel like he could see down to the snippets of her DNA. He asked, "So, what do you think? Care to join us?"

Another mission would ease the strain on her bank account. And truth be told, she felt bottled up and needed release in more ways than one after that sparring session.

"A hunt? Oh, I'm in." She allowed herself a small bounce of anticipatory joy on the balls of her feet. Miles didn't seem to be put off by her enthusiasm in the slightest because he smiled too.

Chapter Twenty-Five

The Hunt

Esme

"First question. A ton of the stories about malevolents aren't that old—two to three hundred years at most. I used to believe that the stories were mere fairy tales, fictional narratives devised to teach children important life lessons. Now that I know the malevolents are here... Is that true?"

As Esme drove toward the hellhound's last known location, Miles kept his eyes fixed on the towering trees that bordered the forest service road. The weather had blessed them with cool cloudy skies and no snow. Only the occasional misty drizzle troubled them as they traversed the wilderness area. His eyes didn't stray from the treeline as he answered, "The oldest records of the Brotherhood note seemingly random returns for centuries."

"Next question. Why are malevolents from other places around the world showing up in the middle of nowhere in the wrong places? Shouldn't they show up where they were when they disappeared?"

Eyes still diverted, he said, "Short answer: We have no idea. Longer answer: The best guess is that they're spun out of wherever they've been for all these years. Sort of like how soda spews out of a spinning bottle on the ground. We assume that wherever they come from rotates just like earth. A brother in Poland recently took out a wendigo and one in Brazil took out a Japanese oni, so it's not just European malevolents popping back into the world."

She replied, "Oh good. Glad to know that it's not just the Caucasian monsters causing problems like normal."

Finn snorted from the back seat. At least he enjoyed her dark humor. It was no longer a surprise to her that the leprechaun kept up with the news cycle and even played games on his phone, which he'd been doing for most of the drive there.

A glance at Miles nodding in her peripheral vision proved that he was listening, but he seemed to be hyper-focused on something outside of the window.

"Did you feel that?" he asked. Lily's huge head raised from her spot in the rear hatch of Esme's car.

"Aye," came from the backseat.

She hadn't felt anything, but driving had also distracted her. "I'll pull over."

The sun hung low in the sky as the days were becoming shorter. Its weak rays cast an eerie glow on the misty forest surroundings.

They'd all kept their jackets on for the trip and had their packs nearby, so getting out of the car should have been an uncomplicated affair. A gasp escaped from Esme as she watched Miles reach under his coat. In the dim glow of the dashboard lights, Miles' hand emerged, holding a no-frills, all-business, matte-black handgun.

"What is that?" she asked, unable to hide all the shock in her voice.

Miles, who had always displayed a calm and reassuring demeanor, locked eyes with her. "A Glock 19."

During their sparring sessions, she had learned about his time in the military, so she understood conceptually that Miles could use a handgun, but she honestly did not consider that he might bring one on a monster hunt. In hindsight, that was probably naïve of her.

Her unease must have shown, because Miles' expression softened. He continued, "I need to protect myself."

She could almost hear the unspoken, "and both of you." His protective instincts were always just beneath the surface. From the time they'd spent together, she'd learned that nothing motivated him as much as caring for and protecting—well, everyone.

"I carry daggers too." He opened his pack to show her one savage-looking piece of metal that he then strapped to his calf. She'd known that he used daggers from the afanc fight, but seeing them up close was a different story.

"I've been doing this for a long time. I don't have Finn's firepower or the ability to summon heavyweight fighters like you do. We've found that since the malevolents don't know what a gun is, we're often able to make clean kills."

Suddenly very interested in the answer, she asked, "You don't rely on your magic much, do you?"

"No," he answered simply.

Finally, he said at last, "This is a precaution."

She made it easy for him. "Okay," she said, meaning it. "I trust you." Miles gave her another approving nod and loaded his weapon.

Still in the backseat, she saw Finn face forward and raise one suspicious eyebrow. He put away his phone, shaking his head a little, and asked, "So, what's the plan, boss?"

From her experience, it was rare for long-lived beings to take most humans seriously unless they were very old or very powerful. The fact that Finn was happy to allow Miles to run the show spoke volumes about the respect between the two. Finn might be old enough to be her great-grandfather twenty times over, but he still maintained his easygoing ways.

"I'll take point. Finn, you take the rear with Esme in between. Lily will be roaming. Esme, if you see, hear, or feel anything, don't think twice before speaking up. We chase false leads all the time, so don't be shy."

He directed that last bit of reassurance at her. She'd opened up about a month ago and told him about her hesitation during the afanc fight. He'd done his best to convince her it was completely normal for someone new to hunting, but some of the shame she felt still lingered.

She popped the back hatch for Lily and they filed out of the car. They walked around the area for at least twenty minutes before anyone spoke. Finally she asked, "I'm not feeling anything or, for that matter, seeing anything either. How about you?"

Not that she had felt anything before, but it was about time someone halted the unfruitful search. The sun was straining by then to keep the forest alight enough for walking without flashlights. Even the ever-vigilant Miles had holstered his gun. Lily was snuffling a clump of leaves about a hundred feet away.

Finn replied, "True enough. Nothin'."

"Fortune's expensive smile is earned," Miles quoted as he leaned over and lifted a clump of black fur from a branch nearby.

Fanning his arms out like a showman, Finn announced, "We have a Shakespeare in our midst, lassie!"

Resigned to being the brunt of the joke, Miles mumbled a quiet, "Emily Dickinson."

They studied the black fur, debating whether it could be the leavings of a black bear instead of their quarry. Esme couldn't tell bear from hellhound fur, so she plopped down on a nearby fallen tree. Then, everything changed.

She spotted glowing red eyes obscured slightly by a bush maybe thirty feet from Lily in the distance. Unfriendly eyes were locked on the dog. From what she learned about these gwyllgi on the drive over, she knew they were fast, agile creatures.

Her decision had to be faster. Her trolls wouldn't do it. They were heroes in a brawl, but they were plodding, heavy creatures, lacking nimble maneuverability. Less than a moment passed as she deliberated. Her latest project would have to make a hasty battle debut.

A tinge of sulfur, the smallest trace of something not of this world, wafted in the air as a creature of shadows tore its way into their reality, as silent as the grave. A feline body of solid shadow with eyes of liquid mercury crouched, awaiting its master.

Not a sound was made, but Miles spun, unholstering his gun. Finn stood ready, hands ablaze as both felt Esme's magic blossom. A blaze of malice burst through the leaves, headed straight at Lily, who had by then crouched with teeth bared, ready to meet her attacker.

From their left, Esme's shadowcat burst into action, leaping across an incredible distance to tackle the hellhound mid-lunge. A flurry of teeth and claws hit the forest floor with a resounding thud.

Caught in the tableau, Lily was hit and knocked off her paws during the initial skirmish. The hellhound and the shadowcat scrambled to their feet and began circling each other. Lily, an intelligent dog, inched slowly back toward her master, not taking her eyes off the two circling creatures.

Miles' finger was poised to shoot. Esme began to whisper, "Do it!" when they spotted a figure with dark hair, dressed in all black, approaching from the direction that the gwyllgi had come from. Was it another Corded Brother?

He wouldn't risk shooting another person. The three of them were there for the malevolent, not a man. Seeing the shadowcat and hellhound locked in a circling stalemate, Miles moved his finger aside but did not lower his aim. Just like Esme, he obviously still thought caution was called for.

As the mysterious man approached, Esme studied his face. From this distance, she could see short, unruly, raven-black hair that contrasted sharply with his pale skin and glacier-blue eyes. Her guess was that they were similar in age. He was tall with a lean build. No beard or mustache concealed his angular jawline or hid his scowling lips. He was handsome in a way that felt strangely familiar.

But those eyes were distracting. Claws of dread tore up her spine as she registered the cold, dangerous, utterly unwavering interest that the mysterious man held for Miles. Was it the gun? She felt a consolidation of magic coming from the man as he raised his right hand.

Her heart pounded, her mind racing with possible responses. But he stopped, mid-movement, just as quickly as he'd begun, sniffing the air. She felt the magic he'd been casting fizzle out as he tilted his head in her direction ever so slightly. A flicker of interest, of something less menacing, flashed through his gaze as he coldly assessed her. A subtle, almost imperceptible lift at the corners of his mouth erased the blanketing menace from his expression.

She cast a wary glance back at him, sensing trouble brewing. Was he smiling at her while looking at Miles like he wanted to slit his throat? As his eyes settled back on Miles, his look of interest was replaced with penetrating calculation.

By this point, Lily was at Finn's side. In slow motion, Esme watched the man's right hand begin to raise again. Miles' finger drifted slowly toward pulling the trigger. It was like watching a standoff in the wild west. Who would shoot first? The trouble was that the power that she felt from the stranger was on par with, if not greater than, what she felt from Jacob when he was casting a real whopper. Given that, would it even matter if Miles got off the first shot?

Then, between one breath and the next, Esme found herself, Miles, Lily, and a collapsed Finn two steps from her car.

She turned to the leprechaun as Miles holstered his gun. Finn grunted a labored "Drive!" as he passed out cold on the ground. Miles was already opening the back door for Lily to jump in.

"Go!" Miles ordered as he unceremoniously shoved Finn's comatose body into the back seat. Esme bolted to the driver's seat and, with a glance to ensure all bodies were in the car, bore down on the accelerator.

After several minutes of tense glances in the rearview mirror, Miles leaned between the front seats to buckle the still-unconscious Finn into a seatbelt. Lily snuffled mournfully at Finn's hair as his body slumped beside her in the seat. Miles was so distracted by ensuring Finn's safety that he didn't see Lily's injury at first. But Esme had.

She forced a sedate tone to her voice, warning, "Miles, Lily's face."

The flesh on Lily's snout was gruesomely torn open from one side to the other, extending all the way to her cheek. Dogs had a survival instinct to hide or mask weakness and pain and Lily hadn't let on that she was suffering throughout the entire ordeal. They likely didn't notice it initially because there somehow wasn't much blood. The injury would be agonizingly painful for a human—Lily was just much better at disguising it.

Esme kept driving. She wanted to put as much distance between them and whatever the hell that was back there. Miles remained turned around in his seat when Esme noticed the illumination coming from behind her in the rearview mirror. The glow was a soft golden hue, like someone had lit a half dozen candles in the backseat. He didn't speak, but turned back around in his seat and grabbed his hiking pack from where it had been sitting on the floor of the car.

She glanced over briefly to see that his hands were smeared with blood. He was scrubbing at them with cleansing wipes, and his expression was completely devoid of emotion. She tilted the rearview mirror down to check on Lily and Finn.

The words popped out of her mouth without volition. "Holy shit." Lily's flesh had bonded back together. Where blood-red flaps of hanging skin had been, only pink lines and fur still matted with blood remained. Lily opened one eye to peer back at Esme in the mirror and closed it for sleep.

If her eyes weren't deceiving her, Miles had healed Lily. That shouldn't be possible. Magic didn't work that way—did it?

The logical part of her brain reasoned that what she saw was something akin to energy transference. She generated her summoned creatures by tapping into the energy of magic. But the unscientific, reactionary part of her mind saw a miracle. She adjusted the rearview mirror back into place and tried to focus on nothing but driving.

The stress of the tense situation they had encountered, coupled with the miracle that she had just witnessed, made the effort fruitless. So, Esme was the first to speak about the other topic that was probably on both their minds. "What the hell, who the hell, was that back there?"

"I don't know. We need to report this to the Bastion."

Esme startled awake from her position in the passenger seat of her car. How could she have fallen asleep?

After they made a pit stop, Miles insisted that he drive the rest of the way back to give her a break. Her initial response was outright denial, but as she reached to open the car door handle, she reluctantly admitted to herself that a break was a good idea. The night before had been restless for her, filled with a mix of anxiety and anticipation for the upcoming hunt.

Taking off his coat as he walked over to the driver's side of her car, Miles said, "I can see it in your eyes," and offered his coat to her as a blanket.

He had no idea how close to the truth his statement felt most days. His ploy to get her to relax had worked as she had woken up two hours later with her face buried in the hood of his coat.

Finn! She startled again, feeling a pang of concern as she realized she had no idea how he was doing.

Noticing her frantic movement to turn around in her seat, Miles said reassuringly, "I've checked his pulse at least three times and his breathing has remained steady. He's fine, I think. I believe that he's just tapped out."

Finn had used too much magic transporting them all to the car, to safety.

Looking out the window, she realized they were already in Seattle. Studying Miles' side profile in the streetlights' illumination, she said, "Thank you."

A slight nod and a tightening of his expression were all that she received at first. He glanced briefly at her face, then returned his eyes to the road. He said, "I'm sorry."

"For?" She let the rest of the question hang in the air.

"I should not have put you in that position. I'm used to working alone, but I let myself get sidetracked. I put you, and Lily, and Finn, at risk. I'm sorry." His Adam's apple bobbed up and down with his swallowed regret.

Thinking that she knew the direction his thoughts were headed, she was determined to head them off. "I volunteered enthusiastically to be here. Finn volunteered probably even more enthusiastically, knowing him."

She was gearing up to defend her magical prowess and continued presence on monster hunts when he surprised her, saying, "I am so glad that you did."

The adrenaline that had bubbled up within her as she prepared for the expected argument fizzled out. Unexpected, but very welcome, warmth replaced it.

Lily leaned forward to lick Miles' ear from the backseat. "And, sincerely, you have my undying gratitude for what you did for Lily. Thank you."

It was past time she learned to not mentally stereotype him. His actions confirmed that he wasn't plagued by toxic masculinity, despite his protective nature. He'd been gracious in her moments of defeat with the afanc and the doppelgänger. Now he was sincerely appreciative in her moment of triumph.

She looked out the window again, feeling a lot better about her relationship with Miles, and saw another very familiar house. They were almost to Jacob's. She facetiously warned him, "Buckle up, Chuck: This is going to be an interesting evening."

Chapter Twenty-Six

Gathering Allies

Gwyn

Gwyn had felt a familiar tugging at the back of his mind shortly after landing in Seattle. At first, he wrote it off as some mysterious result of flight on the human body. But the feeling remained through the night and into the next day.

By midday, the tug became unmistakable. He was being called by a member of the Wild Hunt. Could his retained connection be a sign that all he thought to be lost was not truly gone? The sensation felt like a tease, tormenting him over his lost power. If this piece of his ascended self remained, was it possible that his lost memories were simply hiding somewhere deep within his mind?

There was only one thing to do. He must find what, or who, he was connected to. Brief visions of the Cwn Annwn, the hounds of Annwn, that accompanied him on the Hunt were his most solid recollection. But he couldn't be certain that he was the only man, spirit, ascended one, who rode with them to guide the souls of the dead to the place beyond life.

Locating the being that called to him turned out to be a challenge. Unlike his time in England and Wales, the public transportation system in the United States was scarce. Thankfully, a librarian had taught him how to search the internet. He found a bus that took him in the direction that he felt the pull coming from.

He canceled his hotel room for the night and brought all of his meager worldly possessions with him in a backpack. He needed the money from the hotel to buy boots and gloves for this expedition. The limited transportation schedule meant that he'd miss the last bus back to the city on his return, anyway. He'd have to rough it in the forest. Loyalty to one's own was paramount. He thought the difficulty could very well be worth the reward.

When he'd walked down the dirt and gravel road searching for the one who called for him, he felt something achingly similar to optimism mix with his usual melancholy. The trees that lost their leaves in the autumn stood as naked reminders that loss was inevitable, but they also reminded him that regrowth was a part of life. Perhaps he would never be the same again. Or, perhaps, his journey back to his ascended status had already begun, and this was his first glimpse of it.

His efforts reunited him with Cerys. Finding her had felt like finding a piece of himself that he'd lost. Yet, even this was bittersweet. He knew the basics of his ascended life. They were plain to see in many tales. But, somehow, seeing her unlocked his memory of her and how he could use their connection. It was the slightest memory, consisting of barely more than her name and the hows of communicating with her. But he'd remembered something! Plus, his efforts yielded an unexpected lead.

He'd spent over half a year preparing for his first encounter with Nudd. When he was at his lowest point, literally at the bottom of his cups, chance had smiled upon him. He'd drunkenly stumbled upon his father's picture in a London public house. That had set him on a course to Seattle.

Then, for the second time since his reawakening, he'd felt the warm light of serendipity upon his face when he saw Nudd in the flesh—only for his chance to be snatched away by a flaming leprechaun's mist walking! Once he was feeling more charitable, he'd credit that he had at least gained confirmation that his father was in the area.

He knew that his path to answers, to revenge if need be, would be arduous. Even now, his chest tightened at the thought of confronting Nudd. But he hadn't expected such a banal creature as a leprechaun first to be allied with the arrogant tyrant who was his father, and second to have the strength to step through the mists with so many others in tow.

Gwynn's relentless pursuit had consumed his thoughts since finding that picture in the pub. And then, just when the dark part of himself found its nemesis—if that's what his father was to him, because he still didn't know—his father had looked at him strangely, as though they'd met once in passing, but nothing more. His gaze hadn't drifted, nor had he flinched at the sight of his scorned son. Had Gwyn truly changed so much during their years apart? He didn't think so. Nudd certainly looked younger, but that was easily explained by magic.

And the woman. Everything about her caused him to halt his charm of paralysis on Nudd. The power coursed from her to the shadowcat. The brimstone he smelled. Had Nudd somehow found another begotten to stand by his side? The way she faced him down, a modern shieldmaiden in hiking boots, even her face, was so like Elena that he could believe they were one and the same—if it were possible.

Elena...

Elena was his chosen sister who could always be counted on to show up. She'd been a stalwart ally and confidant amid the intrigue of his father's court. Somehow, history had forgotten her, but he would not.

He suspected—no, he knew—that Elena had meant far more to Nudd. She was the love match that the king could never have without sacrificing his precious morals. His chosen sister's memory and the innocence of the unknown woman who resembled her so closely would provide her protection. He couldn't blame her for falling victim to Nudd's pretty chivalry. So long as she did not force his hand, she'd remain safe.

A thought struck him as he patted the loyal gwyllgi at his heels. The begotten woman deserved to know whether her loyalty to Nudd was misplaced. Her ignorance was no sin. Gwyn would liberate this woman from the tyrant's hold if need be.

If he was right in his suspicion that his father had condemned him to more than a thousand years of unjust imprisonment, or even if he'd just ignored his son's incarceration at another's hand, either way the woman would come to understand what kind of man Nudd was. She would abandon him for it.

If it came to it, the poison that he dipped his sword in before thrusting it through Nudd's heart would be the truth.

Through their shared bond, he urged Cerys to guide him toward a safe spot for rest. She led him to an area protected from the wind. He used his knife to cut evergreen branches and crafted them into a makeshift shelter. He shared the prepackaged food that he'd brought along with her and started a small fire. As he lay with his head nestled against Cerys' warm, coarse fur, the smells of the forest and the crackle of the fire filled the air. He lay awake until the small hours of the morning, crafting a plan for the months ahead.

There was no urgency pushing him to act, so he could afford to be patient. He had to uncover Nudd's purpose here and what his renewed bond with Cerys meant for his lost power and memories. So he'd stay in Seattle, leaving every once in a while to make money in nearby cities.

He'd meet the local mages and find out what they knew of Nudd—no, Miles—and the begotten woman. He could learn what his new magical limits were in the wilderness of the mountains, away from prying eyes.

Even though he was cold and lacked a blanket. Even though his stomach was still more than half empty because, starving, Cerys had eaten the bulk of their meal, he felt contentment. Fortune, serendipity, whatever her name was in this era, had led him to this place at this specific time. Gwyn would keep following her lead.

Chapter Twenty-Seven

Revelations

Esme

History was repeating itself in a familiar pattern, leaving Finn sprawled unconscious in the vicinity while Esme and Miles exchanged words. Although time had changed their positions. Esme was pacing, yet again, in Jacob's library, baffled at what had occurred in the forest earlier that day.

Jacob ordered, "Report." He poured them all chamomile tea and set down the tray of shortbread cookies. "I see Finn is magically depleted. There must be a story behind it."

Miles adjusted his position, his voice calm and direct. He got straight to the point. "I received a communique concerning a sighting of a gwyllgi in the mountains. I brought this information to Finnegan, and he accepted my offer to join the hunt as both firepower and backup for me. As I am certain that you are aware, he agreed to help the Brotherhood with local malevolents on a case-by-case basis. After some discussion, we concluded that there wasn't enough evidence to support or reject the notion that gwyllgi are immune to fire. Therefore, I judged that further offensive strength would only benefit our cause and so I invited Esme to join us."

She liked the sound of "offensive strength" attached to her name.

"We found the target. Esme," he said, looking her in the eyes, "saved all of us with one of her conjurations."

She practically preened.

He continued, "However, the target was not alone. An unknown male—human, I believe—who wore no distinctive clothing, and had no remarkable features that would aid in determining his identity, seemed to accompany the gwyllgi."

Esme piped in. "The man was about my age, tall, Caucasian, with black hair and blue eyes, and not bad to look at if you could get past the whole cold hatred thing."

She caught the hint of displeasure on his face and quickly added, "Sorry, just trying to enrich your reporting."

A small smile played on his lips as he acknowledged her statement, his voice warm and reassuring. "The details might be important, so thank you for that."

Maybe it was the "not bad to look at part" that displeased him then. The possibility of him being jealous was more than she'd hoped for. She was boisterous, sometimes loud, and often playfully dramatic. She knew that her personality could be a lot for pragmatic personalities like his. Miles was one of the most rational people she had ever known. But somehow her "too muchness" didn't seem to faze him at all.

Unaware of the poignant insight occurring in Esme's mind, Miles continued his report. "The unknown man seemed to have either power over, or a relationship with, the malevolent, as he could call the hellhound to heel. From the magic in the air, I could tell that he was preparing to cast something, twice.

Finn teleported us back to the car before we could ascertain his ultimate intentions for the magic."

She tried to hold herself back from interrupting him again but Esme couldn't take the objectivity any longer, even if it was the "balanced" way of reporting their encounter. "His *ultimate intentions*? Miles, the guy had it out for you. He completely dismissed Finn and looked at me like I was an interesting accessory."

At this, Jacob showed no reaction, not even a flicker of surprise. Then, looking at Miles and Esme in equal measure, Jacob prodded them on. "Tell me about the magic that you said this stranger was casting. Could you glean anything from the feel of it?"

Miles answered in his typical precise fashion. "The escalation of power was rapid but lacked the feel of malevolent magic."

Esme agreed and added, "It felt like he was building a whopper. What still bothers me, other than that he clearly had an intense hatred for Miles, was that we didn't hear or see him approach until he was too close for comfort. Could he have camouflaged himself or teleported in like Finn?"

Jacob replied, "Perhaps either. Creating an envelope of illusion would be simpler for him to cast. But I suspect that either of you might have been tipped off earlier, given your particular backgrounds, if that was the case. Mist stepping is not a simple task. I struggle with it myself. So if that occurred, we are, in fact, dealing with a powerful individual."

So the teleportation that Finn did was called "mist stepping." Interesting. She'd have to ask more questions about that later.

Jacob turned to Miles then, bearing down on him with the weight of his stare. "Tell me truthfully. Did you recognize this man? You came here for my...what? My aid, my opinion, or simply information? In all cases, I need the unadulterated truth."

Miles answered, his words sounding like a practiced mantra, "I make no vow, but I tell it true. I do not know, nor do I believe that I have ever met the man that we encountered in the forest today."

Jacob thoughtfully swirled one finger around the rim of his teacup. "Unfortunately, this is scant information to go by in determining the validity of this threat or in determining the identity of this man."

He did not look happy. His worried expression sent Esme to pacing again.

Studying her, Jacob urged, "Esme, darling, you look like you have a thought that should be shared."

She hesitated, then spoke, feeling a little foolish. "The way he sniffed the air and then smiled at me was creepy. I mean, I know my new and improved conjuration has an odd smell to it, but still, it's not that bad."

"Your new conjuration? The smell?" Jacob inquired innocently.

"Yeah, Finn and I have been working on adding to my catalogue of conjurations." She shrugged. "I'll admit that whenever I summon this one, it smells a bit like rotten eggs, but that dissipates quickly."

Jacob showed no reaction, so she went on sharing her thoughts. "Still, it was my smelly cat that saved our asses from the hellhound. The trolls would have been too slow and none of my smaller creatures would have stood a chance in that fight."

The gwyllgi had to have been the size of a world-record-holding Great Dane because it dwarfed Lily, who was probably around one hundred and twenty pounds.

Then she noticed it. The smallest contortion of Jacob's face. His eyebrows arched upward in concern and, she suspected, a hint of surprise. The movement etched the lines around his eyes in deeper. Thinking that this expression was in response to her initiative to try new magic, she said, "We've been practicing like you wanted. Finn suggested that I 'pour a bit of anger' into my casting, and I made a new shadowcat."

She shrugged again. If this kept up, her shoulders would be sore tomorrow morning.

Trying to ignore the feeling of unease building within her, she asked, "Pass me a cookie, Miles?"

Maybe some sugar would help. It seemed to take his brain an extra second to translate "cookie" to "biscuit" as there was a noticeable delay in his action. She accepted the treat with thanks.

A groan erupted from the chaise lounge. Finn certainly had a knack for coming to at opportune times. Food or drink seemed to be the key.

He groaned, "Tell 'er, ya old gobshite. It's time and ya know it."

Her ears perked up at this. Tell her what?

Jacob appeared to dismiss the taunt. He even rolled his eyes! That was a surprising first for Esme. Jacob never performed such a "vulgar" act—his words, not hers—in her presence.

Surely that was all? But no, he kept on talking. "Fine. Ya need convincing. You tell her or I will." The trickster paused for effect and sat up.

Jacob shot daggers with his eyes at the leprechaun.

"I understand ya want to protect her, but ya knew it was time the second ya heard the word brimstone."

Brimstone? No one had mentioned brimstone. Wait...the smell that seemed to spread when she summoned her shadowcat. She had labeled the smell as rotten eggs or sulfur, but she knew that brimstone was supposed to smell the same.

"There is no doubt, Bastion." He said the title mockingly. Esme knew Finn reveled in mischief, but this seemed to be beyond that. Jacob had frustrated him somehow. She needed to know why.

Finn rubbed at the blond stubble on his chin and studied the leader of the mages. "I can see that the deal isn't sweet enough for ya. Let's make a bargain then." He rubbed his hands together excitedly. This appeared to be closer to the attitude of the mischief maker she was used to. "I'll clue you into what ya want to know about Doctor Magic Hands—pardon me, *Hand*—over there. They both deserve to know."

It was Miles' turn to straighten in attention. The energy in the room suddenly felt more like she was on the set of an infamous family drama talk show instead of in a posh private library.

Secrets. More secrets. She buried her head in her hands in defeated frustration. It was all that she could do to hold back the anger. While it was reassuring that Jacob was attempting to protect her from...something, if she didn't know what she needed protection from, how could she stay safe? Plus, it wasn't like she was completely defenseless—just a screw-up half the time.

Could Finn be referring to the miracle, because there were no other words for it, that she had witnessed in the car? She was dead certain that Lily had a gaping wound when she first looked in that rearview mirror. She saw a glow and then when she looked back again, Lily's face was still injured but whole and Miles' hands were covered in blood.

Being upset about yet another secret wouldn't help right then. She grasped at the empathy she felt for Jacob's protectiveness and decided. "Tell me, Jacob."

Jacob straightened his spine and sedately set aside his teacup. He let out a protracted sigh. He squared his eyes on Esme and spoke in the voice that she generally associated with his speeches in the Assembly. "You, my dear, have demon blood."

Her world froze. Her mind stuttered. She couldn't keep up with his words. "You are what people commonly refer to as a cambion."

Now Esme laughed. What he said was utterly ridiculous.

"Okay, Okay, now do Miles." She was giggling like a madwoman. Had Finn infected her brain with his silliness?

Jacob, spine still stiff, raised one eyebrow and said, "I held up my end of the bargain, Fae. I put up with your preposterousness because of your usefulness." He reached for his teacup again and waved at Finn to begin speaking. "Whilst skirting Fae law is undoubtedly one of your favorite pastimes, Mr. Finnegan, this would certainly be beyond that."

Either Jacob was utterly serious or he was performing award-winning level acting to Esme's eyes.

"Aye, I shall keep to my bargain, wean."

Esme briefly recalled hearing Finn use that word before. If she was remembering correctly, Finn was calling Jacob a child! It was bizarre hearing a leprechaun who looked no older than forty say that to a man who appeared so much older than him.

Finn continued, "I swear it. But I think our dear one could use some, uh, clarification because she appears to believe that you're talkin' utter hogwash." For once, Finn didn't break out into a giggle fit but remained stoic.

Esme's stomach dropped. The possibility that Jacob was serious sat like a lead weight in her gut.

"I can assure you, leprechaun, she doesn't need handling with kid gloves. But," Jacob said, rolling his napkin into a tube, "I can see that it was a lot to take in."

He sighed heavily. Finally he said, "Darling, ohhhh, how might I say this in a way that would resonate with you?"

Suddenly, he snapped his fingers, and a spark of vibrant life entered his eyes. "Maureen!"

He remained silent long enough that Esme prompted him, "Maureen?"

Saying that one word took effort. It felt as if the oxygen level in the room had dropped dramatically and she was slowly suffocating. Jacob was still acting like everything he'd said was true.

"Yes, Maureen! I know she's given you trouble over the years. I would beg your forgiveness for not intervening, but I thought it would be best if you could put her in her place yourself."

Esme's mouth hung open. She probably looked ridiculous. He'd just admitted that he'd known how Maureen had treated her on top of saying that she had demon blood.

Jacob continued. "I know she has thrown a slur or two your way, calling you 'tainted.' Darling, she knows your pedigree. Robert and Lauren were both cambion. You are the true-bred daughter of two demon-blooded parents—as were they. If, perhaps, your blood were more diluted, you wouldn't carry around the stigma, but that's why your parents remained on the fringes of mage society. They didn't want you to grow up having to deal with the absurd bias that so many magic users have toward the demon-blooded. Well...at least from those few who know of the heritage. Your type is very, very rare these days."

Finn spoke up softly, nudging Jacob to answer more unknowns with his suggestions, "The brimstone, her athletic progress."

"Ah, yes, very good, thank you." Now the old man seemed downright cordial with the leprechaun. The swing between ice cold and room temperature between the two was bewildering.

"You can thank your blood for your positively Olympian progress in physical training. Likewise, you can thank your blood for your ability to call forth infernals and your ability to maintain multiple conjurations simultaneously."

He read the puzzled expression on her face and clarified, "Esmeralda, your shadowcat smelled that way because it was infernal—the place from whence it comes is tainted by brimstone. You, uniquely, can call it forth because you have a connection to the infernal through your blood."

She stuttered, "D-demon?" The single word contained a multitude of questions. Had malevolent magic always tainted her magic? Maybe she wasn't even thinking of it in the right way. Maybe her magic was something different from malevolent magic altogether. How many people had known what she was and had never said anything to her face?

"Yer not going to sprout horns or anything, lassie." Finn's wry amusement at her bafflement served as an unexpected anchor in the storm of confusion. "If anything, it makes me like you more because we have something in common." He winked and lit one fingertip with ifrit fire.

The flickering heat of the flame snapped her out of her momentary detachment. She had had so much information thrown at her. While it was probably normal and even necessary to gape in astonishment for a short time, that wasn't how she normally behaved.

She looked back down at her feet as Finn finished talking and timed a slow breath in and out. Her parents had taught her to control her emotions through steady breathing from a very young age. Now she wondered if there was more behind those lessons...

After her parents died, Maureen basically ignored her. It wasn't until after Esme started working at the bar that she seemed to take notice. But that still begged the question, why had no one just come out and said what she was?

When she asked, Jacob's response wasn't all that surprising. "I simply made my opinion on that type of bigotry clear in the closed meetings. So, they have defaulted to...what do you call them? Microaggressions since. I actually spoke on the topic of bigotry during one of our quarterly meetings as well." A genuine laugh broke through his words. "But you never go to those."

Regathering himself, Jacob continued, "Very few people know that being demon-blooded is a possibility, so I have always been discreet in my warnings. It is fortunate that the warnings apply to other situations, such as referring to Sasquatch as Bigfoot. I recommend you keep this a close secret. Like an ambidextrous person concealing their left-handed handwriting for subterfuge when needed."

"Ugh." Esme's expression drooped with the sound. "I feel like I've had more information dumped on me in the last six months than in the first thirty years of my life."

Jacob looked positively unburdened by contrast. He said, "When it rains, it pours, I suppose. But, from all I've heard and observed, you have made spectacular progress in your growth. You've made me proud!"

Eight months ago she would have been shocked to learn that Jacob had minions; people who gave him reports on her. Her old response would have been anger at the perceived betrayal. But now she could see his actions through the lens of empathy.

It was a sobering moment when she realized that he saw her as family, just as she saw him. Jacob's watchfulness felt less like control and more like a protective father looking out for a grown daughter. His intelligence gathering was simply more sophisticated than a normal parent's because he had the resources to pull it off. He wasn't directly interfering with her life. He recognized her maturity, but he would seek any information about her well-being that he could.

"While I appreciate the information from *trusted* sources—" she tried, but she couldn't hold back her irritation as she emphasized the 'trusted' part—"the sheer callousness and frankly shitty timing of the big reveal leaves much to be desired. You two had to strike a deal to tell the truth? I get Finn didn't feel like it was his place to tell me, but Jacob? I am far from a child." She felt tears threaten behind her eyes and squashed the feeling with alacrity.

At first Jacob didn't seem even slightly shamefaced as he answered her. "Esmeralda, this information changes nothing. If anything, you can start using it to your—to *our*—advantage. I probably should have mentioned it years ago, but your parents' wishes on this topic were very clear."

His tone changed from august Leader of the Assembly to the kinder, gentler, grandfatherly type that she was used to. "They didn't want you to carry the weight of the stigma like they did.

And I did not want to place it on you until it was necessary. Please try to understand, and please...forgive me."

This was just one more secret piled onto the others. Jacob had a relationship with her parents before she was even born. She could appreciate that the circumstances were complex and that she still didn't know enough to judge him too harshly. After all, looking in the mirror would also show a person who had made questionable choices in the name of what was right. Maybe she was finally learning to see beyond the immediate hurt she felt whenever something like this happened.

Her mind hit on a word that he had said. "Advantage?" The word had sparked a small flicker of hope, and she clung onto it tightly.

"Yes. Like I said, you have unwittingly tapped into the infernal. That could be a font of magic if used correctly. I'm no expert, but I believe that if you do not allow yourself to sink into the darker aspects of your blood—your parents were very clear with me on that topic—it can only be a boon to you."

Esme opened her mouth to ask about the "darker aspects," but the memory of the cold detachment that had taken over when she confronted Miles stilled her tongue. At last, she now understood what had happened when she had allowed herself to be consumed by the darkness. Had she already gone too far?

Jacob continued speaking, perhaps thinking that the consternation on her face was simply because of the news of her birth and not from inner turmoil. "By all accounts, Merlin, the most famous and purportedly the strongest of us all, was a cambion himself. The more conservative of our ilk seems to forget that fact." He said the word "conservative" like it was a slur.

Miles stood, his steps purposeful as he moved behind Esme's chair, a steady presence in the chaotic moment. Then, carefully, he crouched at the side and offered his hands to her. She accepted and squeezed his grip in return. Eventually, when she met his gaze, she saw his eyes searching for something.

Softly smiling, he said, "This answers a lot of questions for me, but nothing has changed. If anything, this is far from bad news. You're kind of a badass." He chuckled softly.

She. Would. Melt.

But was this a show of his bedside manner, or was this something more? The once strict definition of what they were to each other had blurred in her mind since she spoke with Abby and Will after their first sparring session. With her hands in his, it felt like they were moving in a less friendly direction.

Finn dramatically rolled his eyes at the display. Esme pointedly ignored him, as did Miles.

She was demon-blooded.... It was just starting to sink in. She had so many questions, but there wasn't time to ask them because Finn slapped his right hand on the side table nearby. Light erupted from the impact: magic.

Finn announced, "I deem your part of the bargain completed." After a moment's pause, he scoffed, "Tis my turn, I suppose; wouldn't want to detour too far from Fae law."

The weight of disclosure lifted from Esme's shoulders then. Unfortunately, the feeling of relief was short-lived because Miles' revelation was equally earth-shattering.

"You," Finn said, pointing at Miles with a half-awed, half-curious expression, "are god-touched."

"Say what?" Miles asked, standing abruptly.

Lily looked up briefly from the chaise lounge to check on her person. Seeing that all was well, she promptly returned to the very serious business of napping in luxury.

"I suppose I should mention that yer hound is, too. Though not as strongly as you. I'm going to guess that you felt strongly compelled to adopt her?"

Miles nodded, looking as though he were in a trance. Lily didn't react to the news—not that one would expect a dog to. She continued to doze contentedly while all eyes in the room briefly drifted her way.

The leprechaun continued. "C'mon, did ya really think that I was sticking around to help the Brotherhood because it was the *noble* thing to do?" He emphasized "noble" and laughed. Esme thought his words weren't exactly accurate: His deeds had proven otherwise.

Finn went on. "A begotten and a blessed one in the same place, at the same time, who seem to be startin' to work together? I'm stickin' around for the craic!"

He stood up, snatched a couple of tea cookies from the tray and immediately scarfed them down. Crumbs decorated his beard as he continued speaking. "Plus, I know where my magical bread is buttered. Ya both have a connection with this old oaf," he gestured at Jacob, who indignantly stared at the leprechaun's performance, "who I'd rather have on my side than not."

The last part seemed to mollify Jacob slightly, but he still barked out, "Begotten is a slur these days, leprechaun. Mind your tongue."

Finn raised both arms in surrender. "Well, pardon me. I've not spent much time around humans for a couple 'a years." He really seemed to be in a mood to rile up Jacob.

It was Jacob's turn to roll his eyes dramatically. On any normal day, Esme could watch the interplay between the mage and the leprechaun for hours without losing interest. But today was decidedly not a normal day. She could see an encyclopedia's worth of questions written on Miles' face and she definitely had a few herself.

Miles' voice was quiet and slightly unsteady when he asked, "What does that mean? God-touched?" He looked to Jacob for answers, but it was Finn who spoke up first.

The leprechaun swung away from his typical amused banter back to sincerity. "I don't exactly know, but it was somethin' they talked more about when I was a wean than now. I never noticed it until I met you at the pub."

So that was why Finn had stared at Miles, utterly stunned, when they first met at the bar, and perhaps why he called him "sir" for a while.

"You glow with some sort of power. It feels more like sunlight than the golden beams that you see in very old paintings. You know, the ones with the heads of saints lightin' up like Christmas trees? Now, people probably think it was just a bit o' artistic styling from way back in the day. If you know what to look for, ya can sense it." He eyed Jacob, who nodded in agreement.

So Jacob hadn't known or even known what to look for. How? Was this "god-touched" phenomenon that he spoke of something that was so rare, or so old, that Jacob would have no experience with it? This leprechaun was an ungovernable wellspring of information. The Assembly had certainly underestimated him. Esme was glad he was on her side... as far as she could tell, at least.

Meanwhile, Miles seemed both confused and relieved. Perhaps Finn could see this too because he let out a slow breath and said, "Look, lad, I don't know which god or if any 'god' is involved with it at all. It might just be a fancy name for it. I don't know how it works. I just know what I see and what has been handed down to me."

"Hey!" Esme cut in. "If he gets the cool halo effect, what do I get?" It only seemed fair to her. She could wield some levity to slice through the tension in the room. Plus, she genuinely wanted to know. "You knew what I was without being told. There has to be something besides the smell of my magic, right?"

The answer came from an unexpected source. Miles said delicately, "Your eyes turn black."

Every set of eyes, all surprised, swung his way.

"Oooo, now this is gettin' interesting." Finn rubbed his hands in anticipation and practically bounced in his seat. "I was gonna to say that her magic felt different, like mine, but this is gettin' good."

Chapter Twenty-Eight

Alia Iacta Est

Miles

God-touched? Blessed? Hell's bloody bells. Just what did that mean? On the surface, it sounded like a good thing, but was it actually?

His power was a closely guarded secret. Somehow Finn had known. As far as he knew, only his parents and the upper ranks of the Brotherhood and Assembly were aware. If the truth got out, it would be untenable. Miles had witnessed firsthand the desperation in war zones—how people would do anything, risk anything, to save a loved one. In peaceful times, without the barriers of distance or conflict, they wouldn't stop.

He could already imagine the demands and hear the threats, the pleas that would quickly turn violent when he couldn't grant them all. Every plea he refused would haunt him, every life he couldn't save weighing on his conscience. He'd stop being a man and become a tool, or worse—a pawn.

He remembered the first time his healing power manifested. He was eleven years old. It was the night before Christmas. His mother was cleaning the good crystal after that evening's dinner with his grandparents. He was helping her dry them before putting them away. She was normally a teetotaler, but on that special evening every year, she indulged in a hearty glass of brandy with his father. Fumbling, she clipped the side of a glass on the edge of the counter and the stem impaled her hand.

"Oh, Ma!" he remembered shouting as he ran over to help. Instinct took over and his power to heal poured out of him as if it had been waiting for release.

Neither of them knew how it had happened. Normally, only the outcomes of magic are apparent, such as a levitating pencil or a sudden illusion appearing out of nowhere. Yet, the magic that came from his hands shimmered with a soft golden glow.

His mother mumbled, "I...how?" As her flesh knitted together, she found her voice and gathered her wits. "Go on, get your father, and then offer your grandfather some more biscuits while we talk, yeah? I have more to finish here."

The striking dichotomy between her bewildered reaction and his good intentions forever branded the image of her shocked face in his memory. His mother had looked at him as if she had never met him before, and all because he'd been trying to help.

From this, he'd learned to keep his mouth shut and his powers firmly locked away, except in dire circumstances. If his own mother could lose her composure and make up reasons to get his child-self out of the room, others would, and did, react far more troublingly.

Esme had seen him heal Lily, but he trusted her. The look she gave him after Finn's revelation contained a thousand questions and too many emotions to read. But she didn't look at him with distrust or fear, like he was a wholly new man to her. She displayed only curiosity.

Would this change things between them? The lack of outright shock was promising. It would be easier if the answer to that question didn't matter, but it did. The news that she was demon-blooded meant very little to him. It explained a myriad of questions he'd had, but almost nothing could change the way he felt. Ever since he had first seen her, she had captivated him with a hold he couldn't break free from.

The die was cast. There was no turning back. He'd have to see how the cards fell and adjust his expectations accordingly. He'd be damned if he didn't feel like swaying things with her in a certain direction.

As he pondered their future, he also found himself questioning his own abilities. Was being "god-touched" the source of his unique power to heal? Was it also the source of his insane recurring dreams?

He'd halfway lied about not recognizing the man in the forest. But the awful truth was that the possibility of who the man was Miles found almost too much to bear. It was true he didn't know him, nor had he ever met him before. But he had seen him—in his dreams. His was the first face Miles had recognized as a twin to a character from them.

Was he crazy or was there something significant to the fact that before seeing the man in the woods, he'd met two others who reminded him strongly of people from his dreams? Had he been wrong all this time about what the visions were? Could they be some form of premonition?

Esme's mannerisms, her very presence, triggered memories of the shieldmaiden from his dreams. Sure, they didn't look alike, but she felt like a ghost from a forgotten past resurrected into the present.

In his dreams, Miles had felt the king's desperate love for the shieldmaiden. He'd felt the pain that the king felt each time he denied himself, and denied her, the love that simmered between them.

Miles had spent years trying to fight the dreams, trying to fight fate. His days, his nights, and his choices had all been influenced by something that he hadn't chosen for himself. His healing powers, his hand, his dog, his damned face, were a mirror of his! Each time he thought he was making a choice for his life, it seemed that the king had chosen it for him first.

Who was Miles Goodwin without the dreams? He didn't know.

That thought brought up a good question. "Is this something I inherited like Esme?" he asked.

He doubted it. James and Ann Goodwin were normal people who weren't plagued by repeating dreams or unique magic. In fact, they were probably two of the least powerful mages that he'd known. His father was a car salesman in Cardiff and his mother did tours at one of the many castles in the city. But it still needed to be asked.

"Bejesus, no. Well, I don't think so, at least." The lack of confidence that Finn displayed was unlike him. Miles might have been unsettled by it if he hadn't still been reeling from the revelations.

He needed to move. He wasn't normally overcome with the need to let off energy through movement, but the news had shocked him out of sinus rhythm. Restlessness made him pace. Lily stirred and sat to attention, waiting for him to act.

Out of nowhere, he heard a crash. Esme had been grasping the armrests of her chair so hard that the entire structure had collapsed. He understood the feeling that made her do it.

She moaned out, a disheveled pile of disarrayed clothes and a few drops of tea, "Gods below, I'm so sorry, Jacob!" She'd been trying so hard to stay composed. "I'm fine. I'm fine! Just a hot mess, like normal."

She swatted away Finn's reaching hand, as he was the nearest to her. The leprechaun appeared to be puzzled, searching her all over, trying to find out which part of her was too hot.

"Fecking shite, where's the fire?" He didn't understand the slang and was convinced that she was somehow ablaze.

It was impossible not to laugh and so Miles let it out. The hilarity mixed with joy was a wave too strong to not unleash.

His heart hurt. He'd operated alone for so long that the feeling bubbling up in his chest was difficult to place, almost forgotten. In the hospital, he was the doctor. In the medic's tent, he was the attending, not one of the boys. In the shadows, he was death. But here, now, he felt a contentment that had been missing from his life since childhood. He felt at home with these people.

Even amid the savage onslaught of truths, he had two realizations.

First, he realized how fortunate he was with the relationship he had with his parents. While he was an enigma to them, at least they hadn't been lying to him his entire life.

Second, even though he'd tried to fight it, he suspected that he was more than a little in love with Esme.

He decided that the difference between Miles Goodwin and the king was that Miles would not repeat the king's mistake. If she'd have him, he'd get the girl.

Chapter Twenty-Nine

Halo and Horns

Esme

The death knell of the evening was the sound of her ass hitting the floor amid the ruins of Jacob's chair. Seriously, who did that?

Someone tainted, came the unbidden thought. But, really, was that fair? No. It was too easy to be your own harshest critic. Life was hard enough without her adding to her own burden.

Esme felt like she had a truckload of worries dumped on her, and she was willing to bet that Miles felt the same way. He appeared to be fine—relieved, even—but maybe he was just putting on a show. She'd create an exit for them both; it was the least she could do in return for the compassion he'd shown her moments before.

"So you know nothing else about Miles' condition?" she asked.

Finn shook his head. He didn't.

It seemed there was little else for them to learn. Anything they talked about at this point would be poking at a currently very sore spot on Esme's heart. She shot to her feet. "That was... a lot. I need to leave."

She put her hands in the air to forestall any arguments. "This isn't me running. I'm not going to fall apart like your chair. Sorry about that, by the way. I'd offer to fix it, but I'm fairly certain that you'd do a better job than me." She wiggled her fingers in the air in a mock display of casting a spell.

How could she explain what she needed? "This is me taking a step back, to think, to let it sink in. I promise we'll talk soon. But I've had enough of this today. Mister Mysterious Maybe Bad Guy in Black—" she thought for a moment and reconsidered, "Okay, that name is way too long. The bad guy seemed just as surprised to see us as we were him, so we should be safe tonight. I'll put wards up when I get home."

She nodded toward the door. "You coming?"

His eyes questioned without words, *Are you okay? Do you need to talk?*

She could ask him the same question. But no, what she needed was talking-optional. Beating around the bush was never quite her style. The intense look in Miles' eyes as he studied her probably had its roots in his concern about the news she'd received, but there was something else there; something starved.

So, she added in Miles' direction, "Plus, you need to explain the whole 'eyes turn black' thing to me. Do it in the car?"

He had already grabbed his coat, which had been sitting in a disheveled pile on the floor nearby from when he'd carried in an unconscious Finn.

First Jacob stood slowly, then Finn. Jacob started to speak, "Darling, I..."

She cut him off with a soft smile. "I know. I know. I love you, you old curmudgeon."

She leaned in for a hug, certain that she noticed a glint of tears in his eyes. Was that the first time she had said how she felt? Surely not. But if so, it was overdue. He was the found, the chosen, family that she had needed. And if she was right, she was what he needed, too.

She eyed the leprechaun. "I assume you'll find your way home like normal?" Knowing him, he probably used his phone to call a car share to drop him as close to home as possible and mist walked to skip most of the hike back from there.

He sent a devilish smirk her way, eyes seeing too much for her liking. He prodded that wound, saying, "Aye. Have a good night, you two."

Miles addressed the Bastion. "Thank you, Jacob, for everything; for your hospitality." He included Finn in his attention as he said, "We need to reconvene. I'll be in contact. You know how to reach me."

Jacob added, "Finn and I have more to discuss, so I will see you out." With Lily trotting obediently behind, he shuffled them to the door.

Esme's reasons for gesturing to Miles to drive again were unclear, even to her. Maybe, deep down, she craved a sense of security, a way to regain her footing after having her identity shattered. Or perhaps it was the memory of his careful driving after the doppelgänger attack. He didn't seem bothered by her wordless instruction. Miles took it on like he took on every burden, with silent confidence.

She handed him back the keys and waited for him to open the door for her as he gestured for her to proceed ahead. Still in the driveway, they both hesitated before grabbing their seatbelts.

He said, "Thanks for getting us out of there."

She was relieved to hear that she'd made the right call. But when she looked over, Miles locked eyes with her again. Gazing into the green depths, her world seemed to shrink down to a space big enough for only two people. She felt like she was teetering at the edge of something, and she was tempted to fall headfirst into it. It was now or never.

As he reached to put the keys in the ignition, Esme turned in her seat and reached over the armrest to grab his lifted hand. He froze as she eased their hands as one to the armrest. She moved her hand up to gently caress his arm; she wasn't certain that he could feel the small movement on his prosthetic. He responded by placing his left hand over hers and searching her expression for the correct next move.

She didn't overanalyze why she felt compelled to touch him. But it wasn't just about comfort. It was about needing to feel him, needing to know that she wasn't alone in this... whatever this was between them.

"Miles..." she started. As she leaned toward him, he did likewise, bending to accommodate the steering wheel, the two of them drawn together like magnets.

Esme shivered as the stubble on his jaw scraped delicately against her cheek, a contrast to the softness of his lips. She breathed in his scent, fresh with a hint of the ocean. At first, the kiss was tentative. Each move was pensive, each touch a careful exploration. But quickly they fell into a rhythm of sorts and she lost herself in it.

She wrapped one hand around to cup the back of his head, then eventually moved the hand that was wrapped in his hair slowly down his torso to rest high on his thigh. As she felt his body, she realized that his physique matched her mental image perfectly. She smiled as Miles sucked in a surprised breath. She couldn't have made it clearer that her move wasn't an accident.

Eventually coming up for breath, she muttered, "You should definitely drive to your house if you're interested in continuing this."

They were behaving like teenagers making out in the driveway, after all. Gods above and below, she was pretty sure Jacob had security cameras pointed in their direction.

His eyes didn't contain even a flicker of hesitation. They were filled with the same fire as hers. It was a powerful feeling to know that she had stoked it. It was an aphrodisiac.

"So," she asked, "home?"

He reached over and gently squeezed her thigh in reply, snatched the key from where he had dropped it in their interlude, and started the engine.

The drive to his house came and went out of memory: headlights, bridges, a group of night runners on the lake path. He parked in a nondescript parking lot, let Lily out of the hatchback, and tossed Esme her keys. It wasn't until they started walking toward the lake, hand in hand, that she started to question where exactly they were going.

"So you live near the lakefront? Quite swanky, Doctor Goodwin." Her tone was jesting.

"On it," he replied simply.

They walked toward a pier, and she nearly started skipping. She knew exactly where they were headed. "Do you live in a floating house?"

He looked at her quizzically, uncertain as to why this was consequential. "Yes?"

Quietly she muttered, "This is amazing." Esme had lived her entire life in Seattle but had not once been inside one of the iconic houseboats for which the city was famous.

With a quick sideways glance, she caught him grinning like a schoolboy. He added, "It's very small, but I hope you find it to be comfortable."

They walked to the end of a dock and turned toward a light blue one-story houseboat surrounded by hearty chrysanthemums in planters. The house was adorable and not at all what she expected to see. She couldn't wait to get to know this side of Miles: The soft side of him who planted a small garden amid the gloom of autumn and purposefully created a cozy space for himself away from the world and all of its pressures.

Inside, he took her coat and offered her a drink. The interior of his house was an equal mixture of traditional and modern. She liked that it didn't have the frigid, ultra-modern vibe that so many bachelors seemed attracted to when decorating.

When they finally sat down on his couch together, Lily padded over and shoved her snout between them. Miles smiled, patted her head, and stood, saying, "If she's not invited to join, she wants a bribe to leave." He grabbed her a few treats and led her to her dog bed.

As he rejoined Esme on the couch, he picked up where they'd left off, "Now, where were we?" and leaned in for another kiss.

She happily obliged. As time ticked forward, they gradually melted into each other's space. When this had reached the point that one of her knees had crept over his thigh, she needed to be closer to him.

Pulling away from his kiss, she braced herself upward and swung her leg over to straddle his lap on the couch. He wrapped his hands around her waist and pulled her closer, reaching again for her mouth with his. This was nearly where she needed to be. She could tell from his response and from the bulge she sat upon that he would be more than enough for her needs.

She welcomed the feel of his hands on her skin as he reached under her shirt to caress her back. Her enjoyment of his petting was only tempered by one intriguing thought. Trying not to break the mood, she made eye contact with him and asked softly, "Your prosthesis. It feels almost real. It's even warm. Magic?"

A brief arching of his lips upward and a nod while he kissed her again signaled the affirmative. Since she had already temporarily hit pause on their activities, it felt like a good time to ask her next urgent question. She couldn't keep the cheek from her voice as she asked, "So, how do you feel about doing this without pants on?"

At this, the full lazy-eyed smile that only peeked through earlier broke out over his face. He rose smoothly with her in his arms, straddling him, her weight barely a strain as he carried her toward the bedroom. Slowly, he lowered them both to his bed.

Lily took this as her cue to vacate the premises. She picked up her favorite stuffed dragon toy and trotted through the doggy door to seek the peace of the night air on the deck.

If Esme could burn off her clothes with hellfire, she would. There was too much clothing between them. In the haze of lust, she wasn't certain who should start stripping first, but she found herself holding him, shirtless, with his belt unclasped above her.

They'd never turned the lights on when entering the room, so she could only make him out faintly. She traced the lines of his muscles with her hands and discovered raised scars over his chest and one shoulder. One felt like the pattern that claws would make on flesh, another the piercing of a knife. On his right side, a much larger and indented scar flanked his abdominal muscles. She had a feeling that this one had happened when he lost his hand.

As her fingertips explored the scar, he flinched slightly, and for a moment, she worried she had hurt him. But then he released a shuddering breath, leaning into her touch, pulling her closer and kissing her deeper. For Esme, the scars told a story of who he was; of what he valued, not imperfections.

She arched up and swiftly removed her shirt and sports bra. Not to be delayed any longer, she used the space between them to wiggle out of her pants and underwear. He followed her lead. The cold air of the room hit her exposed skin and raised gooseflesh all over.

"Come back," she whispered. Meeting her exposed skin, his body was a warm welcome.

He reassured her, "I'm clean." While there were ways that mages could deal with some communicable diseases and prevent unplanned pregnancies, it still needed to be said.

"Me too. And it's been like five million years, so I'm sure of that. But I don't have a condom," she admitted, half-laughing, half-worried.

"It's been about six million for me," he agreed.

They both chuckled at that. Then he walked to the en suite bathroom, giving her a welcome, if still too dark, view of his backside on the way. He came back to the room with a small box of condoms in his hand. "I promise these aren't paleolithic."

A few dozen kisses and caresses later, she felt the change come over her and understood. Now that she was aware of the possibility, she felt her eyes flicker between their natural color and black, and back again, with the intensity of her desire.

The outside world faded, leaving only the rustle of sheets and soft words of praise between two people lost in each other. In each other, they found their equal, their match. Some moments were tender, others rampant and needy, but each gave when it was needed and took when it was offered.

Meanwhile, on the deck, Lily watched as tiny ripples broke the surface around the houseboat as it bobbed ever so slightly. She covered her eyes with one large paw and set herself on the serious work of falling asleep. It was going to be a long night.

Back inside, sometime later, they both fell asleep, replete and exhausted. For a little while, at least....

Chapter Thirty

The Ambiguous Morning After

Esme

Before the weak light of the autumn morning crept over the curtains, Esme quietly slipped out from under the sheets she'd stolen from Miles during the night. She was thankful that he wasn't the clinging type while sleeping, as it would have made her disappearance that much more difficult.

As she tugged on yesterday's clothes and frantically looked for her shoes, she couldn't help but ask herself, *Why am I disappearing*?

The easiest answer was that she was an idiot. Even before she had first opened her eyes early that morning, anxiety and insecurity had weighed down on her chest.

She wasn't concerned about her boldness the night before. She snickered under her breath as she thought about how she had asked if he wanted to "do this without pants on." That was simply a classic Esme move, and she was okay with that.

No. The disparity in what they'd learned about themselves was why Esme was running. Miles was "god-touched," a discovery that only enhanced his golden boy image. Apparently, he even had a literal halo if viewed a certain way. He was also a doctor and had served in the special forces.

Esme was...Esme. Sure, she had a college degree, but just one. She didn't even use it. She was a bartender and part-time problem handler for the Assembly. Okay, that last bit did sound kind of cool, but still. She was an orphaned bartender who had demon blood. There wasn't anything more antithetical to his halo than her metaphorical horns.

Plus, she'd felt her eyes change. It had to be something brought on by extreme emotions. It was of note, but mostly inconsequential, during her state of ecstasy. The only other time she could imagine Miles seeing her with black eyes was when she had been so furious that she had ordered her minion to hold him while he suffocated slowly. She stifled her whimper of anguish at the thought.

Was she a monster? Sure, Miles had done some reprehensible stuff as well, but he'd never done anything to her like she had to him, and so coldly. He was so understanding—maybe even too understanding, and supportive of her. Everything he'd done after she received the news of her heritage was precisely perfect. She'd never met another person who could make her feel so strong and yet so vulnerable.

All of this flew through Esme's mind as she began tip-toeing out the front door. She was fairly certain that Miles had set no alarms, mundane or magical, last night during their activities, so she could probably sneak out without disturbing him.

He'd barely stirred from where she'd left him in bed. She draped the sheets back over him because he didn't deserve to be left in the cold, too. Leaving him without saying a word was a shitty enough thing for her to do.

Out on the deck, Lily lifted her head and stood on four paws in greeting. The pink line on her snout and cheek hadn't changed much from the day before, but she appeared better rested. Esme spent a few minutes sitting in the chair on the front porch with Lily lounging heavily on her feet, enjoying the view of the water and dreading what she was about to do. She gave the dog a few farewell pets and told her to go back inside. To her astonishment, Lily did just that.

But Esme still couldn't quite get her feet to move. She knew she was stalling the inevitable, but she couldn't help it. Half of her wanted to stay, but the other half knew she didn't deserve him. Remaining there for a little while longer, she rehashed the starkly contrasting natures of their individual "gifts" and the difference in their lives in a spiraling loop of self-pity.

With one step, she began the walk of shame back to her car. She was ashamed because she was too cowardly to face him, the perfect man, in the daylight.

Tainted indeed.

But just as she was about to set foot off the small porch, her phone started ringing with the frantic ringtone that she'd set for Jacob. If he was calling that early in the morning, it was serious.

She heard a muffled thump, then a low groan from inside the house. Maybe, instead of running, the universe was telling her to turn around and talk to him. Would she listen to it?

Miles

The slimy, oversized tongue dragging across one cheek snapped Miles awake. He tried to sit up and push Lily aside, but the dog promptly plopped all one hundred and twenty pounds of herself directly onto his chest. As tufts of fur found their way into his nasal passages, he realized that he also couldn't move his hand. He'd fallen asleep with it on and had neglected to plug it in.

One-handed, he moved the offending creature to the side and realized that he was alone. His house was small enough that he would have heard Esme moving around in the bathroom or kitchen. He let out a long breath as his head fell back onto the pillow.

Esme was gone.

He struggled to keep his disappointment in check. Last night hadn't felt like a one-night stand to him. It was too raw, too real, too vulnerable to have been a throwaway evening of fun. It just didn't seem like something she would do.

Why would she disappear like that?

Bloody hell. The man in the forest. Could he?

Miles scrambled up from the bed, ripped off his useless hand, plugged it in, and called her number. Each ring lasted for an eternity. He nearly threw the phone when it hit her voicemail.

Where was his gun? Had he even properly stored it yesterday? His knives were still in his backpack. He would need to call the Bastion and the ranging Corded Brother stationed out of Spokane. Could his contacts in Portland make it here in good time? His mind was spinning.

He toppled over in the frenzy of trying to put on his jeans, one-handed, when the sound of a call came from the other side of his front door.

It was Esme's phone.

His heart rate immediately slowed. She wasn't in danger. She was taking a phone call outside so he could sleep. Or she was running away. One of the two.

As he heard the front door creak open, he realized he hadn't dreamt at all last night. That was unheard of for him; a miracle.

Esme

Esme walked into Miles' bedroom to see him sprawled, half-dressed on the floor. He smiled up at her sheepishly. Yep, that thump and groan had been him rushing to get dressed. She didn't attempt to quell the knowing smirk that grew on her face.

She placed her phone on the speaker setting, allowing Miles to hear the conversation. She answered, "Jacob? It's early. Is everything okay?"

She watched as Miles sat up smoothly, acting as if nothing had happened. At least now she had confirmation that he was still human.

Then it hit her. Her stomach twisted before Jacob had even spoken the first syllable of her name.

"Esmeralda, my dear, I hate to cut the greeting short, but have you heard from Will? I know that he is the exuberant type, but he didn't come into work last night and no one has seen him or been able to reach him. We're all worried and hoped that you might know what he's up to since you're chums."

She clutched her middle with her free hand and grimaced. She managed, "N-no. I can call his roommate."

Jacob's voice held a bleak certainty. "I already have. They confirmed that he never returned home after his shift the evening before last and also did not return home yesterday."

She sat down abruptly on the closest surface, Miles' bed. She asked dumbly, "What?"

The other end of the phone remained quiet. Jacob was probably giving her time to process what she'd heard.

Miles waved his hand and caught her gaze. He pointed first at her, then at himself, and finally gave the "look" gesture. She nodded decisively. All of this took less than thirty seconds, and a plan was hatched.

She responded more steadily this time, bolstered by Miles' suggestion. "Jacob? Miles and I are going to look for him."

Jacob replied, "Ah." Then he remained silent for a long moment. Her guess was that his sharp mind was thinking through the early hour, exactly what she'd said, and putting two and two together.

Finally he spoke: "It is...good to hear that you have an ally. At this point, I fear it might be wise for us to search for him. I can't reach his parents to confirm their desire for a police report. I will keep asking around on my end. Let me know what you find."

Before Esme could end the call, Miles spoke up. "Jacob, I suggest we inform the non-field Brother in the area that we may need assistance, depending upon what we find."

A sound that was the posh relative of a grunt rattled through the phone's speaker. Esme shot Miles a puzzled look. Why hadn't he mentioned another Corded Brother being around?

Jacob's tone was terse. "Keep me updated. I'll handle my end. I trust you to handle yours."

Jacob's trust in Miles spoke volumes about the relationship between the Bastion of the Corded Brotherhood and the man sitting in front of her.

The sinking pit of dread Esme felt made her want to either curl up in Miles' lap or run away screaming instead of facing the possibility that something had happened to Will—it was too terrible to contemplate. It seemed the hits were going to keep on coming, but she couldn't relax or take a step back. Last night was the only break she was going to get.

Duty called, and Esme would rather fall into a bottomless pit than fail Will. She wanted to reach out and touch Miles again, to be closer to the man who would be there with her every step of the way, but she didn't. He'd proven himself the golden boy yet again.

She needed to apologize to him first. Too bad she'd have to face him and tell him the truth of why she'd been on the other side of the front door when the phone rang. But instead of speaking with him about it then, she said, a bit timidly, "Right...so, I need to change."

Miles gave her an all-too-knowing, considering examination. Then he nodded and made excuses about having to take Lily out anyway, saying that he'd pick her up at her place in an hour.

So, he knew she'd been trying to run. She had exactly one hour to prepare herself for an incredibly difficult conversation.

Entering her bungalow, she collapsed on the couch in her living room, dropping her bag and keys in a heap on the floor nearby. She wanted to scream.

Esme allowed herself a few quiet minutes to acclimate to the crushing weight of so many extraordinary experiences, all unraveling in rapid succession. She did what any woman in such a situation would do. She grabbed the nearest pillow, mindful of her neighbors, and shouted her lungs out into it.

Jacob had placed his trust in her to find Will. She didn't have the option of taking the day off to wallow. The only option was to keep kicking ass and taking names.

The first step on her to-do list was to prioritize acceptance. She had to complete that step right here and right now. With that out of the way, she could focus on what was actually important, on what could be changed.

She had reconciled herself to the fact that monsters were real. She could come to terms with the fact that she was a cambion and had been lied to about it for her entire life. Yes, Miles was amazing in far, far too many ways. The disparity between them made her scared that she'd never be enough, even though that was her deepest wish.

She muttered the catalogue of truths she had to face to herself until the words lost their meaning and her nerves eased with each repetition. Feeling a small bit of satisfaction, she mentally checked off step one of her plans.

She scrubbed at her scalp furiously in the shower, then applied some light makeup as a sort of warpaint. She needed the confidence to get through what would surely be a trying day. While she arranged her hair, she outlined steps two and three of her list. Apologizing would come naturally to her in step two; she was always quick to acknowledge her mistakes. But, when it came to step three, being completely honest with him; well, that would be a tough one.

Time flew and Miles arrived at her front door before she had the chance to rehearse what she would say to him. As she opened the door, she was surprised to see him standing there without his prosthesis. He looked handsome in a fitted sweater with a backpack slung over one shoulder.

"Hey," she greeted him, pausing awkwardly before opening the door wider and gesturing him in. "Where's Lily?"

She couldn't discern anything about his thoughts from his tone and body language when he spoke. "My neighbor is halfway retired and loves Lily. I left her at his house since I wasn't certain how long we'd be out today."

Esme made a sound of understanding and, gathering her composure, offered, "I can whip up some eggs and bacon to make breakfast sandwiches if you want to eat and talk about the plan."

His features scrunched up in mock outrage. "Fairly certain that is supposed to be my job the morning after." He laughed.

The rumbling sound of his laugh released the knot in her abdomen.

"Okay..." she allowed herself a small smile. "I'll let you make it up to me by driving today."

"Deal." He cleared his throat and anxiously scratched his beard. "May I plug my hand in while we're here?" he motioned at his missing hand. "I was distracted and forgot to do it last night."

She relished the idea of being so absorbing that he didn't even notice one that one of his limbs was dead. Still, the anticipation of what she had to admit dampened the pleasure of it.

She led him to the kitchen, and he offered to start a pot of coffee for them. As the first slice of bacon sizzled in the pan, Esme focused squarely on her preparations, avoiding eye contact while she worked up her nerve. Miles leaned back in his seat. She could feel his eyes boring into her back. It felt like he was waiting for her to talk first.

Now or never, she thought. She steeled herself, her hands trembling slightly as she cracked one egg after another into the pan. "I'm sorry," she breathed out the words, trying to imbue them with the sincerity she felt. "I was leaving this morning when Jacob called."

She turned off the stove and faced him, the toaster humming in the background. He deserved to see her face as she told the truth. "Yesterday was just a lot, you know? I'll be the first to admit that I've been a coward. You deserve better than that."

His expression didn't change, and he said nothing. Did he have to be so patient all the time? She wanted him to say something, anything, to end her suffering quickly if need be.

She froze, a rabbit caught in the gaze of a wolf, as he slowly rose and crossed the room. Her only defense against her fear was her voice. "I guess I just see myself as a beater car sitting next to a shiny new foreign model, which is clearly you in this analogy, parked in the same garage, ya know? We're just so different."

He wrapped his arms around her. It felt different because he was lacking one hand, but it still felt incredible, like the sun warming your skin for the first time after a long winter.

She watched as he studied her face. Stripped bare of any pretense, he said, "I've missed you." He held onto her and leaned forward slightly. Unable to resist the temptation, she did the same. He rested his forehead on hers, breathed once, and nuzzled the tip of his nose to hers.

It felt as though every brain cell in her head stopped firing as her body moved to return the bunny kiss. Her caution and nervousness over his acceptance melted away. Slowly, she lifted her hands, which had been hanging stiffly at her sides, to cradle his face. His beard was cut short, but still soft enough that she wanted to massage it affectionately.

He barely spoke the whispered words, "You're perfect," before she took his mouth in a kiss. It felt like heaven after being stuck in purgatory for a lifetime. She sank into the feeling, greedily soaking in the sensation like a starving woman.

She'd spent the morning trying to run away and then walk around the issue like it was a floor covered in glass shards. Only for her to discover that the pathway back to him had always been open—she'd been standing in her own way.

He pulled back slightly to brush his lips, featherlight, over hers. Keeping his voice low with his nose still brushing hers, he said, "I'm with you." He kissed her lips once more and added, "And please never refer to us as automobiles ever again."

She laughed and allowed herself one more comforting kiss before reluctantly pushing away. Steps one through three had gone far better than expected. It might not be the end of her insecurities, but it was a respectable start. As much as she wanted to invite him back to her bedroom for a few hours of reassuring touches, they needed to eat and focus on finding Will. "I'll plate the food and you grab the coffee. Let's plan today."

Lacking a second hand, it took Miles two trips to grab their coffees. His competence in all areas of life was so remarkable that she'd never really thought of how such a disability could make his life difficult in small ways. He'd said that he was with her. What that meant, she wasn't certain, but she promised herself that she'd be there with him too.

Chapter Thirty-One

She Reads

Abby

Abby's curls cascaded backward as she took another sip of her Sidecar cocktail, one hand delicately cradling the glass while the other flipped a page.

She'd spent hours combing through texts, searching for clues about someone named "Glais" for Miles. He'd asked her to look into it as a personal favor, not an official one. He'd asked her months ago, and it had slipped her mind until last night when she realized he hadn't brought it up again. Now she was trying to make up for lost time in quickly figuring out this tiny mystery for him. Even though it was long overdue, she hoped it would still be a pleasant surprise.

She'd found a village in Wales that shared the name, but she doubted that was what he was looking for. Anyone could figure that out. She'd also turned up information on a poet with the same last name, but that also couldn't be what he was looking for. No, he'd asked her for help because she had something that almost no one else did: access to the Assembly's very secret, very private library.

She was considering ordering some hot wings when her eyes strayed back to the page for a moment. Voilà! Finally, a breakthrough. Glais was the grandfather of Peredur. If she recalled the information correctly, Peredur was the Welsh version of Percival, a knight of the Round Table. This must be what Miles was looking for, but she'd keep digging to be certain.

Her ability to hyper-focus on her task, even when sitting in a crowded bar, was mostly a boon to her productivity. Yet it also had the downside of causing her to lose all awareness of her surroundings while she was immersed in work. So, when a male voice broke through her concentration, she jumped in her seat and lost her place on the page. Frustrating.

"What?" she asked, a little grumpily.

"My apologies. I said, 'May I share this table with you for a short while?'" His voice, rich with an accent she'd never encountered before, was confident.

But that confidence quickly changed as he studied her face. Maybe it was that he noticed her surly expression, but he looked like he'd seen a ghost.

He started to turn around to leave, saying, "Oh, please accept my apologies. I can see that you're reading. Umm, thank you."

Only then did she look around and realize that The Sanctuary of Spirits was packed and that she was monopolizing a table for four with her books. She was being a jerk. Once Abby realized this, the unknown man's back was turned to leave.

She stopped him. "No, please! I'm so sorry. My mind was in another place. Please, sit. Join me."

The man turned back around. "Nice to meet you. I'm Gwynn," he rumbled, a confident smile on his face.

She felt her mouth go dry. His presence was almost overwhelming. He was gorgeous—tall, well-built, with raven-black hair and piercing blue eyes.

She had some free time before she needed to go home for the evening. Besides, she could use another drink. Why not enjoy it while getting to know someone new?

Chapter Thirty-Two

Fear Itself

Will

Will startled awake, but he wished he hadn't. His head was throbbing and his mouth felt like sandpaper. This was a hangover from hell, worse than any he'd ever had.

After twenty-five, his body had forced him to limit hard partying. So why did this feel like a hangover when he was pretty sure that he hadn't touched a drop? What the hell had he gotten himself into?

Gods below, was a leaf stuck to his face? What had he done last night? Esme would fall over laughing when he told her about this massive mistake—once he figured out what he'd done, of course.

Wait, didn't he work at the bar last night? He didn't go out at all. Shivering from the cold, he groped blindly for his covers, keeping his eyes shut against the stinging daylight. He blindly reached out to retrieve the covers, to sink back into unconscious, pain-free bliss.

The move proved he wasn't sleeping on his comfortable bed at home. Instead of clean sheets, he clutched handfuls of what felt like sodden, nearly frozen, fir needles and leaves. He opened his eyes all the way.

What he saw was way worse than waking up next to a hideous ogre you mistook for the hottie of your dreams the night before. The light of the sun streamed through hundreds of gaps in the twining vines and roots that formed a sort of natural cage—no, a prison—around him. Surely this was some sort of practical joke gone too far.

A small sound alerted him to the fact that he wasn't alone. A woman, looking as dirty and ragged as he felt, was curled up in a ball at one corner of the enclosure. Pine needles were interwoven between the tangled mats of her brown hair. Patches of the original lilac peeked through the layers of dirt covering her ripped clothing. As the woman lifted her arms from their protective position around her face, Will recognized her. Maureen.

What on earth was he doing in the middle of the forest with a seated member of the Assembly cowering in fear not ten feet away? He licked his dry lips, trying to bring enough life to them so that he could speak. "Maureen?"

The second he spoke, she covered her face again, as if to hide. "Maureen?" he said again. "Where are we?"

She said nothing in response, but whimpered quietly. She curled up into an even tighter ball. Genuine fear settled into his bones. At first it was subtle, but soon it became something that he couldn't ignore. The fear seeped into his mind at the same sluggish pace with which the cold of the air had permeated his light jacket.

From this place of dread, he finally opened his eyes, truly opened them. Will wasn't the strongest mage on the block, but he had a special talent. Most mages could only feel magic as a tingling on their skin, but Will could see magic in all its brilliant magnificence.

It reminded him of what an Impressionist painter would do if the air could be painted with watercolors. Magic looked like streaming mists of color flowing from its source. Or, if it was a stationary sort of magic, it flowed in place, moving like streams of water through the air, never stagnant but also never drifting away.

When Will opened his eyes, he saw a blend of red and green liquid smoke around them, in a macabre Christmas combination. It was swirling across every inch of the enclosure he found himself within. Seeing that jarring shade of blood red for a second time triggered his memory.

Sylas had been wrapped in that same blood-red mist at the bar the night before. Had he done this? The leshy always freaked him out, so it seemed possible. But Sylas was basically Esme's uncle. He wouldn't kidnap them, right? Had Will done something that finally pushed the leshy over the edge? Gods above and below, he hoped not.

The last thing Will remembered from the night before was the beginning of his walk home. The next thing he knew, he'd woken up in a prison somewhere in the mountains with a helluva headache and one Assembly member practically pissing herself in a corner. Experience told him that the green magic was the sort that was deeply tied to nature. That explained the vines of their prison. Given how Maureen was acting, the red magic had to be some sort of bad juju stuff.

And now, somehow, he was mixed up in it.

He knew Maureen. She'd always been kind to him. He had no earthly clue why she'd treated him so well while she spit filth at Esme. Whenever possible, he used her kindness to shield Esme from her cruelty. But ultimately he couldn't do anything about it. He was a no-name mage with no power and weak family connections. Maureen was an incredibly powerful mage with the strongest connections imaginable.

If she was stuck in the cage, prison, whatever, with him…well, he might as well get comfortable because he had zero hope of busting himself out given his meager strength.

He shut his eyes again, tucked his stiff hands back into his pockets, and laid his head back on the cold forest floor.

He'd take waking up with the double whammy of an ogre in his bed and a hangover over this in a second.

Chapter Thirty-Three

Scouring for Clues

Esme

Esme hopped out before the car stopped, already knocking on the door, when Miles caught up. Just as expected, Len quickly swung open the door, their face a blank mask, arms crossed.

Esme had predicted a cold greeting, but she could tell that Miles was taken aback. Will was a brightly shining star of energy and positivity who only looked like the stereotype of a thug on the outside because of his bulging muscles that were covered in tattoos. Len was nearly the opposite: quiet, inexpressive in manner and styling, and unemotional. Esme figured that's why they'd stayed roommates for so long. Their differing personalities fit each other like two interlocking puzzle pieces.

Len opened the door with a curt, "What?" as a way of greeting Esme and Miles.

"Hey, Len! I love the hair," Esme said brightly. Their regular messy pixie cut was dyed blond.

Len stared back at her blankly, not acknowledging the compliment. Unfazed, Esme soldiered on. "I know Will's boss called about him not showing up at work, but I wanted to follow up on that. Can we talk for a minute?"

Even though Len was a mage, Esme seriously doubted that they attended any meetings, so she left out Jacob's name.

Len stepped back and gestured for them to enter, pointing one thumb over a shoulder toward the interior of the apartment. It seemed like an invitation, so she dragged Miles in behind her.

Realizing that she hadn't introduced him, she said lamely, "This is Miles. He knows Will too." She struggled briefly with how to introduce him. They'd just made up after her colossal mistake. Plus, they hadn't had time to iron out what they were to each other yet.

A few steps later, the three of them stood in the crowded living room. Len's work had made the humble space into an art gallery and studio in all but name.

Among all the alteration specialized mages Esme had met, Will's roommate stood out as the most skilled in crafting delicate and complex pieces from materials such as glass, clay, and metal. Len's name in the art world was established through their mixed material sculpture work, as well as their light fixtures, jewelry, and other custom creations.

Because Len didn't require a massive furnace like mundane glass blowers, they could work at home. To protect the carpet and furniture from any flying bits of clay or glass, they covered the center of the living room with thick sheets of plastic. But the shelves lining the walls were uncovered and filled, top to bottom, with creations.

Esme's eye caught on a stunning piece that looked to be pieces of sea glass melted together to make butterfly wings. She walked over to examine it more closely.

Len grumbled in her direction, "Stop. That's part of a five grand commission."

Disappointed, Esme said, "Ugh, I'm sorry. I just love everything that you do! I'm like a moth to a flame when I see this stuff."

Miles knowingly smirked at her. He was starting to learn her idiosyncrasies.

One eyebrow on Len's face arched ever so slightly, and very briefly. Had Esme's compliment cracked their shell just the smallest bit? Encouraged by this, Esme asked, "Will didn't come home last night and not at all today?"

"No. And I already told Jacob that he didn't pack a bag either." So Len knew who Jacob was.

Len slowly rotated the blue glass rod they were holding as they talked. Len continued, "He didn't bring any protein bars. He always does if he plans to stay out."

The thought of Len counting Will's protein bars nearly forced a laugh out of Esme. Still, it was information that let her know that Will hadn't planned on staying out after work.

She asked, "You didn't get a safety call or text?" Will and Len's arrangement to notify each other when either of them was going out with someone new was a detail Esme knew but Jacob wouldn't have known to ask about.

"No." Their grip on the glass bar tightened until their knuckles were white.

"Is there anything else you remember about the last time you saw him that could be useful in finding him?"

Len's eyes cast downward and the glass rod in their hands rotated more rapidly. Voice just above a whisper, they muttered, "No."

Esme watched in amazement as one end of the rod started to bulge and bend slightly upward. She wondered what it must feel like to have the power to change the very structure of something you were holding like that. The subtle, albeit nervous, use of magic was likely an unconscious outlet for their anxiety. Len was genuinely worried.

They probably wouldn't get much else out of Len, so it was time to wrap things up. Esme did what she could to reassure them. "Will is lucky to have you. You're the best kind of roommate; a loyal friend. Thanks for everything. We're going to find him, alright?"

Back at the car, Miles asked, "What was Len shaping toward the end? I noticed the glass moving but couldn't quite guess what it was."

Esme's cheeks heated. But she was an adult; she could answer this question with a straight face. "You didn't notice the pile of them sitting in boxes near one shelf?"

Miles looked confused. "Notice what?"

She smiled through her answer, feeling mischievous, "Len makes most of their money from very personal commissions."

She received the reaction she was hoping for as both eyebrows rose on his face. He shifted the car into drive. "Oh." He cleared his throat and chuckled. "I really didn't see that coming. Talent pays, I suppose."

Esme continued the small game she was playing with him. "Glass is sustainable. Plus, it retains body heat for as loooong as you need it."

She celebrated her victory as his eyes widened in response. She felt herself jerk slightly to one side as Miles swerved the car to avoid running into one of the miniature roundabouts that were common in neighborhoods in the city.

He apologized with a small chuckle, saying, "Sorry. I was a little distracted."

The sinful smile he sent her must have been some sort of payback, because it got a similar reaction out of her.

She remained silent and lost in her thoughts for the rest of the drive to the bar—the last place Will had been seen. It was enough time for her thoughts to turn from teasing to bleak. Normally Esme was the type of woman who skipped straight over sad when something bad was happening and became angry at herself, at the situation, at whatever deserved it. But in this case, she didn't have a direction to channel her negative energy and worries. Len's uncharacteristic display of anxiety had only made hers worse.

The desolate feeling growing within her was familiar, and very unwelcome. She was mourning. It was a premature, pointless emotion to have so early in their investigation, so she made an effort to push it away.

When they parked, Miles' head canted toward her, asking without saying a word. Instead of rejecting the feeling of vulnerability that his attentiveness usually stirred in her, she embraced it. "Thanks for being here today, for helping, like always. You're, like, really great."

Despite her lack of poetic finesse, the sentiment reached him, as his expression shifted to one of understanding. If he always reacted that way, maybe she could make learn to make opening her heart into a habit.

Walking into the dimly lit bar felt like returning home. She'd worked less frequently over the last few months, and she missed her time there.

While Jacob may have set out to decorate The Sanctuary of Spirits like it was a posh club in the Mayfair district of London, its patrons treated it more like a pub in Hounslow. There were a few quiet, intimate conversations going on in the bar, but it was more common to see its patrons arguing good-naturedly or bellowing loudly about their poor luck in some game of chance.

Esme was moderately surprised not to see Finn there. He visited most nights of the week for "the craic." Privately, she thought he was probably lonely, living out in the forest with only his hidden garden to keep him company. She'd texted him to ask if he'd been at the bar when Will was last seen, but Finn told her he'd stayed at home to rest up for the hellhound hunt.

The bar's chef, a púca named Wexley, had worked that evening, so she headed for the kitchen with Miles in tow. Wexley was a skilled and dependable chef who cooked food worthy of any high-end restaurant. In his natural state, he was very short, maybe two or three feet tall, covered in long black fur all over, with striking yellow eyes and large, rabbit-like ears. It wasn't a convenient form for kitchen tasks, so he took on a human shape while working.

The modern stainless steel kitchen gleamed under the much brighter lights of the work area. They'd come in the middle of the family hour's lunch rush. In one corner, a mixer was humming along. The smell of whatever was sizzling in the wok nearby made her mouth water. At the center of it all, Wexley was keeping everything running all on his own like clockwork. No music filled the space, as was common in most commercial kitchens. He said that he could hear when something was done. Given the size of his ears, Esme had no reason not to believe him.

"Wex, my guy, how are you?" Esme's voice sounded urgent, even to her own ears. She pointed at her companion. "You know Miles."

Wexley's striking yellow eyes, a feature he no longer altered when in his human form, darted her way. The vivid yellow sclera of his eyes matched the irises and the color stood out in stark contrast to his dark skin. His startled expression implied that he had been too focused on plating an entrée to notice their entrance.

"Esme!" he said her name, hissing out the S sound dramatically. "You here about Will?"

The púca was aware of Esme's secret role with the Assembly. Seeing how happy he was in his new life always helped her reconcile some of the unsavory choices she'd made for the sake of magekind in the past.

She answered, "Yep, I'm here because Jacob called me about Will. No one has heard from or seen him. We're worried."

The púca involuntarily took a half step back and a shudder ran through his entire body. She'd expected as much. It was the name of the leader of the mages that the púca reacted to. Jacob terrified him out of his wits.

She continued as if she hadn't noticed his loss of composure. "Did you contact Jacob after learning nothing from Len?"

Wexley nodded, his shapeshifted face displaying an inhuman blankness. She guessed that this was a fear response unique to púcas. She offered, "That was the right thing to do. It makes me proud." She wanted to thank him, but she knew well that she had to step around giving direct thanks to a Fae creature, even ones she liked.

Miles leaned against one shiny prep table. He checked his watch, appearing nonchalant as he asked, "Anything feel off last night before Will left?"

While on the surface it sounded like he was asking if Wexley's instincts were piqued at any point, what Miles actually wanted to know was whether the púca sensed the use of malevolent magic. From Finn, she'd learned that most mages and even non-human magic users didn't know what to look for in sensing the difference. The Extinction meant that there was simply no need for them to be taught otherwise—or so they thought.

Wexley thought for a moment, then answered, "He put a lot of eye drops in, but I didn't hear a fight going on in the bar. He seemed like he didn't want to go back on the floor after that, too."

Miles shot a puzzled expression her way. Luckily, Esme understood what Will's use of eyedrops meant. "Will can see magic, mostly when he wants to, sometimes when he doesn't. He says doing it dries his eyes out. Sorry, I thought you knew that."

Miles looked keen to hear more about Will's ability. She hoped he didn't get his hopes up because she knew Will; the likelihood of him joining up with the Corded Brotherhood sat at a negative fifteen on the scale of probable.

Wexley added, "He skedaddled out of here too."

Esme asked, "Do you know if he spent a lot of time talking to any specific customers?"

"I didn't leave the kitchen." Wexley put down the plate that he'd been working on and walked closer to her.

Out of the corner of her eye, she saw Miles flinch at this act of familiarity between them. The flinch wasn't an act of jealousy, though. It looked more like an automatic protective movement since púcas didn't have the best reputation.

Wexley lowered his voice for her ears only and said, "Sometimes the bar feels bad. Like something is off. Last night I didn't want to get near it. I have my babies to think about now." He had a pregnant mate waiting for him at home.

Gods above. That "bad feeling" sounded a lot like the púca felt malevolent magic being used, but didn't have the experience to label it as such. Wexley stepped back from her so he could call the on-duty barback to grab the plates he'd finished preparing while they talked.

What other information could she glean from the chef who never left the kitchen? She was starting to feel desperate to find anything that could lead her closer to finding Will.

Fueled by her rising apprehension, she racked her brain for a creative question to ask. "Did any orders for a regular come in? Maybe someone in the bar that night knows something."

Wexley sniffed, in a manner more akin to an animal than the human he appeared to be, at the stew he was ladling up as he thought. He added more salt to it and spoke. "A few. A bunless burger, caviar fish tacos, and two Fruit de l'arbre."

"Perfect. This was helpful, Wex. We're going to find him."

He bobbed his head upward and announced, "Do."

She led Miles out of the kitchen and back onto the street. Once outside, he feigned an American accent asking, "Ya gonna fill me in, partner?"

She playfully nudged him with one elbow and said, "We need to talk to Sylas and Juniper." But her spirits dropped as she noticed the time on his dashboard. "We can visit one of them today if we can get hiking gear ready quickly. The other will have to wait until tomorrow."

As they buckled their seat belts, Miles asked, "I was able to guess that their orders were the fruit plates. So, who were the other two orders for?"

"The burger was for a guy who couldn't tell you whether an ambulance just passed by. He pays attention to nothing beyond his podcasts most of the time. The tacos were for a water nymph< Beatrice, who is basically the opposite. She could tell you fifteen things about every person around her, but she gets distracted by every pretty face, so any information from her would be iffy."

Miles had known about the malevolent problem for years and had probably killed a couple of dozen, if not more, of them by that point. It was old hat for him, but it was still quite new to her. Malevolents were dangerous—there was no disputing that. She just hoped that they had nothing to do with Will's disappearance and that all of this was just one huge misunderstanding.

Esme found an antacid in her purse and popped it in her mouth. "But get this, when Wexley got all whispery he said that sometimes the bar feels bad. Like something is off. Last night, he didn't want to leave the kitchen because of it. Are you thinking what I'm thinking?"

He huffed out an aggrieved breath. "Another malevolent. Bloody hell. Just what we need."

Her thoughts exactly.

Chapter Thirty-Four

Sylas

Esme

After a decade of knowing Sylas, visiting him first felt like the natural decision. Sylas' territory, his domain, was across the highway from the forest where Juniper and Finn had settled. If their relationship became more serious, Esme suspected that the tree spirit would uproot and move to be with Sylas. However, she doubted that she'd live to see this happen. She'd learned that the longest-lived magical beings, such as dryads and Fae, were in no rush to make the sort of changes that humans leapt at the chance to do, like moving in with your partner or getting married. They simply had more time to make big life changes.

On the way out of town, they'd quickly dropped by Miles' house so that he could change, pack a bag, and check on Lily. Esme always had a bag packed for hiking, so the trip to her house was even shorter.

Hiking in late autumn was nothing to gamble on, so they both came prepared. The trunk was full of overstuffed hiking packs and gear for them both. The early sunset, combined with the possibility that a malevolent was involved in Will's disappearance, ignited a sense of urgency within them both. While Miles was usually a sedate, careful driver, on this occasion he drove over the speed limit all the way to the trailhead.

Esme listened to the crunch of their hurried steps as they hiked up the trail. The memory of how Miles had backed her up to the car slowly while she tested the fit of her ice cleats made her unzip the top of her jacket from the growing warmth. She'd planned on stowing the cleats in her pack, sized and ready to strap on her feet once they were up to the elevation where ice would likely be on the trail. With a flimsy excuse about checking the backward traction, he slowly pressed her backside to the side door and kissed her until her eyes crossed. Needless to say, she hadn't resisted.

The hike reminded her of when she first met Sylas, back in high school, when she was still new to magic. To ensure the safety of both their teens and potential bystanders, mage families would frequently organize hikes or overnight camping excursions in remote locations, granting the kids the freedom to practice their magic without the worry of accidental mishaps.

As serendipity would have it, the day she met the leshy for the first time was the day Esme's father was teaching her how to craft the illusion of fire, of all things. Like any forest-dwelling being, leshies hate fire. They'd hiked away from the trail into a ravine far off the beaten path for practice. Her dad's creation was fantastic. From the lifelike flames, the illusory spectacle of wisps of smoke danced and twirled.

This was before she knew that creating the illusion of scent was possible, like she frequently did with her trolls. So the absence of the telltale smell of smoke meant nothing to her then. Looking back on it, she imagined her dad must have skipped that step to further hide their presence. Try after try, she ended up only making something that looked more like an electronic candle than the lively force of nature that fire was.

She was probably on her twentieth attempt when her father froze, his body tense with anticipation. No sound of leaves crunching or twigs breaking offered any clue that they were no longer alone, but somehow he'd known.

Without warning, a deep voice resonated from behind them. "Magi, let your flames stay illusory, or I'll have no choice but to act."

She halted her casting immediately and studied her father for cues on how to react. At first, he remained stiff and wary, but then his posture suddenly relaxed completely. It was as if a sudden realization had washed over him, allowing him to let his guard down.

He turned toward the voice. Paralyzed with uncertainty, Esme remained rooted to the spot. Her father said, "I once read that leshies granted their companions the boon of seeing the future. Perhaps the stories are mistaken, old friend."

With that "old friend," she turned around to see her first nonhuman. Looking back, she was proud of her past self for keeping it together—mostly. She didn't shriek or run, but her mouth hung open in the most unladylike fashion.

The creature was maybe seven feet tall. His body was lean and vascular in the way that long-distance runners sometimes appear, with all the same parts that a human has. His grayish-brown skin was paired with shaggy hair that looked more like the Spanish moss that she had seen on vacation in Florida than human hair. The antlers that crowned his head added at least two feet to his already impressive height. But his face, and most notably his hazel eyes, were nearly human. The most striking feature of all was that she could see anger all over his alien face.

Sheer terror gripped her as her muscles locked into a rigid stance of panic. But her father wasn't running. For what felt like an eternity, the two faced each other in a tense standoff, though it was likely only a brief moment.

Eventually, she saw recognition flit across the creature's face. His stern expression morphed from murderous to something akin to surprised delight.

He said, "Robert! I had not recognized you. It has been so long. Perhaps too long."

Turning his massive antlers in her direction, the creature asked, "May I be introduced?"

Scuffing his boot in the dirt with a tinge of sadness, her father replied, "You're right, Sylas. That's why we came here today."

Her father gestured at Esme, saying, "I thought it was past time Esmeralda met you."

Knowing her father had hidden so much from her gave the memory a bittersweet edge. Lately, too many memories had left her feeling that way. She knew that it was too late to contain them, like she'd made her third wish and the genie had long escaped its bottle.

Upon reaching the clearing where they should be able to meet up with Sylas, Esme wasted no time in taking off her backpack and preparing them to wait for his arrival. "He should know we're here."

Esme spread out two folding mats to cover the top of a fallen tree trunk so that they could sit in relative comfort. They were at a high enough elevation that the air was frigid and everything was covered in a fine dusting of autumn snow. Looking out over the edge of the mountain, they could see that they were above the cloud line. It was a serene sight. The sun was bright, and the sky was blue above the blanketing grayness below. It wasn't a rare occurrence in the Pacific Northwest for the cloud level to be so low, but it still felt magical.

Miles reached into his pack and handed Esme a thermos and a camping spoon. Then he reached into his pack again and pulled out two more drink thermoses. She had expected to eat a sad, cold lunch of meal bars and old dried fruit. Instead, Miles offered her a warm cup of homemade soup and hot chocolate.

Amazed, she asked, "When did you have time to make this?"

She watched the steam rise from his soup as he replied, "I batch cook sometimes on days off. I try to keep a stock of frozen meals around for when I can't be bothered to cook."

She was starving. Neither of them had eaten since breakfast.

"This is amazing, thank you." Feeling guilty for letting him feed her, she pulled out her stash of cookies and brandished them in the air. "I brought dessert."

He blew on his soup to cool it, then said seriously, "We don't have to be even, lovely."

She tried to laugh it off, but he had been correct in guessing her thoughts. He'd done it again. When he looked at her like that, she felt like he could open her up like a book and page through all of her thoughts and emotions. Sometimes, at unexpected moments like this one, it felt as though they'd already experienced this dance before, and she needed a reminder of what steps came next.

"Okay, okay. Sorry." Still, little did he know she was already planning a dinner date at a wonderful bungalow where she was the chef.

Soon she heard heavy footsteps quickly striding in their direction. She warned Miles, "He's coming."

Esme stood to greet her old friend while Miles put everything away. She waved to Sylas as he approached. "We know you're busy, so I'll make this quick. We came to see if you knew anything about Will's disappearance two nights ago."

Sylas' pleasant pine resin smell enveloped the clearing. She learned that this meant that he was in a fine mood.

"Esmeralda, Miles, greetings." He glanced around the clearing as if looking for something, then said, "I do not recognize this name, Will."

He...what? Will had worked in the bar for four years by that point, and Sylas was a regular. Sylas knew who Will was.

She clarified in case he had misheard her. "Will, the barback. Extroverted, with dark hair, big muscles, tattoos, slightly more tan than me. He's the mage who can see magic."

Sylas' eyes evaded direct contact with hers, choosing instead to survey the treeline. "You say a mage is missing?" he asked dismissively, his body language completely uninterested. "The forest is vast, and I already have many troubles to deal with in preparation for the coming winter. I don't have the time to bother with the whereabouts of a single mage."

Esme stood in slack-jawed astonishment, feeling as though she'd been slapped. Sylas had always had the demeanor of a grumpy uncle, but this was not the leshy she knew. She caught Miles' gaze and furrowed her brow to signal to him that something wasn't right. He nodded infinitesimally, showing that he agreed.

She noticed Miles shifting one hand behind his back, tightly holding onto something. His stance was coiled, ready to spring into action. She knew for a fact that he didn't walk around carrying a gun all the time, but he clearly had his hand on something.

She'd have to try again with Sylas. "Wexley mentioned feeling 'bad magic' in the bar two nights ago. He said that you had dinner with Juniper that evening, so we're wondering if you noticed anything strange."

The leshy hesitated before responding in a low voice, "I did not." He gave her a stern look, then shot Miles a similar scowl. "Something needs my attention. I must go. I look forward to seeing you both again soon."

Sylas, her decade-long friend and one of the few she considered family, stomped away into the forest as if her visit was as inconsequential as a single snowflake in an avalanche.

Alarm bells continued to ring in her mind as they watched the leshy vanish among the trees. Miles' posture finally relaxed. He nodded toward the trail they had arrived on. She agreed it was time to get out of there, pronto.

The same urgency to flee that had infected Esme seemed to affect Miles too. It was much easier going down the mountain than it was going up, so her fast hike transformed into a jog and finally a full-out run the entire way back to the car. Miles stayed with her. Neither said a word, but the glances they shot each other spoke as loudly as words could. Whatever was going on, it was far worse than they'd expected.

As they drove toward the gas station parking lot where they could get a reliable phone signal to check in with Jacob, Esme couldn't keep quiet about what she'd seen Miles do in the clearing with Sylas. She tried but failed to keep the exasperation from her voice. "Did you seriously bring a gun to visit Sylas? Why?"

He answered her steadily. "Yes. I have one with me most of the time. I know you don't like them and frankly, neither do I. Unfortunately, it was my best chance of keeping attention off of you if he decided to..." He trailed off, then took a deep breath.

He parked the car, and she could finally look at him directly. His lips drew a stubborn line across his face and his eyes sparked with something that almost looked like anger. But it wasn't rage directed at her. This was his protective streak again.

Her voice came off a bit piqued when she replied. "I've done a pretty good job protecting myself recently, thank you very much."

He grinned wickedly. She was the mischievous one, not Miles, so this side of him was unfamiliar to her.

He smirked, voice low. "Sorry, you don't get to choose when I protect you."

Being a reasonable adult was a struggle sometimes when it was tempting to be unreasonable. He was right—even if it rankled her pride. He wouldn't have been protective if he didn't think there'd been an actual threat.

"So you felt that too? I didn't feel safe discussing it on the trail, but now…" She rubbed her legs nervously.

He agreed. "It felt too close to malevolent magic to me for comfort. Whatever is affecting Sylas must only be strong enough to distract him or divert his attention. We're lucky because that's probably what got us out of there without a fight. We need to call Jacob."

Esme nodded, too shaken just yet for words, and started dialing. Her fingers trembled with every tap on the screen.

"Hey, Jacob." She steadied her nerves, practicing her breathing exercises, before she said, "Something is very wrong with Sylas. But before I get into that, I think there's something that you and Miles need to know."

Anxiety—and desire—had consumed her since they ran into that stranger in the forest, causing her to make a critical oversight. She swallowed hard and confessed. "Will has been lying to everyone for years now. The Brotherhood and the Assembly should be very interested in finding him, alive and well."

In truth, she'd nearly forgotten what Will had revealed a couple of years ago during a sleep-deprived night at work. She'd been awake the entire night prior handling something inconsequential for the Assembly. For Will, it had been during a challenging period when he was constantly arguing with his family. After closing, he said that he needed to unwind, and had downed three shots of tequila in rapid succession.

Since his apartment was nearby, she walked him home. The reason they started talking about his ability to see magic escaped her now, but he'd drunkenly admitted the truth of his magic to her steps from his front door.

She recounted, "Will wasn't born being able to see magic like he claims. It's a spell. And if it's a spell, he can teach others to do it."

The rest of it poured out of her in an urgent rush. "Imagine what the Brotherhood could do if a more powerful mage than Will learned how to see magic. Because he doesn't just see magic—he can tell who cast it and what sort of magic was used. Will's magic could be the turning point. It could spare us from endless hours of trap-baiting and stakeouts. We could be the hunters, Jacob. We must find him."

Jacob

"This is most troubling, Esmeralda. Please take caution in approaching Juniper tomorrow. If my body would allow it, I would do it myself. Worry not. You're not the only ones I have out looking for Will.

"And I hate to be the bearer of bad news, but Maureen is also missing. There are...reasons why her absence wasn't noted until recently, but I won't go over them right now. Let's determine if her absence is linked to Will's disappearance.

"This should go without saying, but you are not to attempt to contact Sylas again without my say. Miles, ask Juniper all the right questions. Finn will join you tomorrow. Rest well tonight. Although I hope you won't need it in the end."

Jacob hung up the phone and glared at the leprechaun sitting before him. "You've already buggered up Esmeralda's training by teaching her to reach into the infernal. You've also forced my hand to reveal her heritage. I do not count those behaviors as being entirely neighborly, Finnegan."

Finn looked not the least bit disgruntled by Jacob's stare, tone, or words. "Aye, well, 'twas about time she learned the truth of it. I did ya a favor and ya know it."

"If Will truly can teach others how to see magic, his safety could be invaluable. I hope even you, such an unserious creature, can see that."

Gruffly, Jacob switched the topic. "Esmeralda isn't one to wait around, twiddling her thumbs when her friends are in danger. If Juniper was infected with whatever ensorcellment was strong enough to affect Sylas, she would be even deeper within the grasp of the malevolent magic. Your wonderful ifrit gift means that you have more sustainable firepower than even I do. Keep in mind that Juniper is a tree spirit..."

His voice hardened into an ax as he said, "And trees burn." He knew that what he said was ruthless, but he didn't feel like dissembling in the present company.

"I need to know that you will do what Esmeralda will most certainly hesitate to do if required. I trust Miles, but he is better suited to shield her, or you, from harm rather than act offensively against a dryad."

The leprechaun wasn't eager to volunteer. He replied, "I think you might underestimate Esme. But, aye, if I have no choice, I'll do what I must. But I'll be pointin' a finger at you after when she's not happy about it."

So long as she survived, Jacob could live with that.

Esme

The sky back in Seattle was the soft, muted gray of low-lying clouds that the moon's light had trouble penetrating. Miles and Esme stood very close on her front porch, still bundled in their hiking coats, deciding whether they wanted to say goodnight then or later.

Her words puffed out as mist in the cold air. "Oh my gods, I'm such a jerk. I can't believe I didn't even ask if you had to work tomorrow." She buried her face in her frozen hands.

"Well, it is the time of year that I can catch cold with no one questioning it. Please, look at me." He moved one hand slowly to tip her chin up. She allowed it.

The weight in his gaze took her by surprise. "I said that I'm with you."

It was almost too much. His intensity made her feel ruined for anyone else. He had a bad habit of accidentally turning into a fairytale king when it was just the two of them.

She changed the subject to prevent herself from drowning in his eyes. "So, if you're with me... stay with me tonight?"

Once the question was out of her mouth, she regretted it. It came across as being too needy to her own ears. As she felt a creeping disquiet settle in, she couldn't help but draw parallels to the suffocating fear of being alone that had haunted her after her parents' deaths.

She added a bit too hastily for him not to notice her unease, "Or I can go to your house. This way we can leave bright and early to meet Finn and talk to Juniper."

She felt silly for feeling that way, but she comforted herself knowing that at least this time she was running toward him.

His face broke into the same lazy-eyed smile that she had seen the night before when she had asked him to bed. "I'd love nothing more."

Chapter Thirty-Five

No Fire, No Escape

Will

"No, no, no fire!" Maureen rocketed upwards with surprising speed, out of her balled-up position. She tackled Will, easily sixty pounds heavier than her, who was crouched in a squat, making them both roll off their feet sideways onto the ground.

That was the first thing Will had heard Maureen say or do that wasn't cowering in a corner since he woke up in the forest prison. He was freezing cold because his clothing was slightly damp from lying on the forest floor for hours. All he'd been trying to do was start a tiny fire using some magic and a few of the drier leaves and sticks that he could find.

When you were as physically imposing as he was, and not a complete asshole, you learned to make yourself appear to be more tame, more welcoming, and less imposing, so that you didn't make people around you too uncomfortable. Struggling to keep this in mind, Will scrambled back up to his feet and backed away from her, trying to placate her with raised hands. She may be a lot smaller than him, but her reputation was scary.

His energy tank was near zero, he was freezing, and he already had a caffeine withdrawal headache. Plus, he'd just been tackled by a mousey middle-aged woman for trying to help her. So he failed to keep his tone in check when he yelled back, indignant with outrage, "You say nothing for nearly a day and immediately assault me when I try to make us both a bit more comfortable? Maureen, what the hell?"

It dawned on him that she was still lying on the ground where she'd tackled him, protectively clutching her side. She was panting and making a grunting sound every few breaths. It seemed impossible that she could have hurt herself that badly with a simple tackle.

His voice gentled. "Whoa, whoa, are you hurt? Is it on your side?"

She continued to pant rapidly, but nodded slightly. Her hair was matted and had leaves sticking out of it. Her cheeks were sunken, her face dirty, and her eyes... Her eyes looked like they'd seen too much.

"Damn chica, just breathe. What can I do to help?" He chuckled and said a bit sassily, "Since a small fire is out of the question."

Putting one frozen hand to his forehead, he rubbed it anxiously and studied her. "Okay, we're both freezing and you don't look to be in too good of shape right now. I say we share some completely platonic warmth and try to figure this shit out together, yeah?"

To his surprise, she nodded once more. It was probably going to be the most awkward thing that he'd ever done, but at least they would both be a bit more comfortable. She knew she wasn't his type, anyway.

He said, "Okay, I'm coming down, but I don't want to make whatever is going on with you worse. Should I be the big or little spoon?"

She panted out, "Back." Then she gasped and said in a rush, "No arms."

He lowered himself to the ground and inched closer to her back. "I'm going to bring my legs to yours too, okay? Did you hurt your side or something?"

He could hear her make an affirmative grunt. Her clothing and hair stank, but he wagered he smelled little better. All he had to do was pretend like he was cuddling with one of his aunties and everything would be fine. It would be awkward, but fine. He could feel himself thaw slightly from where their bodies were close.

They lay there quietly for a long time. Maureen's breathing shallowed. She was probably asleep. How long they lay there, he wasn't certain. When she woke up, he'd try to get more information from her about what was happening. He wouldn't bother her yet, though. If she felt comfortable enough to sleep, that probably meant that they had time before whoever locked them up came back.

He needed to know where they were, why the hell they'd been captured, and who had locked them up. His stomach growled, and he tried to ignore how long it had been since he last ate or drank anything. He'd seen the little pit lined with leaves that Maureen had dug to drink collected rainwater from. Eventually, he'd have to join her in using it unless his captor started caring for them. The whole situation felt like it was ripped out of a corny horror movie, but his aches and pains proved it was his reality.

Maureen abruptly woke up later, her startled movement causing her to whimper in pain. She panted out, "Maybe broken ribs."

Will had drifted off to sleep at some point too, but this revelation completely woke him up. He asked, still next to her for warmth, "Did our jailer do that to you?"

He saw and felt her head nod. Holy gods. He did not like this.

After what felt like an eternity, she picked the conversation back up in a whisper. "Because I tried to make a fire."

Her tackle had been protective - of him, of herself probably. He needed her to keep talking. If he knew more, maybe they could strategize a way out together.

He whisper-hissed, "Maureen, you are a full-fledged seated member of the Assembly, a freaking girl boss. I need you to get it together. Who the hell tossed you in here and beat you?"

She started shaking her head, agitating more leaves into his face. He tried again. "I know you're scared, but we have to get out of here. There's two of us now."

He could practically hear the tears in her eyes as she whispered back, "You don't know what she's capable of." She carefully lifted her hand to point.

That's when Will noticed the bloodied camouflage jacket outside the cage, with one amputated arm still sticking out of the sleeve. Frantic now, his heart hammering in his chest, he asked, "Who?!"

Chapter Thirty-Six

Blursed Discovery

Esme

The sun hadn't quite risen yet, so Miles' bedroom was still dark but for the light that seeped in through the blinds. Lily was having a doggy dream at the foot of the bed, tiny yips escaping her. In Esme's mind, she could see those huge paws flailing, chasing dream rabbits.

Miles lay on his side, facing away, breathing deeply. His pillow was positioned in a way that offered a tempting spot to lay her head beside his. She edged closer, careful not to wobble the bed. As far as she could tell, the man rarely slept, so she wouldn't wake him yet.

Her head barely touched the pillow before her resolve slipped away. She breathed in the scent of him. He smelled like soap mixed with the traces of their mingled sweat and that indefinable, addictive fragrance that could only be labeled "man." She knew she shouldn't do it, but her lips found their way to the spot where his neck met his shoulders.

"Mmm. Good morning." His words came out groggy, sleep-drunk.

"Morning." She continued her work of drawing a torc of kisses around his neck. She moved her hand around to the front of his body and slowly began to massage his arms and chest.

She could hear the smile in his voice when he warned, "Keep going, and we won't leave this bed for a while, lovely."

If she could freeze time, she would. With Sylas trapped in a malevolent enchantment, the chances of a painless outcome were unfortunately very low. She was avoiding the inevitable pain by seeking pleasure.

"Is that a promise?" Her hand reached lower. This elicited the groan she'd been hoping for.

As quick as lightning, he was on top of her in a grappling mount position, his legs straddling hers and his hips in exactly the right spot. That roguish grin was back on his face.

Sheltered under his weight, she laughed. "Oh, a new type of sparring?" She wiggled her hips and suggested, "Let's see who taps out first."

After a morning of trying to hide from reality, they set out to find Juniper, the seriousness of the mission pulling them back down to earth. Finn dramatically patted his stomach. "So what I'm sayin' is that we should grab a bucket of fried chicken after this. I'm already starvin'."

Out of the corner of her eye, Esme noticed Miles watching her. This act was initially confusing to her until she heard him conspiratorially tell Finn, "If you go for spicy, count me in, mate."

Men and their stomachs.

The mere thought of food made her feel sick. Their morning together had been a much-needed reprieve, but the anxiety still found an opening and had crept back in. That evening would mark a full forty-eight hours since Will had gone missing. The clock was ticking.

Only evergreen trees could grow at the higher elevations in the mountains where winters were harsher and the snow could get deep. Because Juniper appeared to be a deciduous tree spirit, they stuck to the lower elevation areas near the river. The slightly warmer air and reduction of ice and snow made for an easier hike than the one they'd experienced meeting Sylas the day before.

Esme stepped over a large fallen branch and asked Finn, "So, you've seriously never visited Juniper at home? You're neighbors!"

He snorted out a derisive laugh. "Ya act like I've never met her man. I've no wish to be torn into four meaty segments by a leshy."

After Finn eventually scrambled over the same large branch, Esme said, "This feels like a blast from the past, eh? All we need now is for Miles to quote poetry, and it will be like history repeating itself. Miles, do you have anything for us? Maybe that's just what the universe needs to give us a hint about where to go."

She raised her gloved hands to the sky, beseeching the universe to give them a sign, any sign. By this point, they'd already traversed a few ravines that fed into the river.

Miles scratched his head thoughtfully. "Okay, here goes. 'Buy a pup and your money will buy love unflinching that cannot lie.'"

Maybe she should have tried harder to convince him to bring Lily. He'd chosen to leave her at home because of the unknown amount of hiking they'd be doing. She asked, "Who was that one by?"

"Rudyard Kipling."

She was about to comment on her love of the snake in that movie when a finger hit her ribs, hard. The rising frustration from the forceful poking vanished when she noticed the troubled look on Finn's face. He was holding up one finger to his lips in a quieting gesture. Miles had also stopped walking.

Esme opened herself to the magic in the world around her. The shift in the forest's atmosphere in one direction was impossible to ignore—it felt like a neon sign flashing "Magic Straight Ahead." The sickening impression it left was too familiar.

Something or someone was not being subtle with their magic. Either the malevolent was certain that it wasn't risking being caught or, more troublingly, it was confident in its ability to squash any problems that came its way. With Juniper's home somewhere nearby, the outlook for her safety appeared grim.

"Finn," she said with trepidation, barely moving her lips, "Please tell me you can evade notice if you try hard enough. That seems like something a leprechaun should be able to do."

He whispered back, moving closer to her side, "It's a bit necessary, as you can imagine. Though, I'm not as good as I once was, with my impressive height an' all."

"Great. Show us how impressive you are by skulking around toward the magic if you can. Don't get caught."

She had a terrible suspicion that they'd need a concealed card up one sleeve if fighting whatever was out there became necessary.

Miles signaled his approval of her plan by flashing a low thumbs up where his hand hung down by his thigh. Seeing this, she knew that he also felt it was necessary to be discreet. Coming closer, he murmured, "Whatever is out there is highly intelligent, if it has affected Sylas. Let's hope it doesn't have a familiar face."

Icy claws of apprehension raked down her spine. She zipped her coat closed and kept on walking.

Finn visibly shivered, mimicking her sentiment, and mumbled back, "It's a plan."

The next step he took became audibly quieter. Esme felt her attention involuntarily slide away from him as he walked in the direction where the malevolent magic was the strongest.

"Follow and act normal. We might be under surveillance." Miles said the last quietly, with a tone more of a question than a command, as he joined her side. "Smart plan using Finn's talents that way. You sure you don't want to take Brotherhood vows?"

She laughed this off. She appreciated that he tried to make a joke, given the situation. By this point, his continued solicitations to join the Corded Brotherhood were an inside joke between them. He thought that she'd be a perfect fit, and she denied it. Why take vows when she was already doing the dirty work—no vow needed? His demeanor when he asked the first time hinted that the Brotherhood had a similar significance for him as the Assembly did for her.

They walked slightly askew but still toward the direction they felt the malevolent magic most intensely. With each step, Esme felt a different part of her skin turn to gooseflesh.

Please don't let it be a familiar face; please let Juniper be alright.

Miles must have noticed her uneasiness because he tried to reassure her. "Remember what happened with Sylas? He barely registered our presence. If we find Juniper, it will probably be the same. But she's far weaker than he is. We can grab her and bring her back to Jacob to deal with. That way, we can find out what is wrong with both of them and fix it."

It was a good plan. His idea of how things would go was optimistic, but she had no reason to doubt him. Every time she'd seen him in action, he'd done something amazing to her eyes. So she put on a show of having a cheerful conversation and kept walking.

Will

Hearing the faintest crunch of a footstep, Will darted upward from his spot where he'd been cradling Maureen. Instead of standing, she tucked herself into a ball as tightly as her injured ribs would allow and covered her head with her arms.

Still, hope bloomed in his chest when he laid eyes upon a familiar face.

But the spark of hope died a gruesome, bloody, rotten death when the person he thought he knew kicked the severed arm at their cage and hissed, "Quiet!"

He noticed then that his jailer was dragging an ungainly, unidentifiable bundle behind her. She paused, then rapidly sank into a crouch next to the bundle. Looking more like a hungry predator than the woman he'd known, she sniffed hungrily at the bundle while mumbling to herself.

Just as rapidly, she stood and motioned with one gnarled hand to open a small section of their cage with magic. Instinct took over and Will staggered backward, trying to stay as far away from her—from it—as possible. Blessedly, their jailer wasn't interested in either of them. She lifted the bundle and flung it into the cage with them.

In a blink of an eye, the hole in the cage closed again. She—it, because this was not the person Will had known—scuttled away without another word to them, vocalizing a mumbling, broken tune. The only word he could make out of it was "die."

In his naivety, he dared to hope that she'd given them a bundle of food or water. Will walked over to the bundle and brushed away some of the dirt and pine needles caked to it. His fingers came back bloody.

Frantically, he brushed away more of the detritus to reveal pale skin and pointed ears. It was Finn, unconscious but breathing, blood streaming from a head wound and gashes from being dragged across the forest floor.

Esme

Only the breeze and the crunch of their boots disrupted the calm of the autumn forest. It was too quiet without Finn's chattering to fill the silence. The lack of it was profound enough to make her second-guess her decision to send Finn off alone. It didn't help that Miles wasn't given to idle chatter when hunting, either.

Out of nowhere, a sudden rush of air pulled at the loose strands of hair on the side nearest to Miles. Her senses hadn't alerted her to anything approaching. Before she could guess at its cause, Miles crumpled forward bonelessly, collapsing to the ground in a heap.

Time slowed as her brain caught up. Horror gripped her as the reality of what had just happened finally registered. Something, someone had chopped downward with force at the back of his head. With a panicked shriek that only vaguely resembled his name, she dove to his side.

Her relief at the lack of blood in his hair was short-lived.

By instinctively checking on him, she avoided a second attack that whizzed past where her body had been less than a second ago. Glancing up, she saw a massive tree branch arc through the air. She bent backward just in time to watch the impromptu club dance across her chest in a near miss.

Allowing her back to hit the ground, she curved her spine into a C-shape, using it as a fulcrum to roll forward. She landed with one foot under her backside for a ready spring upward. The other foot she planted forward to give her the option of lunging toward her opponent—a classic combat-ready stance.

Fear, anger, and confusion battled for control as she identified their assailant.

"Juniper?!"

Instead of answering, Juniper lunged forward, spittle flying from her mouth, snarling like a wild dog instead of the dryad she was.

What in the name of all the gods was happening?

Esme sprang upward, lunging sideways at the last moment to avoid Juniper's grasping fingers. The tree spirit's bark-like skin was tough, and her fingernails were even tougher, like spikes of ironwood jutting out from old oak.

Esme had to try again. Circling, trying to look relaxed and non-threatening while maintaining a direct line of sight with the rabid dryad, she nearly pleaded, "Juniper, June, it's me,

Esme. I talked to Sylas yesterday. Something is wrong with him, too. We're here to help you."

The creature that Juniper had become lunged forward again, teeth bared, with raking claws outstretched toward her. Esme darted sideways, leaving much more space between them than the first time. Then she hadn't been prepared for the possibility of attack.

She was prepared now, but doubt still crept in, whispering that perhaps she was not strong enough, not skilled enough to face this challenge alone. Her own history proved that she couldn't deal with a malevolent threat without help. She needed to stop this fight, grab Juniper, get Miles to a hospital, and find Finn.

The hollow, hoarse scream that turned into sobs she heard next would echo in her nightmares for years. "Es…me…oh my gods!"

Hoping to get Juniper away from a helpless Miles, Esme made herself a target by running toward the scream. Esme couldn't entertain the possibility that Miles was anything more than knocked out. Anything worse and she couldn't do what she needed to.

She could hear Juniper's feet pounding behind her. The ploy had worked. Now she had to distract her long enough to cast a conjuration.

Ten steps later, her foot hit something that smacked wetly against her calf. In her glance down, she saw that it was a bloody severed arm. She nearly screamed, half in surprise and half in morbid disgust, but before she could, she ran into something much bigger.

A cage. Will. And more.

The person they'd been searching for stood weakly at the bars made of twisting vines and branches. Will was repeating her name over and over like a crazed incantation. A person, probably a woman, was lying on the ground nearby, body tucked tightly into a ball. There was also a bundle lying at Will's feet.

The bundle was wearing Finn's clothing.

Juniper cut short Esme's moment of stunned disbelief by wrapping her arms around her. The suffocating strength of her hold was like the unyielding roots of an ancient tree. As the air left Esme's lungs, she felt an important part of herself, the part that maintained the balance between the darkness and light within her, slide away with her remaining breath.

The relentless, cold numbness held reign over her for a second time. There was a sort of symmetrical, dangerous beauty to it. The last time she'd felt this way, she'd been the one choking Miles, and now she was succumbing to the same fate. The faces she'd failed to protect swam in a haze of regret across the surface of her mind.

She heard Juniper hiss, "A sister...but still meat."

No.

The violet in her eyes was replaced by the black of her rising malice.

Her anger broke through the haze with a violence unique to the infernal, unique to her blood. Cloaked in the darkest shadows of brimstone, her rage tore through the barrier, dividing the infernal and Earth to emerge as something new; something not completely of her own making.

She sensed two tentacles that were lined with rows of sharp, hooked claws creep around Juniper's neck. As they sank into wooden flesh, they jerked backward with a sudden, sharp yank. The suffocating pressure on her ribs released at once.

Slumping to her knees, she felt her body drag in a jagged breath. Feeling detached from reality, she looked around to see what she had conjured. Juniper slashed at the grasping tentacles that streamed from the back of a creature out of nightmares. Its lower body, minus the eldritch abominations that it carried on its back, had the muscular look of her shadowcat. Its neck had a thick scruff, nearly a mane, that ended in a face with the jaws and fangs of an enraged hellhound.

Her hand hit the rough edge of the cage, waking her slightly to the other half of her concern.

"Will," her voice came out toneless, cold, not at all what a survivor needed to hear from his rescuer. "Do whatever it takes to get out of that cage. Is Finn alive?"

She heard a weak, "Yeah."

"Good. Do it."

She pushed herself back to her feet, watching, sensing the eldritch horror harassing the thing that Juniper had become with tentacles and claws. She felt Will kindle a tiny flame near the base of one corner of the cage and heard him say, "Maureen, help me!"

Will

"Maureen, get your shit together and help me burn this cage. Esme is here, fu...fighting Juniper. Gods above. Get up." Will nearly shouted the last, but his throat was too dry for that.

Maureen croaked, "Esme?"

"Yes, you crazy hag, help me now." What he saw outside the cage he had no words for. It looked like a creature from a video game come to life. He poured every ounce of his power into a tiny stream of fire. It wasn't enough. They'd never get out of there.

Again, she asked, "E...Esme is here?"

He snapped, "Open your eyes, woman."

Maureen opened her eyes just in time to see the conjured abomination crash through the underbrush, headed away from them. And just like that, Will saw hope fill her eyes. The feeling was contagious because he felt it too as he watched fire cascade from her hands onto the wooden bars of their cage.

Esme

The moment Esme smelled smoke coming from the cage, Juniper lost the last ounce of sanity she possessed. The rabid tree spirit snarled, bit, and clawed at the still-grasping tentacles in response to the presence of fire nearby. She moved in an erratic flurry of motion that made the tentacles lose purchase on her wooden skin.

Conjured vines snaked out of the ground near Esme's feet while the living cage surrounding her friends groaned behind her. Esme danced out of the way, only for the eager vines to follow her every move. Unable to slap or kick them away, one took her by surprise and wrapped tightly around her left thigh. She tugged and tugged, but she couldn't budge it.

Dread for her impending fate nearly pierced the empty detachment she wore like a second skin when she heard another groan in the distance. Miles was awake.

The problem was that Juniper heard it too.

Her wild green hair whipped around to face the new sound. The vine attached to Esme's leg tightened as Juniper broke free of the eldritch beast's attempt to constrain her.

By the time Juniper had taken two strides toward Miles, Esme had plunged straight back into the darkness—the darkness that whispered sweet words of safety and power. The incredible pain, now coming from both of her legs, soon felt like nothing more problematic than an insect buzzing in her ear.

Miles had held her that morning. With a gentle touch and whispered words, he had comforted her and reminded her he would be by her side through it all. He'd called her "lovely."

In a place of dangerous calm, Esme lost herself in the infernal darkness. She watched as her vision joined the eyes of her eldritch conjuration to become one. On four paws, she and her conjuration sprinted across the forest floor, sending pine needles and dirt flying in their wake. With no need to breathe in this body, they covered the distance without tiring. The surroundings blurred into a disorganized flurry of shades of gray.

They quickly caught up to their prey, crashing through the underbrush ahead. There was Miles, now turned on his side, only a dozen feet away.

Thrusting conjured muscles enhanced with infernal power, they leapt to collide bodily into Juniper's back, bringing them both down into a heap on the ground. The eldritch beast, with Esme in tow, scrambled from the whirlwind of their bodies to overtake the dryad, who was lying face down in the leaf litter.

With cat-like claws and a wolf's bite, they shredded the wooden skin. Something sticky like sap leaked onto their tongue, but that didn't matter. It was still moving.

Their prey *needed* to stop moving.

So they ripped and bit until they saw a thing of smoke and brimstone waft from their prey's body upward, toward the sky.

Only when they heard a familiar name groan out of the other body nearby did their head snap up from ripping and tearing.

Shaking violently from head to toe in shock, Esme barely held onto the phone she had next to her ear.

"Ja…" Her throat tightened, but she fought the sobs, speaking through gritted teeth. "Jacob. Jacob. I…I killed her." She looked over at the place where Juniper's body lay, torn to pieces.

The place within her where the numbing anesthesia had flowed was now filled with too much emotion, with grief and regret. A sob ripped from her throat.

She'd stepped over her line.

No, she'd *leapt* over the line that she'd held as her moral limit for a decade with barely a second thought.

And she'd done it to a friend.

Chapter Thirty-Seven

Living is a Lesson

Miles

For some unknown reason, healing himself had always been less effective than on others. Miles had barely been conscious when he'd done what he could to reduce his concussion and the bruising. He'd woken to see Esme in a heap nearby.

Then he saw the aftermath of what she'd done, and understood. The only thing that he could do for her immediately was ensure that she was uninjured and take charge. She'd just made her first kill, and it was, or rather had been, at some point, a friend. It was the perfect storm of unfortunate circumstances. He'd seen countless injuries before, but nothing compared to the raw devastation in Esme's eyes.

To his astonishment, Esme didn't push him away as he held her tightly, feeling her trembling in his arms. The combination of her tense body language and recent sensitivity about her ability to defend herself made him uncertain how his affection would be received. It was clear from her silence that she wasn't ready to talk yet, so he gently reassured her of his presence before moving on to other matters.

Given the complexity of the situation, triage was necessary. Miles started by giving Finn a quick evaluation. His pulse felt steady and strong. Lacking a stethoscope or pulse oximeter, Miles did what he could to assess Finn's breathing. Lifting the leprechaun's shirt, he saw no evidence of retractions around his neck or at the bottoms of his ribs. Nor did Finn wheeze with each breath. If he had, these would be signs that his lungs were laboring to bring in adequate air. However, he had half-dried blood all over him from a head injury. Miles had only escaped a similar fate by luck.

With Finn stable enough for the moment, Miles grabbed the extra water bottles from his pack and handed them to Will and Maureen. He cautioned them, "Slowly. Take only sips, even if you want to down it all at once. I think Esme has a few leftover biscuits, too." He rummaged around in her pack and handed them out, repeating his warning of restraint.

From a glance, he could tell that Will's main problem was dehydration and cold exposure. Things that would heal well in time. But Maureen sat protectively, cradling her middle, as if hurt.

He asked, "Maureen, what's wrong?"

She barely looked him in the eyes and cringed back like she was afraid that he would lash out at her. He'd seen the woman verbally harass Esme on occasion, so he wasn't her biggest fan, but he'd do what he could to help her without using his healing magic.

Seeing her reaction, he gentled his tone. "Hey, hey, Maureen. Remember, I'm a doctor. I'm here to help. You're safe now. Can I see what is bothering you on your stomach?"

She glanced up at him and back down hastily.

Will lightly touched her shoulder and said, "Boss lady, you can trust him. Let him see your ribs."

Encouraged, she nodded once, resolute. Slowly, Miles lifted the side of her vomit-and-dirt-caked shirt. He thought that he also smelled other biological odors on her, but knew that it would only make matters worse if he mentioned it. Her side was a calico of bruises of varying ages. As far as he could tell without an X-ray, he guessed a few ribs might be fractured. Her recovery would take much longer than Will's.

Both would also require a different type of healing than he was capable of. Finding them therapy was a problem for later.

Next came the tricky part. He hadn't overtaxed himself healing his concussion, but passing out from overextending himself wouldn't help matters right then. He needed to sneak Finn away from the group so he could heal the leprechaun just enough for him to regain consciousness and mobility. Neither Will nor Maureen knew of his healing ability, and he wanted to keep it that way. Getting them all out of the forest discreetly was going to be next to impossible, given Finn's and Maureen's current states. Hopefully, once Finn was healed, Esme would be in a state where she could talk again.

He walked back over to Esme and gritted his teeth, hating what he had to do. Crouching down, he lifted her face to his. He kept his volume low, only for the two of them, but still commanding. "Esmeralda. I need to heal Finn in private. You need to stand up and put on a show of strength for Will and Maureen. Right now, they think that you're the strongest person they've ever met. Act like it."

He wasn't one to give her orders, but she needed some guidance just then. Her big violet eyes bore into his, filled with grief and regret. But behind those, he saw a new sort of hardness there. Good; she'd need to lean into that when times got tough.

Brushing a stray strand of hair from her face, he encouraged her, "You did the right thing." Then he hardened his voice. "Now, up."

She stood without reluctance and looked over at Will and Maureen, then down at Finn. He noted that she had been far less reluctant to order him around. Voice firm, she commanded, "Go."

He could feel a smile tug at his lips, but that could send mixed signals in her present state so, he squashed it before it could grow. His emotions around this woman were crazed, almost too much to contain sometimes. The urge to kiss her was nearly overwhelming, but he settled for stealing a kiss on the cheek.

They walked over to Will and Maureen together. He made his excuses, saying that he was going to carry Finn home to recover. Finally, he saw Esme and Will embrace each other tightly, sobbing anew. Will reached out one arm and pulled Maureen into it.

With them distracted, Miles carefully lifted Finn into a fireman's carry and set off into the forest, leaving them to complete their first step toward recovery.

Will
Two days later

Will was the last to arrive. The empty feeling of The Sanctuary of Spirits was something he'd only experienced when his calves ached from hours of standing and his eyelids began to droop at the end of the night. Everything looked so different being there so early in the day.

Someone had pushed a couple of tables together to form one larger unit near the bar. Jacob sat at the head of the rectangle with Maureen on his right. She looked worlds better than when he'd last seen her. Her hair was brushed and her clothes were immaculate, like normal. Finn perched on a seat next to her, swinging his legs playfully in the air. Across from them, Esme and Miles sat, their expressions a mixture of curiosity and concern. That left the seat facing the man in charge for him. Great.

Will hesitated, then awkwardly took the vacant seat. It was a strange sensation to be back in reality. All he'd done for the past two days was drink, eat, and sleep, on repeat. He knew his roommate was trying to hide their concern, but he could see right through Len's inscrutable act—they were worried about him. Len had nagged him until he relented and went to the gym like normal early that morning.

Will only lasted halfway through a workout before he felt the need to escape. He had returned home to watch more television in his room, bundled under the sheets. All he'd wanted to do was to turn off his brain for a few more hours.

Honestly, he was worried about himself, too. He hoped that this little meeting with the big man would give them all some closure on what had happened with Juniper. Because, seriously, what the hell had happened? She was eating people. She was planning on eating them. He knew he'd missed out on the worst of it. Juniper had been somewhere else for most of the time he was imprisoned. Thank goodness, because that meant that he hadn't been beaten like Maureen had.

Will still couldn't figure out why Esme and her new boyfriend, of all people, had rescued them. He knew that any sort of governing body like the Assembly had to have a group that enforced its rules. But Esme and Miles? He knew she was a badass in a bar fight, but didn't know she could conjure the monster he saw in the forest. Miles was a doctor. He couldn't possibly have time for messing around with Assembly business after hours...right?

Will had seen Esme stress cry before, but not like she had after.... He couldn't think about it. Not right then. It needed to stay in his nightmares, not his waking life. All the same, he was worried about her because she was still off kilter. He'd seen the body afterward. Esme had obliterated Juniper—for him, for Maureen, for Finn.

Finally, the big man spoke, cutting through Will's woolgathering. "Esmeralda, would you please bring in the refreshments I've prepared from the kitchen? They should be obvious when you walk in."

Esme jumped when she heard her name. "Uhh, sure..."

Will shifted in his seat when he saw Miles and Jacob exchange a fleeting look. Alright, he wasn't crazy. The vibe of the room was decidedly off.

Jacob said, "I'll wait for Esmeralda to return before we get started."

She came back out a few moments later with one of her fake smiles plastered on her face and a bead of sweat on her forehead. The tray she carried had six generic lidded coffee cups on it. Will watched the bead of sweat drip down the side of her face to disappear on her neck. Chica only perspired like that on busy weekend nights. Why was she doing it then? Despite his concerns, he accepted his drink with thanks because he was fully intimidated by every single one of the table's occupants.

Jacob took a dignified sip of his beverage and began. "Welcome. I understand it might still be an uncomfortable topic, but we need to talk about what happened with Juniper."

He leaned over to the tidy pile of papers he'd placed off to the side. Leafing through them carefully, he pulled one out. "I have informed the local dryads of Juniper's death. They will hold a ceremony for her at the next full moon. The dryad community—actually, let me be precise—the entire magical community, does not know the circumstances of her death. The word is that she died in a freak forest fire set by lightning."

He gave Esme a sympathetic look.

Jacob's question brooked no arguments. "The story must remain as such. Do each of you understand? I am ordering you to lie."

Esme took a sip of her drink, and Miles rubbed her back. At some point, Will needed to tell her the truth—that she'd done the right thing. But at the moment, he thought his words would sound empty at best.

"Sylas is unharmed, and the curse upon him is now broken. He will be...recovering in his forest for the foreseeable future. It would be best if we left him to it."

Knowing that leshy, Will thought the big boss meant "let him rage alone" but didn't want to say it aloud. His expression left the leshy's future up in the air.

Jacob switched topics abruptly. "Guillermo."

Will shifted nervously once more in his seat. The boss man had just used his real name. This couldn't be good.

"You are now an official employee of the Assembly. Welcome to the team. Keep your lips sealed about everything you saw in that forest. Help us with a tiny project that we have for you and you will be paid."

He placed his hand firmly in the air to forestall anything Will was about to say. "Worry not, you won't be doing anything dangerous. Unfortunately, I cannot condone giving you a choice in the matter, given the circumstances. Am I understood, young man?"

Jacob didn't even have to change his facial expression to make Will nod frantically in agreement. He was starting to understand why Wexley avoided Jacob like the plague. Seeking the comfort of something warm in his hands, he reached for his cup.

So far, Maureen hadn't spoken. She looked spaced out. She was just sitting there as though Jacob subtly threatening him was a normal daily occurrence. For all he knew, it could have been her idea. When she noticed him looking at her, she reached for her cup, too. Will wasn't the best at keeping his mouth shut, even when intimidated. So he raised his cup and said, sarcastically, "Cheers to a second income stream, I guess."

This forced a small smile to bloom on Esme's lips. His sass had been worth it then. Finn enthusiastically cheered, "Sláinte!"

Each put their respective cups to their mouth and sipped. When the liquid touched Will's tongue, the coppery, slightly salty, too-thick liquid assaulted his senses. Blood. Will gagged, nearly losing his breakfast, before he spat it out across the table.

"Uck, Oh my gods!" Will exclaimed, his voice waspish even to his own ears. He looked for a napkin to clean it out of his mouth.

Maureen's gaze snapped toward, him, her eyes widening in realization. Before anyone else could react, Jacob swiftly raised his hand and a surge of magical energy filled the bar. Maureen went rigid, her limbs immobilized as if restrained by invisible ropes.

Simultaneously, Miles, still seated across the table, reacted with a smooth motion of his hand. A mage shield unfolded in place between Maureen and the rest of the table. Finn had pushed back his seat and stood there with his hands holding balls of fire. Esme was standing too, holding a folded piece of paper in one hand—except she just looked sad in Will's eyes.

"Sorry about the test, Will," Esme muttered, eyes fixed on Maureen.

Will's still foul-tasting mouth hung open, pausing mid-reach for the closest napkin. His mind raced with questions that demanded answers, but the look on everyone else's faces stunned him to silence. They were ready for another fight.

Jacob ordered, "Pishacha, leave her and we'll see what we can do about finding you a nice slaughterhouse to live behind. You won't be receiving a second offer."

A low, guttural growl emanated from Maureen's throat, causing Miles to stand up and encircle her completely in the shield. Her eyes flashed a crimson red then back to their normal brown again.

"Enough," Jacob commanded. "Esme will read the exorcism if you do not comply willingly, demon."

Esme held up the paper.

Will's heart was about to gallop right out of his chest. Whatever had been inside Juniper must have jumped to Maureen. Her eyes flashed red once more, then faded. Smoke streamed from her mouth and her body crumpled to the floor like a rag doll. The smoke coalesced next to her into the broad outline of a roughly human-shaped creature. Its grossly distended stomach and too large head proved it was not of human origin.

Gradually, the smoke solidified into a gray creature whose skin looked closer to rock than living flesh. Huge teeth and a pair of tusks jutted out from its lower jaw. The creature glared at them with blood-red eyes. His gaze shifted from the terrifying demon to Jacob. The Archmage had an unyielding expression that suggested this wasn't his first time being involved in such wild circumstances.

In the chaos of the last minute, Will hadn't noticed Finn sneak away until he saw the leprechaun over the demon's shoulder. The two were of a height, so he only spotted Finn's head. He likewise hadn't noticed Miles move, but the other mage had apparently opened his shield to allow Finn through it.

Without preamble, Finn poured a stream of fire onto the demon, pishacha, whatever it was. He saw Esme take a step forward as one of her trolls burst into existence between the gout of fire and Maureen, guarding her from it. A second troll appeared and grabbed the flaming demon, holding it in place, absorbing the inferno just as readily as the demon was. The first troll seized Maureen's body, yanking it away from the conflagration while the other burned.

Miles was still maintaining the shield because it contained the smoke that billowed up from the dying demon. The shield containing the leprechaun, demon, and troll looked like a huge smoke-filled crystal ball.

It felt like an eternity later when Finn exited the shield. He was sweating and gasping for air. Crouching, he bent over and braced his hands on his knees. He looked like he was about to hurl, but there was also a hint of cautious triumph in his eyes.

Jacob ordered, "Miles, maintain the shield until the smoke settles. I'd rather avoid having to conjure water, since we don't have a sprinkler system."

Will couldn't hold it together anymore. His mouth ran away with him when he shrieked, "Gods damn, y'all, what in the nine hells just happened?!"

Esme immediately started giggling uncontrollably. Tears were streaming down her face.

Chapter Thirty-Eight

Coming Clean(er)

Esme

"So," Esme sucked in her bottom lip nervously, "we could probably persuade Miles to write you a script for a single sedative because you're gonna need one to sleep after this."

Esme, Finn, and Will now sat alone in the bar nursing the hot toddies that Finn had insisted on making for them. Jacob and Miles had left a few minutes before to care for Maureen. She was still asleep, but Miles confirmed she was physically fine. But they all suspected that her mental state would be an entirely different matter.

Will rolled his eyes and crossed his arms over his chest, still shaken, grumbling, "I already need drugs to handle all of this. But, okay."

Finn tried for encouragement. "Hey, lad, I think you're doin' better than ya give yourself credit for. Shoulda seen this one when she almost got squashed by a pissed-off afanc."

Will asked incredulously, "A— what?"

Esme groaned and buried her head in her crossed arms on the table.

Finn answered. "It's like what you would get if a monstrous momma crocodile fell in love with an equally horrendous beaver papa. They'll eat anything near the water. Nasty, nasty things."

Esme's muffled voice just barely reached the others. "And this nasty leprechaun dressed up as a very special type of adult actress for said nasty creature."

Finn argued for the sake of arguing, "I was bait!"

Will cut into their banter. "Uh, excuse me. I still don't know what the hell y'all are talking about. Explain it like I'm five years old. Thanks."

Esme kept her head buried in her crossed arms. Finn would answer if she kept up her disappearing act for a little while longer.

"Aye," he huffed out a breath. "Well, lad, it's like this. All the nasty creatures that disappeared in the Extinction are comin' back one by one. The pishacha that possessed Juniper and Maureen was just one of 'em. The Assembly, yours truly included, has been keepin' it quiet by takin' care of the problems when they pop up."

Will looked at him blankly and asked, "So that thing was a malevolent?"

"Righto. I'll admit, I had to look up what a pishacha was myself. Tis the nastiest sort of demon from India, or thereabouts, that has a taste for human flesh. The runnin' theory is that Juniper was unfortunate enough to run into the bear that it had possessed before her. We know it had, uh, killed before, ya see?"

That was news to Esme. Finn must have had a lot of communication with Jacob that she wasn't privy to.

Finn continued. "Anyhow, the problem is that, well, the malevolents are becomin' more of a problem. It used to be that one would pop up occasionally, but lately, it's speedin' up. Truth be told, ya landed yourself in that mess, lad."

Esme looked up to see Will's affronted expression and took action. "Before you start cursing in Spanish, brujo, let me explain what Finn means. You don't remember what happened the night you were taken, right?"

Will shook his head.

Esme explained, "The only thing that makes sense is that you saw something you weren't supposed to see, so the pishacha grabbed you to shut you up."

This seemed to mollify him. What she needed to clarify next, however, would aggravate him all over again.

"It's the same thing that Jacob, and all of us really, needs from you. He knows you weren't born with the ability to see magic. We need you to teach us how to do it."

The curses flew. "Pendej..."

That evening Esme and Miles sat bundled under blankets on his front porch, sheltered from the autumn drizzle, watching the city's lights reflect on the lake. She knew what he was trying to do, and she wanted so badly to make it easier for him. But the only thing she could give him was honesty. No one else was outside, so they could speak in low tones with no one overhearing.

Reflecting on the incident, she confessed, "I've replayed it over and over in my head, wondering if I could have done anything differently." She wiped a stray tear from her cheek and leaned sideways to put her head on his shoulder.

Since finding Will and Maureen in the forest, Esme had spent her days and nights at Miles' house. Being with him, not being alone, was its own form of healing. She'd only been home since to pick up clothes and toiletries.

"I keep dreaming about it. I know that Juniper was basically asleep in her own body after the pishacha possessed her, but still, murder is murder, even if the victim never knew that it occurred. She didn't deserve that."

Miles' quiet response surprised her. "She didn't."

The words made her stomach lurch, forcing her to sit up quickly or risk getting sick all over him.

He noticed and calmly added, "Esme, you didn't deserve to be put into a position where your only choice was to either go nuclear or allow you and your friends to die. I was knocked out, Finn was beaten to an unconscious heap, Maureen had four cracked ribs, frostbite, and dehydration. Will wasn't much better, and they were all stuck in a cage."

His tone changed to the commanding one that he'd used on her in the fight's aftermath. "If anyone is to blame for this, it's me. I allowed myself to get knocked out. My failure left you to face the demon alone. I know you did it to protect me. She was too close to me when I came to, for it to have been anything else."

Not wanting to add to his burden of guilt, she couldn't admit that she'd done it for him. She also wanted to assert that, no, the person who made the choice was at fault, not the unprepared one, but his expression warned her off arguing. So instead, she gave him more of her truth.

"I'm afraid. I'm afraid of myself and the dark place that I hide in when things get tough. It's a cold, bottomless void that I lose myself in and that's what I did, Miles. I lost myself there. What comes out of it, me... I'm tainted."

The truth was, she was afraid of slipping into that dark place again. She'd lost herself to it and had allowed it to control her. In order to kill, she'd gone so low as to unite herself with it.

His eyes pierced through her again, leaving her nowhere to hide. His voice hardened slightly, but it was the intensity in his eyes that made her pause. She noticed a subtle shift in his accent that she had never heard before. "Never use that word when referring to yourself."

She attempted a joke to lighten the mood again, "This is me trying to re-appropriate the word for all cambionkind."

His change in inflection remained in place when he responded. "No, it's not. You actually think that about yourself, don't you?" He didn't pause to allow her to answer. "If your heritage defined you, I can assure you that Juniper would not have been your first kill, Esmeralda."

Maybe the accent thing was something he did when he was angry? Wanting to avoid any more of that, she changed the subject and got comfortable on his shoulder again. "How can I ever face Sylas again?"

Knowing that she'd eventually have to see him again filled her with dread. Would his eyes reflect rage, sorrow, or a blend of the two? The rage would be the easiest to take. She'd already spent every waking and sleeping moment with it directed inward at herself.

His accent was back to normal when he responded to this. "First, know that you won't be alone when you do it. Second, remember that the pishacha had him ensorcelled. He's likely feeling regret for his inability to resist it and stop all of this before it even happened." He grabbed her hand and held on. "Third, lovely: give it time."

The next day

Everything Miles had told her was exactly what she'd expected from him. It was nice to hear, but what made the biggest difference was that he constantly reminded her, "I'm with you," and had proven it repeatedly.

Even though she'd buried her head in her hands to avoid half of it, talking with Will was refreshing. It meant she now had another friend to discuss the new craziness in their lives with. He knew just about everything now, minus the Corded Brotherhood part. Splitting hairs about the distinction between the Assembly and it made little difference.

Will was understandably upset that she'd spilled his secret to Jacob, but seemed to forgive her once he understood that, by teaching them to use the magic, he could make an enormous difference without ever having to face another malevolent.

Esme hoped that today would bring a similar unburdening feeling when she met Abby for a coffee date during her lunch break. Just a brief text message saying "We need to talk" brought Abby straightaway.

Esme's bouncing legs shook the table for two, upsetting the lattes she'd just picked up from the barista. She looked out the window to see the building that Miles and Abby worked in. It felt strange to think that he was somewhere in that building, immersed in his routine doctor's duties, after the last few surreal days together.

Instead of daydreaming, she should've been getting her story straight. She and Miles had gone from friends who sparred occasionally to practically living together in the span of one week. Esme needed to share the news with her friend. The plan was to tell Abby a heavily revised and edited version of events. More importantly, though, she wanted to talk to her about the Turner family secret.

When Esme spotted Abby, she noticed she was either having a tough day or had interpreted the "We need to talk" text as a call to action. Abby marched in, her ponytail askew, sporting scrubs adorned with an outrageous pattern of rainbows, polka dots, and gummy bears. She looked ready for war. The diminutive blonde harpy on a warpath Abby turned into when things got serious would have to be defused. Esme often joked that, in a past life, Abby must have been a nun who either bludgeoned Viking raiders with books or stabbed them with her writing quills.

It felt like forever since they'd spent time together. Abby went in for a hug and, pulling away, demanded, "I'm in the mood for chopping off heads." She slashed her hand forward in a chopping motion. "So tell me who is first in line." She had the whole crazy eyes thing going on too.

"Okay, Abby, here is your latte." Esme gestured calmly at the table and sat down, hoping that Abby would follow. "No one's head needs to come off. Well, I guess I won't complain if you go all stabby on a select few…. But, good news, I think things might get better between me and Maureen. We had a chat recently."

At least Esme hoped that was the case. Time would tell.

Abby settled into her seat with a "spit it out already" expression on her face. She took a long sip of her latte and asked, slightly subdued, "If I'm not chopping off heads, then do you need another hug?"

Esme couldn't fool Abby. Something of what the last few days had done to her must have shown through her forced geniality.

"I don't know, Abby. I'm currently somewhere in the middle of wanting a huge cry-it-out hug and wanting to throw a chair. So, ya know, middling."

Abby asked, "Is this about Juniper?"

Esme resorted to her well-practiced skill of delay and deflect to prevent her voice from cracking or her face from giving her away when she replied, "Umm…" It probably wasn't very effective.

Abby tried to keep the conversation going by commenting, oblivious to Esme's inner turmoil, "Sylas is going to lose his flipping mind. Poor guy."

She agreed mutely. Esme had been trying so hard to avoid thinking about Juniper and Sylas. The familiar sensation of pressure behind her eyes signaled it was time to deflect by switching topics. There was one foolproof subject she had available to divert Abby from the topic.

"Also, I'm having mind-blowing sex," Esme gestured at her head as if it was exploding.

Abby's frown faded slightly. "Okay, I know you. So, you would not have dangled that tasty, nay tantalizing, tidbit in front of me if you didn't want me to bite. Please tell me that Miles is packing. I cannot face him at work if I know he has a tiny—"

"Abby!" Esme's cheeks felt like they were the same temperature as her coffee. Given her irrepressible nature, embarrassing her was typically a rare accomplishment. But everything with Miles was still new, even though it already felt like they'd known each other for a lifetime. Until a few days ago, their relationship had been purely platonic.

Esme narrowed her eyes and asked, "How did you figure out it was Miles?"

"Oh, I don't know," Abby gave her an exasperated look, "Maybe it's the way you two have been inseparable lately? I know for a fact that you didn't work last night, so you didn't pick up some random guy there."

Abby shrugged. "Not that you're big on casual hookups but, still." A sparkle of excitement, the source unknown, entered Abby's eyes as she continued speaking. "I know you weren't there because I stopped by the bar last night to drop off a pile of travel guides for a friend new to the area. But, back to the whole 'mind-blowing' thing. Miles is totally into you, duh. Please, do go on..."

Esme took a sip of her coffee and asked, "Am I allowed to do my full Esme thing or is that going to freak you out because you knew him before I did? I promise not to go full-Guillermo level of details on you."

Blithely Abby replied, "I was captivated the moment you said the 'S' word."

"Gods and goddesses of old, Abby, his hands are magical." She raised her fist to cover her heart. "I am not even kidding. I'm surprised that I was able to walk here!"

Abby clutched at her imaginary pearls in mock surprise, grinning widely.

Esme took another sip of her drink to cover her next words as she spoke, "But then I turned coward and tried to disappear before he woke up after our first night together." Her words slowed. "But don't worry. We talked about it like grown-ups. Other than just to tell you that I'm kind of seeing Miles now, the reason I freaked out is part of why I'm here. "

The words that she was about to say, the truth of her parents and her secret heritage, died on her tongue. Esme immediately snapped her mouth shut and stood at alert attention.

Curious, Abby turned her head to see what had prompted her friend to suddenly stop speaking and stand up.

Esme watched in slow motion while a look of purest bliss stole over her best friend's face as she gazed at the all-too-familiar stranger walking toward their table.

Him.

Chapter Thirty-Nine

VARIED DESIRES

Gwyn

Gwyn had hired a hotel room facing the street to see if he could corner Nudd alone. Unfortunately, he hadn't seen the supposed doctor arrive that morning. Starting the day off with a failed plan was just one more stumble in a series of his missteps. He was bleeding money in his temporary accommodation. He'd have to find a more permanent and cheaper place soon or he'd be sleeping in the forest with Cerys; the hotel hadn't allowed dogs.

Serendipity had nothing to do with his run-in with Abby this time. When he saw her walk into the coffee shop across the street, his day took a turn for the better. He hadn't eaten anything that morning, so it was barely a decision to walk out of the hotel. Perhaps, though, the most magnetic force of all, the force that propelled his feet across the street, was his nearly allergic aversion to further isolation. A thousand years of it, coupled with the grim thoughts that he couldn't seem to escape when he was alone in his bed, bore down on him like an oppressive burden in the quiet of his room.

There was also the sad truth that she reminded him of happier times. The way she tapped her finger excitedly on the table whenever she read something engrossing and the way her smile made the lines around her eyes crease were bittersweet reminders of all that he had lost more than a dozen lifetimes before.

From what he could tell of this era, it was perfectly normal for a man to run into a female friend and settle in for a chat with her. It helped that he had gained a deep appreciation for coffee. As soon as he stepped inside, he was glad to see that it wasn't overly crowded. Soon he thanked the barista for his order, turned, and spotted her.

He didn't expect the uplift of heart and spirit that overcame him simply at the sight of her. It was then that he understood her significance to him, beyond her exceptional nature—she symbolized potential. Hers was the first relationship, of any sort, that he'd cared to cultivate since his reawakening. If she could move him in such a way, perhaps the melancholy that currently held him in its thrall need not be his future.

Everything changed.

His heart skipped a beat. It took every single jot of self-discipline in his body, honed by years of training with the sword and shield, to forestall his steps from faltering as he took in the identity of the woman who was now standing next to Abigail.

The begotten woman.

But Gwyn was light on his feet, mentally and physically. It was a gamble, but he had recently become something of an expert in that area out of financial necessity. There was only one strategy that could gain him each of his desires: the approval of both ladies and an alternative route of access to Nudd.

A great dose of charm and luck, mixed with a little sincerity, could go a long way.

He straightened his spine and fixed his most courtly smile in place. He pitched his voice down half an octave to the level approaching sultry and greeted her. "Abigail! What a pleasant surprise."

Esme

A stream of expletives, plans of action not involving magic, plans of action involving subtle magic, and pure, unadulterated anxiety engulfed Esme's mind. She was on her feet before she realized that her body had reacted without conscious instruction. She took solace in the fact that they were in public because it was unlikely the stranger would do anything overtly violent.

A mellow, deeply accented voice seemed to disrupt the electrical activity in her brain. "Abigail! What a pleasant surprise."

Esme's best friend, Abby, bright-eyed and smiling, answered the man who, less than a week ago, had magic aimed directly at Miles, and perhaps herself.

Abby greeted him. "Gwyn! Hey! How are you?"

Esme felt like she was in a movie scene in which she played the recently shell-shocked victim, complete with ringing ears. Through the din of her internal alarm, she heard herself being introduced to the genial stranger. There was no doubting it. This was the same man. His clothes were different, but she would never forget that face.

On pure reflex, she offered out her hand to shake at the appropriate time. His grip was not overly short, warning, or even clammy. It was precisely socially correct.

"Esme?" he smiled. "A name I've only heard in my country. I'm charmed."

She replied without hesitation, "And where is that?"

Her need for secrecy, combined with their public location, decided her next moves for her. She'd play along with a friendly mask in place. At the very least, she could get more information out of him.

"Wales," he replied simply.

Just like Miles. There were differences, but...well, at least she had a name to add to his identity.

"Gwyn is new to Seattle. We met at The Sanctuary," Abby offered.

Could Abby possibly have a crush on this guy? That would be a second issue piled onto the first, which was that he was standing in front of her like nothing had happened between them. What's more, Esme couldn't say anything about running into this Gwyn character without revealing what she was doing and who she was with. It was for Miles and Finn to reveal their roles in the Corded Brotherhood, not hers. She wouldn't breach their trust.

For this encounter, at least, it didn't seem like Gwyn was hostile. His amiable behavior would make sense if he had only been aiming at Miles. In the forest, he had seemed only mildly interested in her, and now he was being downright pleasant.

She asked, "Oh, when did you two meet? I'm disappointed that I wasn't at the bar that night." Esme needed to know if their meeting had been a sheer coincidence or something much darker.

"Nearly two weeks ago, I think?" Abby looked to Gwyn for confirmation.

"Yes, I learned about the bar from some colleagues back home and headed straight there after flying in. I thought that a tipple would help ease the jet lag. Little did I know that, upon asking to share a table in the crowded room, I would nearly have my head bitten off by a cantankerous woman surrounded by dog-eared books."

Abby laughed with him. "I think I even had a sticky note stuck to my hair. I was in my zone." She groaned. "I'm so sorry about that, Gwyn." She touched his arm as she said it. He smiled back down at her, making eye contact. And that was all the proof that Esme needed to know that Abby was into this guy.

Was she wrong about him? Could they have been wrong about his intentions? She needed to stay and figure that out. "Why don't you join us?" Esme suggested. She gave him a significant look.

Abby hastily reminded her, "But Es, we have that whole business…"

Esme gave her friend a look that combined reassurance with warmth. "Yes, but Gwyn is here now. I can spare a few minutes."

Gwyn presented them with a disarming smile. "Absolutely," he replied.

From the outside, it looked as though they were having a grand time getting to know each other. But, even though she was an active participant in the chat, Esme remained wary. Every few sentences she would start to bristle, her senses heightened with anxiety, only to quickly push the emotions down.

When Abby's phone beeped several times, Esme nearly jumped out of her seat. Abby excused herself. "Oh sorry, sorry!

I probably left something out of a patient hand-off. I'll be right back!"

By the time their conversation was interrupted, Esme had successfully learned two useful things about Gwyn. The first she could ascertain thanks to her time as a bartender and marginally from her work for the Assembly. Being able to study and read people was a necessary skill for both roles. Gwyn was an excellent liar. He didn't lie often, but the times when he did were significant. She'd expected a reek of malice about his falsehoods but didn't sense it. Rather, he was hiding small things; probably a lot of small things.

The second was that every so often he would break into a level of formality or use words in such a way that she would expect from one of the longer-lived non-humans she knew. Perhaps it was that he simply spent more time around non-humans than humans. Or, perhaps, his outdated way of speaking was a calculated method of misleading others about him and his capabilities.

The moment Abby left the table, Gwyn knowingly met Esme's eyes. She didn't see him staring daggers. Still, she needed to keep her guard up and take care of those who might be in danger. She said, "Abby knows nothing. She's innocent."

He answered with a tilt of his head, "I know. And I estimate you are likewise innocent."

The quickness of his answer surprised her. He leaned forward, resting his head on his hand, thoughtful. "But do you know that he isn't? I think you know him by the name of Miles Goodwin. He's not the man he claims to be."

She looked at him, puzzled. "Why are you after him?"

Instead of answering her, he said, "Abigail will be back soon and I can tell that you don't want her to be involved in this. That is how it should be." He emphasized that last word. "Neither do I."

Esme started to interrupt him, but he answered the question that was brimstone burning within her eyes. "I swear to you on my magic that I have no ill intentions toward Ms. Abigail. My meeting her was entirely coincidental, perhaps serendipitous." He tilted his head as if weighing the possibility.

He continued. "Please understand. I have questions for Miles that require answers. You need to know what that arrogant fool is truly capable of. He shouldn't have a chance to bring down a second begotten woman."

There was that word again, begotten. It was considered a slur, but the term held no real sting for her. Her concern was that he somehow knew of her heritage and he'd mentioned that she wasn't Miles' first begotten woman.

He said, "You deserve to know who he truly is. I understand you need to feel secure, so name a time and a place for us to speak, tonight preferably. I'd rather not delay the inevitable any longer."

What exactly was inevitable? She was being bombarded with information and didn't have the time to ask all the necessary clarifying questions. Like, who was he? How did he know Miles? Would she be safe speaking with him alone? Perhaps less importantly, was he saying that Miles had been with another demon-blooded woman before her?

Gwyn must have seen her visibly hesitating because he growled quietly under his breath and then said, "Fine. I swear upon my magic that, for the time between now and the second twilight, I shall halt all hostilities and shall do no harm to you or Miles Goodwin." He practically hissed, "Is that sufficient?"

She studied him, taking in every inch of his expression and posture, and answered, "Yes."

It looked like she would have roughly thirty hours until the next twilight to figure out—well, a whole lot of things.

Chapter Forty

Details, Details...

Esme

Since Esme felt that she had made enough astoundingly bad choices over the last few days, she determined that she wouldn't make one more in dealing with Gwyn. It would be idiotic to meet him alone, even with a binding promise in place. But bringing Miles didn't seem like the best idea, either. Gwyn had gone from calm and genial to furious at the simple mention of his name. She hated it, but she was going to keep Miles in the dark about this meeting until she knew more.

Her safest bet would be to inform Jacob and have him escort her. But Miles was his golden boy and bringing a threatening presence like the Bastion himself could cause Gwyn to tighten his lips instead of opening them. She needed someone who could be underestimated but still stand as a stalwart companion. One quick phone call that ended with Finn excited beyond all reason at "going rogue behind yer man's back ta solve the mystery" later, and they had a plan.

The waning light of the evening cast a warm glow on the water as Esme sat alone on a park bench, listening to the seagulls and the early evening breeze when Finn arrived. To her relief, he didn't pop out of nowhere, sparing her from the usual fright. His height made him distinct, but what he was wearing took her aback. The mundanity of his entire outfit was shocking. He wore a plain knit beanie to cover his ears and blond hair. A hoodie and fashionable rainproof jacket covered his top half. His bottom half sported perfectly tailored jeans and trendy sneakers.

She pointed at his outfit and teasingly said, "Wow, Finn, you've completely nailed the Seattle Bro look."

"Well, it wouldn't quite do to be hangin' out at a beach wearing a proper full getup, would it? At first, I thought this city was full of lumberjacks, but then I understood that ya'all just dress like slobs."

She asked, "It's comfortable though, isn't it?"

"Right-o." He winked. "So, here I am to be your backup to meet this loon. I know ya got the promise from him. But it doesn't extend to me, so let's hope that he remains courteous. I'll be on my best behavior.

"Speaking of my behavior," his demeanor took on a solemn air. "This is long overdue. I apologize for my manner of revealing the truth of your and Mr. Goodwin's status. I could have handled it far better. Since ya've been so straight with me, I feel the need to explain. I saw an injustice bein' done and wanted ta remedy it. The folks around ya have known forever what you are, and yet they didn't seem fit ta train ya or even tell ya? A load of shite! I'll admit, the naughtier side of my nature got the best of me, though. Sorry, lassie."

If he had been more formal with his apology like he had been with Juniper, she probably would have had a hard time taking it seriously. This felt like the perfect mix of sincerity and informality.

Esme shrugged, let out a resigned breath, and said, "Knowing half the story is becoming my M.O."

Finn stood and gazed at the water. It was long enough for her mind to turn its focus inward. She lost herself in the coming sunset. Eventually, she closed the silence, asking tentatively, "Hey, Finn, is what I'm doing here, right?"

The leprechaun pursed his lips and climbed onto the bench beside her. As he gazed out at Elliott Bay, he said, "I don't know, lassie. But I think that he'll forgive ya either way."

She wasn't certain if he was referring to Miles or Jacob, but she hoped for both.

They sat in comfortable silence for a few minutes. The rhythmic sound of the waves, the slightly salty tang in the air, and the cool breeze on a rare dry day in autumn had the power to calm all nerves.

Finn offered, "I get why yer here. I want to know too."

They saw Gwyn approach as the sun sank below the horizon. It wasn't even past dinner time yet, owing to Seattle's latitude, but the sight felt foreboding, nonetheless. Once again, he wore an all-black ensemble, exuding an air of confidence with every step. He was as handsome as before. The same unruly raven black hair, pale skin, and strikingly clear blue eyes.

Gwyn approached and said, "Esmeralda."

Esme and Finn stood in unison to greet him. "Gwyn," she said, feeling as awkward as she'd ever felt.

As composed and collected as she'd ever seen him, Finn proposed they move to the nearby picnic table to have their conversation. Sitting down, Gwyn commented, "You've brought a familiar friend."

Before she could speak, Finn cut in. "The name's Finnegan. The lady sought an escort, as is her right."

Gwyn slowly considered the leprechaun, and wielding his effortlessly friendly air, dipped his head in acknowledgment. "Agreed. And one easily underestimated. I like her more already. She's quite clever."

Finn quickly covered up the shock that briefly blanketed his face. But Esme had seen it and she knew exactly how it felt. He had expected disagreeableness, hostility even, but not this. Despite being someone who should be considered an enemy, Gwyn had willingly set aside his magical for a parley.

Esme cleared her throat and spoke. "So, Gwyn, we've cleared issue number one for me already. Abby is safe, will remain safe, and will have absolutely nothing to do with any of this if we can help it."

"Agreed." His expression, though dark, left her comforted because it told her that he really meant what he said.

He paused, looking as though he were ticking off tasks in his mind, and said, "While we're discussing people we wish to keep safe, I must make something clear. Right now, I do not consider you my enemy. Nor you, Mister Finnegan. Thus far, neither of you has given me any offense nor done me harm. And, as I am uncertain of the custom, I want to assure you I take no offense to your begotten status, Esmeralda."

Finn scrunched up his face and advised, "Well, lad, ya could start off proper by not calling the lady a slur."

The leprechaun and demon-blooded mage shared a fluency in banter. She scrutinized his choice of words. "Okay, Mister Finnegan, you only just learned, like a couple of weeks ago, that 'begotten' is a slur."

The leprechaun looked askance, indignant in his righteousness.

Gwyn's expression remained stoic, but his words conveyed a genuine apology as he said, "Please do accept my apologies. I was...not aware of the insult."

Although she found comfort in the assurance that this stranger had no ill intentions toward her mere existence as someone not completely human, she was eager to address the core of the issue sooner rather than later. She asserted, "You made claims. Time to explain."

"Very well," Gwyn said as he straightened his back and folded his hands on the table. "Let's unravel the illusions you've held about a man who undoubtedly you've seen as noble. A man with a glowing reputation, who appears to be the paragon of virtue and success. You know him by the name of Miles Goodwin."

Gwyn sneered as he said the name. Esme and Finn sat very still, expectant. The beauty of the surrounding scene faded away as the storyteller found his stride.

"For years I rotted alone, wrongfully imprisoned. I committed no crime worthy of such torture. There was no one to share the burden of time with me: only the walls of my prison and the confines of my own mind. I stand before you a greatly diminished man, in mind, body, and spirit.

"He, your Miles, was likely the architect of my wrongful imprisonment. I knew him by another name then. Well, really, by several. He's much, much, older than he appears. Does he not possess unique powers? Have you ever found yourself wondering just how he could be so extraordinary? Well..."

If she had expected hearing anything from Gwyn, it was definitely not this. The formality of this speech matched what she had noted about him before. He spoke with a flair of archaic eloquence. Either he was well acquainted with the art of storytelling or he had practiced this speech before.

"Let this sink in. Nudd—" he pronounced it like "Neeth," "—with all of his supposed nobility, blinded by his righteousness, almost certainly sacrificed his own flesh and blood for the sake of principles." He gestured at his chest with both hands.

Finn jerked suddenly and turned as pale as freshly fallen snow.

Gwyn paused when he saw this. "Ah, so the leprechaun understands. But do you, Esmeralda?" He regarded her.

Seeing that Finn wasn't prepared to speak, she opted for a truthful response. "I don't understand." What she did know is that the last thing they needed, while malevolents were popping back into the world, was further infighting between mages.

"What you need to know, Esmeralda, is that the man you believe you know likely condemned me to rot in mind and spirit. But for what? Any crime so heinous should leave a mark on one's soul. Yet, I remember, I feel, nothing of my sins. I must know the truth from his lips, one way or another."

She heard an implied threat in his words.

Gwyn stood. "I'll allow Mister Finnegan to explain the pertinent details of who we are. Nudd owes answers to you and me, I suspect. For now, our agreement stands."

He handed Esme a sheet of paper with a phone number written on it. "Please call me if you'd like to speak. Or, if Nudd would like to speak with me. I must go. I have a hound to look after."

She felt her head tip in question and then in dawning realization of what hound he meant.

Seeing her look he confirmed her suspicion. "Yes, the gwyllgi from the forest. A pleasant evening to you both."

He turned on his heel and left in a hurry.

As Gwyn's back faded out of sight, Finn returned to himself once more. "Lassie," he said forlornly.

Esme, more than ready to understand what the hell had just happened, perked up. "So…" she started, but quickly noticed that Finn had pursed lips and a worried expression. Recognizing the wisdom in silence, she chose to stop talking. This was not a moment of friendly tête-à-tête.

Speaking didn't change his downcast demeanor. "Aye, sorry. I know how I appear. I think we just met Gwyn ap Nudd."

She stared at him with a puzzled expression.

"Ya heard him say 'Nudd' right? I'm not flippin' bonkers. I did hear him say that name?"

"Yes, something about Nudd and his righteousness. I guess that's supposed to be Miles' real name?" Her frustration grew as she confronted her own ignorance, causing her to act increasingly impatient. "Spit it out, Finn. Gwyn is like his brother or something, right?"

"Nay, lassie." His face looked stricken. "Nudd is his father."

"Okay…" That made absolutely no sense to her.

It turned out she wasn't the only one feeling frustrated. "Aye, you've gotta be coddin' me! He's sayin' that Miles is feckin' Nudd Llaw Eraint of the Silver Hand." He lifted his right arm and wiggled his fingers.

He put his face in his hands and said, trying not to hyperventilate, "An' I'm the scut who called Gwyn ap Nudd himself a 'lad'! By all the magic… what was I thinkin'?" He'd gone pale again.

With gravity in his voice, Finn turned his attention back to Esme and clarified, "He's sayin' that Miles is his father. And," he breathed out quickly and then back in slowly, "they're both the closest things to gods that have ever walked the land."

Abby

Abby closed the volume she'd been leafing through and rested her head on the desk. While certain aspects of her life were winding down, her work for the Corded Brotherhood was just beginning to gain momentum. Her eyes and brain were desperate for a break.

The maternity leave she'd been covering for the past few months had just ended, but her sleep schedule wasn't back to normal. She'd just completed three twelve-hour shifts in a row followed by a full day today. Burning the candle at both ends had left her body feeling like a flu was oncoming, with aches and pains in all of her joints. On the bright side, she'd finally convinced her parents to start therapy. That, combined with spending the entire next day in the bath or on her couch, would finally allow her to relax.

For hours, Abby had pored over ancient texts with a translation dictionary at her side, struggling to stay awake. She couldn't blame anyone but herself; she'd chosen to take on this workload.

Her mind drifted back to her parents. It wasn't just the years of poor communication that had doomed their relationship; it was the secrets. Unbeknownst to her father, her mother had been working undercover for the Corded Brotherhood for a long time. When he found out how she'd been using her magic for them, it was the final straw for their marriage. Seeing the fallout, Abby still hadn't worked up the nerves to tell her father she'd also joined years ago.

Abigail Grace O'Malley vowed not to repeat their mistakes—once she was actually in a relationship, that was.

She felt a small glimmer of hope as she picked up another book and began to turn through it. She had met someone. Gwyn seemed interested in continuing to spend time together, and she felt the same.

They'd already met three times in the past week. The last time they'd met, she'd led him through Pike Place Market's alleys and vendor-filled walkways on an impromptu tour. They started with cappuccinos at a famous coffee shop, a typical tourist activity she expected from their outing. But then he spotted the Greek yogurt bar, mini donuts stand, and chocolate-covered cherries stall and the rest of the day spiraled from there.

He'd been so enthusiastic about trying everything that she couldn't bring herself to refuse him. They practically rolled down the hill to the waterfront park, where they watched the ferries float past. When they parted ways, he presented her with a beautiful bouquet from one of the flower stalls. If that wasn't a date, she didn't know what was.

She could continue daydreaming about another date, but her reality was she was still voluntarily locked up in the Assembly's library after working a full day at the hospital. Her current project involved tracking down malevolent creatures with either the razor-sharp claws of a grizzly bear or the ability to possess one. Whatever they were tracking began its rampage in Montana, where it had slaughtered and eaten parts of a mother and child. The trail picked up westward in the Idaho panhandle, where the creature found a backcountry skier to savage and consume. If it was sticking to the pattern of moving westward, they suspected that the hiker who'd gone missing just east of Seattle was its latest victim.

Maureen had also been missing for a few days. Abby wasn't supposed to know that Maureen had been sent out by the Assembly to investigate a lead, but her mother had let that little detail fly by mistake. Long story short, Abby was getting worried because she hadn't heard an update about Maureen returning yet. Hence, she was working when she could be relaxing.

She had always dealt with her anxiety by doing. When she was in school, she tackled big assignments immediately. Procrastination was the complete opposite of what she needed for her mental well-being. In action, there was security for Abby. If there was a problem, at least she knew she was doing something about it.

She heard the click, click, click of heels approaching the library. It had to be Katia coming in to check up on her. Abby sat up and straightened her clothing and hair. She could at least try to appear less overwhelmed in front of the boss.

The door opened and Katia walked in. She looked far too elegant for a weekend morning of working alone with the rookie. Her dark brown hair was straightened. She wore a thick white sweater with black pants and kitten-heeled booties. Abby could tell that the woman was just a few years her senior, yet her presence exuded a certain elegance and flair that she could only dream of for herself. She was also carrying two travel cups of something that smelled wonderful.

Katia greeted her brightly, "Good evening!" Her accent was subtle but notable. It sounded Russian, but not completely. When Abby had roused the courage to ask, she'd found out that Katia was half-Chinese and half-Russian. Her parents had moved her around a lot growing up, so she ended up speaking

English with hints of her mother's and father's tongues leaking through.

Abby beamed and said, "Wow, thanks!" She couldn't help feeling pulled in by the woman. She had some sort of irresistible appeal that Abby couldn't quite put her finger on.

Katia said, "I just finished a short shift at the library downtown, so I wanted to drop by and see how you were doing on my way home." She smirked. "Plus decaf."

Abby hesitated to be honest with Katia. Acknowledging her imposter syndrome didn't lessen the shame of feeling overwhelmed. She knew she needed to buck up and just ask for advice.

Abby blew out a breath and said, "Honestly, I'm a bit..." She hesitated again, but Katia's patient expression gave her the confidence to speak. "I feel a bit like I'm drowning."

Katia startled her with a tinny laugh. "Abby, you don't have to do it all at once. Look at how many books you have spread around you! Plus, there's a second reason I'm here. You can stop researching that. We caught our malevolent. A few days ago, apparently. Naturally, the support team is the last to know."

"Our malevolent? I saw the photos taken at prior crime scenes by mundane police. It was not pretty."

The expression on Katia's face morphed to one of sorrow. "You heard of Juniper's death, yes? I cannot say this in any other way but bluntly. A pishacha, a type of demon who eats humans, possessed her. Unfortunately, one of our agents was forced to eliminate Juniper in self-defense. The demon had been caging humans, including Maureen, as food stores."

Abby's mind reeled. Katia, with her gentle demeanor, had examined those gruesome crime scene photos? It didn't match the composed, elegant woman before her. Not only that, she'd also delivered the news of it so calmly, as if she'd experienced worse before. This peek into a different side of her made Abby reevaluate her impression of Katia. Maybe she was made of sterner stuff than her outward appearance would suggest.

Abby brushed aside a few papers and the dictionary that she'd been using to place the travel cup down on the table, curiosity sparking. Katia's calmness around grim material intrigued her.

Abby cleared her throat, a nervous habit that bought her a brief moment to muster her courage. Then, she asked, "I'm curious; what led you to start doing this sort of research for the Assembly? I mean, obviously, you're more than qualified, being a real librarian and all, but I doubt a person could accidentally stumble into this work."

Katia gave her a long once over that felt more like an evaluation than one of consideration, then answered, "I wondered how long it would take you to ask."

Abby's face creased with an uncomfortable smile. At least Katia didn't seem to be offended by the question. The other woman emitted a hesitant, contemplative sound that appeared to originate from the linguistically Slavic part of her mind.

With undeniable charm, Katia said, "Let's just say that I have first-hand experience with malevolents. We'll keep it at that for now. Oh, I almost forgot." She reached into her large tote bag to pull out something of Abby's. "Your mother said that you forgot this at her house."

Abby accepted her planner and said goodbye to Katia.

After Katia left, she noticed there was a paper stuck to the back of it. It was a table of Assembly expenses. A thousand horses couldn't tear her eyes away from it. She was weak to the temptation of intriguing information in any form.

As her finger pathed down the line items and associated costs, mainly contractors and services, it caught on one all-too-familiar name.

Esmeralda Turner – Handler – $2,855.00

Surely they weren't siphoning Assembly funds through the bar? The Assembly was listed officially as a nonprofit. Too many eyes were on the money flowing through the organization to allow any form of embezzlement to flourish.

So what exactly was Esme doing for the Assembly? And why did Abby not know about it? She'd known Esme for years, trusted her implicitly. Yet this clandestine payment hinted at something hidden beneath the surface of their friendship.

Abby made up her mind to confront Esme in order to uncover the truth. Maybe they were both keeping one secret too many.

Chapter Forty-One

Rectifying the Truth

Esme

She couldn't run again.

But she also wasn't quite ready to talk. To explain her absence that afternoon while she met with Gwyn, she'd told Miles that she needed to handle a few things at home. He'd been understanding about it, as expected. In all honesty, he most likely thought she was getting cold feet again.

She needed space to think. When she was with him, everything felt too right, too easy. His proximity would only cloud her ability to process Gwyn's revelations. So she texted Abby, "Will you cover for me with Miles if he asks, bestie? I'm trying to work through some stuff right now and don't want him to think I'm running away again."

When Abby didn't respond, Esme forced herself to let it go, telling herself that her friend was probably busy. She found herself too mentally drained to muster up the energy to cook dinner, so "Sad Stew" for one was the only item on the menu that night. As she scraped the can's gloopy beige contents into a microwavable bowl, her mind inevitably wandered back to the conversation with Gwyn. The entire conversation had left her feeling like she was clinging to a buoy adrift in the ocean, and things hadn't improved much since then.

With a sigh, she set the microwave to warm her dinner. Its mechanical hum filled the empty silence of her kitchen, but it couldn't drown out the torrent of thoughts threatening to drown her. Finn had explained everything, but she couldn't quite believe it. Miles was supposed to be a deified legendary Welsh king who predated King Arthur. Gwyn was supposed to be his deified son, leader of the Wild Hunt and escort of souls to the afterlife. Finn bought into the story completely, without questioning a single word. Why? What was she supposed to think?

Miles had never lied to her. When she asked about Finn, he'd been upfront about his ties to the Corded Brotherhood. Even though she'd messed up two encounters with malevolent creatures in a row, he'd extended his trust to her to join their hunt for the hellhound as firepower. Both times she'd asked about his firearm, he had explained. Miles had consistently been honest, understanding, and transparent with her.

She couldn't completely dismiss Gwyn's claims, either. She'd witnessed Miles healing Lily, inexplicably defying the laws of magic as she knew them. Miles' accomplishments were light years ahead of most, but his extraordinary achievements could easily be attributed to his determination and hard work.

Despite all that, he still gave her the impression that he was a normal guy. In the most awkward of moments, he quoted poetry, he laughed, and occasionally cracked jokes. He was exciting. He supported her and surprised her when she thought she'd figured him out. Plus, the pishacha's attack had left him unconscious and sprawled on the ground for several minutes at least. That sounded very human to her.

She took the bowl from the microwave, carried it to the small dining table, and sank into a chair. She stirred the stew absentmindedly, distracted by another thought. Perhaps Gwyn's confusion about Miles being Nudd stemmed from his god-touched aura. It was unfortunate that no one seemed to know anything about his condition. Would Gwyn know anything? He had said that she could contact him if she wanted to talk.

The idea of Miles being over a thousand years old was almost too absurd to consider. But if he was, realizing she might have shared her bed with a demigod shook her to her core. She didn't think her taste in men was that bad—or good, depending upon how you thought about it...

Her meal was bland, the flavor lost in her unease. A part of her couldn't help but wonder if Miles' ordinary facade was a deliberate choice or if it were the genuine reflection of a demigod living among mortals.

The doorbell rang, breaking her out of her swirling, brooding thoughts. Who would be at the door so late?

She must have hesitated a little too long in confronting the visitor because she heard the immediate ping of a text message that read: Esme, open the door, it's me!

The dam burst wide open as she stumbled to the door and turned the lock. She frantically wiped at her eyes but gave up, realizing that it was a losing battle.

She choked out, "Hey."

Abby immediately walked through the door, grabbing Esme by the arm and dragging her to the nearby couch. The blonde disappeared in a flurry from the living room to somewhere else in the house. Esme remained there, unmoving, waiting for the flood to stop. The frustration, the confusion that she had felt just a few moments before, had morphed into despondency. She felt the weight of mourning Juniper's loss, coupled with the bulk of too many revelations dragging her down.

When Abby returned, she was carrying a box of tissues and offered them up. Esme gratefully accepted one and began dabbing at her face. Then Abby asked, "Is this a wine conversation?"

Esme shook her head. It took her a moment to clear her throat, but she eventually said, "I think that I genuinely need to be sober to tell you everything." She noisily blew her nose. "Because it's so much, and more than half of it is unbelievable."

Wonderful, compassionate, Abby replied, "I don't work tomorrow. Tell me everything."

Esme was tired of the constant evasion, the careful dancing around truths. She had reached her breaking point. In the end, the only thing that mattered was that she trusted Abby.

Esme took a shaky breath and began, knowing there would be no turning back after this. "It all started with the Assembly's first requests..."

She told Abby about their slowly increasing expectations. When she spoke, she described the weight of indebtedness she felt towards them. She talked about interrogating Finn and meeting Miles. About her increased training regimen for the rest of the spring and summer.

Esme told Abby about the afanc and the doppelgänger. She revealed the truth of what she was; what her parents were. Confessing her guilt, she admitted to going too far, losing control, and making the worst mistake of her life by killing Juniper.

If she hadn't been so wrapped up in her own grief, she might have noticed sooner that Abby hadn't seemed surprised to hear about the malevolents.

Esme thought she probably looked like a madwoman, her puffy face covered in tears and snot. "I can't do it again. It was Juniper before that thing got to it. Abby, the pishacha called me its sister. I wanted to tell you about the demon-blooded part earlier but then Gwyn walked in…"

Esme sniffed as she struggled to maintain her composure. "I don't know if I can tap into the infernal again without losing my friggin' mind. But I know that I'm going to keep helping the Assembly. I can't turn my back on everything I've learned. At some point, something is going to push me to do it again."

Her voice turned small when she finally asked, "Who am I going to hurt next?"

Abby put both hands on her shoulders and shook her hard, stunning Esme. "No one. You will not lose control again. You know what to avoid now. Juniper was eating people, Esme. Eating them!"

The shaking had stopped, but Esme sat there, stunned into silence at the revelation that her mind was slowly inching toward.

Abby began fidgeting with the ties of her hoodie. "Well, flippin' hell, Esme, I came over here to drag you for not telling me the truth, but before I could even open my mouth, you spilled everything." Her frustrated growl was all the affirmation Esme needed to understand why they were best friends.

But Abby wasn't done yet. "A piece of my mom's paperwork got stuck to my planner. It named you on the Assembly's payroll." A note of hilarity mixed with stress entered her tone and her hands joined in the speech. "I'm struggling with not being indignant over my missed opportunity to be righteously pissy with you. But, as you've probably guessed by now," she snorted, "I've been keeping secrets from you too. So, I have no room to talk."

She stood and walked a complete circle of the living room. Flinging her arms downward in surrender, she said, "Screw it. Let's hash this out."

The harpy-on-a-warpath expression Abby had been wearing faded and was replaced by something approaching culpability. "I'm a Corded Brother too, tattoo and all. Not a field agent like Miles, though. I'm not a badass in a fight like you. I just do research. It's a—" she paused for a moment, as if thinking, "Family thing. I'm sorry for not telling you."

Instead of anger or hurt, the emotion Esme felt upon hearing Abby's confession was a sibling of regret. Instead of feeling alone in their secrets for years, they could have had each other. The burden could have been shared. Understanding why Abby had done it was as simple as looking in a mirror.

It was Abby's turn to let the weight of years of secrets out. They spent the next few minutes blubbering and apologizing. Then, seemingly out of nowhere, Abby abruptly jumped up from where she'd joined Esme on the couch.

"I almost forgot! Be right back."

Abby practically sprinted to the door, returning with an ornate planter overflowing with healthy mint leaves, their invigorating scent heightening the atmosphere of confession. "I found this on your porch."

Attached to it with twine was a small note.

Esme opened the note and read aloud, "I grew it to help you sleep, lassie. I know you prefer mint tea. Thank you for saving me back there."

The last line, coming from a Fae, was equivalent to a declaration of a life debt. She absolutely refused to cry again, but it was a struggle. In only three sentences, Finn had tried to absolve her of the guilt she felt for Juniper's death.

As Esme looked for the perfect spot by a window for the plant, Abby said, "Please tell me that's everything, because, gods, that was a lot."

Esme nearly groaned. "Unfortunately, there's more, and it's the truly unbelievable stuff."

She took a reinforcing breath. "I met with Gwyn last night." She let the breath out and braced herself for what came next, "Which was kind of the tipping point of me losing my marbles. What I'm about to say is going to sound completely batshit insane, so stick with me while I work through it, okay?"

Abby's eyes grew wide. But she nodded, ready to soldier on with this campaign of a conversation.

Esme recounted the unexpected arrival of Gwyn during the gwyllgi hunt, followed by the promises he'd made at the coffee shop while Abby was on the phone. At this, Abby practically collapsed in her seat.

Esme went on to share the bare facts of what Gwyn had told her a few short hours before, of what he'd claimed Miles had done. "The problem is, Finn believes it, Abby! No joke. He was as white as a ghost and practically shaking in his boots afterward."

It was Abby's turn to sit in stunned silence. Eventually, she stirred to look Esme in the eyes, and asked, very seriously, "What have we gotten ourselves into?"

Esme asked, because she needed to know before planning what came next, "Is there something going on between you too? You two seemed cozy at coffee."

Abby fidgeted with her hoodie again. "Yeah, we went on a date. A *really* nice date. And we've hung out a few times."

The prospect of getting them all free of this predicament brought a spark of Esme's usual enthusiasm to her words. "I have a plan. Gwyn said that I could contact him. I have guaranteed safety until tonight. Let's get him talking."

Esme wanted to reassure her because Abby already had the look of a woman mourning a lost relationship. "I get how crazy this sounds, but my gut tells me Gwyn is not a bad guy and I know Miles isn't either. This could all be a huge misunderstanding. There's still a chance that we can settle everything before anything between them escalates."

Abby replied, "Or we find out that Gwyn is completely off his rocker."

"True. I really don't think Gwyn is insane. Neither does Finn and he's at least a few hundred years old. He's proven to know more about certain things than Jacob. Let that sink in." Not being her secret, Esme hadn't revealed Miles' god-touched status.

Abby rolled her eyes. Esme couldn't quite blame her for the reaction; she was still having a hard time believing it herself.

Looking skeptical, Abby threw her hands in the air. "Fine. You've roped me into your little adventure. I'll admit that I'm rusty in my knowledge of the time before King Arthur, so I don't know a lot about either historical figure they're supposed to be."

Esme said, "Well, you should be proud of me then, because I did some research last night. Only one caveat, though..."

Abby looked at her askance.

Esme could hear the cringe in her own voice when she answered, "Gwyn *really* doesn't want you involved in this."

Abby's face morphed back into the angry harpy. It wouldn't be fair to let Abby think it was due to Gwyn seeing her as a problem or as weak, so Esme told her what her impression was. "I think he's trying to keep you safe and away from this whole mess. He's the right kind of interested in you."

Abby's expression turned back just as rapidly. She blushed and replied in a dramatic voice, "Well, damn, I could do worse than a demigod."

Esme nodded fiercely, responding to the note of humor in her friend's tone with a solemn expression on her face. "Mind-blowing, Abby, magic hands, I could continue with the adjectives."

With a hint of defiance, Abby said, "More seriously, though, I can make my own choices. You both need to let me do that."

Esme hugged her friend again, just as fiercely. "Gods, you are *so* right."

Chapter Forty-Two

Conversational Cookies

Esme

After Abby had returned to her apartment the night before, Esme had expected the loneliness to seep back in, but, surprisingly, she'd fallen asleep nearly instantly. She felt so light, unburdened by finally having the weight of so many secrets off her shoulders. All the people who mattered most to her knew the important stuff now.

As far as their plans went, Gwyn had business on the east side that morning, so they planned to meet him at Christi's house around midday. Abby's mother was traveling for work, so it would be empty. The location was ideal for two reasons. It was secluded, offering much more privacy than they could have within the city proper.

"Good news," Esme told Abby as they were leaving her house late the next morning. "I have cookie dough ready to go. So let's hope that some triple chocolate is enough to make Gwyn forget I told you everything. We can bake them at Christi's."

Esme explained what little she knew about Gwyn and Nudd on the drive over. "So, let's start with Miles, since there seems to be a lot less info out there about Nudd. Nudd Llaw Eraint—gosh, I hope I pronounced that correctly—was a legendary king from Welsh myth. He may have been a real guy, he may have not. No one knows."

"Damn. Welsh: that fits Miles so far."

"It gets stranger," Esme replied. "Nudd was worshiped sometime before the common era. Get this, he was famed for having a wolfhound that followed him around as he was healing people. Nudd also had a fake hand, crafted for him by another god after his was amputated in battle. He also had a thing for water."

Abby breathed out, "Gods above: the hand, the dog, the floating house—that fits scarily well. Oh my gods, he had me look up who Glais was a few weeks ago!"

Esme prodded, not knowing the slightest about the name, "And?!"

"The best resource I could find said that he was Sir Percival's grandfather."

If Abby knew about Miles' healing ability, she'd be even more freaked out.

Esme added, "It does fit scarily well. Now stuff is about to get really weird, so buckle up."

"Spit it out, drama queen."

"Fine, ruining my fun," Esme said pouting "Besides being Nudd's son, Gwyn ap Nudd is known for like five thousand different things. He was also deified. He was either the king of the Tylwyth Teg, a Fae people, the ruler of their underworld, or the leader of the Wild Hunt."

Abby asked, "You said Gwyn had a hellhound in the forest, right?"

Esme bobbed her head frantically as she drove. "Yep. This shit is a bit too real for my magical ass."

Abby frantically filled in gaps while reading encyclopedia pages on her phone. "Gwyn knew all the knights of the Round Table and King Arthur himself. Gods and goddesses, Esme, I think I'm going to hurl."

"I'll open a window."

Abby responded by placing her finger on the window button to prevent its lowering. "Do not! You're driving seventy miles per hour."

Esme suggested, "Hey, you could always try my anti-demon breathing exercises." Esme could see Abby's lips straighten into a disapproving line in her peripheral vision.

Abby said, "Glad to see that you can joke about it now. That's how I know you'll be alright. But, seriously, you've always done the whole breathing thing, haven't you?"

Esme nodded, still sore about their years of omissions. "Yep. My parents taught me to do it."

"I've read about cambion before in my work for the Brotherhood, ya know."

"Oh?" Esme made the word a question, trying to hide how desperately she wanted to know more.

"There isn't much about them in the past few hundred years. Maybe they've been hiding or something. Which would fit with what your parents were trying to do. Anyway, pretty sure you're a watered-down version because you don't have fangs or wing nubs."

"Uh, no. Absolutely not. Well," Esme reconsidered. Outside of her magic, all she had was a messed-up psyche when something pushed her too far. "My eyes do turn completely black when I get super pissed off. Or when I'm *really* enjoying myself."

Abby turned in her seat. "Really?"

"Really, really." Esme winked.

Abby squealed with delight. "I can't wait to do more research!"

At least that was confirmation that Abby wasn't afraid of her. Esme didn't realize how much she needed her friend's enthusiastic acceptance until she experienced it. She supposed that when you deal with non-humans regularly, learning that your best friend was only something like ninety percent human wasn't a big deal.

They arrived half an hour before the scheduled meeting time to get everything ready inside the house. Gwyn showed up in a nondescript car, probably a rental, which he drove so slowly that it was painful to watch. He was wearing the same long black coat she'd seen him in before, with jeans, and sturdy looking black boots. Then he opened up the rear door on the driver's side and the gwyllgi she'd seen in the forest hopped out after him.

This did not surprise Esme much, but Abby gasped, peeking out the window. She muttered, "This is so much more real than it was two hours ago."

Esme had mixed feelings about him bringing the gwyllgi, but he had made a promise, so if it was going to harm her, he wouldn't have brought it. While Esme answered the door, Abby stayed out of sight in the kitchen, plating the cookies and pouring drinks for everyone.

Swinging open the door, Gwyn spoke first. "Esmeralda. I'm happily surprised that you chose to meet with me again." He sniffed the air just like he had when she summoned her shadowcat at their fateful first meeting. "What is that smell?"

"Cookies! You're welcome to come in, but," she raised her voice so that Abby could hear while looking at the hellhound at his heels, "Can the hound come inside?"

"If it's housetrained!" Abby said brightly as she walked out of the kitchen into the entryway. "Hey, Gwyn."

It was Gwyn's turn to be surprised. He raised one pert eyebrow at Esme. She shrugged, not trying very hard to appear contrite.

Abby answered his expression for Esme, fibbing wildly with a challenging expression on her face. "I made it impossible for her to deny me."

Cowed, he responded coolly, "I can see how you would have that effect on a person."

His smooth talking caused Esme to remember the way Miles had praised her, his eyes lingering on her with a playful wink when they initially crossed paths. She mused whether that kind of pickup line-slash-compliment was genetic.

She stepped aside to usher him in. The gwyllgi's lambent red eyes were unsettling, to say the least. The great hound prowled on Gwyn's heels as he entered, but sniffed their hands and followed Gwyn into the house just like any other well-trained dog would.

Abby led them to the rear of the house, where she had the cookies and hot tea waiting. Esme loved the sunroom, so she was happy that Abby had chosen it for their meeting. Positioned in a clearing surrounded by towering Douglas fir trees, it had an unobstructed view of the sky thanks to its translucent roof and walls. As they sat around the table with treats, she welcomed the comforting sound of rain pattering on the roof. It was a comforting reminder that, for now, she had nothing to fear from Gwyn. They were there to have a conversation.

As they sat down, the gwyllgi walked over to both women for a second greeting. Esme had to stop herself from flinching as she received a small lick on the hand. When it was her turn for the same, Abby didn't react. She received a wagging tail and several more doggy kisses as her reward. The hellhound's enthusiastic response to her made Abby brave enough to reach for a pat on its head. She asked, "Does it have a name?"

Gwyn smiled at them beatifically. "She's Cerys."

"Beautiful dog, beautiful name. I can't believe that I'm petting a gwyllgi."

The hound unceremoniously flopped onto the floor at her feet, showing her belly. Esme knew Abby was made of stern stuff, but seeing her friend fearlessly pet a hellhound was unequivocal proof.

While this domestic scene was undeniably adorable, they were there for answers, so she did her Esme thing and cut into their reverie. "Gwyn, we asked you here hoping we could get some clarification."

"And with a delightful surprise, too." His eyes shifted to Abby, who grinned back at him with a challenge in her smile. There he did it again. Seriously, were he and Miles actually related?

"Finn filled me in about who you and Miles might be. I also talked to Abby about everything that you said." She stressed the "might" part. "The problem is, there are a few things that don't quite click with me about your story."

"Don't click?" He appeared to be clueless as to what she meant by that.

Esme proceeded cautiously. "I witnessed something that adds weight to your claim that Miles might not be who we think he is. Can you explain why you are so sure about who he is? I'll admit, Cerys' presence lends some credence to your identity."

"I can assure you. He is the same man."

"How?"

Gwyn seemed to have to think through this, so Esme helped him along. "So here's where things get squirrelly for me."

The look on Gwyn's face was priceless. It was almost as much fun to needle him with modern slang as it was Finn.

"I nearly killed Miles. He forgave me. Then he saved my life multiple times. He's been open and honest about things he didn't have to be open and honest about. Since then, he's been training me and helping the mage community. But we barely know you."

Gwyn looked to Abby for confirmation. She shrugged and nodded slightly, lifting her hands in a "well, it's true" gesture.

Esme added, "Then in the forest you started casting something on Miles."

Gwyn sat back heavily in his chair. "Yes; that was not the best opening move. I was casting a spell of paralysis on Nudd, not something to harm him. As I've said, my aim is to ask questions. I didn't trust him to play along. How do I know? The first is that they look exactly alike. But the most damning fact of all is that his unique magic is the same. Your concerns are legitimate. But I have given a promise with heavy consequences. I hope that it still holds some weight with you."

His long black coat remained on, causing his cheeks to redden in the warm room. This was the least confident that Esme had seen him.

Not wanting to get stuck in a circular argument of why she could trust Gwyn, Esme asked, "You also said that I was the second begotten woman. Who was the first?"

This answer came much more readily. "Her name was Elena. She was a shieldmaiden in my father's service. She was only a few years older than myself, but her skill with the sword and shield was beyond question."

His right leg bounced up and down slowly, belying the agitation that he was struggling to hide. "From the moment Elena came into my life, she was a lionhearted ally and a close friend. At every turn, she had my back. She was like a sister to me." His leg stopped bouncing. "And she loved Nudd. She was demon-blooded like you, Esmeralda."

So Nudd had loved a cambion warrior woman. Did Miles have a type?

"Nudd loved her in his own way. But maintaining his precious morals meant more to him than even his own happiness. In disputes, Elena often sided with me. Perhaps that is part of what soured him against me. I know that we often quarreled over various choices that I'd made. I cannot fathom who else but he would have had the power to, and found reason to, incarcerate me for so many years."

That brought up something else Esme had considered in the wee hours of the morning as she struggled to fall back asleep. "Let me get this straight. You claim to have been imprisoned for well over a thousand years, and then suddenly, out of nowhere, you materialized back into reality. How is that unlike what is happening with the malevolents?"

Abby nervously petted Cerys, who was still lying at her feet.

Alarmed, he asked them, "The malevolents are returning? I believed it was only Cerys and me."

Esme nodded at Abby. "I've been personally involved in dispatching an afanc, a doppelgänger, and a pishacha. Abby does research on them so we can hunt them more effectively. We don't know why they're coming back."

If Gwyn was telling the truth, having him as an ally could be a tremendous advantage. He, or some information locked away in his head, could be the key to unlocking the mystery of how the malevolents were returning.

Esme needed him to understand that there was a much bigger problem, an existential threat, that preempted his supposedly righteous fury. "Cerys can be controlled. But the other malevolents are presenting a much greater problem. They're a problem for everyone, including you."

"Their threat would be greater in this soft, magicless world." Gwyn took a long, considering sip of his tea. "I admit, I considered my imprisonment to be a result of this 'Extinction' once I learned of it." He cleared his throat. "It aligns with my suspicion regarding Nudd. Whatever or whoever caused it, the magic involved could be nothing less than spectacular. Could anyone other than an ascended being have wielded such magic? What better way to hide away your recalcitrant son than through an 'accident' of it?"

If he was the real Gwyn ap Nudd and he factually knew people capable of the level of magic needed to rid the entire world of malevolent beings, they needed him on their side.

But still, she felt like she knew Miles, and he was already on their side. He wasn't the man that Gwyn described. She had one last card to play that she hoped would trump Gwyn's arguments. Because, even if she was trying to be impartial, deep down she was arguing in Miles' favor.

She asked, "Do you know what being 'god-touched' means?"

"I do. I understand that it may result from a group's strong belief in an individual. Somehow this belief, this faith in the person grants the individual supernatural ability."

One glance at Abby proved that she, at least, understood what Gwyn was talking about. Abby questioned, "Like a tulpa?" Noticing the blank stares she was receiving, Abby clarified. "Uhh... a tulpa is a being that takes form through collective thought, like if you had an imaginary friend you believed in hard enough that it became real."

Gwyn shrugged. "I have also heard that being 'god-touched' could be because of something beyond the mortal realm, a force greater than ordinary beings, bestowing immense power upon a blessed individual—typically one deeply committed to a specific faith."

Interesting. Everything he said had to do with belief and faith. Esme knew that they were powerful forces, but she hadn't fully appreciated how powerful. But neither of those ideas would explain Miles' supposed aura of blessing—which she still hadn't learned to see. He also didn't have a devoted group of followers, and he wasn't a devotee of any religion that she knew of.

Just as she believed he had finished, Gwyn spoke again. "I received the blessing before what could be termed my ascension."

Finally, he'd given her something to sink her teeth into. "Did Nudd still have the halo or aura, or whatever comes with it after he 'ascended' as you called it? Did you?"

He answered quickly, "No."

Esme's curiosity about how he earned the blessing had to wait until she pressed her point. "Well, Miles has the halo. How could he be Nudd?"

Abby looked at her like she'd just been slapped.

"That is...most interesting." He seemed to turn over that nugget of information in his mind. "However, knowing Nudd, he could be faking it somehow."

It was clear there was no convincing him this way. Esme looked at Abby then, giving her the silent signal that it was her turn. Even though they'd rehearsed this beforehand, she hoped Abby wouldn't falter after learning about Miles' halo.

Abby said, "Fair point. We concede that there are enough similarities between the two to cast doubt on whether Miles is Nudd. Is there some way that you can test Miles to find out?"

"A test." That familiar raised eyebrow returned as he looked at Abby thoughtfully. But Gwyn's thoughts on whether Miles' true identity could undergo testing were doomed to remain incomplete.

At Abby's feet, Cerys gracefully shifted into an alert crouch, her ears perking up attentively. With an inquisitive tilt of her head, the gwyllgi directed her lambent gaze toward the sunroom's walls, through which the forest clearing was visible. Noticing this, Esme asked, "Abby, is there music playing on the patio or in another room?"

"No." Then Abby seemed to hear it, too.

Esme's scan of the backyard revealed nothing out of the ordinary. She noted the wrought-iron chairs and table on the back patio, some potted plants, the gardening shed with tools tucked away for the autumn, and the hot tub covered over for safekeeping.

Where was the sound coming from? Faint at first, the rhythmic beat of distant hoofbeats began to permeate the room. Yet, she still saw nothing.

Gwyn stood from his chair, his muscles tense and his eyes scanning the trees, with Cerys close behind, mirroring his alertness. Even though his expression remained inscrutable, his voice was as grim as the grave when he said, almost pleadingly, "Abigail, Esmeralda. Please go to the interior of the house and shut the doors. These riders are almost certainly here for me."

As puzzled as Esme was, Abby asked, "What? Who?"

He bypassed this question, emphasizing the urgency with further warnings. "Please refrain from leaving the house until the hoofbeats have faded into the distance. Regardless of the outcome, I hope this is short."

Exchanging glances, the women silently concurred that complying with Gwyn's request was not in their plans.

He repeated his plea as he locked eyes with each, "Please."

While Abby looked at Gwyn's eyes searchingly, hoping to find answers there, Esme flippantly remarked, "I'm very good at making bad decisions lately. What's one more?"

Abby ignored her best friend's inanity and said more judiciously, "You've been straight and fair with us so far, Gwyn. You don't seem too thrilled about whatever is coming, and this is my parents' house. We're staying."

Gwyn looked to be a mixture of stricken and furious at their foolhardiness. A great sucking sound, accompanied by the abrupt end of the crescendoing hoofbeats, forced each of their gazes to snap to the area just beyond the sunroom's exit door, where the patio met the forest edge beyond.

Emerging from what looked like a tunnel of shadows as empty as the deepest reaches of space, but was really a pathway through the mists of magic, appeared a troop of undead knights. As the portal closed, the six mounted riders calmed their restless black steeds to stand in a half-circle formation.

Gwyn's hand vanished into his coat and reappeared clutching a plain-looking short sword. So that's why he hadn't removed his jacket. Holding the sword, point angled to the ground, he said, "If you must remain, please stay within the house. Thresholds are essential to their nature."

He turned his attention from them and opened the back door to greet his macabre visitors. Cerys followed in his wake, slipping behind him as a shadow would follow its caster.

Neither Esme nor Abby moved, staring in awestruck silence at the headless riders arrayed in the backyard. With each step closer to the deathless cavalcade, Gwyn appeared to be confident and unhurried. But his warnings to them had belied his fears.

With the two friends left alone to watch the proceedings, Esme was the first to speak as she stared at the rotting heads held in the arm of each rider. She asked quietly, "Headless horsemen?"

Abby, similarly awed, replied, "Dullahan. Irish. They're heralds of death."

"Death? Why are they here for Gwyn?"

Abby hissed, voice still pitched low, "You read the same things I read. Given the whole gwyllgi thing with Gwyn, maybe they're like coworkers or something?"

Esme couldn't help but express her feelings on that topic with a grimace and a single comment. "Gross."

Abby nodded and asked. "Can you make out anything they're saying?"

She answered, "Just barely, but it doesn't sound like English to me." By this point, they'd been watching Gwyn for at least two full minutes.

As Gwyn's grip shifted on the hilt of his sword, Esme felt her last bit of security slip away. His body was tightly coiled, ready for a fight.

Dread—for what she feared might be coming; for what she knew she would do if it happened—snaked around her torso and tightened around her stomach.

Was it too much to ask for one more day without a fight?

Chapter Forty-Three

Reconnaissance

Miles

Prior to losing his hand, Miles had had a future in emergency medicine. But after the amputation, they considered his disability to be too much of a detriment to handle the most life-threatening injuries under pressure. It wasn't like he could explain to the medical boards that his use of magic made his prosthetic just as effective as his own flesh.

Adapting to his new circumstances, Miles transitioned into physiatry, where he could help people with disabilities, both visible and invisible, improve their quality of life. Being a relatively cushy new field of medicine, this specialty allowed him to have a looser schedule compared to his fellow doctors.

This flexibility had allowed him to pursue other more... unorthodox interests, like tracking a mage identified as a person of interest by a member of the Assembly. His search led him to the mountains east of Seattle. The towering trees and snowcapped mountains were such a contrast to where he'd lived for the majority of his life, that he could almost forget about the guilt that was consuming him. Almost.

Guilt over failing to protect Esme and Finn from the pishacha consumed him. The new flood of dreams depicting the king's personal failures only added to his turmoil. Engaging in a manhunt was the diversion Miles thought he needed to occupy his thoughts and ease the overwhelming regret.

Discovering that his target was the same man from the gwyllgi hunt had left him more than just surprised. It made him wary. Perhaps the most cautious he'd been in years.

Miles had passed the driveway where the man had parked his car almost thirty minutes ago, but he hadn't yet left his own vehicle. Lily sat patiently in the backseat, alert. They remained hidden in the shadows down the street, gazing into the treeline, waiting to see his mark's next move.

As time dragged on, Miles began to suspect that this remote stop was a safe house. Perhaps it was time to scout on foot. He strapped back on his weapons and exited the car, with Lily trailing silently behind. He'd rather have her in his sights than risk her safety if the situation turned ugly.

With the driveway far from neighboring houses, he could move without worrying about being seen in the weak daylight. Weaving his way on light feet through the trees, he saw an unfamiliar house. It was a sizeable, slightly older, family home that sat in a small clearing among the trees. Parked next to the mage's rental sat a car he recognized too well.

Esme's.

The same panic he'd felt the morning when he woke up alone and feared she'd been abducted from their bed surged through him once more. The distraction he'd sought through this hunt evaporated, replaced by an icy knot of fear.

Miles forced himself to use reason through the panic: Look for signs of struggle.

Blessed be, Esme had left her car unlocked. He cast a glance around, ensuring he was still unnoticed, and eased the passenger-side door open. Everything looked as it should. He could confirm that it was the same car that he'd driven in with her before. The same hair tie was still sitting in the cupholder. Lily popped her head in and gave it a cursory smell. She quickly turned away, uninterested, signaling that nothing unusual lingered within. A small relief.

Miles silently closed the car door and crouched behind her car. He needed to make some decisions, and he needed to make them fast. He needed to figure out why Esme was here. Was she here willingly, or under duress? It made little sense.

Could his target have lured her there? Miles dropped to the ground, peering beneath the car. From that hidden vantage point, he scanned the driveway to see if there were any marks from dragging or excessive scuffing on the fir needles lining the driveway and sidewalk. Nothing unusual—all he saw were the marks of unhurried footsteps.

Lacking mundane clues, he turned to magic. He wished he had mastered Will's technique for seeing magic directly because the current method of feeling for it was little more than guesswork mixed with intuition.

Lily stuck by his side, barely making a sound as he opened himself up to his sixth sense. The first thing he noticed was the sheer amount of power sunk into the wards encircling the house. This was definitely a mage's house. Beyond that, the smallest hint of the malevolent magic's twisted aura emanated most strongly from the car belonging to his target. That was all the confirmation he needed that something was most definitely wrong.

He hadn't intended to confront his target during this mission. This was supposed to be a reconnaissance foray. But the choices over what to do next warred within him, uncertainty causing him to waste precious time. Should he confront the potential threat inside the house or linger in the shadows, waiting to see if Esme emerged unharmed?

Then the smell hit him. Was that...did he smell biscuits baking?

That's when Lily's ears perked up. A moment later, he heard the sound of hoofbeats too.

Chapter Forty-Four

Dullahan

Gwyn

The timing of the unexpected visit left a sour taste in Gwyn's mouth as he approached the Dullahan. He'd been so close to making an inroad with Nudd.

His thoughts raced, considering various possibilities. Given his recent incarceration, could they be seeking retribution for something he could no longer remember? Now that he was human again, the possibility that they were there to claim him for death did not escape him. Or did they have an entirely different purpose for him in mind?

Caught between curiosity and caution, He took a deep breath and steeled himself for the encounter. There was naught to do but proceed formally. If they were anything like he was, they were greatly diminished in power and possibly even mortal. Perhaps, too, their memories were just as fractured as his own. With such a detriment they might believe the lies his ignorance would force him to tell.

At first glance, they appeared as menacing as the stories described them. With a formal and measured tone, he greeted them in his mother tongue, "Hail, noble Dullahan. To what do I owe the honor of your presence?"

In the place where the otherworldly wisdom of the space between life and death was once held now lived a human's curiosity and a touch of apprehension as he awaited their response.

A horseman from the center of the group nudged his mount forward. Its rotten head, eye sockets gaping horribly, had patches of matted brown hair still clinging to its scalp. The mouth, cradled under one gauntleted arm, spoke a single word carefully, with a sound like a fireplace bellows emptying, "Leader."

A bead of cold sweat dripped down Gwyn's spine under his shirt. The Dullahan had chosen a title for him in place of his name. While ascended, his name on the lips of a Dullahan would not be the death sentence that it could very well be for him now. Could it be as uncertain of his power as he was of theirs?

After an extended pause, it said haltingly, "We seek a common purpose." The creature's steed scuffed the ground impatiently, nostrils flaring, allowing smoke to escape.

Gwyn asked, "Venerable rider, I must know, beyond all doubts, what exactly is your aim with me?"

The provisional leader's stilted voice reverberated through the putrid hollows of its mouth. "Return to our purpose. To sow the Hunt."

With the muscles of his back and legs ready to transfer their power to his arm in an instant, Gwyn shifted his grip on the short sword that he'd stashed in easy reach within the folds of his coat. This he did subtly. The last thing he wanted was for his movement to unravel the precarious balance that the exchange had achieved.

Wrestling with the enormity of their request, he weighed the consequences of his choices. Revealing his weakness, his mortality, could make him a target instead of a potential ally. So instead he deflected, "In times past, we did not ride together." He at least knew that much about the Wild Hunt. It had never included the Dullahan.

Stressing the difference in their roles, he said, "The purpose of the Wild Hunt was never to sow death. My hunt ushered the souls of the dead to the threshold of the afterlife following their natural end."

The bellows of the Dullahan leader's mouth sucked in a great breath. Nothing but magic could transfer the breath from the head to its divorced body and back again. If the creature were human, Gwyn might think that it sounded resentful as it answered his contention. "The same. Harvesting life."

"Noble Dullahan, I disagree." He devised a delicate dance of words, carefully crafting an excuse that both maintained his deified facade and appeased the Dullahan's quest for purpose. He hoped that Cerys' presence at his side deepened the forgery. "Our pursuits may dance in the same realm, but the steps are vastly different. Our paths have not crossed in millennia. Yet, today you come seeking my leadership. Why?"

Three of the six horses shuffled, their hooves grinding into the dirt as they sensed their riders' tension. Gwyn remained still, the picture of composure, but primed nonetheless. His last question was yet another gamble, and he rarely lost those. It would fail if they knew that he, like them, had disappeared into a prison of time. If it worked, they would be unbalanced, reminded of their novel frailty.

The leader seemed to consider Gwyn's words and found them wanting. Unable to speak more than a couple of words at once without taking a breath, the Dullahan replied, "No absolution from your duty. Return to power."

Were they asking him to return to power or were they seeking it for themselves? Or both?

Omitting the proper honorific, since he hadn't been offered one in turn, he replied, "I see that there is some confusion. I once led the Wild Hunt, but those days are long past. The path I tread is different now. The mantle of leadership no longer rests upon my shoulders."

The Dullahan leader's hollow gaze bore into Gwyn, seemingly probing for any hint of deception. "Denial." The others joined in with murmurs of discontent, their steeds shifting impatiently.

As one, each of the Dullahans turned, grabbed their heads by the remaining hair, and lifted them into the air at shoulder level. It was a slow, seeking movement not meant to instigate attack. Each tilted the eyeless faces of their riders to the left for a scant moment, then beyond him toward the sunroom, and then returned their blind, furious gazes back to him.

This time, the stuttering voice of the main speaker emerged with the potency of unbridled rage. "A begotten pet. The blessed hiding in wait!" It took a deep billowing breath and finally spoke the longest string of words that it could manage, "Using them to regain your own power! Denying us!"

The lead Dullahan raised its free arm, hand gripping a nightmare whip made of a human spinal column, held together by malevolent magic. Gwyn instinctively raised his short sword in response, wishing that he had a shield to block the wicked blows that were sure to come, hoping that his sword arm would not bend under the pressure.

But the strike never landed. Gwyn found himself within a protective mage's bubble—a very strong one to have so cleanly deflected the strength of a Dullahan. Simultaneous with this thought came the sound of three loud pops erupting from his right. He watched in awe as the lead rider toppled off his horse.

So far fallen, so long alone, Gwyn now had allies.

Miles

As the curious sound of hoofbeats ceased, Miles sensed the building pressure of magic coming from behind the house. Sneaking around to investigate, he stumbled upon a scene that he had only experienced in his wildest dreams.

Because he had experienced such a nightmare many times before. Yet, this time, his dread was not lessened by his presence in the dream king's mind.

Instinct took over. Miles raised a shield, catching the bone whip's crack just before it struck his would-be assassin. Only time would tell if that was a decision he'd regret until his last breath. With his other hand, he fired two shots at the attacking Dullahan and one at its steed. Horror seized him as Esme darted just out of his firing range to lunge behind a chair.

He was in the thick of it now.

As two familiar trolls popped into existence behind the line of riders, Miles squared to meet the foe nearest to him as it turned to charge in his direction. The knight and steed were both heavily armored. His shots needed to be precise and on target to be effective.

One. Two. Three. Four. Once the fifth and sixth shot met the steed's unarmored legs, it crumpled to the ground, violently unhorsing its rider. The undead knight took no time to regain its feet, still protectively sheltering its head in one arm and the whip in the other. Lily lunged at it, aiming for the head, but missed. The creature kicked, boot landing to move her aside. Lily fell yelping, but was probably only bruised.

Miles had one more shot in the magazine. He aimed and fired. By a blessed miracle, the shot met its mark. The bullet tore through the exposed palm of the raised hand holding the whip. Miles re-holstered his gun, fumbling for a new magazine. But the Dullahan was already on him, closing the distance.

The undead knight came in fast with one ruined hand and the other cradling its head. Unable to hold its whip and its head, it used its fist like a bludgeoning mace, swinging its gauntlet with immense power toward him.

Miles dodged blow after blow. Lily scrambled upward, and lunged again, trying to get a purchase with her teeth between the plates of armor, but only succeeded minimally each time.

Between blows, Miles grunted, "To Esme," and the dog was off in a flash.

Esme

The O'Malley residence's formerly tranquil backyard burst into action. As soon as she saw the lead rider raise his bone whip, Esme was on her feet and out of the sunroom's back door before her brain could utter a word of caution. The presence of walls, even if they were predominantly glass, would hinder the effectiveness of her conjured help in the fight.

The moment she left the safety of the house, she heard three gunshots crack from her right, instinctively prompting her to seek cover behind the nearest wrought-iron chair. As she crouched there, she watched the lead Dullahan fall from his horse.

Which of her summoned companions would best counter what were essentially armored, mounted zombies? She'd try for diversity first and adjust from there.

Power flowed from Esme to the summoned trolls that appeared behind the two closest riders. Bert and George were safe bets who didn't require her to tap into the infernal. They lunged in unison to pull the closest rider off his steed.

Over the years, she'd found that her mind could take the feedback from four conjurations at once. She could push it to five if one of them was only doing a menial task, but this was not a situation where she could push her boundaries safely.

When she looked up at where Gwyn had been bracing to take the whip's lash, she saw with heavy relief that he was still standing, unharmed. He still held his sword in his right hand and his left he'd wreathed with magical fire. Cerys lunged at the nearest Dullahan, teeth bared.

As the trolls struggled to dismount the closest rider, Esme began the call for another helper. Snowbert appeared to the right of her trolls, squarely in front of the next closest Dullahan, who sought to stop the marauding trolls from harming his brethren. Snowbert's icy presence immediately arrested its charge and he lifted one arm to meet the raised whip of his foe.

A light breeze swiftly passed Esme, catching her attention. A blaze of blonde hair streaked across the porch. Abby was running full tilt into the battle. As Esme watched, her friend swerved to open and close the garden shed door behind her. Even as she sighed in relief, Esme prepared for the task she'd been dreading.

Gwyn

Gwyn saw Abigail blaze past him and disappear. By unspoken command, Cerys left her ready stance next to him and trailed after her.

Firearms were not something that he'd experienced before and hoped not to be so close to ever again. The accuracy of the shots hitting the Dullahan's body at the junction of its armor was marksmanship of renown. One shot had taken out the horse as well. He hadn't been able to pause long enough to see the source of his redemption.

However, mounted combat was something that he was intimately familiar with—the dance of blades and horse hooves. Gwyn studied the next Dullahan's movements, watching for a tightened muscle here or a shift in weight there, so that he could respond accordingly.

In three strides, the next Dullahan guided its mount over the prone body of the first. Gwyn watched as it tightened the reins and applied a subtle pressure with its heels. The horse tensed its hind muscles, preparing to rear up and attack him. But Gwyn was ready for this.

The magic, burning bright and hot with brutal force, streamed out of him, catching the horse and rider in a conflagration of fire. He poured as much as he dared into it.

It was enough. But he would not be capable of doing that again so soon.

As he took a moment to breathe, he watched as an ax, a sharp blade, and some sort of farming implement flew with purpose out of the small back building where he'd seen Abigail run. She'd joined the battle.

Soon, he would be forced to rejoin it as a third rider approached.

Esme

The sounds, the smells, the tactile memories of what she'd done while joined with her eldritch beast the last time she'd touched the infernal were a paralytic of her own making.

She wasn't alone this time. Gwyn was there. Abby was there. She needed to be there for them. This time, she would be in control. Esme wouldn't hide in it. She would use her birthright, just like she'd been using it for years unknowingly.

With a deep inhale, she focused her mind, blocking out the doubts and fears that threatened to cloud her thoughts. With measured steps, she cautiously confronted the rage brewing inside her, aware of how easily it could spill over.

These horsemen had come demanding something with whips held ready to punish any answer that they didn't like. That seemed pretty malevolent to her. She couldn't think of anything more poetic than denying them everything.

As Esme completed her summoning, she watched Gwyn obliterate a mounted Dullahan with pyromancy. Impressive. Still, she could tell that it wasn't effortless for him; he teetered to one side, only to regain his footing immediately.

Oatmeal, in all her smelly feline glory, blossomed into being as Esme felt her connection to Bert dissolve. She wasn't overloaded, she'd just taken on her fourth minion, so her addition of the shadowcat was not the cause of Bert's downfall. She hadn't been paying close enough attention.

George was absorbing strike after strike from that horrific whip. Bert must have taken too much damage and lost corporeal stability. Unfortunately, George wasn't close behind, and Snowbert was likewise struggling. Still, they'd effectively removed one horse from the battle.

She sent Oatmeal to harry the floundering knights that had taken out Bert. Oatmeal, now even larger than she'd been when she fought Cerys, rocketed across the patio, narrowly missing being shaved by the enchanted set of tools racing out of the garden shed.

Oatmeal vaulted her massive body onto the back of the armored undead knight, sinking her teeth into the exposed flesh where the neck should have been and digging her claws into the space between the breast and backplates. The Dullahan fell with the weight of the shadowcat on its back as its whip caught George one final time.

Status: both trolls were down, but so was one more Dullahan.

Esme looked around for the best position to send her shadowcat reinforcement. Snowbert was still locked in combat with his foe near the hot tub. Near the... A genius idea struck Esme as she sent the commands to her ice elemental and shadowcat simultaneously.

Snowbert led the Dullahan toward the hot tub, one languorous icy step at a time. His snowy outer layer had protected him somewhat from the blows, but she could feel that he, too, was losing durability. Once the Dullahan was in the correct location, Oatmeal repeated her trick of vaulting onto its back while Snowbert ripped off the protective top of the hot tub. The rider and the shadowcat plunged into the water as one.

She only had eyes for the ice elemental as it climbed in. Leaping once again, Oatmeal propelled herself off the waterlogged undead knight to exit the slowly freezing water.

With only two conjurations running, Esme could experiment with their connection. She needed more power, and she needed it now. She reached down once more, her nails clawing into the darkness where she felt the infernal. The instant she made direct contact with it, shadows eclipsed her eyes. The power she'd grabbed hold of at first came unwillingly, fighting to remain in the dark.

She applied more pressure.

Unlike before, when the power had overwhelmed her—when it had decided for her what came out of the darkness, her eldritch beast—this time Esme controlled it. She forced the dark magic through her link to Snowbert, increasing the dose her conjuration received as if she'd added a heaping spoonful of cayenne pepper to his recipe, instead of a pinch.

Once the brimstone-fueled power contacted the ice elemental, it was changed irrevocably. Untamed, jagged ice spikes of the deepest blue formed all over Snowbert as the snowy exterior of his body hardened. Infernal Snowbert's treacherous-looking arms ensnared the struggling Dullahan against the spikes covering his body, refusing to let it go. The water in the hot tub started to freeze over, bubbling in places as her captive endeavored to break free.

Esme didn't know if a Dullahan could drown, but with her eyes as dark as midnight under a new moon she hoped to find out.

She did the math. The first Dullahan fell in front of Gwyn, another was burned to a crisp, a third fell at the feet of the trolls and Oatmeal, and another was floundering in the cold water of the hot tub. Gwyn was fighting off his second opponent with his sword as two gardening tools aggravated it from behind. He had to leap over the fallen body of the first rider that had perished from gunshots.

She'd almost forgotten about that opening salvo. Where was the sixth Dullahan? Where had the gunshots she'd heard come from?

Because her attention was entirely focused on the fight at the hot tub, Esme failed to notice the dog approaching her side of the patio chair. Esme nearly jumped out of her skin when she felt a warm furry body brush against her legs. She had to do a double take to make certain that her eyes weren't deceiving her as the shadows faded from them. Lily was practically sitting on her feet!

Miles.

It couldn't be. At last, she found him on the far right side of the clearing, grappling with the sixth rider. How was he there? Standing at the cusp of stupefaction, a dangerous place to be in the middle of a battle, she snapped out of her confusion as she watched one of Abby's enchanted tools fly toward him.

His face was dripping sweat as their eyes connected for one eternal moment. He had a way of showing up when she needed him most. Without hesitation, she dispatched her shadowcat to take some of the pressure off him.

Her hands trembled as they stroked Lily's coarse fur. She needed reassurance from Lily as much as she offered it. Esme readied herself for the sprint that would take her to the now-cold hot tub.

Gwyn

Anticipating the whip's lash, Gwyn braced himself with his sword arm raised. He'd used too much magic burning that last Dullahan. His arms sagged under the weight, while his legs trembled with exhaustion. He was still trying to regain the precise control over his magic from his past life, and now he was facing the consequences of his weakened abilities. The Dullahan he was up against had dismounted his horse, likely to send it to trouble Gwyn's allies on the battlefield. He had to believe that they could hold their own.

When the lash came, it menaced the air with a whoosh of speed, exploding like a macabre thunderclap on nothing whatsoever—because Gwyn was ready. He ducked to his left, rolling sideways on the ground, then bounded to his feet, sword outstretched.

The next report cracked toward him. This time he caught it on the edge of his sword, pain ricocheting up his arm all the way to his back. He tried to pull the whip away from the Dullahan, but he wasn't fast or strong enough. Decades of training allowed him tilt his sword at the perfect angle to allow the whip to slide off and not take his weapon with it.

Three enchanted tools launched themselves at the undead knight attacking Gwyn. This purchased him a moment to retreat to the left. He either needed to get in close or keep the Dullahan occupied until he or one of his allies could finish the fight.

Abby

When Abby saw Esme fly out of the sunroom like a shieldmaiden of legend, she felt the same compulsion. But what could she do? She was a nurse and a part-time research assistant; no one special. She wasn't trained for battle, so she couldn't get close enough to the Dullahan to use her unique type of magic to its greatest effect. But testing the range limits of her special, secret power would have to wait; she had to act—now.

Abby wasn't a coward. She sprinted to the garden shed, where her parents kept a stash of tools. No one seemed to notice her flight. That was fine because it gave her time to work. Plundering the cache, she found only three tools suitable for whacking or stabbing at the armored knights.

Enchanting, because Abby would get technical if given half a chance, was a lot like Esme's conjuration in this case. But instead of summoning minions, Abby could compel whatever inanimate object was at hand to do her bidding. With one slide of her finger on the grips of the three tools, she flew them out of the shed, artfully combining telekinesis with enchanting, to harass the nearest Dullahan.

She kept this up for some time, aiding Gwyn in his fight. But then she noticed the large wolfhound run to Esme's side and realized Miles was the one who had shot the gun.

A good commander knew when to split their forces. From her safe spot, Abby sent the ax rocketing toward the Dullahan Miles was struggling with.

But her stomach lurched as she saw fatigue wash over Gwyn's face. His movements became less fluid with each swing of his sword. She was determined to do more to help him. Except the moment she stepped out of the shed, she saw a horse, eyes aglow in the fading daylight, riderless, aiming for a fight.

Miles

How did one fight effectively against a heavily armored foe?

The knife he had strapped to his leg wouldn't be much use against an undead tank, and he needed to create enough time for himself to exchange his magazine. He couldn't take the full force of the blow from a gauntleted fist without risking serious injury. Even grappling had its downfalls. With all that armor, the Dullahan was significantly heavier than him.

He'd have to grab, trip, spin out of the way, rinse, and repeat until something offered him an opening. On its next swing forward, the Dullahan used its sledgehammer of a fist to come at him with a right hook. Miles took the opening to shoot underneath the reaching arm. He drove his right shoulder into the space where the breastplate met the tassets at its waist. The stench wafting from the rotten head that was cradled just above his own nearly made him vomit.

Pushing with all the force available in his body, he heaved upward. Surprised, the Dullahan overcompensated, leaning too far in the opposite direction. It landed on its side and then rolled onto its back. Miles jumped away, aiming to gain distance once again. If conditions were ideal, he would have enough time to erect a shield around himself or reload his gun. Reality wasn't so kind, because his opponent scrambled to its feet, far faster than should be possible when wearing that much plate and chain mail.

The knight sprinted toward him. It sped up shoulders first, carrying its head like a football. Locking both hands on its shoulders, he brought its forward movement to a stop. He narrowly avoided its next punch by ducking his head and jumping backward.

Rather than use the moment he'd gained for self-defense, he scanned the chaos again for Esme. Hiding behind the chair, she was safe, with Lily by her side. When their eyes met, he found exactly what he'd been hoping for. She was in control and kicking ass.

As he squared up to the standing Dullahan again, a surge of newfound strength coursed through his limbs. He watched as an enchanted ax flew their way.

He really hoped that was a present for him.

Esme

Esme took off across the patio with Lily right beside her, keeping up with every step. She screamed, "Abby, give me the trowel!" Ten paces in, they both had to swerve and dodge to avoid Gwyn's backward retreat. Brandishing his sword, he leaped backward, over the body of the bullet-ridden Dullahan, to avoid the long reach of a bone whip.

Abby must have heard her, because she sent the tool gliding her way. As Esme snatched it from the air, Abby ended her enchantment on it, returning it to its natural state of mundanity. Armed with a tool, she could complete the task she began with Snowbert.

Then she was at the edge of the hot tub. Snowbert was holding on, literally and figuratively. By that point, a thin layer of ice had formed on the water's surface, and the Dullahan's movements were sluggish. She wasn't certain how she could kill a headless zombie with a trowel, but she was going to try.

Fortunately, or unfortunately, depending on your perspective, Esme didn't have to solve that specific problem yet. As soon as she lifted the trowel, one of the hellish black steeds charged, puffing smoke out of its nostrils, straight at her.

There was a zero percent chance a trowel would do anything against an armored zombie horse. Desperation forced her hand to reach back down, to try something new.

If this worked, it could change everything for her.

She dropped into a stance from an action movie, one leg forward, the other braced against the ground. By her next heartbeat, she held a pike made of shadows and smoke, ablaze with brimstone. She barely had a moment to acknowledge her accomplishment before she had to brace herself.

The impact of one thousand pounds of horse knocked her cleanly off her knees. She landed backward, head tucked to her chest to prevent a concussion, ass first, onto the ground. Tilting her body to the left, she used the momentum from her fall to continue the roll sideways, finally stopping face down in the dirt. An unbidden groan of pain escaped her throat.

Everything hurt. But she was alive.

Abby

She tried not to look threatening as she slid her fingers along the backs of the two closest wrought-iron chairs and table. The horse shifted into an even more menacing stance. With two of the three tools she'd enchanted free of her control, Abby worked to make the furniture come alive. With a speed she didn't think magic could achieve, she twisted and pulled the objects together, forming a wrought-iron construct with eight legs, a heavy torso, and no head.

Flight wasn't a safe option on its own because one thousand pounds of armored horseflesh were surging right at her, ready to trample and kick, far faster than she could get out of the way. She had to fight. Cerys, who had been by her side, hurled herself at the horse's hindquarters. A rush of epinephrine flooded through Abby's veins like a tsunami. The construct would be her battering ram.

At first, she thought to use the construct to meet the horse head on, but it wasn't fast enough. So it rammed into the side of the steed instead. Abby could hear the thud of the impact. The impromptu T-bone maneuver rocketed the horse sideways. The thrust of so much weight with inertia hitting its body caused the side of the horse's ribs to dent inward with a horrible crunch. It fell with two legs snapping audibly under it.

Abby had to look away.

She'd drawn on too much power, far too quickly.

Her whole body began trembling uncontrollably. Her breaths were ragged, gasping for air as she collapsed to the ground.

She really needed more practice at this sort of thing. If she could just rest for a moment, everything would...

Miles

The Dullahan charged at him again, but this time its perfect momentum was altered by the addition of a massive shadowcat jumping onto its back. As the shadowcat leaped away once more, Miles snatched the arm cradling its head.

Miles gripped the Dullahan's outstretched elbow with his prosthetic hand, locking the metal and wires into place with a surge of magic. At the same time, he slid his other arm beneath its armpit and forcefully drove his shoulder against it. This knocked the putrid head out of place. It squelched as it hit the ground and rolled.

Stepping toe to toe with it, he pivoted while lowering his hips in preparation. He amplified his strength with a burst of magic. With another sudden backward push, he leveraged the Dullahan's momentum, forcing its trapped arm forward. The undead knight arced through the air, landing in an ungainly pile on the ground before him.

Miles snatched the ax from where it had been hanging in the air and chopped downward with all the force he could muster, ending the fight.

Gwyn

Another crack of the whip. Retreat. This dance they repeated ad infinitum. If he could get it to drop its head, he might have a chance for an opening. One tool went flying off elsewhere.

His breaths were coming heavily now. The exertion of the battle was weighing on his muscles. Each time his body struck the ground as he dove or rolled to avoid the wicked strike of the whip, pain shot through him. He was slowly burning himself out by fortifying his body to beyond its dismal human limits. At this rate, he would be incapable of calling forth the smallest stream of pyromantic fire when he needed it most.

Eventually, a second enchanted tool zoomed away from its harassment of his rampaging opponent. Abby must be fighting on multiple fronts. She, Esme, and his unknown savior had most certainly saved his life.

Losing the second enchanted tool was Gwyn's cue to explore imaginative alternatives to their by-then-repetitive dance macabre. Whips could only be defeated by two different types of weapons. While ranged projectiles were ideal, a polearm or a javelin with a long reach would work admirably. His foot hit the edge of a plant pot that had a handle attached.

He'd just have to create his own projectile.

Slipping the tip of his sword under the handle, he fortified the muscles of his wrist, arm, and shoulder with a fragment of the magic remaining in his body and heaved it up into the air. He watched as the arc of his impromptu projectile moved on the proper course. Gwyn sprinted toward the Dullahan, sword arm at the ready.

As the planter hit the undead knight squarely on the head, Gwyn leaped and thrust downward, plunging his sword into the open space where the stub of its neck gaped horribly.

But he fell to the ground with blood pooling around him. In his rush of certain victory, he hadn't felt the whip slice deeply into his side.

Chapter Forty-Five

The Fallout

Esme

As far as Esme knew, the horse was down, but she still had to deal with the Dullahan in the hot tub. Through her connection with Snowbert, Esme sensed it was barely putting up a fight any longer. The freezing water had worked far better than she'd hoped.

She scrambled up, not stopping to wipe the fir needles and grit from her body. Lily rejoined her from wherever she had escaped to avoid the rushing horse. The first thing Esme saw was Abby passed out on the patio next to a gnarled metal behemoth and a second dead horse. Fear of what she might find made her legs move in a stumbling shamble.

Esme kneeled beside Abby, her movements stiff. She placed a trembling hand on Abby's wrist, feeling a steady heartbeat beneath her fingers. Relief flickered through her; Abby was breathing. Esme looked her over carefully, not rocking her or turning her over. Abby had drilled the rules into her—no sudden movements—so she kept her touch gentle. Finding nothing amiss, Esme shook Abby gently.

"Abby. Abby! Wake up!" She urged her friend to re-enter the waking world. It looked a lot like magical burnout, and not too far along because she wasn't standing in a pool of Abby's vomit.

A subtle flutter of her eyelids was the first sign that Abby was coming to. Relief washed over Esme as Abby groggily opened her eyes.

"You okay?" Esme asked, needing to hear the affirmative.

Abby nodded slightly, then sat bolt upright in a state of high alertness. Esme had to dodge out of the way to avoid getting smacked in the face by the movement. "Gwyn! Miles!"

Those were her thoughts precisely. "Yes, let's go."

Both women clambered upright, wobbling, each helping the other. Esme saw Miles a short distance away, standing with the ax raised over the body of a Dullahan. He chopped down, and the ax cleaved into the Dullahan's neck with a wet, heavy crack. This was the ruthless side of him she'd only seen in combat. Finally, he looked their way.

"Miles!" she shouted, her voice coming out strained but relieved. Lily ran to him, barking happily. He seemed whole and uninjured. He started jogging their way.

Once he was closer, she could see that he was just as dirty and bruised as she was, perhaps even more so. Blood splattered the front of his dark clothing and his prosthetic hand looked as if it had frozen in mid-movement from a loss of power or function.

Abby pulled away from Esme in a rush of panic. She shrieked, "Help me get it off him!"

Esme looked over to see that the corpse of a Dullahan was lying on top of Gwyn. Underneath them was a pool of mingled blood, some darker and some lighter in hue. Cerys was lying next to her master's body, panting heavily in agitation. Esme joined Abby in tugging the Dullahan's body out of the way. By the time they finished, Miles had arrived.

Abby crouched down and started her assessment. When her eyes scrunched in concentration, Esme knew that something was terribly wrong. The first thing she noticed was Gwyn's ashen complexion, his eyes closed in unconsciousness. But then she looked down and saw that his skin, muscle, ribs, and probably some of his lung underneath had been shorn cleanly through.

"Gwyn, stay with me!" Abby called out, her voice firm but laced with an undercurrent of urgency. "Miles! Help!"

Despite his exhaustion, Miles sprang into action, his movements quick and precise. Esme's hands twitched at her sides, itching to do something, anything to not feel useless, as she watched them lean over Gwyn. Abby had turned her back to Esme so she couldn't read her friend's face to see exactly how bad things were.

Abby barked out, "Penetrating wound to the side, significant bleeding. Unknown depth." Miles examined the injury briefly. Blessedly unconscious, Gwyn didn't startle or cringe during any of the prodding that he was being subjected to.

Abby turned her attention to Esme and ordered, "Inside there's an emergency medkit to the right of the kitchen sink. Go!"

Esme began to turn, but paused and caught Miles' attention. "Please," she begged, expression filled with meaning. Tears were filling her eyes.

"Esme, go!" Abby barked again.

But Esme only had eyes for Miles. He returned her look. She repeated her plea. "Please, Miles, he might be the only person who can help us stop the malevolents from returning. Please, trust me."

He looked down at Gwyn and shook his head. He clearly did not want to do what she was asking. But then his gaze reconnected with hers and he nodded.

Tears blurred her vision, the frustration and fear streaking down her dirty face. It felt like all she did lately was cry. Trying to maintain her voice through the surge of sadness and fear, Esme said, "Abby, Miles needs to work. Move your hands."

At first, Abby resisted, voicing incoherent rejections as she tried to speak, but Esme grabbed her by the shoulders and pulled her backward forcefully. Stunned into stillness by Esme's rough handling of her, Abby stopped fighting to return to Gwyn.

While both women watched, Miles placed his hands on Gwyn's wound. A soft golden glow blazed from his palms—even the prosthetic one. The magic knit blood vessels together, decreasing Gwyn's blood loss until it finally ceased. A rib shifted under the glow, a fragment rejoining the body of the bone, as it slithered back into place like a pale snake finding its nest. Next, muscle fibers reconnected beneath the skin.

With every flicker of glowing magic coming from his hands, Miles grew paler until he grunted, "The skin, fascia, I can't..." He lifted his arms to cradle his head and he, too, passed out cold. He fell sideways into the pool of blood next to Gwyn's prone body. Miles had used too much magic in a short period, but Gwyn might just live to see another day.

Esme turned Abby around bodily and grabbed her shoulders. Abby's expression was as stunned as Esme's probably had been the first time she saw Miles heal Lily. Compared to this, that healing had been trivial.

She looked Abby squarely in the eyes and said as calmly as she could muster, "Go get that medkit. You need to clean and stitch Gwyn up. Now."

Years of experience working in emergency situations made Abby nod once, definitively. Instead of asking the million questions Esme knew were spiraling in her head about what she'd just witnessed, Abby sprinted back into the house.

There was one final task to do. Throughout all this, Esme had successfully maintained her link with Snowbert, keeping the final Dullahan under control.

Esme walked over to the hot tub and dismissed her ice elemental. The Dullahan was practically motionless at that point, so she didn't think that it needed to be restrained any longer. As she embraced the familiar darkness, in some ways, she accepted herself a bit more. Drawing the power back into herself, she remained steady and in control.

Esme's violet eyes darkened once again. The change was starting to feel natural to her. She should have been surprised when the icy surface of the hot tub broke with the abrupt upward surge of the Dullahan, but she wasn't. The numbing clarity of the infernal magic had sharpened her focus to her task. The undead knight lunged forward to attack her.

But, to its surprise, Esme had already come back from that place of anger and shadows, holding a sword made of brimstone and hatred.

The Dullahan impaled itself on her sword, knocking her down with it. Its body fell on top of her in a violent crash of plate armor on soft flesh. It didn't struggle or make a single movement as she pushed its carcass off her.

As she shook off the infernal magic and scraped the leaves from her clothing, Esme's attention returned to less violent concerns. Finn would riot when he learned what he'd missed out on. And, just in case Jacob had a heart attack while listening to the story, she would have a baby aspirin ready.

It had been an exceptionally bad day for Esmeralda Morgana Turner, and she still needed to ask her boyfriend if he was over a thousand years old.

Gwyn

The next morning, Gwyn woke up in an unfamiliar room. His bed was rocking ever so slightly and his mouth was as dry as salted fish in the middle of summer. He felt familiar fur under with the fingertips of his left hand—Cerys.

As he engaged his abdominal muscles to sit up, wild pain electrocuted his body. He relented, falling back into his place of rest. He must have groaned loudly, because answering footsteps started his way.

Gwyn's heart sank through the floorboards as he saw Nudd walk through the open door wearing sweatpants and a T-shirt. Contrasting with this outfit of modern comfort, he was carrying a wicked-looking dagger.

"You," Gwyn croaked out accusingly through dry lips. The lazy, untroubled look Cerys gave the other man made Gwyn briefly question her loyalty. But then he remembered the effect his father had on dogs...

"Me," said Nudd, holding his arms out wide, hands splayed in a gesture of challenge. "So let's talk about some house rules, eh, Gwyn? Since we might be roommates for a while."

Nudd performed a threatening trick of spinning the dagger in one hand rapidly. Then he floated it in the air using magic.

The weapon picked up speed, rotating at sufficient velocity and at just the right angle to spear Gwyn through the heart. But he was powerless against it.

The wolfhound that Gwyn had seen in the forest sauntered into the room and walked over to sniff him. The blade kept whirling. When the hound licked his hand, he felt a flicker of calming, pleasantly warm magic transfer to him. He hadn't expected the pleasant gesture from his father's hound. Although this wasn't the hound he remembered, he could sense that the new one was just as valuable.

Nudd spoke. "Rule number one. You act against me or Lily in this house, you die."

So her name was Lily. The dog was a ray of light in the dark of this new prison of his father's making.

Nudd paused to see if Gwyn was still listening. Satisfied, he continued, "Rule number two. If you act against Esme or Abby, you die. Rule number three. You harm anyone else, you die." He grabbed the spinning dagger from the air, pointed it at Gwyn again, and asked, "See the pattern? It's very simple."

Before turning to walk away, he warned, "I didn't want to heal you, but she asked. Don't make me regret that."

Chapter Forty-Six

An Epiphany

Gwyn

He knew he should feel the deep, sharply cutting teeth of the winter wind on his skin. That he should feel the pit of his stomach gnawing away at him with hunger in its emptiness, with need. Gwyn remembered physical pain, if only vaguely.

But something else sustained him now. Magic. He'd begun to despise it as deeply as he'd once worshiped it. Because for all that magic had given him—near immortality and power beyond his wildest imagination—it had likewise taken away the thing that matters more to man than he can comprehend, until it is snatched from his hands: choice.

He saw pain on the faces of those alive and dead as he passed through their lands. Sunken cheeks, bulging eyes, shoulders jutting squarely through their clothing.

If the Wild Hunt could tire, it would be ragged, panting, with lungs heaving for breath on the side of the muddy tracks that passed for roads in the wilds of Wales. Two years of too much rain at the wrong time, not enough when it was needed, and frost after the flowers had bloomed, left men starving. As Gwyn had learned, there were few other things in this world that could turn a righteous man into a beast in the same way that a hollow belly did.

War had ravaged the island from top to bottom. Men stole from and retaliated against their neighbors for the slightest offenses. So death by deprivation birthed grizzly death in battle, which only served to fill winter's greedy mouth with more and more death. By the droves, they came. It was Gwyn's duty to guide them, but it was no longer his honor.

What his body could no longer feel, his soul ached with: despair. His soul cried out in frustration at the suffering of the world. It ached with the agony of a thousand mourning voices pleading for even the smallest bit of comfort. However, the anguish caused by a single death broke through the cries of the many to shatter his already fragile grasp on reason.

As he walked through the wood and stone halls of his father's keep, Gwyn ap Nudd passed unnoticed by the human guardsmen. He sought Nudd Llaw Eraint, his namesake, who, like him, had received the gift of power to better serve humanity. For reasons unknown to Gwyn, Nudd still inhabited the place where his humanity had ended and ruled there as though he were still wholly a man.

When Gwyn found his father, he was sitting alone in his room. The hearth was cold and unused. Ice had formed on the rim of the chalice containing his favorite sloeberry liquor. No feminine touches graced this bare place. No tapestries brightened the walls, as would befit the king that Nudd was. For Gwyn's mother had perished many, many years ago, and he had never remarried.

Whenever Gwyn entered his presence, Nudd always felt to him like a great torch, burning brightly with just the right amount of heat to make a man feel comfortable against the day's chill.

His magic was for healing, for the waters, for ruling. But on this day, Nudd was closed off, his power contained. Likewise, his loyal hound was nowhere to be seen. It was puzzling.

It was at that moment that he realized Nudd already knew. But how?

He only knew because of his duties. He'd taken her by the hand to the door himself. She'd walked next to him, resplendent in her household armor, head held high like the queen she was in all but name. She took off her helm, revealing her bright amethyst eyes to him.

The gray hairs that made up her braid had disappeared in the space of souls, outshone by the spirit of her vitality. Gwyn allowed a sob to convulse his body as she embraced him one last time. She'd left him with a parting message for his father. One that he'd traveled to deliver in person.

Gwyn greeted him simply. "Father."

Nudd stirred enough to raise his gaze in acknowledgment of his son's presence in the empty shell of a room that seemed to contain the empty shell of a man. He looked to be frozen in time. To the world, he appeared to be a man in his early fifties, with a beard more white than brown but still strong and capable. Yet, if he were still a man, Nudd would be dust in the ground by then.

"Son." Nudd barely spoke the word.

Gwyn said heavily, "I came to deliver a message."

"Yes, but let's address something crucial that has come to my attention first," Nudd said, his voice slipping into a tone Gwyn knew all too well.

So he'd rather pick a fight with Gwyn than hear the love of his life's parting words. So be it. He'd give his father this respite in anger, for anger was far easier to sit with than sadness.

Nudd began, "Your purpose is to serve humanity."

Flippantly, more out of the habit of being lectured than an actual feeling, Gwyn said, "Agreed."

Voice rising, Nudd said, "Your purpose is to guide souls. You occasionally lead the hunt. You fight when required for a higher purpose." Nudd stood and banged his hand on the table where the icy chalice sit, rattling it nearly to the floor. If Gwyn had been less trained, he'd have jumped in surprise.

His father continued ranting. "Your purpose is not to interfere in mortal affairs outside of the realm of your duties!"

Gwyn had quarreled with him about this very topic in the past. About his love for Creiddylad and his hiding her away from her abusive husband. Nudd had not approved of "abusing their powers to meddle with the affairs of men" as he put it. Saving her was never a choice: it was a duty. But that was long past now. Creiddylad had passed away a few years prior. Guiding her spirit had been the hardest thing he'd ever done.

Gwyn could think of many things that he'd done recently that would offend Nudd's sanctimonious morality. He only needed to be quiet long enough for his father to reveal his supposed trespass.

"You revealed your true self and your retinue to a man deep in the throes of the battle sickness! Why? Were you playing with him? Seeing how far you could take him to the edge of madness? There will be a point when something, when someone, punishes you for your interference."

Nudd was speaking of Myrddin Wyllt, the madman. Had that even been this year? Gwyn couldn't recall, but he did not regret his actions. Should he tell his father his true reason for what he'd done? That he saw within Myrddin the ability to overcome his madness and the potential to prevent future bloodshed? That Gwyn's heart was sick from visiting battlefields brimming with suffering and needless death?

Instead of answering Nudd, because he knew that this argument would go nowhere, he asked, prodding an open wound, "Why did you send her out, father?"

If Nudd could choose to fight, then so could Gwyn. Elena had fallen in battle. She'd fallen honorably to a foe who used trickery to prevail against her, aided regrettably by the weakness of her advancing age.

Nudd's posture stiffened, as if slapped, but he somehow maintained his regal air. He answered, tone registering lower, "You know as well as I that I cannot force that woman." He corrected himself, "That I could not force that woman to do anything that she disagreed with."

"You acknowledge this and yet somehow you refuse to apply the same logic to your ascended son." Gwyn shook his head sadly.

"The message, dear father, she gave to me for you, and I quote it truly, 'I have and always will love you.'"

Nudd made a strangled, angry sound, but Gwyn refused to look at him. He was used to the lines of anger written on his father's face, placed there by his actions. But he wasn't certain what he would do if he saw anguish written there instead.

Rather than chance seeing, Gwyn turned and walked through the mists of magic away from Nudd.

He walked to the door that separated this world from the next and considered it. He thought about who was behind that door and wondered if it was really necessary that they remain on the other side, separated from the ones they loved.

Gwyn bolted awake. Pain ripped through his side as he felt the blood seeping through his shirt from the stitches he'd ripped in his abrupt movement.

The faces of four women, two from his past and two from his present, combined to make an individual of each. Creiddylad, Abigail. Elena, Esmeralda.

His thoughts as he stared at the door...

Gwyn had a terrible, boiling-acid-in-the-gut feeling the dream had just told him why he'd been imprisoned, and not unjustly.

The End

The Condemned and Crowned

Sneak Preview

It Does the Body Good

Esme

"Hey, Jacob, so do you remember when you asked if you needed to grab your tarp, shovel, and rope to help me hide a body?"

Jacob, Esme's long-suffering mentor, local Archmage in all but name, and grandfather in all but blood, let out a deep, exasperated sigh through her car's speakers. He replied, "Well, good evening to you too, Esmeralda. Please try to remember your manners, darling."

Unfazed by his reprimand, Esme soldiered on. "We have twelve."

From the passenger seat, Abby added, "Six are horses, though."

A small sputtering sound reached their ears. "Is that Christi's daughter?"

"Yes, Jacob. Abby is with me," Esme replied, her voice tight with impatience.

Esme rolled her eyes. Her grip tightened on the wheel as she focused on staying right at the speed limit. A traffic stop while covered in blood would be a disaster.

"Long story short, I know she's a Corded Brother. But the thing is, there really are a dozen dead bodies in Christi's backyard right now. We need a clean-up crew or something. I don't know—whatever you all do when more than one malevolent gets killed at once."

Abby lightly tapped Esme's arm, a silent rebuke for her impatience, and reported to her superior, "Bastion, we arranged a parley with the man Esme, Miles, and Finn ran into while hunting the gwyllgi a few weeks back. The purpose was to learn more about his motives for seeking out Miles. We got the information we needed and even established a potential alliance with Gwyn. But our meeting was disrupted by an attack from six Dullahan."

The other end of the line went so quiet, Esme thought Jacob had accidentally hung up. By this point, she was so tired and sore from getting knocked on her ass by a charging horse and tackled by its three-hundred-pound, fully armored undead rider that she just wanted the conversation over with and the corpse problem solved.

She said, "They attacked Gwyn. So, I did what I always do and ran in without thinking. I wasn't about to let Abby's boyfriend die in front of us. Oh, yeah, she didn't know Gwyn was our guy until last night, so that's a whole other thing..."

Esme chewed her lip, realizing she was completely botching this report. "Anyway, Abby helped too. You should have seen the metal behemoth she used to T-bone one horse."

Despite Abby's groan, Esme continued. "Miles had been following Gwyn after a lead he got about a new mage matching the description you'd been circulating. He showed up and joined the fight, which was lucky because Gwyn almost died. Gwyn is in Miles' car right now, headed back to Seattle.

"Miles healed Gwyn as much as he could, and Abby stitched him up." Esme took a breath, trying to keep her tone light. "So, we really need that clean-up crew. Pretty please with a cherry on top?"

Jacob's slightly intimidating, official Assembly voice came through the speakers. "Abigail O'Malley, upon your honor as a Corded Brother, I require an honest answer."

In her peripheral vision, Esme saw Abby sit up straighter in her seat.

Jacob asked, "Are you working with that leprechaun to play a trick on me, or is this a genuine issue?"

Esme wanted to laugh but bit her lip to stop what would probably come out as a mad giggle. Jacob thought Finn, Esme's magic mentor and infamous thorn in his side, was behind it all. To be fair, she wouldn't put it past the leprechaun to do something like that.

Abby slapped both hands over her face and muttered, "Jacob, this isn't a joke. At all."

In his upper-crust British accent, Jacob replied, "Well, bloody hell," and the giggle Esme had been holding back finally escaped.

Abby had kindly offered to let Gwyn recover at her apartment, but both Esme and Miles vehemently objected. Although Esme now had a great deal of respect for Gwyn, they just didn't know enough about him to trust him. Esme argued that the man who healed him would be the better caregiver during his recovery, while Miles maintained that Abby's safety was their primary concern. Abby fell silent at that—she'd been just as dumbstruck to see Miles' healing powers at work, knitting Gwyn's lung and bones back together, as Esme had been the first time she'd seen it.

Miles lived in one of Seattle's famous floating houses. It was small, but the view from the dock was unparalleled. When they reached the parking lot, they realized they had a blood-covered, Gwyn-sized problem. He was still unconscious, and they needed to get him down the dock without anyone calling the cops. Luckily, it was dark, so the simplest non-magical solution was to carry him like he was blackout drunk. The Dullahan's whip had sliced through his muscles, ribs, and into his lung, so carrying him like that, even after the healing, would have been excruciating if he were awake.

With Lily and Cerys trailing behind, Abby rushed ahead to open the door and prepare the guest bed. Esme and Miles carried Gwyn between them, but as they tried to lay him down, her arms wobbled with fatigue, and he flopped onto the bed like a sack of potatoes. She wasn't surprised she managed to mess up something so simple with how drained she was feeling.

"Sorry," she muttered into the silence.

"He'll recover," Miles replied, his voice colder than she'd heard in months. Cerys' lambent eyes studied them for a moment, hopped onto the bed and curled protectively around her master.

They all stood there for a pensive moment, looking at Gwyn and Cerys. The past twenty-four hours had been a living nightmare, and they were all completely spent.

Letting her shoulders sag, Esme suggested, "Can we all just go to bed now?"

Face determined, Abby insisted, "I'm not leaving Gwyn."

Miles shrugged weakly. A bruise was forming under his left eye. "I've got a sleeping bag."

Abby surprised him with a hug. "Great. I can sleep anywhere. My bag's in Esme's car, and I can just...jump in the lake to clean off."

Miles gave her a quizzical look. "It's eight degrees Celsius outside. And I have a shower, Abby."

A bit sadly, Esme commented, "So we're having a bestie sleepover at Miles' and all we're going to do is sleep. Lame."

Abby and Miles both looked at her wearily.

She sighed. "Yeah, you're right. Honestly, a full night of sleep sounds like heaven right now. Being over thirty has definite drawbacks."

Even though she was exhausted, Esme's mind refused to rest as she lay next to Miles. The room was quiet, save for Lily's soft breaths at the foot of the bed. Esme shifted, watching the steady rise and fall of Miles' chest. If things were different, she would have reached out for his warmth, but her hand hesitated in the space between them.

Gwyn had claimed Miles was his father, the legendary Welsh king, Nudd Llaw Eraint. It was impossible to dismiss the idea completely—everything they'd learned about Miles lined up with what was known about Nudd. She had seen Gwyn fight with a sword against the Dullahan like he was born to it, and then Miles had done the impossible, re-knitting Gwyn's organs, bones, and muscles with magic. As far as she knew, magic wasn't supposed to work that way.

She pulled the blanket tighter around herself, trying to ward off the doubts creeping into her mind. Even if he was Nudd, it wasn't like he'd lied to her. He just hadn't told her everything, and they hadn't even been together that long.

Esme rolled onto her back, staring blankly up at the ceiling. The minutes dragged into hours, and the cold expanse of mattress between them became a chasm she couldn't cross. The night felt endless as her silent battle between weariness and doubt raged on.

***

The next morning

"How much longer can you hold out?" Esme muttered, more than a little annoyed as she was already half-covered in dust from the early morning battle. Her grip tightened on her opponent and her weapon.

She'd be the first to admit she was taking her frustration out on something that didn't deserve it, but it felt damn good. The lack of sleep and the bruises covering her from head to toe after the previous day only made her grumpier.

The next twelve hours offered no hope for improvement, either. Miles and Abby had to work. Since Esme was the only one with a job she could skip, she would act as Gwyn's nurse for the day. Something had to give. They had to talk about this. It was eating her up inside.

Earlier that morning only Lily rose to say goodbye as Esme slipped out of Miles' house a little before dawn to return home.

When she woke up, Miles was still fast asleep next to her, his body looking as battered as she felt. Peeking through the cracked door, she saw Abby asleep on the floor next to Gwyn's bed.

Now, back at home, Esme was taking out some of her frustration while planning on indulging in copious amounts of sugar. The dust she was covered in was flour and her weapon was a grater. She tossed the stump of the carrot she'd been grating into the batter and grabbed a muffin pan.

Carrot and walnut muffins for the health nuts and double chocolate for her. She had just enough time to get both batches baked before she needed to head back over to Miles' house to take over nursing duty.

Carrying twenty-two muffins, having already eaten two of the chocolate ones, she tiptoed through his front door. She found Miles awake, dressed for work, and standing by the coffeemaker. He looked pensive, maybe even a bit miserable, but his face transformed upon seeing her and her baked burden.

"Hey there," he greeted her quietly.

She cracked a smile at his relieved expression. "You thought I'd left again, didn't you?" she teased.

"Technically, you did." He pointed at what she was carrying. "I'm just glad you're back."

"Is Abby awake yet?"

"You just missed her. She's off already."

"Ugh, now I have all these muffins and too few stomachs to fill."

He walked toward her and exaggerated his Welsh accent as he asked, "Hang on now, what kind of muffins?"

By the time he reached her, she could feel herself being pulled into his gravitational field. She set the muffins down and hugged him close, holding him tightly. For a long moment, they simply stood there, breathing and existing together in the little time their responsibilities allowed.

She'd known him for less than a year, but somehow, he already felt like home—warm, safe, and comforting. With each heartbeat, her doubts whispered louder, turning the warmth of his embrace into a question she couldn't ignore: What if he wasn't the man she wanted, needed, or even the man she thought he was?

He could be the jailer of the injured man in the guestroom, his father. He could be a man older than gunpowder or paper money. A legend who had become part of mythology itself.

"When you get home, we have to talk." With all the finesse of a wrecking ball, she shattered the tranquility they'd shared.

"Should I be scared?" he asked, jangling his house keys in one hand and sending her a crooked smile. "Those are terrifying words for any male."

Unable to find the right words, she kissed him instead, filling the space where her answer should have been. She feared the right response to his question was, "I'm probably the one who should be."

Esme brought a book to keep herself entertained while taking care of Gwyn. She'd waited for months to get it from the library, but she didn't mind if she accidentally drifted off to sleep after the abysmal night she'd had.

Just as she reached the most gripping part of her book, a low, pained groan broke through the quiet, pulling her back to reality. Trying not to overreact to his discomfort, she walked to the spare bedroom that doubled as Miles' office and knocked. "Hey, sleepyhead, how are you doing?"

"Esmeralda!" His voice was strained, but underneath it, she heard a hint of relief at seeing a familiar face. "It is nice to hear your voice this morning."

She cracked the door open wider. Cerys glanced at her with mild interest before settling back down to rest.

"May I come in? I'm your nurse today." She allowed a small laugh to color her statement because, of everyone who'd been there when Gwyn was injured, she was the only one vastly underqualified for the job.

"Yes, of course. But I should warn you, I seem to be somewhat underdressed." He looked around himself. "Do you know where my shirt went? And, uh...where exactly am I?"

She opened the door fully to see him lying in bed, bandages covering half his chest. He looked exhausted. Trying to lighten the mood, she said, "I'm surprised Miles didn't heal you completely this morning. You're in his guest room."

Gwyn clearly didn't consider her statement to be a joke. He responded ruefully, "Your man is a psychopath. I hope you understand that."

Esme didn't know the limitations of Miles' healing and she refused to make assumptions about the whys of this whole situation. She was trying to be congenial with Gwyn. But damn it, he hit a nerve first thing.

She snapped back, "I'm part demon. Is there even a difference? And whether or not he's 'my man' is still up in the air." Her voice carried the sharp edge of irritation she couldn't quite keep in check.

Offhandedly, Gwyn replied, "Of course, there is a difference. He is enjoying my suffering."

Her sarcasm came out in full force. "Wow, I did not take you for the 'woe is me' type. But here we are."

That seemed to have struck a nerve with him as well, because his face fell. He said, "Apologies, Esmeralda. You're so much like her. I..."

He let out a long breath. The movement tugged at his bandages, causing fresh blood to stain them.

As if summoned by this, Lily pattered into the room and sat by Gwyn's bed. Apparently, the gwyllgi and the wolfhound had become fast friends because Cerys looked at her new roommate with unmitigated adoration.

Esme rummaged in the medical kit for fresh bandages and sat on the edge of the bed without asking for permission. "Let's change this out, shall we?"

She knew she should have been more cautious, but she couldn't muster any fear. She should have been on guard, but instead, she found herself slipping into the routine of caring for him. Despite his injuries, she knew what he was capable of. She'd seen the fierce power he wielded in battle. But in this quiet space, his presence felt oddly gentle, and her caution faded away.

As she removed the tape with one hand and held his bandage in place with the other, she couldn't help noticing the artificial smile he displayed for her.

With manufactured levity, he said, "I believe you are in a dangerous area. I'm quite certain that I smell horribly. I commend you for your bravery and for your aid."

She scrunched her nose in mock-horror. "Only a little smelly."

She'd learned during her work with the Assembly that switching topics without warning often caught people off guard, making them answer more truthfully. "Real talk time, bud. It's hard to believe the things you said about who you are when this injury suggests otherwise."

"Yes. After I broke free from my confinement, I was surprised by my newfound ability to bleed." He started chuckling but quickly restrained his movement, trying to cover his wince of pain. "What I said when we talked near the beach with your leprechaun friend wasn't me playing the dramatic bard. I am not the Gwyn ap Nudd I once was."

He paused for a long moment, wincing again as she pulled away the most sodden part of the bandage. Finally, he added, "I have lost my ascension. I am less. Now, I am nothing but a man."

It made her wonder if something similar had stripped Nudd of his power, turning him into the man she knew as Miles? She tried to reject the thought, but the uncertainty lingered. She rolled her eyes at her own thoughts. They seemed too far-fetched to even consider.

"N—" he started, then corrected himself, "Miles told me you requested my healing. Sincerely, thank you, Esmeralda."

His tone made it sound like she'd threatened to fall on her own infernal sword if Miles didn't heal him. She muttered, "Uh, yeah. We couldn't exactly let you die."

Out of nowhere, Gwyn said, "Your eyes... they're just like hers. That same impossible shade, a blue so dark it is almost purple."

The combination of fatigue, pain, or emotion had made his accent so thick that Esme couldn't be sure if she understood him correctly. "I didn't quite catch that," she urged.

"Elena."

According to Gwyn, Elena was the woman Nudd had loved but couldn't be with due to societal pressures. Esme did not try to hide the glare she was giving him, which clearly communicated her desire for him to stop talking about Miles' supposed ex.

"Gwyn, Gwyn, Gwyn, I feel like we keep stepping off the path I want to travel down right now. You say you've lost your ascension, I understand. But how can we know Miles is Nudd?"

There was a hint of sadness in his response, but he made it clear that he understood her intentions. "Honestly, Esmeralda, I don't know how to prove it. He'll talk to you..."

Lily moved closer to Gwyn's injury, her snout twitching as she sniffed. Esme shifted, positioning herself between Lily and his wound. She couldn't blame Lily for following her instincts. Petting the wolfhound to redirect her attention, Esme said, "No, silly girl. I'll get you a treat in a minute."

Of course, what she needed from the medical kit next was the farthest away from her. She had to lean off the bed to reach it. In the split second between leaning over and reseating herself, Lily had wedged her body between them—an easy feat for a massive dog—and was already licking at Gwyn's stitches. Cerys, watching from Gywn's other side, seemed to approve.

When Esme reached to redirect Lily, her hands stopped mid-movement. Then her heart skipped two full beats as she saw the faintest candlelight glow emit from Lily's tongue as she licked at the blood on Gwyn's torso.

Neither of them moved, as if afraid they'd break whatever spell was happening. They gawked as the skin under the stitches slowly knitted itself together beneath Lily's ministrations.

Esme remembered what Finn had said the night she learned about her demon heritage and Miles' god-touched status: "I suppose I can be fair and mention that his hound is too."

She must have been staring blankly, because Gwyn's quiet murmur of "Diolch" startled her. It seemed like he was thanking the dog.

Gwyn's face darkened as he addressed her. "If I needed more proof that Miles is Nudd, Lily's healing power would be more than enough."

Gods below, was it true?

Her mouth shot off, defending Miles again, even after what she'd just witnessed. "Whoa now, Finn said that Lily was also god-touched too, with a weak halo, just like Miles. Which, remember, Nudd did not have. In case you haven't noticed, I trust Finn."

She ended her tirade by standing abruptly, her frustration seeping into every word, pushing past the embarrassment she might have felt.

She didn't need to finish bandaging him now, because Gwyn sat up smoothly, already apologizing. "Esmeralda, I'm so—"

She cut him off. "But, hey, Gwyn, you had six freaking Dullahan come after you and you have a pet gwyllgi. Plus, you can fight with a sword—people can't do that anymore! So maybe you're not a complete lunatic. I'm somewhere halfway between believing you and thinking that you're a basket-case."

She walked out of the room and quickly grabbed a random T-shirt of Miles'. Returning, she tossed the replacement shirt at the no-longer-invalid. She knew she wasn't being fair to him, but she was too exhausted in mind and body to hold it back.

"Your shirt and jacket are in pieces. While you hop in the shower, I'll warm up a couple of muffins and make some more coffee. The four of us are talking about this tonight, calmly, like friggin' adults! Do you understand?"

When she looked at him for a response to her scolding, she saw he was holding back a laugh that bordered on tears.

"I'll look for some scissors and tweezers so you can pull the stitches out. I'll find your shoes too, because I'm pretty sure poor Cerys is long overdue for a potty break. I was too afraid to take her out."

She hastily shut the door and walked back into the kitchen, still flustered but not truly angry with Gwyn. She needed that chocolate muffin because every word that had come out her mouth combined with the tone... Esme was turning into her mother.

They spent the afternoon in uneasy silence. She buried herself in her book while he brooded in his bed. The peace only lasted until Miles got home.

About the Author

Urban Fantasy author Stella Hope blends myth, romance, and non-stop action in each of her novels. Her favorite stories feature strong female protagonists, their loyal companions, and a generous sprinkle of humor.

Before embracing her passion for writing, Stella embarked on an academic journey that began with bachelor's degrees in Latin and geography. Afterwards, she pursued a graduate degree in environmental science and worked as a scientist for a few years. Stella's love for books eventually led her out of the forest and into the world of libraries, where she had the pleasure of running two public school libraries.

She lives in the PNW with her family, where she occasionally has to leave her writing cave to thwart the neighborhood bear's attempts at pilfering food from her bird feeder. When she's not writing, she's doing her best to stay away from bears, bobcats, deer, and sometimes coyotes during her trail runs and hikes. Her efforts are frequently less successful than one might suppose.

If you'd like to receive sneak previews, updates from Stella, and content available only to subscribers, please join her mailing list at stellahopeauthor.com

Milton Keynes UK
Ingram Content Group UK Ltd.
UKHW041823131124
451149UK00001B/69